I0599668

BOOKS BY KIMBERLY R. VARGAS

The Dance

Fallin' for the Fame

KIMBERLY R. VARGAS

Cover design by Gowtham Thangaraj
Interior design and formatting by Jose Pepito Jr.
Edited by Katharine Bost and Raquel Brown

First Edition: January 2026
ISBN: 979-8-9995198-1-8

For content guidance, please see the Sensitive Content note at the front of this book.

Published by Kimberly R. Vargas
www.kimberlyrvargas.com

Printed in the United States of America

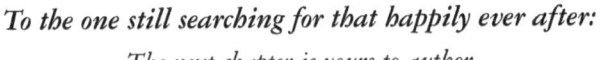

To the one still searching for that happily ever after:
The next chapter is yours to author

AUTHOR'S NOTE

Thank you for reading *Fallin' for the Fame*. This story was born from a question I think many of us have wrestled with in private: What do you do when the life you built feels safe, but something in you still aches for more?

Sam's journey is messy, loud, tender, and human. She wants comfort. She wants predictability. She wants to do the right thing. But she also wants to feel alive again, and that longing pulls her into a world she never planned to enter.

At its heart, this book isn't really about fame or Hollywood. It's about the quiet, unspoken decisions we make when we're caught between what feels steady and what feels like possibility. It's about the stories we tell ourselves to stay put, and the ones we chase when standing still starts to hurt.

If you've ever found yourself torn between comfort and curiosity, this story was written for you. ♥

With all my heart,
Kimberly R. Vargas

CONTENT NOTE

This novel contains mention of sensitive topics, including:

- Drugging / spiked drink
- Drug use
- Parental death (x3)
- Reference to suicide (off page)
- Reference to sexual exploitation of a minor
- Presence of a firearm

Reader discretion is advised.

1

Empire State Building with mimosas,
watching the sunrise over Manhattan.

My usual Friday morning never looked like that. Instead, I lie in my bed, reading Legend Blake's message again and again, wondering if the fantasy could ever be real.

Would he take me there? Really?

I tap my thumb against the edge of my phone, trying to think up how to reply. The early rays of the sun stream in through the apartment's half-moon window, warming my shoulders and shimmering across the screen.

The conversation started last night with a little game he proposed. It reminded me of *Would You Rather,* but he insisted it wasn't quite the same.

It began with simple questions like: *Ferris Wheel or a bouncy house?*

Bouncy house. Definitely.

New York Pizza or Po' Boys?

New York, all the way.

LEGEND: *Ok Ok. I got another one.*
SAM: *Shoot.*
LEGEND: *3 ingredients that would make for the perfect first date.*

After all the flirting—and him claiming we were so alike we must be soulmates—my stomach had already been through its share of tumbles and twists. He kept going before I could ask what he meant.

LEGEND: *I'll tell you mine: Yacht in the Caribbean, during sunset, couple of glasses of Moët & Chandon.*
SAM: *LOL You're so extra!*
LEGEND: *What?! Girl, you KNOW you want it!*
SAM: 😬
LEGEND: *Aiight. I see you. So tell me, what would you want?*

I held my breath, cheeks burning hot. In all the time we've talked, he's never been so straightforward with me. No way was he suggesting taking me out for real. I teased in response.

SAM: *Guess.*

But for whatever reason, he didn't respond. At least, not until now.

I figured I'd said too much, but looking at his response, I guess he decided to play along.

Every word, every flirtatious text is starting to feel less like a game these days. Honestly, I'm not sure how much longer I can keep pretending it's harmless.

Inhaling a deep breath, I stare at the screen, a mass of hazelnut hair falling into my face. I brush it back, running over how I might respond.

Option 1: *That sounds beautiful.*

Option 2: *You know me so well!*

Option 3: *It would be perfect... if you were there.*

No. Can't say that. I could never say that. I'm just another fan. Only one of more than fifteen million followers on IG. He'd probably blow me off anyway.

Then again, how many fans has he entertained nearly every day for the past three years? Maybe I should go with Option Three...

Out of nowhere, my boyfriend, Justin, pounces on my back, his six-foot frame knocking the wind out of me. I choke and wheeze as my phone slips from my hands and tumbles into the sheets.

"Good morning, beautiful!"

The phone rests beside my pillow, Legend's message staring back at me. I scramble to turn off the screen. "Teddy, you nearly scared the crap out of me."

He sucks his teeth and flips me over, knocking off my cozy blankets. He gazes at me with soft brown eyes, a million-dollar smile on his round, handsome face. He proceeds to saturate my cheeks and jaw with wet, indulgent kisses.

"Justin... Justin! Your stubble tickles. You need to shave!" I laugh, struggling to come up for air, but his hickory brown arms envelop my waist as he holds me close.

I nudge him back, admiring his chocolate bald head and dimpled chin. With my honey-gold skin and slim frame, most people see us as an odd couple. But after seven years of dating—not to mention fifteen years of friendship—I have more in common with him than anyone I've ever met.

A grin plays on my lips as I look him over. He's got on nothing but a pair of plaid boxers, and his skin is still damp from the shower. "What are you up to?"

He continues on his mission, nuzzling me with his nose. "I'm sorry about last night. The team hit a snag and wanted to go out for drinks afterward." He eliminates what's left of the space between us, whispering in my ear, "I missed you." He runs his robust hands across my belly, making a trail down my sweat shorts, and headed for the back of my thigh.

A clear mating call.

I gnaw my lip, studying the vaulted ceiling. "It's all right. I packed up the leftovers, so you can take them for lunch today." Wiggling out of his grasp, I sit up on the pillows.

I'm no match for my boyfriend when it comes to strength. Mom swears I got my lanky arms and legs from Dad's side of the family. But Justin's always been a gentle giant, following my lead. Wonder what's gotten into him this morning.

I brush some hair behind my ear and adjust the straps of my tank top. "So, dinner at Mom's tonight?"

Justin purses his lips, blinking at me.

I know he's frustrated, but after my recent conversation with Legend, I just... can't right now! I cross my arms, waiting for his answer. It isn't long before his pout melts into a genuine smile.

"Can't wait," he says.

My shoulders slump as the reality of our evening plans start to sink in. "Wish I could say the same."

"Aw, come on." Justin joins me on the pillows, wrapping an arm around me, rubbing my shoulder. "I love your mom's cooking."

"It's not my *mom* that I'm worried about, or her cooking."

He looks me square in the eye. "Really, Sam I Am? You not gonna let this go?"

"You don't understand. Your dad never remarried."

"Even if he did, I'd at least give the woman a shot. That's all your mom wants from you. Trey's cool people."

"You're biased," I say. "Both of you are software geeks."

"That *does* give us plenty to talk about." Justin is a software engineer for Apple, my stepdad, Trey, designed a traveling app. The two of them could go on about zeros and ones for hours.

Justin squeezes my arm. "But I bet y'all have a lot in common too."

"Such as?"

He gazes out at the living room just below our loft. "Well... you both love your mom."

I scoff, gathering sheets around my waist, praying that maybe they'll put a barrier between us.

Justin laughs. "Look, I'm sure that there's more. But Sam, you can't do this forever. I mean, he's been with your mom nearly as long as we've been together." He pulls the sheets from my grasp, making his way back to my neck, lowering his voice to its sexiest bass. "And if he's into your mom even *half* as much as I'm into you, ain't no way he's backing out *anytime* soon."

He returns to planting sweet kisses along my jaw, his fingers wandering into my hair. He's always loved my hair. And I've always loved him.

The scent of his Old Spice body wash lingers in the air, hints of cinnamon tickling my nose as I run my hands over his broad shoulders and kiss him back. Justin's always been on the bigger side, but in recent years he's started working out, and most of his excess cushion has transformed into pure muscle. I can't say I'm disappointed with the results. I curl my fingers around his beefy biceps.

A sigh escapes me as my body grows warm. "What time is it?"

He moans. "Who cares?"

I chuckle, glancing at my phone. "Justin! It's almost six-thirty!" I shuffle back, preparing to jump out of bed. I've got *so much* to do!

But Justin slips the phone out of my hand. My entire body tenses as I clasp the air, trying to get it back. "What are you... What are you doing?" If he sees my DMs with Legend, I am *so* dead. Thankfully, he sets the phone on the nightstand without looking.

"I thought you missed me..." He drowns his words as he swallows my lips with his.

I pull back. "Teddy, I gotta get in my—"

"I know. I know. You gotta get in your morning jog." But his eyes are ravenous. "I was just hoping maybe we could have a little fun instead." It isn't a question. His hand makes its way under my shirt as he suffocates me with pecks and moans.

I close my eyes, forcing back the image of Legend Blake's gaze as the sun rises over the Empire State Building.

Ugh! I can't do this right now.

I nudge my boyfriend back. "Teddy, you know I can't. I've gotta work out, and then—"

"Shower."

"And then—"

"Breakfast before work." He grins at my sidelong stare. "I know you better than you know yourself."

"After seven years, you better." I smile, kissing him. "I owe you. All right?"

Justin bobs his head, seeming to accept defeat.

I pat his sculpted shoulders and hop out of bed. If I hurry, maybe I'll find a moment to respond to Legend in peace.

2

"It always helps to frame your interview with a few ques tions that will warm up the individual..." My boss, Professor Natalie Cooper, squints at her PowerPoint presentation on broadcast journalism strategies as if she might need glasses. Her slide is missing a few words at the end. "The individual, um, being interviewed." She nods and clears her throat. "Moving on."

Behind me, papers shuffle and notebooks flip as the *tap-tap-taps* of laptops echo throughout the lecture hall. The class watches intently from cushioned stadium seats, chins in hand, fingers drumming. Professor Natalie clicks her remote, transitioning to the next slide.

I've been a graduate assistant at the University of Washington for the past two years while working on a master's in communications, and thankfully Professor Natalie has been kind enough to keep me at her side the entire time. There's no way I'd survive without her.

As an award-winning journalist from London, Professor Natalie rose to fame on the evening news here in the States. Viewers fell in love with her warm smiles and endearing English accent. I, on the other hand, adored her investigative reporting and her ability to hold people's feet to the fire during an interview. She started teaching at UW at the prime age of forty, and she's been with the university for the past eight years. The woman's brilliant writing and weekly reports inspired me to go after my degree. She almost had me wanting to go into broadcast journalism, but I've never been the type to jump in front of a camera.

Humor fills my chest as Legend and I continue our conversation about the perfect fantasy date at the Empire State Building.

> **SAM:** *Yeah right! I bet that place is SO crowded every day!*
> **LEGEND:** *Maybe it would be on that secret floor.*
> **SAM:** *And how would I get access to that exactly?*

We've been chatting like this for a while now. And though we've yet to meet face-to-face since it began, I'd say we've become good friends over the years.

I've been on every one of his social media accounts since high school. I know his favorite hobbies, favorite food… everything there is to know about him. There's something about the way his voice wraps around a lyric—smooth, deep, intimate—that makes it impossible not to listen. Paired with those bedroom eyes? I was a goner. But I never worked up the courage to connect with him until a few years ago.

I was scrolling through Instagram one day when his latest post pulled up in my feed: a black and white photo of Legend with his eyes cast low, as if he were deep in thought, and maybe a little sad. Beneath, the caption read: *I wish I didn't care so much.*

I zoomed in, admiring his athletic build and low-cut waves. He'd recently trimmed his goatee, which only served to define his chiseled jaw that much more. The post was already filled with hundreds of thousands of likes, several fire and heart emojis posted in response.

My thumb hovered over the photo, just a breath away from a double-tap. But this picture was different. Something was off. Legend wasn't reflecting. His gaze seemed clouded, like something was pulling at him from the inside.

It couldn't have been easy, putting on a happy face for the cameras all the time. But people would drag me if I posted about it in the comments. And what if my boyfriend saw it or something? Though I doubted Justin would ever follow Legend Blake.

I went to his DMs instead.

It took me ten minutes to get over my nerves, but after reading and rereading my message, I hit send.

SAM: *Some days are like that. But it gets better.*

With a heavy sigh, I set my phone aside. I had no idea why I was so uptight about it. I highly doubted he would respond.

But he did. He responded right away.

After screaming at the top of my lungs—and reminding myself to breathe—I sat down and read his message.

LEGEND: *How'd you know?*

How did I know? What did he mean, how did I know? I was his biggest fan. Of course, I knew!

SAM: *Just a hunch. But if you need an ear, I'm here. I swear, I'm not paparazzi!*

He responded within seconds.

LEGEND: *lol*

I held my breath as a full five minutes passed.

LEGEND: *You from Seattle?*

OMG. He was checking out my profile. He'd seen my picture! It was as if I'd slid on a patch of ice, smacked my head on the pavement, and slipped into a coma where Legend Blake actually wanted to talk to me. *Me!* Samara Allen, of all people!

> **SAM:** *Yep. Graduated from Tyler Prep in '17.*
> **LEGEND:** *'Ey! I went there too! Would've graduated in '16 but... you see how that went.*😬

Oh wow, I thought. *He sent an emoji.* But I had no clue if he remembered me. I closed my eyes, trying to calm my racing heart. *Please, God, don't let me mess this up.*

> **SAM:** *Destiny awaits, right?* ☺

It was a phrase he often used in his interviews. I couldn't believe I'd just quoted him with a winky-face emoji. Maybe it was too forward. I read the message again and again. *What if it was too forward?* I counted every minute that passed.

And then he said the one thing I never thought he'd say.

> **LEGEND:** *So tell me about you.*

I didn't hesitate. I mentioned that I was a student at UW, on my way to a degree in communications. A nobody from Seattle... But one of his biggest fans.

He humored me, asking me to tell him something only one of his *biggest fans* would know. I mentioned how he hated pepperoni on his pizza and had been playing piano since he was five. But he wasn't impressed. Those things had been covered in several interviews.

I studied his profile photo, thinking... *When you're sad, your mouth turns down just a bit and you get this little crinkle over your brow like it physically pains you to feel anything but joy.*

Of course, I couldn't tell him that. I brought up the Care Bear he slept with until he was twelve.

Two minutes went by.

> **LEGEND:** *Yo! I only mentioned that like 1 time on YouTube!*

I laughed.

> **SAM:** *Told you. One of your biggest fans.*
> **LEGEND:** *Wow. You starting to sound like my #1!*

And now, I'm one of his closest friends. But I could never tell my boyfriend that.

As usual, there's a draft in the spacious lecture hall. Even with wall-to-wall carpet, and three hundred bodies in the seats, the space rarely stays at room temperature. I tug on the sleeves of my acid wash denim jacket, awaiting Legend's response. My vintage bangle bracelets slide and clink as I lean my elbow on the arm of my seat.

"And if the individual being interviewed seems... antsy," Professor Natalie continues, "you might want to work your way up to the, um... the hot-topic question." I frown as she paces at the podium.

What is going on with her today?

Professor Natalie is usually composed, her tall frame and curvy hips commanding attention with zero effort. Her flawless caramel skin practically glows beneath the lecture hall lights, her jet-black curls spilling down her back in soft waves. But today, there's something off. The way she taps the remote in her palm, the heavy sigh slipping from her lips. "Next…"

Maybe she needs water or something.

I close my eyes and take a breath, wishing Legend would respond already. He's probably with his choreographer. He said he had rehearsal.

Professor Natalie switches slides, and a photo of an adorable kitten pulls up on the screen. Students cover their mouths, snickering as she gazes up at the massive screen with scrunched eyebrows. "Now that wasn't supposed to be there…" she says.

Legend finally returns to my question about the Empire State Building's secret floor.

LEGEND: *With a celebrity, it's no problem.*

I stare at the screen, long and hard. There's no way he's suggesting that the two of us…

"Well, that's it for today." Professor Natalie nods, signaling the end of her lecture, and I tuck my phone away. "We'll review next week."

An eager student on the front row raises her hand, and Professor Natalie points for her to go ahead.

"What about the quiz we were supposed to have?"

Students groan at the reminder, but Natalie blinks at her like some amnesia patient in a telenovela. It's as if she's just learned that her husband was dating her twin sister all along.

She completely forgot. Thankfully, I didn't.

I wave to the professor, signaling I've got it covered. She offers a grateful smile as I grab the copies I made earlier and pass them out.

"Thanks for the rescue," says Natalie as we head to her office after class.

"That's what I'm here for."

Something was definitely off with her today. And I know just the remedy.

We enter the Communications Department, and the aroma of a fresh mocha latte calls my name. "I'm gonna get some coffee. You want the usual?"

Professor Natalie places a hand on my shoulder as we part ways. "You're a lifesaver."

I toss her a smile as I head for the coffee station near the front desk.

The banquet table—adorned with a frilly white skirt and a plastic cover to catch spills—looks more like a wedding reception set up than a break area, complete with neatly arranged stirrers and a towering pyramid of sugar packets. The staff around here takes their refreshments *seriously*. There are four single-serve machines—each one set up for tea, cappuccino, espresso, or coffee—and at least seven different types of creamer. I didn't discover how much my taste buds had been missing until I started working here. Professor Natalie insisted I take my first sip when I joined the team, and I have never looked back.

I like my coffee with one sugar and a hint of French Vanilla. Just like Justin, the Professor prefers hers black. And Legend? He rarely drinks coffee, but if he does, he likes it loaded up with four sugars, minimum, and as much cream as possible. I've told him he may as well have a milkshake. He says that's exactly the point.

I check my phone while the coffee maker generously pours a fresh, tall cup of Raspberry Chocolate Lava, Medium Roast. I still have no idea how to respond to Legend. And if I don't soon, I might just miss my chance… again.

My screen lights up with a message. But it's not from Legend, it's Justin.

It's an old GIF of Issa Rae in *Insecure*, wide-eyed and nervously finger-gunning in the mirror. The caption reads: *"Everything's fine. Totally fine."*

He follows with a text:

> **JUSTIN:** *Your Monday energy had me like...* 😄*But I still love you.*

A reluctant smile pulls at my lips as he sends another:

> **JUSTIN:** *Being real, I hope you're feeling better. Try to not stress about tonight. It might go better than you think.*

He's such a sweetheart. Which only makes this entire situation worse.

Instead of responding, I heart the message and tuck my phone away. Because all I can think about is this... "thing" with Legend. And how my boyfriend deserves so much better.

———— ✦✦✦✦✦✦ ————

Professor Natalie is at her L-shaped desk studying her phone, a grin tugging at her lips as I rejoin her. She thanks me as I pass over her cup.

I've come to enjoy these private meetings between us over the years. Her office is on the busier side of the communications department, near the end of the hall. Instructors are always coming and going, sharing donuts and lame jokes. I admire their ability to be so relaxed despite all the nervous undergrads popping up, moping and whining about their assignments. It's rare to see Professor Natalie with a frown on her face.

Even when I'd drop by, full of anxiety and questions, she'd take the time to listen to my concerns, never hesitating to share a selection from one of her several "bookcases of wisdom" lining the back wall. She keeps a degree on display at the top of each one, inspiring apprehensive students like me to never give up.

My phone buzzes as I take a seat across from her.

Great. He waits until I can't get to my phone to say something else.

I'm itching to check the message, but business comes first.

Crossing my legs, I take my first sip of the morning. My entire body relaxes as the sweet caffeine rushes through my veins, making me feel complete. "Is everything okay?"

Professor Natalie feverishly types on her phone, her little grin growing into a full-blown bride-on-her-wedding-day smile. "Mmhmm."

Well, this is a world of difference from the scatterbrained professor I witnessed just moments ago. She's yet to even sip her coffee.

She sets her phone aside and breathes a happy sigh. She notices me staring and her eyebrows rise. "Hmm?"

"I didn't say anything."

"Oh." She nods, reaching for her cup. "So, Samara, I've been meaning to ask about your future plans. You're graduating next month, correct?"

"Yes. Two more weeks to complete my thesis, then finals, and that master's degree is mine." The two of us tap our disposable coffee cups in celebration.

"Have you applied for any jobs or internships?"

"Not yet." I take a slow sip, the warmth doing little to ease the tightness in my chest. "But I've been thinking it might be a good idea for me to sharpen a few more skills before putting myself out there. Maybe enroll in a few enrichment courses over the summer, that sort of thing."

Professor Natalie bobs her head.

"Actually," I sit up straight, tugging on my denim mini skirt. "I'm considering pursuing a PhD. In the meantime, if you're interested, maybe I can work with you again this summer."

I've already applied for the position.

Professor Natalie stares at me. "A PhD? You want to teach Communications?"

I shrug. "Maybe."

Okay, so I'm still not *one hundred* percent sure about what I want to do for a living, but I enjoy working for Professor Natalie. She was the first instructor who truly expressed interest in my efforts in journalism. She taught me how to make an article shine and really dig for the "story behind the story".

I remember the way she walked me through delivering a proposal for a feature. I've always been overwhelmed at the thought of presenting in front of people—I wasn't exactly looking forward to delivering my idea before a class of three hundred. The professor didn't give me a hard time about it. She invited me to her office *every day* for a week to prepare for the assignment.

By the time it was my turn to give a presentation, I knew every word by heart. It was the most confident I felt in all my undergrad years, and it was all thanks to her. It would be a shame to part ways when we've grown so close.

Professor Natalie's smile doesn't quite reach her eyes. She leans back in her swiveling leather chair, fingers laced tightly around her cup.

"Well, I have some news... I won't be teaching over the summer, or any future semesters at UW."

My nervous system grinds to a halt. The words echo, but don't land. "I'm sorry, what?"

She exhales through her nose, glancing toward the window like she wants to be anywhere else. "I'm, uh... resigning."

I set my coffee on the desk. "Resigning? But, why?" I whisper. I glance over my shoulder to ensure no one's passing in the hall.

Professor Natalie waves her hand. "No, no, nothing scandalous! It's Paul. You remember Paul?"

"Ex-boyfriend Paul? The one you reconnected with on Facebook last year?" The two broke up years ago when she moved to the States.

She nods. "We're still… reconnecting."

No. She can't mean… I stare at the professor, willing her to admit she's joking.

She taps her thumbs at the lip of her coffee cup. "We've decided to give it another go. So I'm returning to the UK. There's a BBC station near my old house with the perfect producer role opening up. I'm really as good as… hired." She reaches across the desk. "Samara, are you okay?"

There's a soft buzz in my ears. My chest heaves up and down as the room shifts on a tilt.

"Mmhmm. That's wonderful. I am so, so happy for you."

This is awful! It's no wonder she's been so distracted. The only thing on her mind is… *shagging* her old flame or whatever. How could she do this to me? I could use a paper bag right now.

Professor Natalie steps around to my side of the desk and rubs my back. "It's okay. Now, just breathe… Breathe, Samara."

It's been a while since I've had an episode like this. The last time was a year ago when Justin sent a text saying he was in a car accident. He didn't respond to a single call or text for over an hour. It turned out to be a fender bender, and he was wrapped up in conversations with insurance people and the other driver. I nearly passed out during the wait. Thankfully, Professor Natalie was there to pull me back from the edge.

Just like she taught me before, I close my eyes, inhaling through my nose, exhaling long and hard. "I'm good. Really."

"Are you sure?"

I nod. I just don't know what I'll do without her, or how I'll manage to find another job, for that matter. Résumés, interviews, and all those new people... I cringe at the thought of shaking complete strangers' hands.

Professor Natalie looks me in the eye. "Samara, it's been wonderful working with you these past two years. I might've lost my head otherwise! But there comes a time when we all have to move on. You know, a season for everything and all that."

She's right. I know she's right. I just don't understand why everything has to change *now*.

Professor Natalie pats my hand. "You're a very smart girl. And though it might seem like an uphill climb right now, you *can* do this without me. I'm one hundred percent certain that you'll figure things out."

I'm still trying to regain my composure when I leave the professor's office. She wants me to check her PowerPoint slides, so hopefully, she won't embarrass herself next week. I'm headed to the library where I can work on my laptop in peace.

Throngs of students with heavy backpacks shuffle by on my left and right, vibing to music or chatting on their phones. Others sit on the manicured grass, catching up with friends, the branches of newly budded cherry blossoms arching over brick-paved walkways.

I inhale the sweet scent of spring in bloom, the cool breeze wafting over my face, calming my fears.

I struggled with the idea of moving to campus when Justin and I were freshmen. But once I got here, I fell in love with the massive libraries and gothic architecture, the majestic fountain spouting at the center of campus each summer. By the time we graduated, I couldn't imagine leaving. Now we live just ten minutes away.

I check my message from Legend as I walk.

> **LEGEND:** *Wish I could get out of here right now!*
> **SAM:** *Rough day?*

I know I've got plenty to share. But I'm sure his situation's more pressing.

> **LEGEND:** *Understatement. Practice. Lunch Meeting. Dress Rehearsal. The show doesn't start until 8 PM.*
> **SAM:** ☺ *I know.*

I keep track of every show he does, though it's been forever since I made it to one. I'd never ask Justin to take me—he'd see through me in a heartbeat. But honestly... I'd give anything to see Legend in person again.

> **LEGEND:** *Just a little down right now. Ya know?*

It isn't rare for Legend to have his moments. But I know exactly what's got him down. I'd be a fool to bring it up at this point.

> **SAM:** *Just keep your head up, ok?*
> **LEGEND:** I *know, I know. One step at a time.*

There's only one reminder that never fails to cheer him up.

> **SAM:** *I'm always here if you need me.*

I can picture the handsome grin on his charming face.

LEGEND: *I know that too.*

The dancing wind tickles my cheeks, and visions of his alluring gaze float off in the breeze.

If only...

I clutch the collar of my jacket with a sigh and head on my way. Guess I'll be updating my résumé this weekend.

3

The sun is just setting when Justin and I head to my mom's in his Durango. Hues of lavender and tangerine gleam like dancing strobe lights on a tree-lined street, long shadows stretching across the pavement. A few neighbors have already stepped out on their evening walks, their dogs on leashes, tails wagging happily as they trot along with a steady, timeless ease.

I shake my head, wrapping up my tale of Professor Natalie's latest announcement. "The least she could've done was give me a heads up. This is so last minute."

"You're about to graduate," says Justin, flashing me a crooked grin. "It's not like she expected you to hang around campus." When I blink at him, he busts out laughing. "You didn't think she *did*, did you?"

I purse my lips. "You wouldn't understand."

"Oh, really?" Justin scoffs in amusement.

I don't have anything else to say to him, so I casually check my messages.

Nothing new from Legend since his bout of depression this morning... Ugh. He hasn't behaved this way in months. Maybe I should drop a message about Professor Natalie's latest bombshell.

But Justin gives me a nudge, his V-neck sweater pulling tight across his shoulders. "Everything okay?" He glances at me, eyes full of concern.

Justin's been there during some of my worst breakdowns. If anyone knows how difficult it can be for me, it's him. He was the one who kept me from passing out when we had to take the SAT. He literally held my hand when we entered junior high. Even back in elementary school, the boy had a way of sensing when my day had been good or bad... especially when everything fell apart.

His eyes drift to my phone, and I quickly turn it off.

"It's just... Simone being silly again."

He nods, returning his attention to the road.

My poor boyfriend. I've been lying to him for *years*, and he's completely oblivious.

"She comin' to dinner tonight?" he asks.

I wave my hand. "You know my sister, 'Life is too short for boring people!'" I let out a light chuckle and gaze at the Dogwood and Maple trees passing by. *If I could just sneak off to the bathroom before his dress rehearsal, we could talk. He needs to be in a good headspace tonight.*

"So what's going on?" asks Justin.

"Hmm?"

He nods at my phone. "With Simone. I hardly see y'all talking lately."

"Oh, um, she was just warning me not to try this organic shampoo she found. Smells like prune juice and a baby's bottom."

His nose curls as he laughs. "What?"

"I know, right?" With burning cheeks, I force a chuckle, gazing out the passenger window. After all this time, I still suck at this. And I hate lying to my best friend.

Justin and I have been tight since the second grade. Before we even entered high school, he knew he'd developed feelings for me. Of course, he didn't fill me in until junior year. A soft kiss during a study session and the two of us became a thing. A *real* thing. A *beautiful* thing. By the time we graduated and entered college, I knew I'd fallen for him too.

Through all of my ups and downs, Teddy's always been there for me—a giant, cuddly shoulder to lean on when times get rough.

But all of the cuddles and kisses in the world couldn't cure me of my little infatuation.

To this day, I still follow Legend's every move. Every promotion, every song. The two of us have formed a real bond. And if Justin were to ever find out, it would break his heart.

Justin taps his fingers on the steering wheel, humming along to Bruno Mars's "That's What I Like." He glances back my way. "You feeling better about seeing the fam tonight?"

"Now that my future is hanging in the balance? I guess I'll be okay."

"Honestly, Sam I Am, it's not the end of the world," says Justin. "You never know what the future holds." He gives me that salesman smile, and I roll my eyes.

"Pressure. A ton of pressure is what the future holds for me. Like a giant latex balloon, stretched to the brink with helium, rising high into the sky, and headed straight for the mesosphere—if a jet doesn't hit it first."

My boyfriend frowns. "That's a morbid way of looking at balloons."

"It's true!"

"Well, I'll tell you one thing, I am thoroughly looking forward to having something besides the *Divine Six* this week." Justin chuckles to himself, but I'm not amused in the least.

The Divine Six is his little nickname for the meals I cook for dinner because they're *always the same six,* according to him. We typically go out to eat once a week.

He settles down when he notices my stern gaze.

"There's nothing wrong with having a set menu, Justin. I just like my routine, okay?"

"Okay, okay!" He shrinks away, a grin still on his lips. But I don't slap him. Not this time, anyway.

Justin takes me by the hand, so I put my phone away. Legend will just have to wait.

Meanwhile, Justin wiggles my hand in his, tapping my knuckles along with the beat.

Why's he so amped up today? He's like a kid on his way to McDonald's or something.

We round the corner, turning into my mom's subdivision, the neighborhood where Justin and I grew up: playing tag together, riding bikes together, taking late evening walks and talks together.

We pass a charming colonial house on the corner with brown vinyl siding and multi-pane windows. It's Justin's old house, and up until a couple years ago, his dad still lived there.

Justin firmly sets his eyes on the road as we pass. I still can't believe he sold it. But Justin made it clear that he didn't want to relive the memory of finding his father, still and lifeless, in his favorite living room chair, a lukewarm bottle of beer next to him on the table.

I'll never forget the way Teddy fell on my shoulders, sobbing at the hospital.

A brain aneurysm, he'd said. *You're my only family now,* he'd whispered, holding me tight.

Ever since he's never been the same.

It's not just the workouts or the sudden interest in designer jeans. It's the little suggestions that we do things differently, the grating moments of spontaneous inspiration to "walk on the wild side" or whatever.

"Let's go snowboarding," he says.

"We should try a new restaurant."

"What do you say we make love at that secluded beach tonight?"

And every time, I have to tell him no. We *used* to be on the same page. I was comfortable with my routine, and so was he. But lately, it seems like it isn't enough.

I gaze at the sky. Dark clouds push in like the smoke of a locomotive on the horizon. "You think it's gonna rain?"

Justin shrugs as he whistles to himself, content in his own little world.

Since the passing of his dad, Justin *definitely* hasn't been the same. But I guess I should give him a break because, after the death of my father, my life changed too.

———————— ✦✦✦✦✦ ————————

Of course, with my luck, Trey is the one to answer the door.

"Hey, guys!" He throws his arms out wide, a glass of champagne in his right hand, an unlit cigar in the other.

Trey is a retired ladies' man, at least that's what Mom says. He's got walnut brown skin with thick dark eyebrows, and struts around in khakis and open-collared dress shirts as if he's waiting to be invited for a round of golf. Apparently, he's working on growing a mustache, again.

I step in and give him a light side-hug, pulling away as his lips attempt to graze my cheek. "Where's Mom?"

"In the kitchen," he says. "You want me to take your jacket?"

"I'm good." I make my way back to the kitchen, as he and Justin slap fives.

The house where I grew up sits on an expansive lot full of novelty plants and is as tall as the old weeping willow in the backyard. These days, the inside of the place is decorated like a page out of *Better Homes & Gardens*: polished hardwood floors, classy artwork on the walls, and fake orchids on every table. Back when I was little, the floors never shined, and the walls definitely weren't stark white.

Despite her decision to remarry, my mom decided to stay here, even after Simone and I moved out. This was the first place my parents bought after my dad got his job, working for *The World News*—the country's *number one international news provider*. I was only five when we moved in. Simone was four.

Mom is chopping potatoes at the center island when I enter the industrial-style kitchen, seasonings and vegetables sprawled everywhere. Water bubbles in a large pot on the stove, the aroma of butter and warm apple pie dancing through the air.

"Hey, Mom." I greet her with a kiss on the cheek.

"Oh!" She startles as if she didn't hear or see me coming. Throwing a hand over her chest, she catches her breath. "Hey, honey. Can you check on that pie for me, please?" She casts a half-glance toward the stove before returning to her intense chopping.

I step behind her, peering into the double oven. "Nothing oozing out yet."

"Great. That means I have more time." Mom rushes across the kitchen and dumps her potatoes into the pot of boiling water. She stands on her tiptoes as she stirs.

She's always been the petite one in the family. Any height Simone and I have came from my dad. Unlike the three of us, Mom has more curves in all the right places. Dark chocolate skin with burgundy undertones, classy shoulder-length curls that perfectly frame her face. Tonight, she's wearing a casual, but sophisticated, empire waist dress.

I take a seat at the breakfast bar. "Seafood chowder tonight?"

A lengthy moment passes as she shuffles back and forth, turning down the heat on the stove, adding seasonings, stirring the pot, readjusting the heat.

"Mmhmm," she finally says, drawing out the syllables as she cooks.

Back when she was raising Simone and me, she worked full-time in a nearby district as a seventh-grade math teacher. It was rare that she found time to cook, so we grew up on fried chicken and mashed potatoes. She only made her seafood chowder occasionally on the weekends. But that was before she met Trey and became… this.

My baby sisters, Talia and Tatiana, scream at the top of their lungs, chasing one another through the kitchen, and headed for the dining room.

Mom shouts after them, *"Girls, no running!"*

They giggle as they circle the dining room table and take off for the stairs.

Mom stops and throws a hand to her forehead. "Samara, honey, have you seen my oven mitt anywhere?" I point. It's sitting right behind her on the counter. She closes her eyes, releasing a heavy breath. "Thank you."

I take off my jacket and lean on my elbows. "You need any help, Mom?"

"No, honey. I just…" She doesn't finish her sentence. She's reading over her recipe on the fridge.

Mom was still working when she married Trey, but then they had Talia and Tatiana, just one year apart, like Simone and me. Mom decided she'd be staying home with Talia before she even left the hospital. She swore she *wouldn't let strangers raise her babies in some daycare.* Simone and I went to daycare, and we turned out just fine.

I grab an apple from the fruit bowl and take a bite.

Mom glances over her shoulder. "Samara, don't ruin your appetite, okay?"

"Okay, Mom."

"So how's school?" she asks.

"Good. But Professor Natalie threw me for a loop today."

"Oh, yeah?" She adds the rest of her ingredients to the pot.

"Yeah. She's moving back to the UK."

"Hmm." Mom's not listening. She's stirring her pot and reading her recipe at the same time. "That's good."

"Mmhmm." I take another bite of my apple. "So after she puts her parrot up for adoption, she'll be free to join the circus."

"That's great, honey."

I swear she's the master of pretending to listen these days. Frankly, it'll be a miracle if Talia and Tatiana make it through childhood with all their limbs intact.

Trey and Justin stroll in, chuckling and speaking in binary code.

"How's it goin', Sam?" asks Trey, showing off his bicuspids. "You ready for graduation?"

"Ready as I'll ever be," I say with a plastic grin.

He pats my shoulder. "That reminds me. A client of mine passed me some tickets to the Mariners game next month. You should come with me and the girls. It'll be our way to celebrate."

"Ah," I nod, exchanging glances with Teddy. "I'm fully booked next month, but I'm sure that Justin would love to go."

Justin blinks at me, but I hold his gaze. He promptly nods at Trey. "Yeah, sure. I'm down."

Trey frowns. "You sure you can't make it, Sam? It'll be fun—"

"Trey, she said she's busy," Mom interjects.

Suddenly, the woman is listening.

She and Trey connect eyes as she reaches into the stove… without her oven mitt. "YOUCH!" Mom drops the pie on the rack and grabs her hand, sucking air through her teeth.

"Mom!" My body tenses and I shoot up from my seat.

Trey rushes to her side before I can. "Carissa, what were you thinking?"

She shakes her head. "I wasn't."

Trey moves her to the sink and runs cool water on her fingers. Mom breathes a heavy sigh as Trey gazes at her tenderly.

"What'd I tell you about getting distracted, huh?" His voice is low as he makes googly eyes at my Mom, kissing her fingers. She nods, grinning back at him.

Gross.

Justin tilts his head as he watches them, a charmed grin on his face. I jab him with an elbow, and he stands up straight.

The doorbell rings, rescuing me from my nightmare.

"I'll get it!" I shout. "Not that anyone's listening..."

A curly-haired version of myself yanks off her helmet as I open the door.

"Simone?"

"Hey, slut. You gonna let me in?" Not bothering to wait for an answer, my sister pushes me aside and heads over to Justin in the foyer. She smiles, throwing an arm around him. "What's up, nerd?" Justin chuckles, hugging her back.

I thought I heard a motorcycle outside. I purse my lips, staring out at Simone's Kawasaki Ninja in the driveway. I can't help rolling my eyes as I shut the door.

Though she's only a year younger than me, Simone prides herself on being the original *baby of the family*. At least until Tatiana was born. When she isn't racing around the country on her bike, making trouble with strangers, she likes to try odd jobs like bartending and floral arranging. She even tried stripping one night for some quick cash. But she's never been the type to stick with anything for long. She walked away from a full-ride scholarship for Cheer & Tumbling, claiming that she didn't want to be *nailed down*. She's been a nomad for the past four years.

Justin takes Simone's helmet and jacket, scrunching his eyebrows at me. "I thought you said she wasn't coming."

I open and shut my mouth.

Simone nods, reading my eyes. "I wasn't... But then I heard about the..."

"Seafood chowder," I say.

"Exactly!" She shrugs at Justin. "*Love* Mom's seafood chowder."

Justin is none the wiser. He heads to the front closet as I mouth, *Thank you*, to my sister.

She slinks up beside me the second Justin's out of earshot. "You using me as an alibi, Sam?"

"What? No." When I scoff, she slaps me in the chest. "Ouch!" I pout, throwing a hand over my boob.

"Don't give me that," she whispers. She looks me over with big almond eyes. "Please, tell me you finally grew some balls and had a one-night stand."

"We can't all be like you, Simmy."

"Right." She runs her fingers through her unruly head of curls. "I forget how boring you are with your boring life and your boring-as-a-corkscrew boyfriend."

I suck my teeth. "That's not true. Justin's great."

"Yeah," she says. "Only 'cause he's just as boring as you. Tell me, how many positions does he have? Two?"

I take a swipe at her but miss. "Shut up!"

Simone's cracking up. "It's true! Isn't it?!"

Mom calls from the kitchen. "Simone, is that you?"

My sister calms down with her chuckles, tossing an exasperated glance my way. "Yeah, Ma. It's me." She takes her time, heading back to greet her.

4

*A*s I sink onto the living room sofa, Simone's words still echo in my mind. I shove aside a few scratchy pillows and feign interest in the game show flashing across the TV screen.

My relationship with Justin isn't boring. Not really. I mean, maybe we could switch up our favorite date locations and be a little more spontaneous, but we stick with what works. I don't see a problem with that.

Over in the kitchen, Simone greets Talia and Tatiana, hugging one while tickling the other. Just like our baby sisters, people often assumed we were twins when we were little. But nowadays, it's easy to tell us apart. Simone prefers to wear her curls natural and says I should do the same. It's the main feature that came from our dad's Irish and Afro-Brazilian roots. But I've been straightening my hair since I was twelve. I simply prefer a more sophisticated look.

I'm readjusting my side ponytail when Talia and Tatiana come scampering into the living room.

"Hey, guys."

The two girls climb into my lap, and I hug them close, the bows of their pigtails brushing against my cheeks. Each of them has the perfect combination of Mom's long princess lashes and Trey's bushy eyebrows. They're wearing adorable summer dresses with ribbons at the waist. Little Tatiana is carrying a stuffed dolphin. She passes it my way, and I hug him too.

"He isn't real," Talia says with a giggle. "He doesn't need a hug."

I stare at her with wounded eyes. "Well, maybe I need a hug."

The two girls jump down and run off laughing, not a care in the world… I remember when Simone and I were like that.

Back in the kitchen, my sister shrugs at Mom and Trey. "You really think I give a crap?"

Mom shushes her. "The girls can hear you!"

Simone rolls her eyes as she continues sharing her latest road trip adventures.

Justin is propped in the doorway that leads to the dining room, his hands stuffed in the pockets of his dark-washed jeans. I catch his eye, and he grins my way, giving me that same familiar, charming smile.

For fifteen years, it's always been that same smile.

I nod, and he returns his attention to Simone's dramatic story. She's going on about some woman in a wedding gown that hitched a ride on her bike, insisting that she drop her off at a Buffalo Wild Wings. I'll have to hear that one later.

The game show on TV fades to black, and the trailer for Legend's latest movie, *Heist in the Hills,* pops up onscreen. My stomach flutters, and I sit up straight. The movie's about a couple of teenage girls who get mixed up in the plans for a Hollywood heist before stepping in to save the day. Legend plays an arrogant, sultry version of himself. A small, but significant, cameo that I'm sure is driving sales at the box office. I must've seen this commercial a hundred times by now.

Everyone's focused on Simone in the kitchen, but I cross my arms, determined to maintain self-control. Just in case anyone's watching. I sit back and watch the TV, prepared to indulge in the eye candy.

"Legend Blake," he says, flashing an irresistible smile. *"Pleasure's all mine."* Understandably, the girls are drooling onscreen.

Goodness, the Lord made him handsome. My temperature rises as I continue watching.

Most girls fawn all over these guys in Hollywood whom they've never met, but that isn't the case for me. Legend and I met in high school. I was a sophomore. He was a junior. The unforgettable moment just may have slipped his mind.

From the second I saw Legend, I wanted him *bad.* I had a *huge* crush on him, but he had no clue I existed. He'd transferred to our school the year before and with his handsome looks and sexy singing voice, it was no time before he became the most popular guy in school. I honestly don't think it could've gone any other way. Confidence was in the boy's genes.

We'd passed several times in the hall, but I never got a chance to talk to him. Not that I would've, had the opportunity arrived. I rarely talked to anyone besides Justin or Simone.

Then, out of nowhere, my chance arrived. A talent show was coming up, and they were looking for stagehands. Everyone knew how seriously Legend took his singing—his YouTube channel had already racked up thousands of subscribers. The boy was determined to become the world's next R&B star. It only made sense that he'd sign up for the talent show. The publicity would get him one step closer to the record deal of his dreams. So I signed up too. But not as a performer—that would be a disaster—I signed up to help backstage. And then I could gaze at his gorgeous face and admire his sultry singing voice as much as I wanted every day.

One afternoon, I found myself backstage, watching him rehearse for the show. He was pouring his soul into a romantic rendition of Ne-Yo's "So Sick" while playing an acoustic piano, making my heart race with every note. Settling on the backstage stairs, I swayed to the melody, mesmerized as his voice drifted through the empty auditorium.

But just as he moved to note his sheet music, he looked up and noticed me. I stood abruptly, trying to play it off by making my way down the steps, but I totally missed one and went sliding on my butt.

Legend rushed over to me. "You all right?" His hand was soft and firm. He smelled like fresh rain.

I forced myself to exhale. "Yeah, I—"

Before I could say another word, a man who looked like an older version of him appeared at the front of the stage. "Yo, L, we gotta go. Vocal coach will be at the house in thirty."

I'd later learn the man was his dad.

Legend looked back at me. "Take it easy, okay?" I nodded, and he rushed off.

And as I watched the sexiest boy I'd ever met head out with his dad, it hit me: *I just talked to Legend Blake… and somehow I didn't die.* I promised myself if I ever got another chance, I'd make a proper introduction.

I got that chance the next day.

I was making my way up the hall when I spotted him a few lockers away. He stopped and smiled before heading in my direction.

This was it. This was my opportunity! I took a deep breath, brushing some hair behind my ear. And then he walked right past me. He stopped just a few feet away and started chatting up some girl at her locker. My heart ripped in two.

I never got another chance like that. The talent show came and went, and of course, Legend won. By the time we returned from Christmas Break, he was gone. He entered the televised singing competition, *Lucky Star*, and his career took off.

I, on the other hand, settled into my quiet and much duller life...
But I've never forgotten about him.

"*Holy beefsteak!*" Simone pops up behind the sofa, nearly scaring
the confetti out of me. "Someone's been working out."

She points to a lengthy slow-mo shot of Legend stepping out of
a pool on TV, drops of water glistening across his chiseled chest like
lucky little diamonds. "I bet the guy's got an insurance policy on each
butt cheek." Simone winks at me, and I swat at her head, somehow
missing again.

"*Shhhh!*"

No one knows about my little thing for Legend besides her.
Thankfully, Justin is preoccupied with showing Trey something on
his phone.

My sister falls next to me, laughing. "You still aren't over him, hmm?"

I scowl at her. "Shut up, Simmy."

She rests her chin in her hand, glancing back and forth at the
TV and me. "Can we both agree that this little infatuation is beyond
ridiculous?"

I roll my eyes and stand. I don't need her blowing up my life with
her irritating comments.

She throws out her hands as I head for the stairs. "It's just an
observation!"

I march up the steps, heading straight for my old bedroom. I need
some space... and I need to talk to Legend. But as I round the corner,
a wall of Pepto-Bismol pink hits me like a slap to the face. I stagger
back, peering left and right. It looks like a dizzy unicorn trotted inside
and barfed cotton candy all over my room.

I inch inside looking around. "What the—?"

"What do you think?" asks Mom. She's standing behind me with
a load of laundry in her arms, beaming like a child who just doodled
her first crappy drawing.

"What happened to my room, Mom?"

"Well, the girls kept butting heads, and Trey and I figured Talia was big enough for her own space, so..." She sweeps her hand, presenting her little project. "Don't you like it?"

Someone has painted a fairytale castle on the wall. Vines are dangling from the ceiling, and a giant rocking horse sits in the corner. The four-year-old has a queen-sized bed. I never had a queen-sized bed. I *still* don't have a queen-sized bed. "What about Simone's room?"

Mom waves her newly bandaged hand. "You know she drops in and needs a place to stay sometimes. You're much more independent."

She heads off, humming to herself, not the least concerned about my feelings.

It's gone. All of my things, all of the memories, gone.

The desk where I'd study and write in my diary, the reading corner where I shared secrets with Simone, the bed where me and Justin had our first make-out session, gone.

I sink down on my baby sister's massive bed, and the fluffy pink blankets nearly swallow me whole. Shaking myself aright, I scoot toward the edge, my head throbbing as I stare blankly at the wall.

Wait... No. My breath catches in my chest as I scan the room.

My favorite portrait that hangs in the center of the wall has vanished. The photo of me wrapped up in my dad's arms is nowhere... to... be found. In its place hangs a happy picture of my mom, Trey, and the girls.

It's as if he never existed at all.

My eyes sting with tears as I swallow and turn away. Over by the window, I see a vision of my nine-year-old self, gazing at the stars.

Dad snuck up behind me and hugged me tight, nuzzling my cheeks with his goatee. He was a slender man with wavy black hair and the arms of a center basketball player. His skin was light, like butter mint candy, and he smelled like cinnamon apples.

It was a chilly night in January, and he'd come to check up on his *ten-year-old.*

I giggled. "I'm not ten yet, Daddy!"

He smiled, brushing back my curls. "I know, but tomorrow you will be..." His words trailed off as he gazed at the floor. At the time, I was too young to know what his silence meant, but I knew that something wasn't right.

"We're going to the movies tomorrow," I said.

Daddy nodded. "I know, Sweet Pea."

"Justin's coming too."

He let out a soft chuckle. "That's great. I'm glad you've got such a good friend."

"You're coming, right?"

"Actually, I got a last-minute assignment in Tokyo. You remember where that is?"

I nodded, trying my best not to pout.

Daddy lifted my chin. "But I promise, I'm gonna be back to take you out for ice cream, just like we do every year." My little heart was already sinking.

Daddy dusted my forehead with light kisses. "You're gonna have a *great* birthday. Be sure to have your mom record you blowing out your candles. And *just you*, all right? Not Justin this time."

I agreed. But the thought of Justin gave me pause. "He's been kinda sad lately. He misses his mom, so I've been trying to cheer him up."

Daddy smiled with sad eyes. "That's sweet of you to care so much, honey."

"They found her last week... She was in the water." Justin's mom had been missing for a while, and everyone thought she'd run away. But that wasn't the case.

Daddy pulled my face into his chest, breathing a heavy sigh. "I'm sorry you had to hear about that, Sweet Pea. Sometimes parents just... have a hard time."

I'd heard Justin's dad talking to my mom. They said she jumped off a bridge. I figured that maybe she wasn't a good swimmer.

"He's just been so sad, Daddy." I looked up, blinking into his eyes. "I don't want you to go away and never come back."

"Of course not, honey." Daddy pulled me back into his chest. "I might go away sometimes, but I'll always come back. I'll always be here for you."

As a naïve child who knew nothing about the harsh realities of life, I believed him.

And then his plane disappeared over the Pacific Ocean.

I press my palms against my eyes, willing the tears to leave. I let out a deep breath and take out my phone, but Legend still hasn't hit me up.

My temples throb as my heart sinks into my belly.

Simone always says, *"I'll never understand this obnoxious obsession. His singing is trash and his acting sucks."*

Simone wouldn't recognize true talent if it hit her in the face. Her idea of quality music is someone who hasn't washed their hair in a week, imitating demonic growls while their death metal guitar shrills at eardrum-piercing decibels.

But she's right about one thing: This *is* an obnoxious obsession. How much longer can I do this? Until I have children? Until he starts dating again? I run my tongue across my teeth, shaking my head. Maybe I should just let this go.

I'm leisurely scrolling through my feed on Instagram when I receive a new message. I go to my DMs without thinking. But it isn't from Legend at all. It's Professor Natalie, forwarding some lame chain letter:

Today your life is going to change!
Give a double-tap and forward to four people.
Make a wish and watch it come true!

I hate this sort of thing. Downstairs, Simone has started another tickling session with the girls. Justin's going on and on about some software glitch with Trey. It isn't like I'm in a rush to head back down. I forward the letter to my mom, two of my cousins, and Simone. Then I close my eyes and make a wish:

One more shot with Legend Blake.

A few seconds pass before I open an eye, peeking out. Nope. No Legend Blake with washboard abs standing before me in a shimmering haze.

I giggle and toss my phone on the bed. Such a silly idea. I really should consider distancing myself from Legend before I lose my mind. I mean, I'm a *nobody*. Why would he even...?

And then my phone chimes.

My fingers tremble as I check the message...

LEGEND: *Let's meet.*

5

*A*nother hour passes before dinner is ready.

Simone tramps into the dining room, her lace-up riding boots squishing across the handmade Oriental rug. "Sheesh! It's raining sewage and fish guts outside." She's just returning from covering her bike.

I, on the other hand, have no clue how to handle the poop storm headed for me. I honestly can't believe Legend would suggest such a thing. There's no way this could ever work.

Simone plops down next to me, her soggy curls dripping all over a white dining chair. Our mother frowns, and Simone flings out her hands. "What, Mom?!"

"Let's not start our evening like this, okay?" says Mom, struggling to hide the pout forming on her lips.

Simone grabs a dinner roll from the center of the table. "It's not like *I'm* the one with my thong twisted up tight."

Trey drops his spoon. "Simone, please. That's enough."

She's actually cut back significantly on her f-bombs in recent months.

My sister snorts. "Trey, I'm twenty-two. I didn't listen to you at sixteen. I'm certainly not gonna start now."

To me, our stepdad is sort of like a persistent bill collector. Always checking up, pretending to care, probing with questions no one wants to answer. But to Simone, the man may as well be Hitler. She and my mom have been butting heads since the day he walked into our lives.

Mom exhales deeply. "Come on, Simmy. Don't talk to him that way."

"You're right." Simone leans back, her champagne in hand. She gives Trey a curt nod. "I'm sorry for bringing up the obvious."

Down at the other end of the table, Talia and Tatiana are sketching soupy landscapes on their salad plates, using their bread as paintbrushes.

"Girls," Mom chides with weary eyes. "Please don't play with your food."

The crystal chandelier, dangling over our heads, casts shadows on sheer white curtains. Outside, raindrops plunk against the windows like rogue pebbles.

"So, Sam, I was talking with some of the guys at the office, and they suggested that we get a little more exposure before we release this new app next year." Trey flashes a smile, fishing a lump of shrimp from his chowder. "How about you and your boss help us out? We could put together one of those press packages or something."

Trey's travel app has taken off in recent years, and now he has over fifty employees. They're currently developing a companion app that's kind of like TikTok for travelers. It's too bad they can't design an app that'll help your stepdad take a hike. Figuratively, of course.

"My boss won't be around next year, or next month," I say. "She's moving back to London."

Mom gasps, eyes bulging. "Professor Natalie? You're kidding!"

It's only been an hour since I told her this.

Trey leans on his elbow, his brow wrinkling in concern. "That's really too bad. So you'll be looking for another job soon?"

"Guess so." I gaze at the table as I take a sip of my champagne.

Justin squeezes my knee with a reassuring glance, the way he always does when I need to chill out. There's a rhythm to us I don't have to think about. Sometimes I wish I did. I take a deep breath to steady myself.

Trey clears his throat. "So Justin, any update on that interview?"

Interview? What interview?

Justin exchanges a look with me and sits up straight. "Uh, yeah. Thanks for hooking me up, T."

"It's no problem."

Hooking him up? What the heck is Teddy talking about? I stare at him, puzzled.

Justin wipes his mouth with a napkin and gives me a tense grin. "So, I have an announcement, everyone. I've received an opportunity. A job opportunity."

Trey chuckles, pointing as if he's in on some inside joke. "You serious?"

Justin nods. "You're looking at Apple's next potential senior software engineer."

Mom is thrilled. "Justin, that's wonderful!"

"Congratulations, man," says Trey.

"And here I thought you were getting a vasectomy," says Simone. Mom whacks her on the arm.

"So will you be managing your current colleagues?" asks Trey, excitement dancing in his eyes.

"No," says Justin. "Actually, the job isn't in the same building, or the same state." He looks my way. "It's in Silicon Valley."

My heart deflates and slumps into my abdomen. A sharp chill races down my back.

The entire table is silent until Simone busts out laughing.

"But Justin, that's so far away," says Mom.

Over thirteen hours away. At least two hours by plane. And I hate planes.

"I think it's great," says Trey. "He'll be at the headquarters. Right in the thick of it."

Justin studies me with a wavering smile, hesitating to respond.

Silicon Valley?

He wants to move to Silicon Valley? Like it's that simple?

"But what about Sam?" says Mom.

"Yeah," says Simmy, her tone taking on a sarcastic bite. "We know her schedule is *jam-packed.*"

"Sam is about to graduate," says Trey. "I bet she'd love working in California. Besides"—he smiles my way—"a little change would do her good."

Talia and Tatiana giggle, throwing bread at one another.

"Trey, she's happy here," says Mom, nodding at me. "Aren't you, honey?"

"No, she's not!" shouts Simone, a mouth full of bread.

Mom turns back to Trey. "That's asking a lot of someone to simply walk away from everything they've ever known in the last twenty-three years."

"It isn't like they're moving to Australia, honey. They'll visit over the summer and during the holidays." Trey nods at Justin and me. "Won't you, guys?"

I give him a look as warm as an arctic breeze.

"I say, screw Justin." Simone tosses an arm across my shoulders. "Come with me, Sam, and I'll introduce you to a *fine* variety of charming, ravenous men."

Teddy leans back, casting a stern look at my sister on the opposite side of me.

"Simone, don't be crude," says Mom.

"I'm just being honest."

"That's not who Sam is," Mom says. "She's slow and steady. You're wild and... loose."

Simone chokes and nearly spits out her drink.

"Is anyone thinking about Justin, right now?" says Trey. "This is a *major* opportunity for him."

But Justin's eyes are back on me. "Actually, I've got something else to say." Teddy stands and pulls out a little black box... then gets down on one knee.

Simone's spoon clanks into her bowl, splattering chowder across the table. Mom gasps and her hands go over her mouth. Even Talia and Tatiana have settled down.

I'm boxed in... by the chandelier light, by their expectant faces. By the way Justin's hand shakes just enough for me to see it. There's no room left to breathe.

He's brought up the conversation so many times before. And I've deflected time and time again.

"After I finish school," I'd tell him.

"Once things calm down."

Anything to put off that next *major* step.

Justin opens the box, revealing a gold solitaire diamond ring. The exact ring I pointed out years ago at a jeweler downtown.

One day, I'd said with a smile.

But today? Of all days?

Of course he remembered the ring.

The part of me that used to fantasize about this moment—about this proposal—feels numb.

He gently takes me by the hand. "Sam I Am, we've been thick as thieves for more than half our lives now. Back in second grade, I spotted you alone in the cafeteria, and I knew I had to be your friend.

I decided that day to be the one to make you smile. And if you'll let me, I'll do that for the rest of our lives."

"This is so incredibly cheesy," says Simone.

Mom swats the air. *"Shhh!"*

Chewing on his lip, Justin gently traces his thumb across the back of my hand. "Samara Allen, will you marry me?"

I gape at him, my lungs about to explode.

How could he do this to me... in front of everyone?

Mom starts whimpering, and Trey rubs her shoulder.

"Why are you crying right now?" asks Simone. "She hasn't even answered!"

"It's just... my baby..." Mom waves her hand and grabs a napkin to blow her nose. "I'm sorry. Go on."

Justin's too nervous to laugh. "What do you say? You ready to make this thing official?"

My mom, Simone, and Trey lean in, waiting for my answer. Even the girls are holding their breath.

Who am I kidding? This was inevitable. It's everything I've worked for. Everything I'm supposed to want.

Justin stares at me lovingly, his charming eyes locked on mine.

So I let out a heavy breath and say, "No."

⋯✦✦✦⋯

The late spring rain is pouring down in heavy sheets as the two of us drive off into the night. The SUV is silent, and all that can be heard is the *thump, thump, thump* of rain droplets, threatening to plop on our heads.

Justin's not speaking. And neither am I.

He shouldn't have asked me. He *had* to know what my answer would be.

I stare out the window at the thick grey clouds. Streaks of lightning flash overhead. "I'm sorry. Okay?"

He scoffs. Then he shakes his head, chuckling. "I knew you'd do this. You *always* do this."

My muscles tense as I look at him. "I always do what?"

"This!" He punches a button, and the windshield wipers pick up speed. The blades swipe back and forth, squeaking and thumping, pounding against the glass. "Anytime a new opportunity presents itself, you shrink away. Like it's some sorta curse."

An opportunity? Is that how he sees his proposal? Like some offer I could never refuse? He is *not* the only bachelor in Seattle. And I am *not* some desperate maid, who couldn't survive without him. At least, I don't think. "I'm not shrinking away. I'm just… not ready. That's all."

"Seven years, Sam. *Seven years*, and you still aren't sure?"

I roll my eyes. "Why didn't you tell me about the interview?"

"I didn't wanna get you worked up if I didn't get the job."

"You *know* how I am, Justin. You shouldn't have put me in that position. *Especially* in front of everyone!"

"Yeah, I know that now." His jaw tenses beneath the passing streetlights. "It's just… ever since my dad—" He stops and looks at me. "I just thought marriage would bring you around to the idea. That's all."

I don't know what he wants me to say.

He sighs, staring out at the road. "Look, I know change freaks you out, but I couldn't pass this up."

"Wait… you took the job?"

He glances my way with a shrug that splinters my heart.

So not only did Justin receive this job offer… He accepted it? It's as if he doesn't care about how I feel at all.

I blink and turn away. Droplets of rain cling to the passenger window, gingerly rolling down its surface. My eyes burn as I cross my arms.

When Justin places a hand on my knee, I brush it away.

"Sam, I... I just wanna go for something. For once," he says.

I gaze at the crescent moon peeking through ominous clouds, wondering when it stopped being *us* and started being *him*. He would only make such a drastic decision if he were okay with the chance that I'd say no.

I wipe away the tears. "It's fine. You should totally go for it."

I'm sure there are plenty of less boring people in Silicon Valley.

He reaches over and takes me by the hand. Against all my pain and doubt, I slip from his grasp.

Lightning streaks across the sky. Thunder booms and crackles.

Justin stares at me as he pulls up to a red light. "Come on, Sam. What am I supposed to do—go on without you?"

<hr />

Two days later, he's moving out. He plans to room with one of his colleagues from work until his new job starts in two weeks.

Justin tapes up the final box and lifts it on his shoulder. I remember how much he grumbled about lugging our things up to the loft when we moved in, carrying our bed up the ladder, one piece at a time. But the location was perfect. Not too far from school, just the right distance from Mom's. And even though he wanted a house at twenty-frickin' years old, he was willing to wait... for me. But he could only wait for so long.

Justin flashes his signature-charming smile as we meet in the living room. "We're good, right?"

"Best friends forever," I say.

He nods, sighing through his nose, his hopeful brown eyes scanning the apartment. "Then I guess this is it." He extends an arm, and we exchange an awkward hug.

For a moment, the two of us stand in silence, neither of us saying a word.

Justin rubs a palm on his jeans, clearing his throat. "You gonna be good with the lease and all that?"

"Yeah. I'll get out of here soon. Mom says I can stay at her place until I figure things out."

"Okay. Well, here goes nothing." His voice quivers and cracks. He swallows and heads for the door.

"Bye, Teddy."

"See you later, Sam I Am."

He opens the door and stops. Then he sets the box down on the floor and turns back with glistening eyes. In three giant steps, Justin's back at my side. He swallows me up in his arms and holds me for what seems like forever.

He hasn't held me like this since that day in the hospital... when he learned that his father would never wake up again.

"Sam..." he whispers through broken sobs. "If... you want me to stay..."

I close my eyes, letting his words settle heavy in the air. My chest tightens as everything inside me shifts. Toward him, away from him. Part of me wants to nod, tell him we'll work this out. That's what we do. That's how it's always been. But I can't hold him back anymore.

"No," I whisper, the words coming out more certain than I feel. "This is your chance. You gotta go after your dream."

His eyes shine with unshed tears. "But I can't—"

"Yes, you can."

We lock eyes, the silence thick with everything we can't say.

Finally, he takes a step back, dabbing at his face with the back of his hand. "Promise you'll take my calls?"

"Of course. And hey, this is the twenty-first century. Email, text, whatever." I'm chuckling as my heart wrenches in my chest, forcing tears to my eyes.

Justin nods and heads out. And this time, he doesn't look back.

As the door shuts behind him, a heavy breath escapes me.

How the heck am I gonna do this?

Simone hops off the loft ladder. She slowly applauds as she steps my way. "You two should audition for a soap opera or something. That was some sappy stuff."

My sister decided to hang around for a few days and be my support system. As expected, she's doing a horrible job. She slaps me on the back as tears roll down my cheeks.

"Simmy, not right now, okay?" I rush over to the kitchen to grab some paper towel. Simone chuckles as I wipe my face.

"Okay, okay. I know it's sad. But don't act like this isn't an answer to prayer."

I frown at her. "Simone, what are you talking about?"

She leans against the island with her arms crossed, the REBEL logo on her tank top peeking out. "How many years now have you been stringing that poor guy along, when you clearly had eyes for somebody else?"

I shake my head and blow my nose. "That's not what this is about."

"That's *exactly* what this is about. Honey, I know it sucks the way it played out, but Mr. Cuddles is handing you the opportunity of a lifetime on a silver frickin' platter right now."

Oh no. I'd recognize that devilish smirk anywhere. "I'm not hitting the road with you."

"And why not?" Simone crosses the kitchen and throws an arm around my shoulders. "Just imagine: You and me, two *hot* girls—who may as well be twins—traveling from coast to coast on our sexy bikes, wreaking havoc and stomping on men's hearts."

"I'm pretty sure that movie's been done before."

"Come on, Sam!" She juts out her bottom lip like a toddler. "You act like you can't have any fun unless it's planned twelve weeks ahead with an itinerary!"

I pinch her cheek. "You remind me of when you were little, whining like that."

"Both of us were little, Sam."

"The answer is no." I ball up what's left of my damp paper towel and toss it in the trash. "Besides, I have enough on my plate right now."

"What do you mean?" Simone follows me across the kitchen. "Your boss just announced she's leaving the country. Clearly, you're out of a job."

"Yeah, but…" I take out my phone, staring at Legend's message.

LEGEND: *I'm still waiting…*

"Wait a minute." Simone frowns at the screen. "Is that—? *Seriously?* You're still talking to that guy?"

I turn to her with a wince. "Almost every single day for the past three years."

Her lips curl in a dubious smirk. "You mean to tell me this hot celebrity wants to talk to my Saltine-cracker sister?" She snatches the phone from my hand and begins scrolling. "Wow. *Empire State Building?* Sounds like somebody's horny for you."

"Would you— Wait. What? You think so?"

"Well, he's an R&B singer. Those guys are always in heat." She spins around, her curls smacking me in the face. "'*Let's meet?*' What does he mean, '*Let's meet?*'"

"That's what I said. Apparently, he plans to stop in town on his way to Vancouver. And he wants to meet me for dinner."

Simone's jaw drops. "Dinner?"

I nod.

"I am so incredibly proud of you. Of course, you said yes."

"Actually..." I rub the back of my neck. "I told him I'd think about it."

"*Think about it?*" Simone frowns. "What the hell is there to think about? Legend Blake is finally offering to get between your legs and you're choosing *now* to think things through?"

Heat rushes up my neck. "Simmy, it isn't like that."

"And how the hell do you know?" She's scrolling again. "From the looks of things, the two of you have been dancing around the idea for months. Clearly, you were giving the man digital blue balls."

I snatch back my phone. "You don't know anything about our relationship."

"Uh-huh." Simone grabs a bottle of apple juice from the fridge and takes a seat on the arm of the sofa. "So, did Mr. Cuddles have any clue about your little computer love?"

I gently shake my head.

"I knew you were tired of His Royal Dullness." She swallows a chuckle with a nice long gulp of my juice.

"Honestly..." I cross the room and sink next to her on the sofa. "I'm starting to think the dull one is me."

Simone surveys me with sober eyes. "So why don't you do something about it?"

I glance at my phone and throw my head back on the sofa.

How did I get myself mixed up in this mess?

"Look," says Simone. "Though you and Justin are as bland as unseasoned chicken, you're clearly letting go of a good thing."

"You think so?"

She nods. "If you're gonna walk away, may as well make it worth the heartache."

Simone has never been much for relationships. The closest she's ever gotten to a committed boyfriend is Kyle, this guy she met at a bar in LA. He said he liked her bike. He was a thrill-seeker just like her. The two connected and have been on and off for two years now. But lately, he wants to be exclusive, which Simone says is the easiest way to turn her off.

My copy of *Keanu* rests on the table—a hilarious movie with the comedians Key and Peele racing against time to rescue some kingpin's cat. Justin and I must've watched it thirty times.

"Just a few days ago, everything was fine." I shrug. "Then I made a wish on this... *stupid* chain letter, and everything fell apart."

Simmy nods. "Well, that's some superstitious bullcrap, but I can't say the Hollywood stars aren't aligning." Simone sinks into the sofa, pushing me over with her hip.

"Ow! You don't have to sit on me!"

She laughs, giving my shoulder a nudge. "Just give it a shot. What have you got to lose?"

6

"*R*ight this way, ma'am," the hostess says, holding the door open and guiding me outside.

I step over the threshold, my gaze sweeping across the packed patio. Diners laugh and indulge in heaping plates of classic dishes, the rich scent of salmon and baked potatoes curling in the evening air. A gentle lakeside breeze brushes my cheeks, carrying the mellow strum of soft rock drifting from speakers above.

I agreed to meet Legend at TK's Seafood, one of his favorite spots downtown. He reserved a prime table for us out on the deck, where the lake shimmers under the glow of yacht lights.

I can't believe this is happening. I've imagined this moment for nearly a decade, and now, somehow, Legend Blake wants to meet with me. *Me.*

I brush some hair behind my ear as I settle into my seat. Overhead, string lights dangle like ornaments, their golden glow soft against the saffron-streaked sky. The sun, sinking low, casts its final glimmers over glossy tabletops and oversized umbrellas, tipping its hat to the Space Needle in the distance.

Tonight, I've chosen one of my favorite outfits: a black off-the-shoulder top, a sleek, flirty skirt, and ankle boots that make me feel unstoppable. My hair cascades over one shoulder in thick, beachy waves, the kind that make me feel like I belong in a moment like this. I gaze out at the water as I wait, my stomach bobbing like a buoy on the waves.

A server materializes out of nowhere, and I nearly jump out of my seat. He offers a polite smile as he fills our wine glasses with ice water, then neatly places rolled silverware before me. With a practiced nod, he assures me he'll return once the "other half of my party" arrives.

The other half of my party… Legend Blake is in a "party" with me.

Yeesh! I don't know which would be worse, getting here first and facing the gut-wrenching possibility that he might stand me up or arriving late only for him to realize that this was a *major* mistake.

And then, the air changes. A cool breeze rolls across the deck, raising goosebumps on my skin. People shift, whispering, their gaze locked on the patio door.

It's him.

Legend Blake in the flesh.

Of course, he's dressed to kill. An open-collared black dress shirt, perfectly tailored slacks, and a burgundy blazer that screams luxury. A pair of sleek designer boots, polished to perfection, complete the look. I swear, I've never seen a more flawless human being in my life.

Flanking him are two towering, muscle-bound men in all-black, their sunglasses giving them an air of silent authority. Bodyguards, no doubt.

A woman approaches, phone in hand, but the larger guard thrusts out an arm, stopping her cold. Before tension can build, Legend offers him a light pat on the shoulder and gestures her forward with an easy wave. A dazzling smile—effortless, magnetic—graces his lips as he grants her a selfie. But the guards, ever watchful, hold everyone else back.

Jeez, how did I not see this coming? Of course, things would be this complicated. Everyone on the planet knows who he is!

And then he looks up, and our eyes meet. A slow, knowing smile spreads across his lips, and just like that, he's moving—confident, effortless—his two guards shadowing his every step.

I jolt upright, smoothing down the ruffled layers of my cheetah-print rah-rah skirt.

Okay, Sam. Breathe. Stay cool. And for the love of all things holy, don't screw this up again!

But he spins on his heels and turns back to his guards.

Oh no. Is he changing his mind now that he's seen me in person?

He leans in, murmuring something to the guards, but the larger one responds with a firm shake of his head. With an exaggerated eye roll, Legend pivots and heads my way.

Maybe he was asking for space or something… I hope he wasn't trying to leave.

The charming smile returns to his face as he makes his way over. "Sam!"

"Legend!"

I stand, and he pulls me into a hug—warm, soft, and all-consuming, like rose petals, hot cocoa, and seventeen Snuggies all rolled into one. He smells like a tropical waterfall, fresh and intoxicating. My knees threaten to give out, but I refuse to let them.

"Dang…" He takes a step back, his hands still on my shoulders. "After looking at you every day on IG, I thought I'd know exactly what to expect. But you're a lot taller in person—and a whole lot more gorgeous."

My mouth falls open, but no words come out, only a light chuckle. *Legend Blake just called me 'gorgeous.'* My cheeks grow hot.

He places a hand on my back, introducing the two men accompanying him. The shorter one is Alex, and the bigger one is Lorenzo. "You don't mind if they hang around while we eat, do ya?"

I shake my head. "Of course not."

The two guards turn their backs and take position just a few feet away on each side of our table. They raise their hands, requesting that the other diners give *"the star his privacy."* Who knew a simple meeting would take such choreography?

Legend pushes in my chair like a perfect gentleman and takes a seat across from me. "I can't believe we're just now doing this," he says.

"I know, right?" My voice comes out thin and squeaky. With a dry throat, I take a sip of water.

Legend studies me for a moment, stroking his goatee, and making my cheeks prickle. *Maybe he finally recognizes me from school?*

I set down my glass, my pulse kicking up as I risk a glance at him. "What?"

He shakes his head, but he's still staring.

Okay, maybe he doesn't recognize me. "Is there something on my face?"

He sits up and chuckles. "Nah, you're… You're perfect."

My tummy flips and flutters. *Okay, Sam, don't pass out. You can do this, girl!*

"Thanks." I reach for my glass again, but my fingers betray me, knocking it over with a clumsy swipe. Water rushes toward the table's edge, and Legend jolts upright, but I manage to grab the glass before it tumbles to the ground. "Sorry, I… I'm just a little nervous."

The taller guard, Lorenzo, casts a glance over his shoulder, a brow creeping up over his shades. He returns to his post, unfazed, adjusting his shoulders.

Legend smiles and grabs a napkin, helping me mop up the spill. "I am too." I pause, eyeing him skeptically, but he shrugs. "I mean, it's been, what—three years now?"

I nod.

"And you know all my dirty little secrets," he says, in this really low and sexy voice.

I wave my hand and snort.

Oh my gosh, I did not just do that!

I bounce my knee, stomach twisting tight, as Legend stares at me in amusement. "Sorry. I'm just full of nerves."

"Just think of it this way," he says, "*If this was a complete nightmare, what's the worst that could happen? A giant gummy bear with sharp, pointy teeth runs out and bites your head off?*"

I laugh, recalling the idea I gave him over a year ago. He was performing at a royal wedding in Ghana for the first time and he was terrified. My silly suggestion got him back on his feet. "I suppose you're right," I say.

"And if that doesn't work"—he says with a James Bond-esque brow—"you could always picture me in my underwear."

I bust out laughing, another snort slipping out before I can stop it. "I'm sorry!" I gasp, throwing up a hand as I struggle to regain control.

"No apologies. It's adorable," he says. He leans back in his seat, a flicker in his eye. "It's nice to finally hear that laugh out loud."

The tension eases as the waiter returns to take our order, and soon, we're diving into plates of smoked salmon and buttery crab cakes. Rich red wine flows as we trade laughter and stories, reminiscing about old times like no time has passed at all.

As the sun melts into the horizon, the boldest of the stars begin to emerge, twinkling like tiny little secrets. And before I know it, I'm at ease, savoring the moment, the meal, and the company.

Legend laughs as we continue our talk. "Man, I can't believe I still did that show!"

"Right? I thought for sure you were gonna blow chunks all over your bass player!"

He throws a hand over his mouth, struggling to hold back his drink. "I almost didn't make it."

"But you did." I shrug. "Like only Legend Blake could."

He tilts his head slightly, a soft smile forming. "There's no way I could've done it without my Number One."

Refusing to let myself blush, I shove a piece of crab cake into my mouth, focusing on the rhythm of chewing.

All this time, I've longed for a moment where he'd look at me just like that. Now that it's finally here, I have no idea how to handle it. For the first time, I can actually imagine a future with Legend. Maybe my wish is coming true after all.

Legend dabs his mouth with a napkin, then glances at the guards. They've been keeping an eye out, blocking the other diners from snapping photos or videos. He leans forward, elbows on the table, this sober look in his eye.

"Sam," he says, his voice quieter now, "I've been meaning to ask you something. And it only felt right asking you face-to-face."

Wait. There's no way that Legend Blake officially wants to ask me out... Right?

I swallow the lump in my throat, praying that he does. "Okay. Sure. Go ahead."

"Okay. So, you remember how a few months back, I had that fallout with Indigo Taylor?"

I nod. How could I forget? Indigo Taylor is only one of the most influential entertainers in the world. She was a child actress who launched a singing career in her teenage years and has over twenty million followers on Instagram. I must've cried for two weeks straight when she and Legend started going out.

"And you remember how after that I said I'd back off with chicks for a bit?"

As long as he was available to me, I was thrilled. I nod again.

"Well," he says. "I'm thinking that maybe I changed my mind."

EEEEE! Pick me! Pick me!

I swallow. "You're ready to start dating again?"

He nods, a sly grin playing on his lips.

Okay, Sam. This is it. Don't screw up now.

I brush some hair behind my ear, watching him with a racing heart. He reaches across the table and places his hand on mine.

Oh my—! Please God, help me keep this crab cake down.

"Sam, after everything that went down before, I honestly wasn't sure I'd bounce back. If it hadn't been for you, I don't know how I would've made it."

I'm trying to resist the urge to grab a fork and gnaw on it. "I'm glad I could be there for you, L."

Maybe he does remember that day backstage. This could finally be our moment.

He runs a thumb across my knuckles, and my heart leaps. I hold my breath, waiting for him to ask me...

"That's why I need your help."

I blink. "Hmm?"

He pats my hand, sitting up straight. "I know it sounds crazy, but I gotta get her back, Sam. And I can only do that if you help me."

"I'm sorry. What are we talking about now?"

"Indigo. I know I said I would move on, but I *can't*, Sam. She's the love of my life. I can't just walk away like nothing ever happened. I'll never be able to live with myself if I don't give it all I got. Know what I mean?"

I bob my head, my heart sinking into the depths of despair.

"So," he says on an exhale, "I want you to come to LA."

"*LA?* Legend, what do you mean?"

"Look, if I'm gonna win her back, I need some *serious* intel."

"*Intel?* You mean like a spy?"

"Exactly!"

I'm in a daze as Legend goes on to describe this little plan of his. He needs someone to talk to Indigo. A close friend. A confidant who can get the diva to spill all her little secrets without slipping up and snitching on him. Legend wants to know about her feelings for him, and why she decided to end things between them three months ago.

His eyes spark with passion as he goes on about the idea. "And once I know that I'll be able to make things right."

I push a smile onto my face. "But L, don't you think this is a bit much? And what does any of this have to do with me?"

He grins.

I draw a sharp breath, shaking my head. "Legend, no. This? This is crazy!"

"Sam, she's looking for a personal assistant. You're the best assistant I know! And don't worry about the cost. I'll cover everything."

I shake my head like a stubborn toddler, leaning back in my seat. "L, I can't—" I glance around and lower my voice. "I can't spy on Indigo Taylor! I'll get arrested or something."

"No, you won't," he says. "I know some people who know some people. It'll all be legit, I promise you."

I fix my gaze on him, my throat tight with emotion.

He wants me to spy on Indigo? After all this time, he's still pining for her? What about me? What about *us*?

No. This... this is insane. This is illegal!

But also... this is Legend.

And the last time someone asked me to take a risk for them, I ended up alone.

Do I really want to lose Legend too?

Legend's gaze holds mine, laden with quiet anticipation. "Come on, Sam. Please?"

7

This place looks like a Disney Resort.

I shield my eyes against the blazing noon sun as I wait at a red light. The heat feels almost unbearable, but I try to ignore it.

Sunny Hollywood Apartments stands tall on the corner of a busy intersection, reaching into the cloudless blue sky. Along the sidewalk, a row of palm trees lines the edge, guarding its border like the moat of a castle. I glance at my phone, double-checking the address.

"This can't be right."

But it's what Legend gave me. I turn the corner into a parking structure, still second-guessing every part of this ridiculous plan.

I'm only a week out of grad school, yet here I am. I refused to get on a plane to come to LA, so I drove my Corolla hatchback. Not that it was any easier to leave Seattle. Simone had to escort me halfway here before I finally agreed to part ways.

Mom was already heartbroken over me and Justin breaking up after so many years. So when I told her I was leaving to chase a "job opportunity" in LA, she could barely conceal her anxiety. She wanted me close to the family, being a good influence on my little sisters. Not across the country, working with some Hollywood celebrity.

Some Hollywood celebrity being an understatement. I'm not supposed to tell a soul that it's Legend Blake. Of course, I told Simone, but she doesn't count. I tell her everything.

And Trey, of course, has his two cents to add. Despite always pushing me to spread my wings, even he's confused. "You couldn't go the mile for Justin, but you're doing it now?"

He'll always be Team Justin. For once, I need to be Team Me.

I know it's crazy. I'm not exactly known for being *spontaneous.* Technically, I don't even have the job yet. And that would justify me freaking out about this entire situation had Legend not already volunteered to cover *everything.*

I'm not even sure I can pull this off. But some part of me feels like I have to.

This could be my only shot.

I loop the parking structure for what feels like hours before nearly taking out the back of a Lamborghini. Finally, I find a spot and park. Here's hoping this all pays off.

Legend left the keys at the front desk. I sign what's left of the paperwork and take the elevator to my new apartment on the ninth floor. I step inside and nearly lose my balance, my breath catching at the sight.

The apartment looks like something straight out of a luxury travel magazine. Sleek, stylish, and effortlessly sophisticated. It's fully furnished with mid-century modern pieces, plush wall-to-wall carpet, and towering floor-to-ceiling windows. I tiptoe around glass tables, admiring bright shades of teal and orange decor. The fridge is fully stocked, and the Hollywood sign can be spotted from my bedroom window.

I slap a hand over my mouth, laughing.

My own queen-sized bed! This has got to be a dream!

I'm seconds away from pinching myself when the door buzzer goes off. I peer through the peephole… and nearly pass out.

Legend Blake is standing right outside my door. He's waiting in the hall with Lorenzo. The two exchange glances, and Legend knocks.

"Yo, Sam, where you at? The front desk said you just got in."

My tie-dye tank top and jogging shorts are *so* not ready for this. I dart to the mirror, fumbling with my side-ponytail. Not much better. I grab the cardigan draped over my luggage and throw it on, hoping it's enough to make me look like I've got my life together.

"Maybe I missed her outside," Legend mumbles out in the hall. "I'll call and see what's up."

My phone rings on the kitchen counter just as I yank open the door. "Hey!"

Legend pauses, the phone still pressed to his ear, his eyes sweeping over me. "Hey, beautiful." Realizing he's still on the call, he quickly hangs up and steps inside, pulling me into a hug.

If only I'd had time to shower…

This town is obnoxiously hot. I feel so sticky and gross.

Legend doesn't seem to care. He gives a casual nod to his guard, and Lorenzo immediately turns his back to us.

My eyes flick between the two of them. "Does… he want to come in?"

"Nah," says Legend. "He'll wait."

Lorenzo is like a statue as I slowly shut the door.

"So…" Legend rubs his hands together, looking around. "You like it?"

"I love it. But you didn't have to do all this."

The assignment is supposed to be temporary. I can't imagine what this all must've cost him.

Legend spins back, taking me by both hands, sending a jolt of electricity through my arms. "Of course I did." He drapes an arm over my shoulders, pulling me toward the balcony window. "I mean, this view, right?"

I nod, my mind a blur. He's got on a light bomber jacket with jeans today, and he smells like a fresh sea breeze. A leather briefcase is slung across his chest.

He turns, lowering his head to meet my gaze. "You all right?"

"Mmhmm." I waver on my feet and start to fall, but he catches me.

"Yo! Sam, what's going on?"

My eyes flutter as I gaze up at his handsome face, everything around us spinning. He manages to get me to the sofa, then rushes to the fridge.

"Here, drink this." He opens a bottle of sparkling water and helps me drink. I can't look at anything but him. "That better?" he asks.

I nod. "Thanks."

He exhales deeply, his gaze softening. "You do realize we'll be seeing a lot more of each other, right?"

That's why I'm here.

"You gonna fangirl every time you see me?" he asks.

"I might."

Legend chuckles and encourages me to drink some more, so I do. He leans his elbows on his lap, chin in hand. "You know this means the world to me, right?"

I nod, knowing how much *Indigo* means to him. When he started seeing her, our daily conversations dropped to nothing but brief updates. For six miserable months, all he could talk about was *her*, and how "head over heels" he was. And when she broke his heart—falling into the lap of a world-renowned boxer at a nightclub—he ghosted me for nearly a week.

I'm not here for her. I'm here for him.

But hopefully, with a little more time, I'll prove to him that she's not all she seems.

Legend and I exchange smiles, the kind that linger just a little too long. But we're interrupted when the door buzzes again, cutting through the stillness between us

He jumps up before I can move. "I bet that's for me."

Lorenzo hands him a paper bag, and Legend thanks him before shutting the door. He proudly presents the bag to me. "Ordered lunch."

A few minutes later, I find myself sharing another meal with Legend Blake. Containers of fried rice sit in front of us, an array of sushi spread across the glass coffee table.

"Help yourself," he says.

"I don't know where to start." I stare at the different options, and some of them seem to be staring back at me. *Maybe I should stick to my water.*

Legend frowns. "You've had sushi before, right?"

I softly shake my head. I've never been a fan of trying new foods. Even when I'd go to restaurants with Justin, salmon and rice pilaf were generally my go-to.

Legend groans dramatically, throwing a hand over his heart. "We've gotta fix that, right now!" He grabs a pair of chopsticks and picks up a piece of sushi like he's done it a thousand times. "California Roll. I never met a soul that ain't like it." He holds it up to my lips, a playful gleam in his eye.

Well... *this* is what I came for.

I give him a quick once-over before taking a bite. The moment the flavors hit my tongue, I cover my mouth, barely able to contain my delight. "That's actually really good."

"What I tell you?" He offers the rest of the roll to me, and I swallow it whole. "Maybe now you won't be passing out on my watch."

"I didn't pass out! I just got a little... dizzy. It's hot out here, you know!"

"Uh-huh." Legend arranges a few more sushi on a plate and passes it my way. I fumble with my chopsticks, trying to get a grip as he goes over the plan.

"I got it all worked out," he says, pulling a piece of paper from his briefcase. "Here's your résumé. You're an aspiring screenwriter trying to get your foot in the door. For now, you're working with multiple temp agencies until you get your big break. Just tell her Ruby sent you."

I nod, scanning the résumé. "Ruby. Got it." According to this piece of paper, I'm a Long Beach native, who's been grinding in Hollywood for three years. I've worked with celebrities like Keke Palmer and Emma Roberts. I even walked Zoë Kravitz's dog. "You really think she'll buy this?"

"It's foolproof," says Legend, sitting back with his rice. "Trust. The people I know are excellent at reinventing identities."

Suddenly, I'm not so hungry anymore. I set everything down and take another sip of water.

Changing my identity. Lying from day one. The thought makes me want to vomit.

First it was Justin—lying to him about why I needed space, about why we weren't right for each other. And there's so much Legend doesn't know. If I'm pretending to be someone I'm not, it won't get any easier.

But I don't want to lose him. I don't want to be the one to mess this up.

Legend rests a hand on my knee, and I get goosebumps all over. "Hey, there's no way I can pull this off without you."

"Except going to Indigo yourself and telling her how you feel."

"You think I ain't tried that?"

I purse my lips.

"Look," he says. "She's not gonna open up to just anybody. And from what I hear, she could really use a friend right now."

"You want me to be *friends* with Indigo Taylor?"

His grin is irresistible. "You been a great friend to me."

Darn it! Why does he have to be so frickin' gorgeous?

Staring into his twinkling brown eyes, I know there's nothing I wouldn't do for him. But this feels wrong. I just want to prove to him that Indigo Taylor is nothing more than a little, promiscuous nightmare. And then, maybe he'll realize that I'm the girl of his dreams.

I duck my head with a shy smile and grab another piece of sushi. "You owe me several dinners."

"Of course." He shoots me a wink as his phone buzzes. "Plus, a trip to Disneyland." We laugh as he answers his phone. "'Sup?"

But the warmth drains from his face as he breathes a heavy sigh. He stands and steps over to the balcony window, his shoulders tense.

There's only one person who could suck all the life out of him like that… Victoria Austin. Legend's manager.

His eyes squeeze shut as he rubs his temples. "Yeah, I hear you. I'm on my way." He hangs up and turns back to me, regret written all over his face. His lips press into an adorable pout.

"You gotta go?" I ask.

"Unfortunately," he says. "You know the boss. If we ain't slaving away, making her money, we better be strategizing how to make her *more* money." He lets out a light chuckle, but his smile isn't nearly as bright.

I sit up on the sofa. "You ever talk to her about that idea you had?"

"Launching my own label?" He shakes his head. "I always tell her, if I knew it would mean the end of my creative freedom, I never would've signed that stupid contract. She says, 'You win some, you lose some.' But she don't know what it's like to lose."

Legend grabs his things, and I stand to hug him goodbye.

"I'm sorry about rushing off like this," he says, his warm voice brushing against my cheek.

I close my eyes, inhaling his fresh shower scent one last time. I'll be on a high for days. "It's okay. You do what you gotta do."

He lingers for a moment, then steps back, his thumb grazing my jaw in a touch so soft it sends a shiver down my spine. "You're amazing."

I barely manage a smile before he's gone.

The door clicks shut, and I stand frozen, the silence rushing in like a cold tide.

It's like he's taken a part of me with him, and I'm not sure how to get it back.

With a slow breath, I release the tightness in my chest and sink into the massive pile of sofa pillows as if I'm floating in a dream.

8

ake nice. Be a friend. Take notes.

I take a deep, measured breath—in, then out—just like Professor Natalie taught me, as the steel entry gate to Indigo Taylor's mansion glides open. Her estate stretches across an expansive lot, partially hidden behind towering sycamores. The house itself is a striking art deco masterpiece, all clean lines, a flat roof, and stark white concrete exterior.

I can't believe I'm doing this. God, why am I doing this?

Maybe because three years of secret DMs add up to something.

Because even though he's a celebrity, he's the only one who called—*actually called*—when I had a panic attack during finals.

Because the night Trey said I should be more like my dad—*chasing stories worth dying for*—Legend sent me a voice note at midnight. Just six words: *He'd be proud of you, Sam.*

I squeeze my steering wheel tight and force myself out of the car. *You can do this, Sam. Do it for Legend!*

Making my way up the stamped concrete walkway, I step up to the door. I reach for the doorbell with trembling fingers but stop and throw my hands on my knees.

Oh, I can't breathe… I think I'm gonna pass out, or barf, or both… She'll step out, on her way to a meeting or Pilates, and she'll find some random, twiggy chick, covered in green chunks, passed out on her walkway.

I'm preparing to turn and run when the door swings open.

A stocky Hispanic woman with rosy cheeks and side-swept bangs stares down at me. "You here for Ms. Indigo?"

I raise a brow, my stomach still churning like ice cream. "Hmm?"

"Ms. Indigo? You here to help?"

I stand up straight, forcing a nod, and she invites me in.

The woman—Eva, the house manager—barely spares me a glance as she informs me that Indigo's upstairs and has a meeting in twenty minutes. She needs help getting ready. With a quick gesture down the long hallway toward a grand, winding staircase at the center of the house, Eva vanishes before I can ask a single question.

"Okay…" *Inhale slow, exhale hard.* "Here goes."

Brushing some hair out of my face, I smooth my hands over my vinyl jacket and jeans. Then, with a deep breath, I make my way down the hall, wobbling in my slouch boots.

The glistening hardwood floors seem to stretch endlessly beneath my feet, the staircase drifting farther and farther away. The hallway feels infinite, lined with a repeating pattern of mirrors and self-portraits. Indigo smiling. Indigo pouting. Indigo captured in a charcoal sketch, a strand of hair curled around her finger.

At last, the hall opens into a grand space. A high-end living room sprawls to the right, and at the back, a sleek kitchen gleams with black countertops and matte-finish oak cabinets. More portraits of Indigo dominate the walls, surrounded by bold animal prints and tribal figurines, giving off this African-queen vibe.

This place isn't just a house. This place is like a frickin' museum.

"Hello?" I call softly.

Upstairs, hip-hop music thumps through the ceiling. I close my eyes and sigh, gripping the rail.

I am doing this for Legend. And Legend alone.

The bass grows heavier as I climb the stairs, leading me straight to the first room on the left. The door is slightly ajar.

I knock. "Ma'am?"

She doesn't answer. I take a step inside.

Indigo's bedroom—easily the size of a three-car garage—is bathed in rich hues of purple and pink. The lights are dim, slivers of sunlight peeking beneath plush velvet curtains. The floor is a mess of discarded underwear and empty liquor bottles, thick scents of whiskey and lavender in the air.

At the center of it all, sprawled across a massive California king-size bed, lies a figure, a cascade of platinum blonde curls with dark roots obscuring her face.

Indigo?

My pulse kicks up as I rush to the lush pink carpet lining the bed. A colossal portrait of Indigo Taylor hangs above the headboard, gazing down at me with critical eyes. I jostle a glistening, golden arm.

Oh, my gosh! If she OD'd, they'll totally put it on me. They'll drag me in front of a grand jury on one of those nationally broadcast trials on TV, and no one will believe my story when I *swear* that I didn't do a thing to harm Hollywood's Sweetheart. They'll throw the book at me. They'll say that I wanted her dead because I wanted her man, and that's something I couldn't deny. Then they'll lock me up, for the rest of my life, and no one will ever visit me… Not even Legend Blake.

Then a low groan escapes her. She shifts, rubbing her face into the purple satin sheets before going still. Slowly, she lifts her head, one thick feathery brow arching high. "Is there a Madonna concert in town or something?"

Huh?

Not seeming to care, she rolls back on the bed, running a hand down her face, her black lace bra peeking out from a silk emerald blouse.

I clear my throat. "Ma'am, I've been informed that you have a meeting in about twenty minutes. If you'd like my help—"

Indigo groans again, flopping onto her belly. "Shut up! Nobody needs your help." She tries to push herself up, but her hands slip, and she faceplants right back into the sheets with a muffled *oof.*

I take a step forward, grabbing her arm. "Here, let me—"

"Get your sticky hands off me!" She snatches out of my grasp. "I said I don't need your damn help!" Then she gags… and hurls all over my boots.

I freeze, stomach twisting as warm, lumpy brown vomit trickles across my feet.

Indigo hiccups, staring down at the mess. "They were ugly anyway."

From what I've seen in the headlines and on social media, Indigo is known for her partying and late wild nights. But since she ended things with Legend, it's been on another level. I had no idea that things were this bad.

"What the…?"

A woman stands in the doorway, frowning. She's Asian, with bold blue eyeshadow and ruby-red lips, rocking a leather jacket and thigh-high boots. Her black shoulder-length hair is razor-sharp.

The woman pinches her nose, fanning the air. "Ugh! It smells like potpourri and beer in here." Her assessing gaze rests on me. "Who are you?"

"I'm Samara Allen." I'd step over and shake her hand, but… boots. I give a gentle wave. "Temporary assistant."

Emphasis on the temporary.

The woman couldn't care less. She rushes to the other side of the bed, barks a command at the wireless speaker to cut the music, and grabs Indigo's ankles. With a firm tug, she slides her down to the edge of the mattress, then lightly pats her cheek.

"Indigo, honey, it's Kelly. You've gotta wake up, sweetheart."

Oh! This is Kelly! Legend mentioned her. The publicist... or was it the manager? Either way, she's clearly the one who cleans up the mess.

Indigo releases a guttural whine, her head thrashing back and forth. "I'm up. I'm up!"

Kelly doesn't look convinced. "The media team will be here any minute. We've gotta get you cleaned up." Kelly flicks her stern gaze to me. "Can you help?"

Ten minutes later, we've got her in a marble, luxury alcove tub as Kelly helps her bathe. "How many times are you gonna do this, Indigo? You keep this up, and you'll tank your career," says Kelly.

I quietly rinse my boots in one of several black granite sinks, watching murky water swirl down the drain. The stench still clings to my shoes. Not to mention my dignity.

Meanwhile, Indigo reclines in the tub like some tragic queen—mascara smudged, platinum curls damp and lifeless—as Kelly scrubs her down.

What did Legend ever see in this train wreck?

Indigo glowers at my reflection in the mirror. "Who's that?"

Kelly glances back at me, exhaustion etched in her features. "That's, uh..."

"Samara. Allen," I say.

"Samara Allen," Kelly nods, seeming to remember. "She's here to, uh—"

"Help," I say.

"*Help?*" Indigo scowls, her plump lips drooping. "I don't need *help.*"

She needed my help getting off her face a few minutes ago.

I turn, plastering on my best smile. "I heard you needed a personal assistant. Ruby sent me."

"Ruby?" Kelly's brow shoots up. *"Ruby* sent you?"

I nod. "Mmhmm."

They both stare at me as I return to my boots.

—————— ✦✦✦✦✦ ——————

A few minutes later, I'm sitting in the living room on a lengthy camelback sofa. Across from me, a brass vintage coffee table rests atop a zebra skin rug, its bold stripes clashing with the room's otherwise sleek aesthetic.

Above the fireplace, a TV the size of a baby elephant looms, dark and silent. Floor-to-ceiling windows stretch across the entire room, framing the outdoor pool like a museum exhibit, shimmering, pristine, and completely unnecessary.

I exhale slowly, glancing toward the front door. I could get up and walk out right now, and I doubt anyone would notice or care.

Before I can decide whether to make my covert exit, my phone chimes.

LEGEND: *How's it going, beautiful?*

I close my eyes and breathe a heavy sigh. That's right... No one would care but *him*.

SAM: *Great! We'll be BFFs in no time.* ☺

I throw my head back against the sofa, squeezing my eyes shut, hoping to block out the feeling of being trapped in this world that isn't mine.

"Why would you do that?" shouts Indigo, making her way down the stairs with Kelly in tow. "I would've been fine!"

"You would've been a mess," says Kelly. "We'll just have to reschedule."

I guess the meeting is canceled.

Indigo halts when she spots me in the living room, her gaze zeroing in like a hawk's. She charges my way, the silk of her kimono trailing behind her like a cape.

I sit up straight as she takes a seat in the throne-like armchair across from me, crossing her sculpted dancer legs. Her high-waist athletic booty shorts make them appear ten times longer. The loose white crop top she's wearing shows off her perfectly chiseled midriff, as if she was born in a gym and molded by angels.

At least she seems sober now.

She gives me a once-over, tilting her head like I'm some kind of puzzle. "Ruby sent you, hmm?"

Okay, Sam. Get this right!

"Yes," I say, reaching into my bag. "I was told you needed a temporary assistant, and there's potential for a permanent position." I pull out my phony polished résumé and pass it over.

She rips it to pieces without a second glance, her expression stone cold. No emotion, just a flick of her wrist as she tosses the tiny shreds of paper over her shoulder. They flutter to the floor like confetti.

"Tell me about yourself."

My throat goes dry. "Okay, um, I was born in Long Beach. I've been working in Hollywood for three years…" I recite the rest of my bogus experience with a straight face, fingers clasped in my lap, refusing to scratch or show any sign of nerves.

Kelly leans against the banister, watching the impromptu interview—the same way a bored lifeguard watches the hundredth kid cannonball into the pool.

Indigo leans back in her chair, arms crossed, her shimmering brown eyes studying me. She runs her tongue across her teeth, the diamond stud in her nose gleaming beneath chandelier lights.

"Okay," she says. "Let's see how much you can help me."

⁘

She has me sign an NDA, and the rest of my day is hell.

"Give me breakfast," she says.

"What kind of breakfast?"

"Figure it out."

It turns out that the chef only comes in to make dinner, so the rest is on me. I throw together some scrambled eggs, fresh strawberries, and toast. "Here's your breakfast."

Without so much as a glance, she heads downstairs to the gym. "I'm not hungry anymore."

She's finishing her Brazilian Jiu-Jitsu training when I return from the kitchen. "Bring me a warm towel," she says.

"A warm towel? Where are the warm towels?"

"Figure it out."

I find Eva in the laundry room, and she tosses a towel my way. She casually informs me that next time, I should have the towels in the dryer before breakfast. I thank her, then sprint back across the mansion.

"Here's your towel."

"I've already got one," says Indigo. "Next time, pick up the pace. What's on my schedule this afternoon?"

"Um..."

"Figure it out."

I find Kelly in the library. "Do you know Ms. Indigo's schedule?"

She glances up, scrolling through her phone. "Nothing special today. But there's a magazine interview tomorrow."

I let out a quiet sigh of relief. "Thank you."

As I turn to leave, she grabs my arm. Extending a hand, she says, "Kelly Watson. Publicist."

Publicist! I knew it!

"Nice to meet you," I say, shaking her hand.

"So, you know Ruby?" she asks, sizing me up. "From Rihanna's team?"

My stomach drops and bounces like a carnival ride. I blink, forcing a smile. "Of course."

Kelly nods, her gaze lingering just a second too long, and I make my escape.

Shoot! Shoot! Shoot!

"Nothing special on the schedule today," I tell Indigo. "But there's a magazine interview tomorrow."

She's lying beside the pool, a masseuse giving her some sort of drainage massage. "Do better. Keep up."

"Yes, ma'am."

"And, uh—what's your name again?"

"Sam."

"Sam." She points at her phone on the patio table. "Check my DMs."

"Huh?"

"Delete the useless ones."

"How do I know which ones—?"

"Figure it out."

By lunchtime, I'm completely spent, and my feet are killing me. I honestly have no idea what Legend sees in this chick. She's rude, spoiled, and an all-around nightmare to work for. Sure, she's gorgeous and famous, but up close? She's even worse than her online persona.

Maybe getting rid of her will be easier than I thought...

I'm just delivering her lunch—a Caesar salad that her personal chef left in the fridge last night—when I overhear her and Kelly talking in the dressing room. And yes, she has an *entire room* dedicated to clothes and makeup.

"Look, I hate to tell you this," says Kelly. "But I spoke with your agent. She hasn't received a single decent offer for you in a month."

Indigo waves a dismissive hand. "They'll come around. It's only a matter of time before they start craving *real* talent again." She sits at the vanity, idly scraping at the rhinestones on her pink chrome nails with tweezers.

Kelly leans in, lowering her voice as she meets the starlet's gaze in the mirror. "Indigo, the word 'difficult' is starting to get attached to your name. You *know* what that means in this town."

Indigo stills, staring at Kelly's reflection, the color draining from her face. "What should I do?" She whips around, panic creeping into her voice. "Kelly, acting is my life. I can't fall off now."

Kelly studies the floor, her lips pressed into a pensive frown. "Lay low. Get cleaned up. More exercise, no social media besides sponsored posts... Keep your image tight."

Indigo nods, dropping her gaze to her hands.

"I'll make some calls," says Kelly, giving her shoulder a squeeze, "see what I can work out." Kelly turns and nearly jumps when she spots me at the door.

With a small nod, she moves past me.

Indigo's glassy eyes darken as they meet mine in the mirror. "What do you want?"

I lift the plate an inch. "I, uh—have your lunch—"

"Oh my gosh, Cyndi Lauper. *Get lost!*" She grabs a brush and hurls it at me. It clips the doorframe as I duck into the hall.

She barricades herself in her room for the rest of the day. I don't know if I'm supposed to leave or stick around, so I hover, helping Eva with small tasks and making sure the chef delivers food to Indigo's door. Not that she ever opens it.

It's 7 p.m. when I slip into the kitchen. I haven't eaten all day. Hunger gnaws at my stomach like a feral cat as I yank open the fridge. Why didn't I eat those eggs she rejected?

"You still here?"

I slam the fridge, standing up straight. Indigo is at the end of the counter, her hair wrapped in a towel.

"I figured you left with Kelly," she says.

"No, ma'am. I'm here to assist with whatever you need."

"Please." She waves a hand. "Stop calling me that."

"Yes, ma'am. I mean—Okay, Miss."

She lets out a small laugh. "Indigo is fine. I honestly thought you quit this afternoon."

I shrug. "Everyone's entitled to a bad day."

"Are you talking about me? 'Cause I'm not having a bad day."

"Uh..."

Indigo busts out laughing. "Anybody ever tell you that you look just like a chihuahua?"

This chick... "No, Ma—I mean, no, Ms. Indigo."

She stares me down, her full lips still curved in amusement.

Just grin and bear it, Sam. No complaints... just like Daddy taught you.

I clasp my hands in front of me, keeping my voice even. "Would you like anything else, Ms. Indigo? I could page the chef to send up more food if you like."

"So, what—you trying to make me fat now?"

I blink, scrambling for the right response, but she's already rolling her eyes.

With a swift step, she brushes past me, bumping me out of the way like I'm just another kitchen appliance. She yanks open the fridge and grabs a bottle of water. "Come back tomorrow. Seven a.m. sharp. Show up late and you're fired. Got it?"

I nod as she heads up the stairs, her silk robe billowing behind her like it's got its own attitude.

———————— ✦✦✦✦✦ ————————

I fall into my bed, every muscle in my body aching. The drive home took nearly an hour thanks to traffic, and now I feel like I've run a marathon in heels.

Oh… Why did I ever agree to do this? I throw a pillow over my face. And then my phone rings.

Oh no! What if she needs something!

Tumbling out of bed, I scramble across the floor to my bag. But when I see the name on the screen, my breath catches. "Hello?"

"Hey, beautiful."

"Hey… handsome." It sounds like Legend is outside somewhere. The wind gusts in my ear. "You hang gliding or something?"

"Ha-ha," he says. "I'm on my balcony."

"Oh…" I fall silent, suddenly at a loss for words. We usually stick to texts and DMs. This is maybe the third time he's actually called. And that voice… smooth as melted chocolate, rich enough to make me weak.

"Just wanted to check on you," he says. "See how your first day went."

Awful! It was an awful, horrific nightmare! She yelled at me. She barfed on me. She threw a frickin' brush at my face!

"Wonderful," I say. "She's so sweet."

"Really? From what I've heard she's kind of a nightmare."

"*Whaaat?*" My pitch couldn't be any higher. "No way."

Legend chuckles. "You two hit it off, huh?"

"Mmhmm. In fact, she wants me to come back tomorrow."

"That's great!" he says.

I fall back on the thick, luxurious carpet, rubbing my temples.

I'd give almost anything to go back home right now. Almost.

Legend exhales into the phone. "So, any news yet?"

Of course, that's why he's calling. He wants to know if I've dug up any dirt. But how am I supposed to get intel when I can't get within three feet of the chick without her projectile vomiting in my face?

"Not quite," I say softly.

The line goes silent for a moment. Finally, he says, "It's cool. You know, I really appreciate you doing this, Sam."

"I know." *I just hope the near-death-by-hairbrush and verbal are worth it.*

There's another pause on the line.

I'm just about to make it clear that I'd do it all again in a heart-beat, when he says, "So tell me more about your day."

A smile slips across my lips.

It's silly, how one voice can make all the chaos feel worth it.

9

The interview's in full swing when I slip quietly into the back of the room, careful not to disturb the scene. Indigo's had me running through her chaotic schedule all morning, managing calls and answering emails. It's only been a couple hours, but I feel like I've already earned my paycheck today.

Indigo's perched on her camelback sofa, looking like a different person. The woman I've seen ripping through the mansion like a tornado is nowhere to be found. Instead, there's a softer, more polished version of her, elegant, collected. The lights gleam off her sleek black dress, and her platinum curls fall perfectly around her shoulders.

She's chatting with—*Gasp!* It's Nina Banks!

I've been following Nina for years. She was a top amateur investigative journalist on YouTube before she got picked up by *The Spotlight Report*, the nationally televised entertainment show. She didn't even have a degree, but she uncovered some of the *wildest* celebrity scandals in LA, from exposing a pop star's secret marriage to breaking the news of a notorious actor's cheating scandal during a live award show. She's young, Black, and absolutely gorgeous, with sharp eyes and a ruby-red bob that's as iconic as her fearless interviews.

Every time I see her drop a bombshell on someone, I can't help but admire her hustle. I'm just hoping I can get through this and sneak in a selfie with her without Indigo flipping out.

Kelly gives me a quick, silent wave from the edge of the living room, just out of camera view. She's standing in the shadows, guiding Indigo, giving subtle instructions with nothing more than a shift of her head.

"So, Indigo," Nina's voice lilts, smooth as silk, "you've been through *a lot* in the public eye. But you seem to be in a better place these days. How have you been handling the ups and downs of fame?"

Indigo smiles softly, almost like she's trying to forget the world around her. She seems so genuine, it's easy to believe she's America's sweetheart. "You know, it's not easy. But at the end of the day, I've learned to protect my peace. Surrounding myself with the right people has made *all* the difference."

I can't help but roll my eyes. She's so full of it. But damn, I can't deny how convincing she sounds. She must've reviewed these questions with Kelly a dozen times.

Nina exchanges a brief glance with her producer beside the cameraman, the mood in the room tightening. Kelly sees them too. She unfolds her arms, pinning them with a hard stare that says they better not try anything funny.

But Nina's not paying attention.

"So, you know all of us was eating up your relationship with Legend Blake. Y'all were *total* relationship goals!" Nina says, her tone playful. "Not that long ago, you two seemed inseparable. Is there anything he could do to maybe… get you to give him another shot?"

I lean forward, intrigued. I'd love to have a juicy tidbit to finally take back to Legend. Something that won't come between us, of course.

But the mention of his name turns Indigo's entire posture rigid. Her smile fades as quickly as it appeared, and for a second, she looks like she's going to break.

I almost feel bad for her... until she jerks to her feet.

"Get out." Her eyes narrow, her glare sharp enough to cut glass.

Kelly inches forward, her hands held up in a quiet plea for calm. But Indigo doesn't care.

"I said... *Get. Out.*"

Nina blinks, clearly caught off guard by the harshness. She looks around—to her producer, to Kelly, even *me* for help—but we're all at a loss. "Indigo, I—I just thought—"

"No." Indigo interrupts, her tone icy. "You were told. *No* questions about Legend."

The entire room freezes. Nina's face hardens, the confidence in her expression faltering just slightly. But Indigo's already up, striding toward the door like she's just wrapped up a perfect day at the spa. Nina scrambles to follow, stammering a final apology, but it's no use. Indigo's made her decision.

Kelly's hands fly up in a gesture of helplessness as she calls after her. "Indigo, wait!" She trails after Indigo, her heels clicking on the floor as she follows her out of the room.

I don't even know if I feel bad for Nina, but I sure as hell feel the weight of the tension in the room as the crew whispers.

This is the real Indigo, and she *does not* play.

✦✦✦✦✦

From then on, it's another day of Indigo-induced torture. She's got me prepping her meals, scheduling appointments, and—because she clearly enjoys watching me suffer—standing in as her Jiu-Jitsu partner.

I don't know a thing about Jiu-Jitsu, but that doesn't stop Indigo from flipping me like a ragdoll. The mat and I become close, intimate friends as she hip-tosses me, arm-drags me, and somehow folds me into a position that defies basic human anatomy.

At the end of it all, I find myself sprawled across the floor, staring at the ceiling, questioning my life choices. My back is screaming, my limbs are noodles, and Indigo? She's scrolling through her phone like she just wrapped up a light yoga session.

A while later, I'm collapsed on the camelback sofa, gingerly stretching my sore limbs, as she struts toward the door, freshly changed and effortlessly put together. She gives me a once-over, wrinkling her nose as she passes. "I'm out. Tomorrow, do better."

Wait. She's letting me go early?

The door clicks shut behind her, and I make a wobbly escape for my things.

⊹ ✦✦✦✦✦ ⊹

Legend Blake lives in a mansion on a hill. No, literally, he lives in a mansion on a frickin' hill. The place is part cruise ship, part private jet, and so far above the city it might as well have its own zip code. Up here, privacy isn't a concern, it's a given. When he heard I was off early, he invited me over to catch up.

The second I step inside, he pulls me into a heartfelt squeeze, the scent of his cologne, warm and addictive. Without hesitation, I inhale all I can, refueling for the week.

"You're more gorgeous every time I see you," he says.

I shove his shoulder, giggling like a teenager. "Stop!" But I totally want him to go on.

Just behind him is an open floor plan the size of a gymnasium. On one end sits a theater-sized TV with white lounge sofas big enough to seat a wedding party. On the other is a modern kitchen with a lengthy breakfast bar. A stark white staircase branches off the center of the gigantic living space, while panoramic windows and glass doors frame a breathtaking view of the Hollywood Hills. Seriously, not a single curtain on the first floor.

At the bar, two guys and a girl sip drinks, their conversation fading as they note my arrival. Legend takes me by the hand—*he takes me by the hand!*—and leads me over for introductions. The bulky guy is his homeboy, Hunter, the short guy in the baseball cap is his assistant, Cam, and the curvy girl with the long black hair and flawless mocha skin is his stylist, Jackie. "They're my entourage," says Legend with a smile.

"Man, whatever," says Hunter, a dimple appearing in his cheek. "I don't get paid to babysit your ass!" Hunter socks him in the arm, and Legend winces at me.

"You see how hard it is to find good help these days?" Everyone laughs as Legend rubs his shoulder with a pout.

He leads me through the rest of the house, and while he insists it's only two stories, with the pool and basketball court, it feels like three. Five bedrooms, six bathrooms, bordered by terrace walkways on every floor. Downstairs, we pass a billiard room with a pool table and bar. He gestures to a door across the hall. "And here's where the magic happens."

Legend throws his arms out wide as we step inside the studio. He spins in the open space between his grand piano and vocal booth window. "Welcome to the heart of it all."

It's like I'm on one of those old episodes of *MTV Cribs*.

I'm simultaneously awestruck and a little overwhelmed to finally see how Legend lives. Being this close to him, in a space that's clearly his sanctuary, is almost surreal. Does he really trust me that much?

I run my fingers along the acoustic panels of the recording booth, glancing at the headphones hanging on the wall. "Wow. If I had a setup like this, I bet I'd make beautiful music too—and I can't sing 'Happy Birthday' in key." I chuckle at my own lame joke, but I stop when I notice Legend watching me with a quiet intensity... the way parents do when their kids open that one special gift on Christmas morning.

"It's real cool finally sharing this with you," he says.

My cheeks flush, and I quickly drop my head, trying to hide the warmth spreading across my face. I lean against the wall, just in case my knees decide to betray me again.

Legend takes a seat at the piano and begins to play, his fingers gliding across the keys like a baker's hands kneading dough. Notes bloom from the piano strings, rich and smooth, making my pulse quicken.

He begins to sing, his voice a soft, irresistible drawl that curls around me like a warm ocean current.

> *"How about you and me?*
> *Can you think of us together?*
> *Baby, it's chemistry...*
> *Honey, you and me together..."*

It's his hit song, "Us Together." I exhale a breathless sigh, my heart lifting and tumbling with every note. His voice is velvet, wrapping around me, making it impossible to think of anything but him. Our eyes meet, and a quiet smile tugs at his lips.

He knows that this is my favorite song.

He continues to play and sing, presenting a little concert, just for me. The melody swirls around us as I sway to the rhythm, wondering if at some point I fell and hit my head. 'Cause there's no way this is reality.

Then he stops. He extends a hand, a clear invitation in his gaze. I bite my lip, stepping forward, and with a gentle tug, he draws me closer, pulling me beside him on the bench.

Inhale. Exhale. He smells so unbelievably good. Refreshing almost... and dangerously addictive.

His fingers return to their natural rhythm, stroking the keys with ease, as he plays a slower, unfamiliar melody.

> *"Honey, you're... just right.*
> *You make me higher than... a kite.*
> *When I think of you... at night.*
> *I don't wanna stop. Baby, I can't stop..."*

It's gentle. Sweet. A quiet, aching kind of song. And it's captivating.

I've never heard this before, but I'm already in love with it. His passion for his craft is undeniable. The music feels like it's spilling from his soul.

Legend holds out the notes, his voice low and smooth as he croons into the air. His eyes are closed, his face tilted back, fully immersed in the melody.

> *"Baby, you... and I,*
> *you know I need you in... my life.*
> *You got me spinning 'round.*
> *Was lost and now I'm found.*
> *And in time... I'mma find your light."*

He slows to a stop, opening his eyes to meet mine. His gaze is burning with something deeper, something that reaches straight to my heart. A charming grin lifts his lips, but it's softer, sweeter than I've seen before. "What do you think?"

"I think… it's beautiful," I say, my voice barely above a whisper.

He nods, a shadow passing over his face, as he refocuses on the keys. "I wrote it for Indigo… Never got a chance to let her hear it though."

The words hang heavy between us, the air suddenly thick. My heart gives an unexpected thud as I swallow.

"Maybe soon she will," I say softly.

Legend offers a weak smile, but it doesn't reach his eyes. "How'd the job go today?"

"Well… I learned a little Jiu-Jitsu."

He chuckles. "She's still into that, huh?"

I rub the crook in my neck. "Very much so."

Legend's eyes sparkle and dance, almost the way they did when he was singing just now. "She giving you a hard time?"

Up until now, I've been biting my tongue, but maybe this is a good time to let him know just how awful his sweet princess can be. "Let's just say she has some… high standards."

Legend scratches his nose, amused. "Yeah. I could see that."

"I mean, she's impatient, she's rude. L, she insists that her bath water be 'precisely 102 degrees Fahrenheit—or else!'" I realize all too late that I'm imitating Indigo's whiny little voice.

Thankfully, Legend laughs. "Man, that *does* sound like her." He shakes his head with an irresistible smile. "I'm sorry, Sam. I know it's a lot."

I roll my eyes to the ceiling. "Anything for Legend Blake!"

He laughs again. But I don't.

"Honestly, L, the girl has a *serious* wall up."

"I know," he says, studying his piano keys. "But don't give up." His eyes lift to mine, filled with an intensity that leaves no room for doubt. He's not just encouraging me, he's pleading.

What's it gonna take for him to see that this girl is all wrong for him?

The only silver lining? For every additional day of torture with Indigo Taylor, I'm one step closer to my fantasy of dating Legend Blake. I just hope that I live to enjoy it.

"Ya know, my boys kept clowning me when I started dating her," he says, the words dripping with nostalgia. "All the gossip blogs were taking bets on how long it would last."

I remember. I bet fifty bucks that they wouldn't make it a month.

I glance at him, taking in his effortless vibe—ripped jeans and a fitted Henley T-shirt that hugs his chest in all the right places. "So how'd you know?"

He arches a brow, looking at me. "How'd I know what?"

"That she was the one for you, when everyone said it wouldn't work?"

He chuckles to himself. "It seems like we're total opposites, right?"

That's an understatement.

Legend stares at the ceiling, thinking. "I remember the night I met her, at the *Mending Time* premiere. You remember how nervous I was?"

I nod. The movie blew up *way* more than he expected. The poor guy was a wreck that night.

Legend's eyes are distant as he reflects. "And then I saw her. Dressed to kill on the red carpet, looking like some sorta glamorous Hollywood statue in that silky white gown. I didn't care if I shook another exec's hand that night, she was the only one I wanted to get next to." His eyes twinkle. "I swear, I could barely put together two sentences that night. But somehow... she was feeling me."

Legend drops his head, a smile tugging at the corners of his lips. Almost the same way I smile when I think of the first time he spoke to me, all those years ago. I guess even Legend Blake gets star-struck sometimes.

"Anyway," he says. "We got to talking, and we had way more in common than I thought. She knew what it was like to see the dark side of Hollywood. To have agents and fans trying to dictate your every move. It was just... real refreshing to click with someone like that." He looks my way, reading my mind. "Kinda like when I started talking to you."

My cheeks burn, a wave of heat rushing through me.

Legend's gaze drifts back to the piano, his fingers absently tracing the keys. "And then, she told me about the scandal with her dad, and I told her about the scandal with mine."

How could I forget? Indigo's dad was caught in a scandalous sex tape with some woman who *wasn't* her mom, while Legend's dad had a whole secret family. Poor Legend didn't even find out until after he won *Lucky Star.*

"I mean, this dude went and had *three other kids* with another chick," he says, sorrow clouding his handsome brown eyes. "Had 'em set up in a house just a few blocks away. What the hell did he think would happen?"

I get it. We're not gonna agree with all of our parents' decisions. When my mom and Trey announced that they were getting married, I must've cried for three days. Simone didn't talk to Mom for a week. I couldn't imagine trying to handle something like that in the public eye.

"Indigo found out about her dad's nonsense during a live interview," says Legend. "Can you believe that? She had to play it off, making some lame PR statement about giving her family privacy at the time. That's when I knew... she wasn't all that different from me."

Usually, when I ask about his family, he changes the subject. Maybe there's more to this thing with Indigo than I thought.

Seeming to push off the memories, Legend nudges me with an elbow. "What do ya say we head back upstairs and chill with the crew?"

Another evening with Legend Blake? I'd be crazy to turn him down.

◆◆◆◆◆◆

Two days later, I'm in Indigo's shoe closet, waist-deep in Louboutins. "Are you sure you trust me to do this, Miss Indigo? I don't want to toss anything important."

She cocks her head as she crosses the dressing room, a stack of sponsored makeup kits in her arms. "I'll let you know if you screw up."

I nod and get back to work. There's a new shipment of designer heels arriving today, and Indigo needs to make room in her closet. Guess who gets the special job of sorting through all her old ones to make room for the new?

I glance back and forth between two nearly identical pairs of heels. One pair to the shelf, the other to the donation box. Only 299 pairs to go.

Against my better judgment, I've decided to stick around—if only for a few more precious moments with Legend. But despite his feelings, Indigo is… a lot. She's obnoxious, self-absorbed, and has a laundry list of demands that could rival any diva on world tour.

I've already reached out to Eva and Kelly, but Eva's out "sick". And after the Nina-Banks-Interview-Gone-Wrong, Kelly's got her hands full. I'm still trying to make sense of Indigo's schedule—not to mention figure out what she does or doesn't like without help from her or anyone else.

"Here's your breakfast, Ms. Indigo."

"Gross! Eggs aren't plant-based!"

She wrinkled her nose when I presented a delicious-looking vegan pad thai at lunchtime.

"Ugh! All those carbs! Bring me a cold-pressed green juice."

How am I supposed to get intel for Legend if I can't even get the chick to eat? Let alone hold a full conversation...

Now, let's see pink pumps with crystals or purple with crystals...

Indigo saunters across the room in her jogging pants and bra, humming along to one of her old hits, "Your Kiss." A love ballad about finding one's true love.

Since going off on poor Nina, it seems she's taken Kelly's advice on laying low and cleaning up her image. She hasn't been out much. So, when she isn't busy scrolling through social media—groaning about all the things she wishes she could comment to the "chicks she don't like"—she fills her time making my life a living hell.

"Remind me to have you go through my social media later," she says. "I need you to like the posts for all of my sponsors and cast members today."

"Yes, Miss Indigo." I need to get down to business. The sooner I get the intel for Legend, the sooner I can get out of *this*. But how to do so without ending up decapitated?

I casually pick up a glittering pair of Jimmy Choos, examining them with interest. "These are cute... Do you have a favorite pair?"

Indigo stops mid-stroll and purses her lips as she surveys the mountain of shoes. She strides into the closet and grabs a pair of four-inch stilettos. They're beaded with chandelier-style crystals that snake up glittery ankle straps. With the briefest hesitation, she thrusts them into my arms. "Those. I wore them at the *Mending Time* film premiere."

A smile edges on my lips as I set the stilettos on a shelf. Keeping my tone casual, I cast a small glance her way. "That's when you met Legend Blake, right?"

Indigo stills, staring at me.

Dear God, don't let her fire me for saying the man's name.

Thankfully, she gives a stiff nod.

Phew! I'm sure to appear indifferent as I return to sorting. "I always thought you two were the cutest couple." I pause just long enough to make it seem like an afterthought. "My friends and I were shattered when you two split up... Always wondered what happened, ya know?"

A charged silence lingers between us as she studies my face, her gaze sharp, searching. I hold my breath, keeping my smile light, open, easy. The kind that says, *You can trust me.*

For a second, I think she might.

Instead, something shifts, a dark cloud creeping into her eyes.

"You and your friends should mind your damn business."

"Sorry, I was just—"

"Get back to work."

I bite back a sigh and do as she says. *At least I'm still breathing.*

I've just managed to whittle my pile down to two hundred fifty pairs when she asks the time.

"Just past one-thirty," I say, checking my watch.

She cuts the music and grabs a remote, flipping on the mounted TV in the corner. *The Spotlight Report* pops up onscreen.

"All of the hottest celebrity gossip and news," says Nina Banks, a flawless smile on her face. *"And wait 'til you hear what we've learned today!"*

I used to watch this show all the time between classes. Indigo's been checking it out every day since the disastrous interview, just to ensure they don't air it against her wishes.

"Taylor Swift," says the male announcer. *"Will she or won't she?"*

"And the hottest star of Heist in the Hills *reveals all of his criminal workout secrets,"* Nina adds.

My attention is drawn to the screen as the title of Legend's movie is announced. And sure enough, there he is, approaching the camera in slow motion with smoldering eyes. His infamous pool scene.

But Indigo... she's frozen, staring at the TV. She doesn't blink once, not even a subtle shift of her gaze. I think she's forgotten how to breathe.

That's funny... It's kinda the way I behave whenever I see him.

Indigo doesn't snap out of her trance until he's vanished from the screen, her shoulders drooping with a quiet sigh. She turns to me, her expression hard.

"What are you looking at?"

I lower my head and get back to work. Maybe she isn't quite over Legend after all.

10

"No, no," Mom scolds gently on the other end of the line. "It's gotta simmer at least five more minutes. Then add parsley."

"Got it. Thanks, Mom."

The chowder bubbles thick and creamy on the stove, the scent of Old Bay and briny shrimp curling around me like a hug. I turn down the heat and stir the pot hard. My phone slips against my cheek, as I press it between my ear and shoulder. This call is taking much longer than expected. Luckily, Legend is across the living room on a call of his own, pacing near the sofas.

I'm at his place, attempting to make Mom's seafood chowder. He sent a text earlier, asking if I had plans. Of course I didn't, so he invited me over. His staff is off for the night, so I offered to bring food. Now if I could just get this to taste like home…

"You know," says Mom, her usually calm tone on the brink of a lecture, "if you were here, I'd teach you how to make some proper crab cakes to go with it. But I suppose I'll send you the recipe."

I've only been out here a week, but it's clear she must miss me a ton. This is only the fifth hint she's dropped in our conversation that I'd be better off at home, which certainly isn't helping me get over being homesick. I already miss the Storyville espresso, my old loft, and the U-Dub campus. Not to mention, Mom and my sisters. But if I can just get this soup right, perhaps I'll head back soon with a handsome celebrity to introduce to them all.

"That reminds me. Honey, have you seen that Squatty Potty I ordered last fall? I've been looking all over for it."

"Sorry, Mom. I have no idea where you'd put that."

She clicks her tongue. "'Cause when Trey doesn't have it—"

"How is Trey doing, by the way?" Better his feelings than his bathroom habits.

"He's well... for the most part," she says. Then relenting with a sigh, she adds, "Honestly, he seems pretty down in the dumps since you left. And Justin heading to Silicon Valley did not help."

I go still at the sound of the name. *Justin.* It stings like lemon on a papercut.

Of course Trey was devastated when we broke up, but I'm more haunted by the look in Justin's eyes the day I left. I wonder if he's doing okay... 'Cause I still can't say I am.

I casually glimpse over my shoulder, noting that Legend still seems to be wrapped up in his conversation. With a lowered voice, I ask, "Has... Justin given him a call or anything?"

He called me this week. Just once. Of course, I missed it while alphabetizing Indigo's handbag collection. But I didn't call him back. I didn't know what to say. I mean, how do you tell your ex-high school sweetheart that you're out in LA, kicking it with your celebrity crush who you've been secretly DMing for three frickin' years? Not to mention going incognito to spy on his ex. Besides, after the way we broke up, I figured it would just be… weird. I hold my breath, anticipating Mom's response.

"No…" Mom says, slow and careful. "But if there's a message you want to relay, we can—"

"No, Mom." I shoot the ceiling a look, kicking myself for even asking. "It's fine." I wipe my hand on my jeans, then stir the soup again.

'Cause if you want—"

"Mom, please." Checking to ensure Legend's still distracted, I hiss into the phone, "Just—He's fine. I'm fine. It's fine."

The line goes silent, and I swallow hard, the guilt as thick as chowder in my throat. First real conversation we've had all week, and I'm snapping at her like Simone.

"Anyway, I better go," I say, forcing a lighter tone.

Her voice softens to match. "Okay, honey. But if you need anything, anything at all… I'm right here. If you change your mind. If you wanna come home—"

"Got it," I choke out. "Love you, Mom. Bye." I rush off the phone before the tears can fall.

The soup bubbles, warm and fragrant… but it does nothing for the cold sitting behind my ribs. I add salt anyway. Because I don't know what else to do.

"Look, I said I'd do it, aiight?" Legend runs a hand over his head, pacing like he wants to punch a wall but can't afford drywall repair.

I bet he's talking to Victoria.

He's been running around like a maniac this week, prepping for some private concert. It seems like he's constantly racing around town for fittings, meetings, and rehearsals. I'm surprised he's even free tonight.

He ends the call and blows out some air. His shoulders rise and fall, like they've carried the entire week.

"Just picture her naked!" I call over my shoulder.

He lets out a soft laugh and heads my way with an effortless, heart-stopping smile. "That would be a nightmare."

"That's the point. There's absolutely nothing she could say or do that would be worse than that."

Legend chuckles, stepping up behind me. "I hear you." He peers over my shoulder. "*Yo!* Is that what I think it is?"

"Your favorite."

"Ah, man! You're amazing." He throws his arm around my neck and kisses my cheek.

Oh. My. Gosh.

"I swear, Sam. You're the sweetest chick I know." Grabbing a carrot from the counter, he heads over to the wine rack behind the bar. Meanwhile, I'm frozen, spoon in hand.

I'm gonna be smiling for days. I'll never wash my face again.

"Feels like the only time I get a chance to chill is with you these days." Legend grins as he grabs two glasses and uncorks a bottle of wine.

I stir like it's the soup I'm flustered about. "Victoria's working you hard, huh?"

"Like a mule." He returns and passes a glass of red wine my way, raising a toast with his own. "To chilling with longtime friends."

"And a break from tyrant bosses," I add.

The two of us laugh and clink glasses.

++++++

Legend's still filling me in on the upcoming show when we sit down to eat on one of his terraces. The golden sun dips lower, casting long shadows across the table. The city hums below, but up here, it's just us—quiet, warm, and more intimate than expected.

"At first, I told her no—these guys fund sweatshops in India! But she wants to turn a blind eye to the whole thing. Says that's *none of our business* or whatever." Legend sighs as I pass him a spoon. Wisps of steam coil and dance, rising from the bowl of chowder. "This smells amazing, by the way."

I smile, praying it tastes just as good.

"You still swear by this chowder, huh?"

My lips part in hesitation. "Still?"

He grins. "You used to say it was 'liquid love' during finals. Every time you were stressed or homesick, you talked about your mom's chowder like it could save your life."

The memory hits unexpectedly. "Wow. I forgot I told you that."

"I didn't."

My stomach flips. It's just soup. Just a memory. But the way he says it—soft, certain... it throws me off balance. I glance down, suddenly too aware of my own breath.

"So... it's a private concert for these politicians?"

"Technically. They're sponsors of the label," he says, placing a napkin on his lap. "So according to her, I don't really have a choice."

"That sucks," I say softly. "I'm sorry, L."

He lifts his wine glass to his lips, eyes distant. "Not as sorry as I am."

I understand how difficult it must be for him, having the job of his dreams but no real say on his commitments. At least he's getting paid to do what he loves to do. This morning, Indigo had me voice-record all the lines for an audition she has coming up. She's planning on listening to them while she sleeps.

"*Not animated enough,*" she said. "*Do it again.*"

I'd rather shovel cow manure for a living.

The trouble is, being around Legend always flips some switch in me. With him, hope doesn't just whisper... it shouts. One look, one laugh, and my heart completely forgets how messy this could get. I nearly passed out when he kissed my cheek in the kitchen.

Legend blows on his spoon and takes a sip so effortlessly sexy, he could make cafeteria food look five-star. His eyes spark like firecrackers. "Wow. That's good!"

"Really?" I scrunch my nose, not quite buying it.

He nods, encouraging me to have a taste.

I take a sip and throw a hand over my mouth. "Oh man, it is good... and *really* hot!" I fan my lips as Legend chuckles.

"You all right?"

"Mmhmm."

I gulp down half my wine before Legend tugs the glass from my hand.

"Slow down, tiger. I'm trying to wine and dine you, not carry you to bed."

Oh, if only... I dab at my lips with a napkin.

"Enough of me griping," he says, swirling the wine in his glass. "I heard you on the phone with your mom. How's it feel being away from home?"

My stomach knots. *Crap. How much did he hear?*

I shift in my seat and rest my elbows on the table, exhaling like my heart *isn't* doing somersaults in my chest. Between Mom's latest guilt trips and Simone's raunchy texts, it's not like they've let me forget them.

But still... the quiet here is louder than I thought it'd be.

Especially without... my best friend.

"It's different," I say, batting the depressing thought away. "I've never been this far away from my family before. I honestly miss them more than I thought I would."

I look out past the railing, past the hills, past the ache clawing at my chest.

"Think of it as a summer vacation." Legend blows his soup and takes another sip. "You know I got you."

I glance up. "What?"

"I know it's a lot being out here." He shrugs. "Just sayin'... you don't have to carry it all by yourself."

He says it so casually, like it's nothing. But it lands like *everything*. It's not a grand gesture. Just steady. Quiet. And exactly what I didn't know I needed to hear.

"In the meantime, I'll do my best to make LA your home away from home. Aiight?"

His words settle deep in my chest, warm and steady, like the super-salty chowder in my bowl. I smile, my heart doing that thing where it forgets its normal rhythm.

I take another careful sip, being sure to blow this time. When I look up, I find Legend studying me. His gaze drops—first to my lips, then my torso—slow and deliberate, like he's memorizing something he shouldn't. The moment our eyes meet, he looks away, almost bashful.

Wait. Was he checking me out just now?

He clears his throat like *he's* the one trying to recover.

"So, you owe me an explanation, Sam." He says it like a tease, but the look he gives says otherwise.

I blink, curious. "An explanation for what exactly?"

He tilts his head, eyes gleaming under the terrace lights. "As beautiful as you are, you've never *once* mentioned your love life."

I inhale wrong, choking on a mouthful of soup. I grab my napkin and cough into it, mortified.

Legend drops his spoon. "You okay? Still too hot?"

I wave him off, still sputtering. "I'm fine," I croak, trying to breathe and speak at the same time. "Really."

He watches me closely, concern etched between his brows as I straighten up and cough once more, doing everything I can not to melt into the floor.

"I, um… I recently got out of a relationship, actually. A long-term boyfriend."

Legend doesn't say anything at first. Just nods. Once. "How long?"

"Long." I drum my fingers on the table. "It was… long. Um, he recently got a job in Silicon Valley, and—you know what they say about long-distance relationships."

"You didn't wanna move?"

I shift in my seat, gripping my wine glass a little tighter than necessary. "He, uh… moved out of our place just before you invited me out here."

Both of Legend's brows rise as he crosses his arms. "So, y'all was kickin' it, fa' real, fa' real?"

I nod, then take a lengthy sip of my wine.

"Why'd you never say anything?" he asks, leaning in, elbows on the table like he's piecing together a puzzle.

"It… never came up," I murmur. "And—I don't know—Maybe I've just always been a private person. Kinda like you."

Legend lets out a dry chuckle, his gaze falling to the table. "I couldn't keep that kind of secret if I tried."

"It wasn't a secret," I say, picking at the edges of my napkin. "Not really."

Legend stares at me soberly. "What's his name?"

My eyes drift over his shoulder, focusing on the electric blue pool glowing a story below. "Justin."

There's that sting again.

"He know about me?"

My stomach tightens. I set my spoon down gently. "Not exactly," I say, voice a little tight.

He doesn't speak. Just watches me. Waiting.

"You know," I blurt, pushing to my feet, "this would be great with some bread. You want some bread?" I head for the kitchen before he can answer.

———— ✦✦✦✦✦ ————

May 29th
From: Justin C.
To: Samara A.

Congratulations, Sam I Am!

I wish I could've been at your graduation. I know the hype isn't nearly as big for grad school, but I would've loved to see you walk just the same.

Silicon Valley is something else. Giant parks are everywhere, and the beaches are incredible! And get this—my roommate's a Trekkie too! But the guy is almost never home. Around here, there's a conference or tech convention every week!

I start the new job tomorrow, and I'm terrified, Sam.
Wish me luck!

~Teddy

June 3rd
From: Justin C.
To: Samara A.

Hey, Sam I Am!

Well, I've survived my first week. And I've gotta say it hasn't been nearly as bad as I thought it would be.

Working at Apple Park is honestly a dream come true. I love my new job, and there are a ton of cool people here. I even got to meet Tim Cook yesterday,

Sam. TIM FRICKIN' COOK!!! Now I know how those BTS groupies must feel.

Anyway, I'll do my best not to freak out too much and keep my cool. Let me know how you've been.

~Teddy

June 12th
From: Justin C.
To: Samara A.

Sam! What's up?

I tried to call, but somebody's too busy to pick up... You really gonna leave me hanging, Sam I Am? I thought our friendship meant more to you than that.

I'm settling into life in Silicon Valley, and I think you'd love it here. The theaters and museums are unbelievable. The place is real cool. Oh! And there's this nice ice cream spot, not too far from my apartment. I go there alone sometimes and order your favorite: birthday cake with a cherry on top. Maybe one day you'll visit, and I can take you there.

I miss you, Sam I Am.

~Teddy

June 14th
From: Samara A.
To: Justin C.

Hey Justin!

Sorry it took me so long to respond. Life's been crazy busy! I'm glad you're enjoying Silicon Valley. You always said you belonged there.

I actually have some news of my own. I've found a job. It's temporary for the summer, but it pays great. I've been hired as Indigo Taylor's personal assistant. I know, crazy right?

Anyway, thanks for letting me know you haven't forgotten about me.

Miss you too, Teddy.

~Sam

June 14th
From: Justin C.
To: Samara A.

Excuse me? Who are you and what have you done with my best friend?

You mean to tell me that Samara Allen, who's too afraid to fly to Portland, traveled to Hollywood to serve one of the craziest divas in the world?

This is a joke, right?

~Teddy

June 14th
From: Samara A.
To: Justin C.

No. It's true.

Of course, I didn't fly! I drove the hatchback.

I question the decision every day.

~Sam

June 14th

From: Justin C.

To: Samara A.

Wow. I'm shocked. After you turned me down, I never thought you'd leave Seattle.

[REPLY TO THIS MESSAGE?]
[CANCEL]

11

"*H*ow's it going, Indigo? You look beautiful today."

She bows her head, her smile dazzling as she strolls down the sidewalk, a Fendi shopping bag swinging from her hand. Her voice is as sweet and soft as sugar. "Thank you."

"Indigo, over here!"

"Indigo, we love you!"

She giggles, running her long, perfectly manicured nails through her hair, her gaze lifting to admire the towering buildings around us. DIOR, GUCCI, and BVLGARI gleam in the sunlight, like proof she belongs here. Photographers circle us like sharks, their cameras *snap, snap, snapping* away.

Kelly must've made a few calls to give the paparazzi a heads-up about Indigo's Friday shopping spree on Rodeo Drive, because they've come out in full force. Three whole stores have shut down for her.

As we weave down the sidewalk, I keep my head low, hoping to blend in. Tourists clog the cobblestone street, some too busy snapping pics of the rare celebrity sighting to notice me, others striking their own poses for selfies. Palm trees sway lazily in the breeze, tulips bursting with color along the edges of the boulevard. Effortlessly picture-perfect. Pop music spills from every boutique, blending with the low growl of luxury cars rolling past, as if the entire street is showing off.

I switch the heavy bags to my other hand and flex my fingers. Man, these things are *heavy*. And this girl has a *serious* shoe addiction.

Indigo gives a dainty wave as more photographers snap away, her frohawked bodyguard, Chloe, at her side, ensuring the crowd keeps their distance. Kelly and I trail behind them, playing the role of a low-key entourage.

"Here's a note," says Kelly, elbowing me, a playful grin hidden behind her Cartier sunglasses. "Always carry shades."

I laugh softly, but my neck heats. "How could I forget?" I glance away, pretending to study the window display. Someone who's been in the industry a while should *know* that sort of thing. *Stupid, stupid, stupid.*

"You look great, by the way," says Kelly, her tone casual but sincere.

"Oh? Thanks."

Indigo drove us in her Continental GT convertible today, and by some miracle, we arrived in one piece. We were just about to get out when she looked over my strapless jumpsuit and insisted I stay in the car. A few moments later, she returned with this flowy camisole and white cut-off shorts—a gift from the nearest store. She raised the collapsible roof, demanding that I change before stepping out of the car. Honestly, I didn't see what was wrong with what I was wearing. In my opinion, vintage is *always* in style.

We're headed into another designer clothing shop when my phone chimes. It's Legend, shooting me a photo of Indigo looking gorgeous while shopping. The photographers are already posting them online.

A second message pops up. It's the same photo but zoomed in to catch me in the background. I'm squinting in the sun, making a face like I smell something awful, looking like a total dork. Legend hearts the photo.

SAM: *OMG I couldn't look worse!*
LEGEND: *You look beautiful.* ☺

My stomach spins like a carousel on overdrive. I reply with an LOL. I want to believe him.

The store employees glide around the space, moving furniture with practiced ease, setting out crystal trays of champagne and sparkling water, catering to Indigo's every whim. The whole place feels like it's been transformed into a personal runway just for her, the polished floors gleaming under the soft, golden lights. Every movement, every gesture is part of the show. The kind of world I've only seen in movies or on a theater stage.

LEGEND: *How's it going?*

The twisted paper shopping bag handles dig into my wrists as I type.

SAM: *Not gonna lie. Kinda wanna quit right now.*
LEGEND: *Aw.* ☹ *Come on, beautiful! You gonna leave me hanging?*

Indigo cackles as one of the employees passes her a tall glass of champagne.

SAM: *Never.*

"You can set the bags right there on the sofa, as long as you stay close," Kelly whispers, sliding off her shades. "Your hands are turning red."

With a slow breath, I gladly take advantage of the opportunity. "Thanks."

A server passes me a champagne flute, but before I can sip, Kelly swipes it from my hand.

"You know better! Indigo needs you one hundred percent sober in case you have to drive. Also, in case of a random drug test." She tosses back her own glass and sets it aside, then takes a seat on the sofa with mine. She pats the spot beside her, inviting me to take a load off.

Indigo is chatting with the manager while the employees roll out a long line of designer dresses. I nod and take a seat.

"So," Kelly smirks, tugging at the denim jacket she's paired with her black maxi dress. "Almost two weeks with Indigo now. How you feelin'?"

"Good. It's been… really nice," I say, my voice a little too light.

"Really? 'Cause the bags under your eyes speak volumes."

I throw a hand to my cheek, and she busts out laughing.

"Oh my gosh! I'm just messing with you." She grins. "But seriously, I've been working with Indigo for years. You really think I don't know how she treats her staff?"

I go still, a knot forming in my throat. I rack my brain for a clever response but draw nothing but blanks.

Kelly chuckles again, patting my knee. "It's fine. You don't have to answer."

A weight lifts off my shoulders as I release a quiet breath.

Keeping up with this job has been more difficult than I ever thought it would be. If it weren't for Legend, I would've quit days ago. But he's infatuated with the girl. And if I want to protect him, I need to stay close enough to see the train wreck coming.

Kelly takes a swig of my champagne. "Look, I know Indigo can be... a lot."

Across the room, an employee presents a dress to Indigo. She scowls, snatching it from the hanger and crumpling it in her hands before tossing it back in the employee's face.

Kelly rolls her brown eyes back to me. "But she's a talented girl, been through more than most."

Okay. I'm curious. "How long have you worked with her?"

"A little over seven years now."

Wow. So if anyone knows about Indigo, it would be her.

"That's a long time," I say. "You must be a fan."

She smiles at her glass. "Guess you could say that."

Okay. Here's my chance. I need to get to the bottom of what keeps guys like Legend sniffing around. And who better to ask than the one person who's been promoting Indigo for nearly a decade? "So, what's your secret? To sticking around, I mean."

Kelly tilts her head, watching Indigo lounge on a chaise like Cleopatra. "Most people stop at the surface. The stuff they see on social media and TV. They only see what they *want* to see. I see her for who she is."

I watch as Kelly takes another sip. "And who *is* she?" I ask.

Kelly smiles, her smoky eyeshadow dancing. "She's human. Just like you and me."

Meanwhile, Indigo purses her lips, pouring what's left of her drink down the front of another dress. I guess more people care for this chick than I thought.

"That's why you're perfect for her," says Kelly.

I blink, my brain scrambling. "Excuse me?" I'm not sure if I'm supposed to laugh or be offended.

"Look, you're not fooling anyone. It's clear that you've never worked for Rihanna—or *anyone* close to her team. But I can tell, you've got a genuine heart." Kelly slaps me on the arm with a little too much force. "You're the first assistant she's had who isn't just out for themselves."

I swallow hard. If only she knew. Getting close to Indigo is just the means to an end.

Kelly studies me for a beat, then leans in. "So, I need your help."

"My help?" The words come out slower than I intend. "What do you—what do you mean?"

"Indigo's hitting a club tonight, and I need you to keep her out of trouble."

I frown. "But I thought you told her to lay low. For PR and all that."

"Yeah, but when Indigo wants what she wants..." She shrugs, her nonchalance almost irritating. "Just be a friend. Gentle reminders. That sort of thing."

Gentle? That's not exactly Indigo's speed. She's a walking hurricane, leaving destruction in her wake with a smile on her face. Still, I don't want anything bad to happen to her.

"Obviously, I know exactly who you are," says Kelly.

And my stomach bottoms out.

I hold her gaze, refusing to blink or even breathe.

"Who I am?" I manage to croak, but Kelly doesn't answer right away. She takes her time, lifting my champagne flute and swirling what's left. Her fingers trace the rim, lingering. Deliberate. Testing.

"Yeah," she finally says. "The way you've gone out of your way to get this job?" She pins me with a sober gaze. "You clearly stan her."

The tension snaps like a rubber band. I force out a laugh—too light, too breezy. "You got me."

Kelly leans in, dropping her voice just above a whisper. "So just remember *everything* you love about her. And do whatever you can to protect that image for all her other fans. The Indies will thank you."

That's right. *The Indies*. Indigo's die-hard fan club. The ones that'll kill me if I let anything happen to their precious princess.

I'm just resigning to my assignment when Indigo snatches a dress off the rack.

"Hey, new girl! Come try this on for me!"

I'm checking my phone as Indigo tosses back her third shot.

"*Whoo! Let's go, ladies!*" She pounds against the window of her limo, bouncing in her seat like a firecracker ready to explode.

She's like a dam about to burst, all the frustration from being cooped up for a week flooding out.

> **SAM:** *I think she's drinking vodka. Should I say something?*

I tap my phone, glancing at her out the corner of my eye.

> **KELLY:** *Wow. She's going hard tonight. Don't let her do more than that.*
> **SAM:** *I'll do my best.*

I shiver, tugging at the hem of my satin red cowl-neck dress as Indigo dances in the seat across from me. She insisted that if I was going to travel with her, I had to look the part. At least she let me keep my high ponytail tonight.

Legend finally responds to the selfie I sent him earlier.

> **LEGEND:** ☺ *Hey!* 🔥🔥🔥*Look at you! Got one of Indigo?*

Of course. Still orbiting her.

SAM: *Not yet. But I'll try to get one for you.*

We pass the crowd out front and pull into VIP. Flashes burst like fireworks, velvet ropes rippling with tension.

SAM: *We're here. Good luck with your show!*

Legend's giving that private concert tonight and has been pretty down about it.

LEGEND: *Good luck to you too! Keep my girl out of trouble. Aiight?*

I'm mid-reply when Indigo plucks the phone from my hands.
"Wait, wait, wait—"
She stares at me blankly as she shuts the phone off and drops it in the bin beside her. She and Chloe's phones are in the bin as well. "No cameras," she says. "Not tonight."
I gaze at the bin, my pulse kicking up. No phone? No lifeline? What if I need help? What if Legend texts me something sweet, and I miss it forever? I swallow hard.
"Now, let's party!" Indigo tosses her hands in the air, gyrating in her Louis Vuitton halter-top as Chloe jumps out to open her door.
The paparazzi descend like wild dogs, their voices rising in a chaotic chorus. Snapping shutters, shouting over each other, jostling for the best angle.
"Indigo! Indigo!"
"Ms. Taylor, over here!"
"Indigo! You lookin' to have a good time tonight?"

The flashes strobe like a disco ball on overdrive, casting Indigo in a flickering spotlight made for red carpets and chaos.

She steps out like a queen entering her court, gliding through the frenzy like she was born for it. Tossing megawatt smiles left and right, her diamond-studded nails catching the light as she waves. She doesn't rush, doesn't flinch, just basks in the attention like it's warm sunshine.

The club is one of Hollywood's most exclusive spots. A playground for the rich, famous, and those lucky enough to slip past the velvet rope. Not so private that it's a secret, but exclusive enough that just getting through the doors is a status symbol. At least, that's what Legend tells me.

Then, as if the chaos outside never existed, we step into the club, swallowed by darkness and the steady thump of bass.

I can't figure out if all the pounding is from my chest or the music inside. The bass rattles the walls, vibrating through the floor like a heartbeat in my toes. Neon lights flicker in a dizzying swirl of purples and blues, casting hazy shadows over a packed dance floor where bodies move like liquid.

In all my years with Justin, I never thought about stepping foot in a place like this… Neither of us was the partying type. Now, under the strobe lights and the weight of a hundred eyes sizing us up, I have no idea what to do with myself. Indigo also had me leave my purse in the car, so I'm stuck with my arms, awkward and misplaced. I cross them, then drop them to my sides. Nope, too stiff. Hands on my hips? Too posey. I settle for shoving them in my pockets… only to remember, I don't have any.

Awesome. I'm just one accidental robot dance away from completely embarrassing myself.

The place is alive, buzzing with heat, sound, and way too much money in one room. It's a swirling mix of sweaty bodies, flashing lights, and designer everything. A sea of gorgeous women in barely-there dresses, guys dripping in chains and flexing like they own the place. Up on platforms, dancers twist under neon lights, moving like they don't have a single care in the world.

Waitresses weave through the crowd in stilettos, carrying champagne bottles topped with sparklers flickering in the dim light. A DJ is at the center of a towering platform, head bobbing to the thumping rhythm, as he mixes a relentless stream of trap music.

Indigo makes her way through the throng, her body moving effortlessly to the bass-heavy beat. Meanwhile, I'm stuck behind Chloe, who's strolling like she's in a museum on a Sunday afternoon, scanning the crowd like a security camera on legs.

"Excuse me. Chloe!" I tap her shoulder.

Big mistake. She whips around, staring me down like some sort of pissed Rottweiler.

I give my best smile. "Would you mind if I jumped in front of you? I'm trying to keep up with Ms. Indigo." My voice is practically a yell over the music.

Chloe blinks once. Slow. Silent.

O-kay. I take a step back. "Never mind. Go ahead."

By the time I finally squeeze past a group of overexcited clubbers, Indigo's already at the bar, laughing with some girls I'm sure I've seen on TV.

The bartender slides a drink her way, and she tosses it back.

"Indigo! Indigo!" I wave an arm, squeezing in the huddle. "Maybe you shouldn't—"

The starlet and her group of associates stop and stare at me.

Is... this not allowed or something?

In an instant, all of them are howling with laughter.

Indigo doubles over, clutching her bare midriff. "I'm sorry, y'all. This is my new *basic* assistant. Obviously, she ain't used to this yet!"

"She 'bout to get turnt up tonight!" One friend cackles, and the other ladies join in.

"Right?!" Indigo slings an arm around me, still grinning as she waves them goodbye. Her voice drops low and venomous in my ear. "Keep out of my way, or your scrawny ass is fired. Got it?"

My gaze fixes on the sticky floor as I nod.

"Gabriel!" Indigo tugs me toward a guy with low-cut waves, sharp cheekbones, and hazel eyes. The diamond studs in his ears glint under the shifting lights as he pulls her into a slow lingering hug, his hands resting low on her waist.

"It's been *forever!*" she purrs. "Where ya been?"

He shrugs, dragging his gaze down her body and back up again. "You know me. Always in the studio."

"*Always!*" Indigo smirks, directing his attention to me. "Gabe, this is my girl, Samara. Gabe's a music producer, Sam."

Before I can react, she eases behind him, winking as she mouths something like *Great lay!* Then, with a playful thumbs-up, she backs away into the crowd.

Shoot. I'd go after her, but Gabe is in my way.

He steps closer, taking my hand, his fingers trailing over my palm before he lifts it to his lips. His mouth is warm, lingering just long enough to make my pulse jump. "What's up, Samara?" His voice is rich, low, like a slow bassline. "You new to Hollywood?"

My eyes drift over his shoulder, catching the last glimpse of Indigo's platinum ponytail weaving through the crowd, Chloe's fro-hawk trailing behind her. "I guess you could say that."

I should've known she'd pull something like this. I'd leave now, but I gave Kelly and Legend my word. Plus, I left my phone with the girl's driver.

Gabe watches me, his smirk lazy, full of quiet confidence. "Fame or fortune?"

"Excuse me?"

He leans in, his breath warm against my ear, the spicy scent of his cologne teasing like a dare. "Fame or Fortune? You tryna get famous off your talents, or make some money?"

Gabe flashes a smile so captivating, it almost pulls me in. I catch a glimpse of his Cuban link chain, shining in the strobe lights, and the silk of his designer shirt sliding across his broad chest. He's a charmer. Confident. Easy on the eyes. A vibe.

But he's not Legend. Legend doesn't have to try this hard. He just... shows up. Says the right thing. Smirks, and my whole system resets.

Gabe holds a fist in his hand, waiting for my answer.

"Honestly? I don't have a single skill that would make me famous. And money wouldn't solve my problems."

He raises an eyebrow. "So, neither?"

I shake my head, Legend's laugh echoing in the back of my mind like one of his hit songs.

"I guess you could say I'm looking for fortune."

A grin stretches across Gabe's lips, an unspoken gleam in his eye. "Me too."

The music shifts, and a popular Dua Lipa song pulses through the speakers. Gabe and I start bobbing our heads at the same time, the rhythm syncing effortlessly.

He leans closer, connecting eyes with me. "Wanna dance?"

My heart stutters in my chest. Is this hot, semi-famous guy trying to hook up with me right now? Frankly, I'm flattered.

But Legend's the reason I'm here in the first place. And I've got a job to do.

I smile politely, stepping back. "I'd love to, but—"

I'm interrupted by a loud crash ringing through the air, followed by the collective gasp of the crowd.

"*Always running that mouth. I'm about to shut it for you!*"

I turn, barely able to catch my balance. My blood goes cold.

That voice is undeniable. I draw in a long breath, turning back to Gabe. "Will you excuse me, please?" I head into the swarm of people before Gabe can answer.

The music dims, and the crowd parts, as I make my way to the center of the dance floor. Indigo is screaming, a broken vodka bottle clutched in her hand like a dagger. *Oh no.*

Selina Auber, from *Let's Have Tea*—the daily Hollywood gossip show—is standing off to the side, her feather boa bunched at her throat like a shield.

"Indigo, honey, no one is here to fight with you!" says Selina, her voice trembling like she's holding back tears.

"Could've fooled me," Indigo shouts. "What you got to say now, huh?!"

She lunges forward, and the crowd releases another dramatic gasp. Everyone, including Selina, takes a step back. Indigo lets out a bitter laugh. "You scared now, huh? Got a *whole* lot to say on your little panel. What you got to say now? Huh?!"

Chloe, looking more exhausted than concerned, rolls her eyes and gingerly grabs Indigo's arm. But Indigo yanks out of her grip like a toddler having a tantrum in the toy store.

I can't say I'm surprised to see Indigo flare up with Selina in the room. The clip of the panelist giving her opinion of Indigo went viral months ago. The girl broke my man's heart and even I've gotta admit, the woman dragged Indigo *hard*.

"I'll show you a 'washed-up child actress!' Come here!" Indigo screeches, charging at Selina again, but Chloe snatches her up this time, yanking the bottle from her hands.

Selina, like the smart woman she is, scampers off into the crowd.

"*Yeah!*" screams Indigo. "*You better run, bi-atch! I'mma catch you outside!*"

Chloe shushes her, trying not to draw any more attention.

But it's already too late. Because unlike us... nobody else left their phone in the car.

12

INDIGO STRIKES AGAIN!
HOLLYWOOD'S BAD GIRL MAKES GOOD ON HER PROMISE.

A grin plays on Legend's lips as I read the headline on his phone the next afternoon. Pictured below is a frightening image of Indigo, face twisted in fury, vodka bottle raised, charging at Selina like she's in a Scorsese film.

Of course, she made the front page.

Legend lets out an incredulous chuckle as he slips the phone back in his pocket.

I lean on the pool table, the hush of the billiard room pressing in. "I told you this was a bad idea."

He lines up the shot with lazy precision. Sinks the five-ball without blinking. *Show-off.*

It's effortless for him, like everything else he does.

"You said you'd try your best. I didn't even see you in the picture." His glance is quick, almost kind. But it lands like disappointment anyway.

My stomach twists.

What if he thinks I'm a liability now?

One reckless night, and he decides I'm not cut out for this. That I don't belong in his world. That I should've stayed in Seattle, grading freshman essays and daydreaming about someone who was never supposed to text me back.

"L, you don't understand. She had this whole plan. She took my phone, dodged me all night, changed my look—"

"You looked gorgeous by the way."

I falter.

Of all the things he could've said, I didn't expect that. Not now.

"Thanks."

I've imagined him saying those words a hundred ways. But never this casually. I blink, chasing the swirl of emotion back down.

Focus, Sam.

"She even abandoned me with some random producer guy who had the hots for me."

Legend chalks the tip of his cue stick, brow raised. "What producer guy?"

"Gabe something..."

"Oh, fa' real?" He leans back, eyes dragging down my frame. "So what happened?" The question feels more pointed than nonchalant. But I'm too worked up to decipher it now.

"*Page Six* happened! Frickin' *TMZ* happened, Legend!" I flop on the sofa, draping an arm over my face. "Ugh! I'll be lucky if I have a job on Monday!"

"Hmph." Legend goes quiet. I look up and find an irresistible smirk on his lips.

"What?"

"It's just interesting to see you worried about the ice queen potentially firing you."

My mouth falls open. "Well—I, uh..."

He busts out laughing as he strides over to me and perches on the arm of the sofa. "Admit it," he grins. "She's got you shook."

I scoff in denial. "It's not that I care so much about *her...*"

He nudges me with his foot, his voice softer this time. "Then what is it you care about?" His gaze holds steady, reeling me in.

I try to catch my breath, but it's difficult with him this close. My mind races. Years of things left unsaid. Things that have been lingering on the tip of my tongue for so long.

But what would that mean? What could that change? For better... or worse.

"Legend, I—"

But there's a knock at the door. It's his assistant, Cam. "Hey, boss, I took the GT-R to the detailer. It's sparkling and ready to go." He tosses the keys, and Legend thanks him. Cam gives me a nod. "What's up, Sam?"

"Not much, Cam."

Both of us laugh.

Once the two of us realized the irony of our rhyming nicknames, we took to greeting one another in this cheesy way. Legend says he loves that the best dude and the best girl in his life sound like twins.

But he's not smiling right now. "Yo, Cam, why don't you go ahead and dip early, bruh? I know you got a shorty dressing up for you tonight."

Cam sticks out his tongue and slaps the door. "You know me, boss! I'll check y'all later." He's gone just as quickly as he came.

"That was nice of you," I say, looking back at Legend. "Doesn't seem like you lean on your staff nearly as much as Indigo."

He nods slowly, studying the cue stick in his hands. "She's much more high maintenance."

I wait for him to look at me, to flash that easy grin, to throw out some teasing remark that makes all of this feel lighter. But he doesn't.

"Is something wrong?" I ask.

He shrugs, staring toward the hall. It sounds like Cam is long gone. "Just trying to figure out what to do with this new ride," he says, something heavy in his eyes.

"You don't like it?"

He exhales through his nose, rolling the cue stick between his palms. "It's a gift from Victoria... A *'thank you'* for my private performance last night."

"That's... generous."

He exhales deeper this time. "All that glitters ain't gold, Sam."

That's something coming from someone who sells out arenas and lives like a BET awards after-party.

I'd laugh if his shoulders weren't sagging like he just missed a high note on live TV. I wonder what's going on.

Before I can ask, my phone chimes.

INDIGO: *Where did you put my cross-wrap bikini???*

Legend catches my eye roll.

"That your boy from the club?"

My boy? He stares at me expectantly, a curious crease in his brow.

"Uh, no..." I mutter, typing out a reply.

SAM: *Which one?*

Legend leans closer, his arm brushing mine as he tries to peek at my screen.

"It's not the ex, is it?"

I huff a laugh. "Mine or yours?"

He stills. "Oh! That's Indigo?"

I nod, returning to her messages.

INDIGO: *The pink one. DUH!*

I throw my head back with a sigh. Everything's an emergency with this woman. But when I glance up, Legend's still watching me.

Wait. Did he think I was talking to Justin or something?

He stands and grabs his glass of Cognac off the bar. His sip is slow. Pensive. "Based on your reaction, it seems like you still got a job."

I purse my lips, my thumb hovering over the screen. "Unfortunately."

Legend chuckles. "It'll get easier. You still got your training pants on."

"So, you're saying that at some point I'll stop crapping myself and go full commando?"

Legend chokes mid-sip, laughing so hard he coughs out his drink.

I groan, covering my face. "Wow. That sounded way less disturbing in my head. I think Indigo's rubbing off on me."

I bite back a smile as he dabs at his Givenchy tee, still laughing. He always did have the softest laugh.

He shakes his head in amusement. "In what analogy that makes sense is *beyond* me."

I shrug. "I just like making you smile."

He's quiet for a beat, his gaze steady. "You always have."

My stomach flips. Like it used to, back when all I had was a username and a dream.

The words hang in the air between us, soft and unexpected. Our gazes lock with a weight that feels heavier than it should. He's the one who ends it.

"We'll figure this out soon enough," he says, focusing on the glass in his hands. "Just... Don't give up. Aiight?"

He looks at me, his brow set, and I nod.

"I'm gonna go get some more ice." He sets down his glass and heads for the door.

"But Legend…"

He turns back, almost expectantly.

"What can I do? The girl hates my guts."

He stares at me for a second, his expression faltering before it fades into a more pensive frown. "Just win her over, the same way you did me."

He disappears into the hall before I can reply.

And that's when it hits me. Of course. That's *exactly* what I need to do.

Study. Adapt. Win her over. Even if it kills me.

That's how I became Professor Natalie's closest confidant, and Legend's too. Why didn't I think of this before? If I'm gonna get on Indigo's good side, that starts with proving I'm a *real* fan.

+ + + + + + +

I spend the entire weekend consumed by research, turning over every stone I can find. I dig into her childhood, analyze each snippet of her career, and watch every interview I can get my hands on. I even reach out to Kelly for a few extra details.

By the time I head to work on Monday, I know Indigo inside and out. The girl's a triple threat. Started taking voice and dance lessons at the age of three, was homeschooled with private tutors her *entire* life. And go figure, her favorite food is sushi. Can't say I'm surprised. She's also a sucker for the color pink. Kelly's right. The girl is a lot more human than I thought.

She steps out to the pool, stopping short when she spots me waiting beneath the lattice pergola. She peers over her shades at the patio table, where I've set out her favorite organic protein bar on a plate, perfectly arranged beside a fresh glass of cold-pressed green juice. Adorned with a pink straw, of course.

I pull out her chair as she approaches more slowly, her silk kimono fluttering in the summer breeze.

"Is there anything else I can get for you, Miss Indigo?"

She flicks a dismissive hand, already reaching for the juice. With a reserved nod, I turn toward the house.

"Hey, Sam!"

OMG, she actually remembered my name! I turn. "Yes, Miss Indigo?"

She doesn't even glance up from her phone. "I don't need you for Jiu-Jitsu today. Sort my lingerie drawers instead."

Yes! Not a bark. Not a glare. Just delegation. That's growth... right?

The rest of the day moves like clockwork. I keep up with her schedule, anticipating her needs before she even asks. A fresh towel, still warm from the dryer, is waiting the moment she steps out of the shower. I test the bathwater twice before she so much as dips in a toe.

No complaints. No sharp remarks. Just a nod of approval here and there.

Progress.

Folding the last of her silk robes and smoothing my hands over the fabric, I steal a glance toward the hall. She's in the lounge now, scrolling through her phone, her second green juice of the day in hand.

Maybe now's my chance. I chew my lip, debating. I need to start a conversation. Something easy, something casual—before she shoos me away or, worse, remembers another ridiculous task for me.

I glance around her dressing room, searching for an opening. And then I see it.

A delicate heart-shaped locket glints in the shadows, half-hidden between a bottle of Chanel perfume and a tangle of velvet scrunchies on her vanity.

Even in the dim glow of the dressing room, with soft slivers of light cutting in from the hallway, it gleams like it holds a secret.

My fingertips skim the cool metal as I lift it from its resting place. It's delicate, lighter than expected, with the kind of vintage charm that doesn't fit Indigo's usual modern style.

"You do know theft is grounds for automatic dismissal, right?"

My spine snaps straight. "Miss Indigo."

She leans against the doorway, arms crossed.

I clasp my hands behind my back like a sneaky toddler. "I thought you had a meeting to prepare for."

"Cancelled." She steps inside, flipping on the lights. The room floods with a soft glow, revealing the Hollywood-style vanity mirror, rows of meticulously arranged makeup, and a fuzzy pink sofa piled with faux fur pillows.

She shifts her weight, arms still folded over the crop tank that shows off her toned stomach, joggers draping effortlessly over long, lean legs. "Why are you in my stuff?"

I swallow. *Think. Fast.*

"I'm sorry. I was just…" I gesture toward the vanity, specifically the delicate heart-shaped locket gleaming under the lights. "Admiring."

Her expression doesn't budge.

I push forward, my voice steady but careful. "This is the same locket you wore during the first season of *Treasure*, right?"

Silence.

She studies me with a steely gaze, and my stomach clenches, lungs seizing like I've walked straight into a trap. I force myself to hold her stare, willing the moment to tilt in my favor.

Finally, she nods. "You recognize it, huh?"

Relief untangles in my chest as she crosses the room, picking up the locket and lowering into her vanity chair.

"How could anyone miss it?" I say on an exhale. "You wore it in almost every episode."

I hold my breath. *Please. Just let this work.*

Her eyes meet mine in the mirror. "You watched my show?"

Just binge-watched twenty episodes last night. "Of course!" I give her my brightest smile. "What else was worth watching at thirteen?"

Indigo turns the locket over in her fingers, a flicker of nostalgia passing over her face.

I watch her carefully, my pulse kicking up. This is it. An opening. If I can get her talking, get her to let her guard down, maybe I can find something useful for Legend. Something real. And maybe, just maybe, a reason why he shouldn't still want her.

With a small shrug, Indigo holds the locket up to her neck.

"I never wear this tacky thing anymore. My stylist would kill me."

"I remember reading about how much it meant to you. But you never said why in your interviews."

She stares back at me in the mirror. "Okay, stalker. I haven't talked about this thing in, like, a decade."

A tense silence stretches between us. My pulse thrums in my ears as I force myself to stay still beneath her pointed gaze. If she kicks me out now, I'll have nothing. No way to help Legend, no way to prove I belong here.

I softly bob my head, praying that she'll buy it.

Thankfully, it seems she does. Indigo leans her elbows on the vanity, running her thumbs across the golden pendant. "It was from my favorite nanny. The main one who took care of me since I was a baby." She opens the locket, presenting the picture inside—a photo of a young Indigo, hugging a middle-aged Hispanic woman tight.

"Her name was Nadia," says Indigo, studying the picture with a charmed grin. "Honestly, I was so close to the woman that sometimes I thought she was family. Maybe a close aunt or even my abuela.

Actually, she'd left her entire family in Mexico just to come work for me. I didn't even know how to tie my shoes, but I was her boss."

I swallow hard. This woman has a vault under all that glam. And I just cracked it.

Indigo lets out a light chuckle, and for just a moment, her eyes seem to glisten. She blinks, staring up at the ceiling. "She kept me eating right. Made sure I got to *every* voice and dance lesson... Man, she nearly passed out when she heard I got the lead role for *Treasure*. She was *so* proud of me. And her support meant more to me than anything from Mamí or Daddy." She stares at the locket, a faraway look in her eye. "This was a gift to congratulate me. I told her she shouldn't, but she insisted. *'Remember your old nanny when you blow up,'* she said." Indigo lets out a thin laugh, brushing away a tear before it can fall. "Daddy fired her the week I started filming."

I'm not supposed to feel sorry for her.

She's spoiled, chaotic, rude on a good day.

But something in her voice, raw and almost childlike, unravels that narrative. The air in my lungs turns thick.

"That's awful. Did he ever tell you why?"

"He thought she'd stolen one of his favorite watches. Had her deported in a heartbeat." She glances at me in the mirror, her expression cold. "Turns out it was just one of his mistresses. Nadia died a few years back."

I wince as she replaces the necklace on its rack.

"My parents and me never really saw eye-to-eye," she says.

That's another thing about Indigo. She filed for emancipation at sixteen. She hasn't spoken to either of her celebrity parents since.

Indigo eyes me like I tracked mud across her marble floors. "Seriously, Sam! What is this crap?"

I glance down at my overalls and Reebok Classics. "What's wrong with vintage?"

She flicks her wrist, already over it. "Ugh. Enough of this!"

Two hours and twelve wardrobe changes later, I'm in her styling chair as she dries my hair. I scroll through her social media, half-listening to the music videos flashing across her mounted TV.

"Oh! Before I forget—" I flick back to her DMs. "Travis says he 'saw you last week at the Grove, and that poolside bikini post was...' Several tongue emojis. He's got a Maserati and wants to take you to dinner."

"Tap on his profile." Indigo leans in, squinting over my shoulder as I scroll through his feed—shirtless selfies, luxury cars, bottle service flexes. She scoffs. "Hard pass."

I delete the message and keep scrolling.

Indigo runs her chrome nails through my hair, sifting through the strands like she's inspecting a hidden treasure. "Sam, why are you hiding all these fabulous curls? With thick hair like this, I'd *never* wear weave."

"I'm just used to wearing it straight." Which explains why I'm giving full Simone circa freshman year.

She tuts, shaking her head as she gathers my dark hair in her hands. She releases the spirals in layers and fluffs them. "Honey, I'm gonna have so much fun with this."

"Can we just avoid cutting it?" I ask, my wary gaze meeting hers in the mirror. "My sister Simone gave me a makeover at ten, and I ended up with lopsided pink hair."

Indigo laughs. "Chick, if I wanna cut your hair then I will. You *my* baby doll now!"

My scalp tightens. *Lord, what have I gotten myself into?*

"Keep scrolling," she says, staring at her phone in my hand. "Stop. Zoom in."

I pinch and enlarge a paparazzi shot of two A-listers strolling hand-in-hand along a sunlit beach. The ocean glows behind them, waves lapping at their ankles like a perfectly staged romance novel cover.

Indigo rolls her eyes. "Ugh! I can't *believe* they're together again. She acts like his package is a frickin' golden Oscar."

I arch a brow. The girl's got a point.

She tugs my hair absently, twisting a curl around her finger. "Keep scrolling." I do as she says, but her focus shifts to my reflection in the mirror. "You got a man?"

"Not really."

I mean, I did. But I left him. Then came to LA chasing something—or someone—who was never really mine to begin with. But who really wants to go there?

"*Not really?* What's that supposed to mean?" A smirk tugs at her mouth. "You screwing somebody with a wife and kids? Into some *Fifty Shades of Grey* behind closed doors or something?" She wags her tongue, laughing.

I crack a smile myself.

I should keep it light. Legend told me not to share too much. But with Indigo, it's tough. There's something disarming about the gleam in her eye, the way her laugh fills the room like she owns it—which she does. But still, here? In this moment? We aren't celebrity and assistant. Not two women in a tug-of-war for the same guy.

We're just two girls swapping stories. Like she could almost be... a friend.

It kinda reminds me of those late nights with Simone, when she'd sneak into my room, and we'd stay up giggling over one of mom's

Cosmo magazines. One of those soft, fleeting pockets of time when the weight of losing our dad didn't feel quite so heavy.

I rest Indigo's phone in my lap, tension easing from my shoulders.

"I just… recently got out of a long-term relationship, actually. His name was Justin. We were together for seven years."

"Oh." She frowns. "So you're the Bible camp committed type?"

"I guess you could say that."

She leans in, curious. "He cheat?"

I wince, then say it anyway. "No."

Indigo gasps with wide eyes. "Wait—*you* stepped out?"

"No! It wasn't like that. Not really," I blurt. "I, um, just had an old crush I couldn't shake. Figured it was for the best."

Indigo snorts, raking the comb through my curls with a little more force than necessary. "A *crush?* So you dumped the guy you were with for some dude that doesn't even know you caught feelings?"

I softly nod. "Even rejected a proposal."

Her sharp laugh cracks through the air. "You're dumb."

Heat rises in my neck. "You think it was fair to string the guy along while I was infatuated with someone else?"

"Hell, yeah! Girl, how many of us would give our right butt cheek to have a guy that devoted to us? And your stupid ass threw it away for somebody you can't even be sure likes you! You're a dummy."

Okay, maybe it sounds bad. Maybe it is bad. But I made peace with this decision… Didn't I?

I exhale, staring at my reflection. "I had to make a choice. It was, *stay with the man of my life,* or *take a chance with the guy of my dreams.* So, I stepped out on faith and went for it."

Indigo pauses, her hand still in my hair. "So, what? You think getting with this new guy would make you less of a nobody?"

The words sting more than I want to admit. "I guess."

Indigo sucks her teeth. "You're stupid for letting a good thing go."

There's always the possibility that she could be right. Maybe I did let something good slip through my fingers. But so did she. I read about it again last night. It turns out that the rumors were much worse than what actually went down that night at the club. She was grinding on the professional boxer C. K. Boston, but that was it. The question is... Why?

I study her in the mirror. "Can I ask you something?"

I'm expecting a glare or some sort of rude remark, but instead, she nods for me to go ahead.

"Why'd you let Legend Blake go?"

I brace myself as she yanks the ponytail holder from my hair, my scalp stinging under her grip. Her eyes track the fall of my curls, tension coiling in the air between us. I hold my breath, hoping I haven't said something that'll shove me right back to the starting line.

Then, with a slow, deliberate shake of her head, she exhales a humorless laugh. "You know, it only took a few relationships for them to label me a 'heartbreaker'. 'Indigo the *man-eater* strikes again!'" She scoffs. "People always blame me. Nobody ever thinks about my feelings. Can't I get hurt? Can't I be scared?"

She combs my hair in silence, her smile not quite reaching her eyes. "I swear... that boy would flirt with a houseplant."

Both of us chuckle. She's right. But something about the way she says it—with that wistful, almost nostalgic look in her eye—has got me wondering if she's really over Legend.

"Keep scrolling," she says. "I have more hearts to give."

She scrunches my hair, telling me when to double-tap.

Then she raises a hand. "Stop. Scroll back up." I slide my finger back, landing on a clip of some guy singing on a theater stage. According to the caption, he stepped out during the final number of a musical, excusing himself to the restroom, only to surprise his girlfriend with a sweet serenade after curtain call. His voice is really good.

Indigo watches intently, her eyes fixed on the screen as the cast pulls the lucky girl onstage. Her boyfriend kneels in front of her, proposing with a ring in hand. I catch the quiet change in Indigo's expression through the mirror, a flicker of sadness passing over her face before she quickly masks it.

Maybe this is my chance.

I tilt my head, pretending to admire the clip. "Wow. This is so romantic. I, on the other hand, was proposed to over a random family dinner. My mom sniffled through the entire thing." I casually look up at Indigo's reflection. "Has anyone ever done something like this for you?"

Indigo shakes her head softly, her gaze locked on the screen. There's something raw in her eyes. Something aching and unspoken, like a wound that hasn't quite healed, still tender to the touch.

Abruptly, she snaps out of her trance with a scoff. "All those cameras in my face with me blubbering and junk? Please. That's corny as hell!" She shakes her head, more forcefully this time. "Keep scrolling."

A lengthy silence hovers between us, and I begin to wonder if maybe I've crossed a line. The tension hangs in the air, thick and awkward, making me second-guess every word I've said up until now.

Then, quietly, she says, "I blame Lydia."

I stare at her reflection. "Lydia?"

Indigo nods. "My old personal assistant. I just wanted to have a little fun that night with C.K. Get people talking."

OMG, she's talking about the breakup. I don't dare say a word.

She sighs heavily, fluffing the last of my curls into place. "Somebody paid her off though. Got her to film the whole thing and paint me as a slut. I never meant for things to go that far." A small pout buds on her lips. "I was just fooling around."

I go completely still. "You mean, your personal assistant leaked that video?"

Indigo nods, lips pressed tight. "I never should've trusted that chick."

13

*L*egend's eyes nearly fall out of his head when he opens the door the next afternoon. His gaze flickers from head to toe, taking in my curly hair, high-waisted shorts, and silk plunging blouse. Indigo even donated a pair of slinky designer heels.

I can't help smiling as I remove my shades. "Surprise!"

"Damn, Sam…" He lets out a breathy laugh, still staring. "You tryna give a man a heart attack?"

"Just trying something different," I say, trying not to beam. "Can I come in?"

"By all means…" He opens the door wide, his eyes glued as I walk in. If I'd known this little makeover would have such an effect, I would've switched up my look weeks ago.

His attention never wavers as I take a seat on the living room sofa. He clears his throat, finally blinking himself back to reality. "You want a drink or something?"

"Nah. I'm good." I reach into my Prada handbag. "I was thinking… maybe we could watch something."

"Oh, yeah?" His curiosity flares as he drops onto the sofa beside me, close enough that our knees nearly brush.

I turn my phone screen toward him, *Hamilton* queued up and ready to play.

"*Yo!*" Legend throws a fist over his mouth. "Fa' real?" He leans in, checking out the movie on my phone screen. "I was just thinking about this the other day. I ain't seen it in a minute."

"I know. Legend Blake is *much too cool* for musicals."

"Exactly," he says with a sly grin. Both of us know they're his secret guilty pleasure. He moves a little closer. "But... I guess I could make an exception for a hot chick that wants to check it out with me."

The warmth in his gaze stirs something deep in my chest.

———— ✦✦✦✦ ————

He sends his staff home, and within minutes, we're curled up on the sofa, the flickering light from the TV casting a soft glow across the dimly lit room. Legend stretches an arm across the back of the sofa, his fingers grazing my shoulder every time he shifts. The screen's low light casts shadows across his face, highlighting the smirk tugging at his lips.

OMG, this feels like a date. Am I on a frickin' date with Legend Blake right now?

I'm sitting beside the man who was never supposed to text me back. In his mansion. Like this is normal. Like I belong here. Like he didn't just invite me to keep tabs on Indigo.

He swirls a glass of brandy in his hand, taking a slow sip as the opening beats of "The Schuyler Sisters" pulse through the room. "Ah, man. I remember this number. It's dope!" He sets his glass aside, settling into the sofa with a casual ease, his hand drifting to rest on my shoulder.

I'm gonna faint, or I'm gonna barf... or both. Okay, Sam, get it together, girl! Inhale. Exhale. You're only chilling with the hottest R&B star on the planet.

Suddenly, Legend turns, and his eyes meet mine, his thick lips mere inches from my face.

Yep. Definitely gonna barf.

His handsome eyebrows knit together. "You good?"

"Mmhmm." *Just feeling a little woozy... Inhale. Exhale.*

He pauses the show, studying me. "You sure? 'Cause you look a little buzzed."

"Me? Buzzed?" I let out a laugh that sounds a little like a Kookaburra. "Ha! Yeah right!"

He bobs his head, his eyes lingering on my wine-colored lips. "I like that color on you."

"Really?" My cheeks grow hot. "I told Indigo it was too dark, but she insisted."

Big mistake.

He blinks, his eyes seeming to wake from their daze. "Indigo fixed you up like this?"

"Yeah. We had a moment yesterday and she decided to give me a makeover... About time, hmm?"

Legend nods, his gaze shifting to the floor. "Yeah. You look really good." He lets out a light chuckle. "Not that you didn't always look good." Slowly, he removes his arm and leans down on his knees, rubs his knuckles in his hand.

He doesn't have to say a word. I already know. He's thinking about *her* again. And for once, I sorta get it. Because when I mention his name, she gets the same look in her eye.

Ugh! Sam, don't get a guilty conscience now! What the heck is wrong with you?

"I'm glad to hear the two of y'all are getting along," he says.

"Mmhmm. Actually, we had a nice long talk yesterday."

He looks back to me, intrigued. "Yeah?"

Great! Now you've done it. So much for keeping him all to yourself.

He nudges me, his gaze locking onto mine with the earnestness of a child waiting for an answer. "Anything to report?"

I scrunch my face in denial, but he sees right through me.

Sitting up straight, he stares me down, his deep brown eyes twinkling with mischief. I glance away, throwing a hand over my face, and he busts out laughing.

"Nah! Don't get all cute now. You got something to say then say it, Sam."

There's an edge to his voice that cuts to the heart. *Shoot! I need to play this off, redirect, say something charming.*

But the way he's looking at me—hopeful, vulnerable, like he *needs* to hear whatever I might say—I can't stay quiet.

I *want* to. I should.

But with him I just... can't.

"She... *did* bring you up yesterday."

He pauses the movie, then leans back. "I'm all ears."

So, despite the NDA I signed, I spill it. I tell him all about the locket, the viral video, Indigo's thoughts on the TMZ scandal, and Lydia. Each word feels heavier than the last, and I can't shake the feeling that I'm treading on dangerous ground.

Legend nods pensively as I finish relating the details. "So, she's still yet to explain why she dumped me?"

"Unfortunately."

Legend throws back his head, letting out a deep, frustrated sigh. He runs his hands down his face. "Man. I had to fall for *the most* complicated chick in Hollywood."

"You got that right." *In only six months, no less. And I doubt they exchanged nearly as many DMs as he and I have over the years.*

"All you chicks are complicated," he says, tossing me a bitter grin.

"No, we're not! You boys just don't know how to give us what we want."

His eyes trace over my outfit, lingering on the coils of my hair. "And what do beautiful girls like you want?"

The world seems to quiet around us, the space between us thick with unspoken thoughts.

I shrug, trying to keep my voice steady. "We wanna feel special. Like you've got eyes for no one else."

His gaze flickers downward as he bobs his head, seeming to snap out of... whatever just happened.

My stomach tightens. *Stupid, stupid, stupid! Why'd you have to go and say that, Sam?! Goodness, you're dumb.* I gnaw at my freshly polished nails, wishing I'd said anything else.

Legend sighs, the sounds soft but heavy. "So what should I do?"

My eyes slide shut as the weight of his misery presses against my chest. I don't wanna say... But the sight of the boy drowning in his own thoughts wrenches something deep in my gut. It *physically* hurts to breathe the words. "I think I know what would win her over."

Legend listens intently as I share the plan. By the time I finish, he's nodding to himself, his thumb tracing the edge of his goatee as he considers my words.

"You really think this could work, huh?"

"I'm sure." I stand, gathering my things. Suddenly, I'm no longer in the mood for musicals.

Legend stands too. "All right. I'll give it a shot." He pulls me into a hug, enveloping me in his fresh mountain scent. With a light kiss to my forehead, he presses his cheek against mine. "You're the best, Sam."

I nod, the words feeling like a cruel joke. *If only that were true.*

His eyes are humming as we move toward the door. "I got a lot of planning to do."

"Yeah, just let me know how I can help. Raincheck on *Hamilton*."

At least, I hope that'll be the case.

Legend turns to face me as we reach the door. "I can't thank you enough, Sam." His smile is warm and enchanting. "Is there anything else I should know?"

I grip the strap of my bag, my pulse thrumming in my throat.

Years I've spent, swallowing my feelings, pretending that my heart doesn't crack every time he says Indigo's name like it still tastes sweet on his tongue. And now, look at me, handing him over, piece by piece, like I haven't spent every late night and every secret daydream imagining what it would be like if, just once, he looked at me the same way he looks at her.

Years, I never changed anything. Same town, same routine, same boyfriend… Safe. Predictable. But then *he* happened. Legend Blake, pulling me into his world like gravity. And suddenly, the life I thought I wanted wasn't enough anymore.

I left everything. *Everything* I ever knew behind. For what? To help him run back to *her*?

He has no clue how many times I've typed and deleted messages I'll never send, how many times I've rehearsed confessions I'll never say.

It isn't fair. It isn't fair that he can't see what's right in front of him.

A rush of selfish desires flood my thoughts as I stare at him, my heart racing.

"Actually, there is one more thing…"

◆◆◆◆◆

Indigo glances left and right as we enter the Japanese restaurant on Thursday. A full sushi bar in the corner is manned by smiling chefs in boat-shaped hats, and dining tables are set with crisp white cloths and scarlet napkins.

"This place is dead," says Indigo. "You sure this is the right address?"

"This is the location Kelly gave me." I shoot a text to Legend as the waiter ushers us toward the back.

SAM: *Headed down the hall now.*

Legend responds with a thumbs-up, and in the distance, the faint tinkling of piano keys begins to fill the air. Indigo, however, is too focused on the rose petals scattered across the floor to notice.

"What's all this about? Somebody having a wedding or something?"

The waitress gives Indigo a coy grin in response, then continues on her way. Indigo glares back at me, and I respond with an innocent smile.

"Right this way, ma'am," the waitress says with a polite nod, guiding us forward.

We step out onto the restaurant patio, and the scene instantly feels different. Special.

All around the dining area sits a bouquet of roses on every table, votive candles scattered like fireflies, interspersed with red and pink petals. Large floral bouquets and tall candelabras border us on every side, the aroma of perfume and burning candles dancing on a gentle evening breeze.

Legend sits behind the piano, on a raised platform, in a handsome gray blazer and jeans. His fingers glide across the keys as his full, deep voice drifts into the evening sky.

> *"One look at you.*
> *Your eyes, they sparkle and they shine—*
> *No doubt about it.*
> *I want you.*
> *Been thinking about you all the time—*
> *'Cause girl, you got it..."*

It's the song he wrote just for her. And it's even more beautiful than the first time I heard it.

Legend lifts his eyes, gazing at Indigo as he sings the chorus.

"Honey, you're... just right.
You make me higher than... a kite.
When I think of you... at night.
I don't wanna stop. Baby, I can't stop..."

Indigo stares at him with gaping eyes, a hand over her mouth. She's dressed casually in ripped jeans and a simple tank, topped with a long zebra-print cardigan. She's not even trying, yet somehow, she still looks effortlessly stunning. As suspected, she's captivated.

My gaze drops, my chest tightening.

Please, let this work.

Cam's already live-streaming, Legend's phone angled high as he inches closer.

Indigo does a double-take when she sees him. "What the—?!"

She snatches the phone from his grip and hurls it into the cement. The moment it lands, she drives her heel into it, the crunch of splintering glass wincing beneath her platform heels.

Cam's jaw falls open, his eyes wide with disbelief. Panic flashes across his face as he looks back at Legend.

This is honestly going better than I ever could've imagined. I hide my smile as I stand by, waiting for the fireworks.

Suddenly, the music comes to a stop. Legend stands, squinting in our direction. "What's going on?"

"Really, Legend?" Indigo's voice cracks as she backs away, eyes glassing over.

Legend steps toward her, his voice tight with panic. "Indigo, wait—"

But she's already turning, heels clacking hard against the floor as she storms back inside.

Legend looks at me, eyes wide, confused, like he's waiting for me to explain. Maybe even fix it.

I give a quick shrug, as if at a complete loss, then take off after her.

My legs are moving before the guilt can rise any higher. But by the time I push through the doors, her car's already peeling off down the street.

Great. Now how am I gonna get home?

I can't shake the image of her face, the hurt in her eyes. What if she fires me?

Legend jogs up behind me. "Sam, what the hell?"

"I know," I throw a dramatic hand to my forehead. "I'm sorry."

"I thought you said she'd be down for this sorta thing!"

"I thought she would! She seemed impressed… at first—"

"Yeah, until she straight-up wrecked my phone!"

Shoot. Legend is really pissed.

He paces back and forth, his hands on his waist, frustration radiating off him.

Geez… I mean, this was the goal. Distance. Damage. I wanted her ticked. Wanted them done. But I didn't expect things to blow up like this. Didn't expect tears in her eyes. Or that look on his face… like something sacred just shattered.

I cross my arms, my gaze drifting down the street. "I'm sorry, Legend. I really am."

He glowers at me, but I mean it.

Not because I regret what I did. But because it had to be done. Because if I hadn't stepped in, I might've lost him for good.

Still…

I never thought it'd wreck him like this.

Suddenly tears are stinging my eyes.

I sniffle, forcing a half-laugh. "If it helps, she ditched me. I'll probably get abducted trying to take an Uber or something."

He stares at me with dull eyes. Then, with a heavy breath, he waves me over. "You can ride with me."

———— ✦✦✦✦✦ ————

Legend needs to grab his backup phone, so we stop by his place first. He's still fuming as we head inside.

"Legend, I am so sorry. I'm not sure what went—"

He throws up a hand, making a beeline for the bar. "Save it, Sam. Fa' real."

The clink of glass and the slosh of whiskey cut through the silence as he pours himself a generous amount.

"But, L—"

"Just… drop it." He exhales hard, finally looking at me. The raw disappointment in his eyes is gut-wrenching. "It was a fail. That's that." He downs half the glass like it's water.

He's much more upset than I thought he'd be. And it's all my fault. I drop my head, my eyes burning.

But before I can even process it, he's by my side, pulling me into his arms.

I suck a shaky breath, my voice barely above a whisper. "Legend, I… I never—"

He hushes me, his grip firm but warm. "It's cool, Sam. I know you meant well."

I stare up at him, my face damp, my chest tight. Thank God Indigo gave me that waterproof eyeliner. I sniffle, rubbing at my cheeks. "You shouldn't be comforting me. *I* should be comforting *you*."

I was supposed to have his back. To help him win her over. Instead, I betrayed him. Now he's sitting here with a broken phone *and* a broken heart. And it's all my fault.

Shame burns through me. "You have every right to throw me out on my ass right now."

Legend exhales, his gaze softening. "Nah. You drove all the way here to help me out. I can't be mad at you for trying."

But he should be. He totally, totally should be.

Yet, instead of pushing me away, he pulls me closer. And I don't resist, I melt into him, my cheek pressing against his chest, listening to the steady rhythm of his heartbeat.

I just want to stay here. Just for a little while.

And maybe... maybe if I stay long enough, he'll realize that he likes me here too.

I wrap my arms around him and hug him tight, praying I can somehow keep this moment from slipping away.

His chest rises and falls with a heavy sigh. "I think it was the phone that freaked her out."

My eyes spring open. "The phone?"

He nods, letting me go. "Now that shit was your idea."

I tilt my head, scratching my neck. "Was it?"

"Actually," he takes a step back, crossing his arms, "I *distinctly* recall you suggesting that detail."

Heat creeps up my neck as I shrink beneath his stern gaze.

In all fairness, I didn't twist his arm. I just... played the angle. Told him it was a romantic gesture. That Indigo would see the heart behind it. I think part of him wanted to believe that. The rest? He probably just wanted to believe me.

To his credit, he asked if I was sure this wouldn't backfire. But I sold it to him like a promise. That it'd be the one thing to get through to her. He trusted me. And now I'm not so sure I deserved it.

And then, the doorbell rings.

Legend freezes, his jaw still clenched. He steps over to the wall monitor and his eyes grow two sizes. "It's Indigo."

My breath catches. "What? What is she doing here?"

His voice is low. Almost hesitant. "I... Your guess is as good as mine."

I stumble back, scanning the room in a panic. "If she sees me, we are *so* dead!"

He grabs me by the hand, tugging me toward the staircase. "Hide up here while I get her to go."

I nod and dash up the steps, pressing myself into the shadows just around the corner. Blood thuds loud in my ears as Legend opens the door.

"Indigo—"

"You stupid idiot!" Her heels click-clack like a warning shot across the marble floor. "Who the hell do you think you are?"

"Listen, I—"

"I don't give a crap what you were trying to do! You *never, ever* film Indigo Taylor without her permission. Do you hear me?"

Legend doesn't respond, but I assume he's nodding. At this rate, he'll be running into my arms in no time.

I peek around the corner, and I can just barely spot them at the center of the living room. Legend has ditched his jacket and is leaning against the back of the sofa, while Indigo paces back and forth.

"Thanks to you, everyone's gonna be in my business by sunrise!" Indigo stamps her foot like a child. "Ugh! What the hell were you thinking?"

He shrugs. "I was just trying to let you know how I feel."

"Right," says Indigo, "And now everybody's gonna think I'm just as soft as your fro-yo ass."

Legend stares at her.

She scoffs. "What?"

"Why you so stuck on what they all think? Why can't we just be us?"

"*Us?*" Indigo lets out a sharp laugh. "There is no *us!*"

"And why the hell not?"

A tense silence hangs between them, and my stomach twists in knots. Squeezing my eyes tight, I press my back against the wall, praying that she'll just leave.

Thankfully, her heels echo across the floor as if she's backing away.

"Indigo, come on!" says Legend. "Don't run away."

Her footsteps falter. "You. Leave me. Alone. And keep your stupid cameras off me!"

"Indigo—Wait, wait, wait!"

There's a scuffle, and she slaps him. I throw a hand over my mouth, willing myself to stay still.

"Everybody blames me for what went down. But you *know* it wasn't all me, L!"

"Indigo, what are you talking about?"

The girl goes quiet. Then she sniffs. "I saw you on that interview with Bethany Mathis. Everybody did."

Bethany Mathis? His co-star from *Mending Time?*

Legend lets out a dry chuckle. "I have no clue what you're getting at. Can you fill me in?"

"Really, L? 'Cause from what I remember, there wasn't a single blog that didn't cover the two of y'all flirting all over Europe."

They're silent again. Indigo moves toward the door.

"Indigo, wait—"

"*Get off me!*"

"Please!"

"No! I'm sick of you making a fool of me! And after the last time, I swore it would be the last."

Last time? What is she talking about?

I remember the rumors going around about Legend and Bethany back then. The two of us joked about it. But obviously, it had no merit. Bethany got engaged two weeks later.

But from the sounds of things, this fight isn't ending in a clean break. Legend's heart will be completely shattered... Luckily, I'll be here to pick up all the pieces.

There's another scuffle, but this time Indigo doesn't say a word.

"Come on, Di-Di..."

Di-Di? He calls her Di-Di?

Legend's voice is quiet, almost pleading. "You know how I feel about you."

I roll my eyes, feeling sick to my stomach. I'm not sure how much more of this I can take. But the two of them are quiet.

I inch forward, breath caught in my throat, only to find there's no need to hide. Their eyes are closed. And they're not fighting anymore... they're kissing. Folded into each other like a scene I was never meant to watch.

I fall back against the wall, pressing a hand to my mouth as a soft sob escapes me.

And just like that, I know. I've lost him.

14

June 23rd
From: Samara A.
To: Justin C.

Hey Justin!

I'm sorry. I know it's been forever! Working for Indigo Taylor has been… challenging, to say the least.

I dunno. LA's nothing like home. It seems like everyone needs to be Someone, and no one is happy with who they are. Even Indigo has these moments when she's pissed at the world, and no one really knows why. Those days are the worst, 'cause she always takes it out on her staff. Don't get me wrong. The girl can step down from her throne from time to time. She gave me an amazing makeover. You should see my hair. It's wilder than Simone's!

Anyway, keep me in your prayers. And let me know how things are going with you.

~Sam

June 23rd
From: Justin C.
To: Samara A.

Sam I Am! Long time, no hear.

Things have been cool on this end. We've got a major project deadline that's been kicking my butt, but with the team's help, I know we'll blow it out of the water.

I'm sorry things have been so tough with Indigo. I looked her up and found some REAL horror stories from people who said they've worked for her. Her bathwater has to be a specific temperature, or something like that? I don't know how much of it is true, but it sounds like a nightmare. Anyway, if anyone can stick it out, it's you.

Hey! You remember when we were freshmen at UW, and it was time to move out of your mom's? I found you curled up in the corner of your bedroom, hyperventilating and all that. You said you couldn't do it. Swore you'd have to enroll in online classes and would never leave the house again.

But then I reminded you about all the times you overcame your fears: That time you tried out for Little League softball, the first week of junior high, when I was out sick with the flu. And standing at your mom's side when she married Trey. I told you your dad would want you to push through and stick it out. So, you took me by the hand and stood tall. And that year, you KILLED it! Even with that nightmare dorm mate who couldn't sleep without music on! You remember that? But just like every other time, you overcame that fear. And even though I was shocked to hear you struck out on this journey on your own, I'm not that surprised you did. 'Cause that's just you, Sam I Am. You're so much stronger than you realize.

Prayers up, for sure!

~Teddy

June 23rd
From: Samara A.
To: Justin C.

Thanks, Justin.

I'm not gonna lie, your email brought tears to my eyes. I remember that day when I was terrified to move out. Ugh! If you hadn't been there, I'm not sure I ever would've gotten out of that corner. But just like every other time, you were always by my side, pushing me, reminding me I could do it. I swear, it's like you were placed in my life just at the time I would need you.

Your words mean more than you know.

~Sam

June 23rd
From: Justin C.
To: Samara A.

I miss you.

June 23rd
From: Samara A.
To: Justin C.

Okay. So, you remember when we talked about celebrity hall passes?

You said yours was Beyoncé, and I said mine was Chris Brown. I lied. For the longest time, I've had a crush on Legend Blake. You know the one. He went to high school with us for a bit.

Anyway, what I neglected to mention is, Legend and I are sorta friends. Good friends, actually. We've been talking for a while now. A lot. It started as casual DMs, but… it's complicated.

I'm sorry. I know I should've told you. I just didn't know how.

The worst part is, he's kinda the one who got me the job here in LA. Please forgive me?

June 23rd

[NO NEW MESSAGES]

June 24th

[NO NEW MESSAGES]

‹‹‹‹‹‹‹‹‹‹

Indigo drops her rollerblades on the dining room table with a thud. "You've got a lot of nerve showing up here." Her ponytail is still damp with sweat, evidence of her recent lap around the estate.

Kelly arches a brow as Indigo sinks into the chair across from her. "Excuse me?"

"You really didn't think I'd put two and two together?" Indigo leans back, drumming her nails against the armrest. "You gave Sam the address to the restaurant last night."

My hands go still. *Crap. Crap. Crap.*

I fumble with ribbon, pretending not to hear, but the panic's already bubbling up. The thank-you kits in front of me blur—candies shaped like pink tubes of lip gloss and mascara—and I can barely tie the bow.

At a loss, I shoot Kelly a pleading glance.

Indigo snatches an apple from the fruit bowl and takes a slow, deliberate bite. "Lucky for you and Legend, your little stunt worked. We're getting back together."

Kelly blinks at her. "You are?"

Indigo tilts her chin, cool and casual. "We hashed things out last night and... we're gonna give it another shot."

They hashed things out? More like they made out.

It must've been a good twenty minutes before Legend finally came up for air and remembered I was hiding at the top of his staircase. He told her he was just heading out to meet with Victoria—she had his new phone. Indigo nodded that she understood, and apologized for *losing her temper,* or whatever... It took her another ten minutes to leave.

And me? I just sat there. Invisible. Forgotten. Disposable.

Probably exactly how Justin felt when he read my last message. Like a damn joke.

Meanwhile, Legend practically floated the whole drive back to my place.

"That's great, Indigo. I know how much you *hate* surprises," Kelly says, flicking a glance at me.

Indigo waves her off as she stands. "Yeah, but the rose petals were a nice touch. Just... no cameras the next time you pull some crap like this, okay? My outfit was trash."

Kelly nods as Indigo heads upstairs.

I keep my head low, folding the next box, but Kelly appears over my shoulder. "Got a minute?"

Before I can answer, she grabs my arm and hauls me to the library. "Talk. Now."

My throat goes dry. I need a script, a plan, a lifeline. But all I've got is panic.

"Okay, so... something happened last night—"

"I'm aware." She holds up the phone in her hand. "Twenty million people are aware of what happened last night. I want to know what *you* had to do with it."

I pick at my nails, my throat tightening. "Legend Blake may or may not have asked for my help..."

Her expression doesn't change much. But her silence is intimidating as hell.

"How do you know Legend Blake?"

My stomach knots at her narrowing eyes. I need a red carpet-worthy performance right now. Oscar-worthy. A role that screams *casual acquaintance.* But I'm no actress.

The truth leaks out before I can stop it. "We're sorta, kinda friends, I guess."

"*Friends?*" Kelly tilts her head, folding her arms. Her laugh comes low and sharp. "I should've known."

"Kelly, please don't tell Indigo—"

"I *knew* you weren't who you said you were. At first, I figured you were just some obsessed stan. Some rando from Seattle. But you were a mole?"

I lurch forward, pressing my palms together. "Kelly, please. If Indigo finds out—" I stop, her words catching up to me. "You know where I'm from?"

Her smirk widens. "You really think I'd be stupid enough to let you get this close to Indigo Taylor without checking you out? The minute you brought up your phony little connection with Rihanna's staff, I ran a background check. But it never occurred to me that you were working undercover."

My stomach drops.

If Indigo learns the truth, Legend will be dead to her. And maybe that wouldn't be the worst thing. But once Legend realizes it's all my fault? He'll never speak to me again.

And then, *everything*—leaving home, trading real life for a fantasy… breaking Justin's heart—will have been for nothing.

Kelly's sharp nails tap against her sleeve. "You *do* realize you could be sued for this, right? Like, actual legal repercussions?"

"I know." My stomach coils tight, like someone's twisting the lens of a camera, blurring the edges until I can't see the next move.

She's probably deciding whether to laugh or call security.

"But it seems like you mean well," she says with a sigh. "Only a *true* Indie would drive 1,100 miles for a stunt like this."

I hold my breath as Kelly scrolls through the viral post, her gaze flicking across the screen. Finally, she clicks her tongue. "You're *so* lucky this is good for PR," she says.

"So… you won't tell her?" My voice is barely above a whisper.

Kelly glances up, eyes sharp. "I haven't seen her this happy in a while." She points a crimson red fingernail in my face. "But if I hear that you're running back to Legend Blake telling him *anything* else, you may as well start shopping for a lawyer."

I nod, the weight in my chest loosening. "Thanks, Kelly."

"No, thank *you*." A slow, knowing smile creeps across her lips as she gazes at her phone. "You just may have saved Indigo Taylor's career."

+ + + + + + +

"Sounds like we're in the clear to me," says Legend on Sunday. "Kelly won't snitch."

He makes his best pitch, hurling a giant foam kernel of candy corn at Heimlich the Caterpillar's mouth. He misses.

"How can you be so sure?" I ask, sinking another shot. "One false move, and she might blow this whole thing up." I toss in my final oversized kernel… and win.

Legend throws his head back and groans.

Tucking away a smirk, I claim my prize: Flik, the blue ant from *A Bug's Life*. "Softball. Remember?"

He eyes the plush toy, then looks at me. "Rematch."

One nod, and the attendant starts resetting the game.

Indigo's on a wellness retreat this weekend and doesn't need my help, so Legend decided to make good on his promise and rented out Pixar Pier at Disneyland for a few hours. His entourage is sampling the Incredicoaster while we play Heimlich's Candy Corn Toss. His bodyguards are over by the bridge, watching the gate.

Legend throws another air ball—or corn, in this case. "Nah, Kelly wants her happy. Plus, she likes seeing the views go up on that video. That's more dollars in her pocket."

"If you say so. I just don't want anyone to end up in a lawsuit if this whole thing goes belly up."

"It won't," he says. "'Cause I've got you in my corner."

I open my mouth, but the words tangle in my throat. "About that..."

The smile falls from his face as he looks at me. "Sam, no."

"Look, Legend. I did what I came here to do. Maybe I should head back home."

It sounds brave. But it isn't. Not even close.

Even as I say it, the taste curdles on my tongue. But I can't ignore the truth.

This whole thing... Legend. The glitz. The rush. None of it was ever real. And the only solid thing I've ever come close to? I've shattered it.

Obviously, destiny has decided to play a cruel trick on me. Every day I stay, I sink deeper. And if I don't leave now, I'm not sure I'll be able to at all.

Legend drops the foam corn and takes my hand. "Sam, don't. I want you to stay."

His eyes are locked on mine. No cameras. No act. Just him.

The attendant sweeps something up in the corner, pretending not to listen. I lower my voice anyway. "What about Indigo? You can't hide our friendship forever, Legend."

His thumb traces the back of my hand, sending my heart into a stumble. And he's looking at me like I matter. Like *this* matters… the same way Justin always did.

"I know," he says with an adorable pout. "But I like having you around. I'm not ready for you to go. Not yet."

I can feel the weight of his words, the sincerity behind them. I couldn't help grinning if I tried. "I like being around, too."

He smiles, a slow, warm thing that reaches his eyes. His thumb continues to trace my knuckles as he steps closer. He's about to say something. I can feel it.

But his phone chimes, slicing through… whatever was about to take place.

Legend bites his lip for a moment before releasing my hand to check the message. "It's Victoria."

I hate the way her name changes him. One ping, and he's back to factory setting.

He sighs, reading the screen. "'Indigo Taylor. Again? Call me.'"

I wince. "Sounds like she has some reservations."

Legend runs his tongue across his teeth, shoving his phone back in his pocket. "I don't give a shit what she thinks. She controls nearly everything. The least she could give me is this." He gets that little crinkle over his brow and his mouth turns down a bit. With a sharp nod, he has the attendant reload the game.

"I'm sorry, L. I know it's gotta be tough."

He glances at me, his gaze heavy, almost defeated. "You've got no idea."

Something deep in me twists. Hesitating for half a second, I finally rest my hand on his shoulder, then his back. Gentle, steady. A flicker of nerves sparks through me, but I push it down. He needs comfort right now, not my jitters.

The way he talks about her... it's like she's a chain around his neck. Signing a contract with Victoria Austin's label was *supposed* to be a dream come true.

He shakes his head, his fingers curling around the candy corn, but his distant stare says he's somewhere else entirely. "I know it sounds dumb, but I'd give anything to breathe without her shadow everywhere."

It might be too much. Too soon. But I press my cheek to his shoulder anyway. His clean cologne steadies me. I breathe it in. "That's not dumb at all," I whisper.

"You don't think so?" he asks, his lips centimeters from my forehead.

"Nah." I look up, attempting a slow, Indigo-style gaze. Hopefully, it reads as flirty. Bare minimum. "If it's what you want, you should go for it."

He grins slow, unraveling me. "If only it were that easy," he says softly.

A burst of laughter erupts behind us. Legend turns as his entourage stumbles back from the Incredicoaster, loud and rowdy as ever.

I nod once and shift my stance, aiming blindly for the next toss. But Legend's studying me like some sort of complicated roadmap. "How do you do that?"

"Do what?"

"Be... you?" He lets out a low laugh, rubbing the back of his neck. "Indigo says I should just suck it up. That it's the price of fame. But with you... it's different. Sometimes, I think you get me better than anyone else."

A flutter sparks low in my stomach. I don't know how long I've been waiting for him to see that. To *feel* that. And as the carnival lights flicker around us, and the distant cartoon music warbles through the air, I know deep down...

He doesn't belong with her. He belongs with me.

And I think he knows it too.

His eyes linger, tracing the curve of my lips, the fall of my hair...
Like he's memorizing me.

"Just keep tossin', just keep tossin'!" shouts Cam in his best Dory voice,
followed by a chorus of exaggerated "Ooooooohs" from the entourage.
"Don't make me call Indigo!"

Laughter ripples down the boardwalk as Legend shoots a mock
glare at his assistant. "You're fired, Cam!"

He turns back to me, the sound of his entourage still echoing
behind us. The moment flickers and fades, his grin settling into place
like armor.

Like nothing's changed. Like my heart didn't just swell.

"Okay, beautiful. Watch me whoop yo' ass on this corn toss!"

He hurls another foam candy corn with all his might. It bounces
off Heimlich's foam-board face, lands on the floor, and rolls away
in defeat.

Everyone howls with laughter. And the air between us shifts, like
nothing ever happened.

15

*O*n Friday evening, I burst through the door like my apartment owes me answers, yanking off my shirt like I've got exactly twenty minutes to become someone new. And I've got no idea what to wear.

I was just heading out today when Indigo insisted that I join her and Legend for dinner.

"It'll be a group thing," she said. *"Cam will be there."*

I tried to back out, telling her I had plans, but she wasn't buying it.

"Please," she said. *"Don't pretend you have a life."*

So here I am, brushing my teeth while trying to stuff my feet into a pair of Manolos. I'm just catching myself, after slipping on a rogue towel, when my door buzzes.

Shoot! I don't have time for this! I zip my pencil skirt and go to answer. "Simmy?"

"Damn." Simone yanks off her shades, squinting like I've offended her eyes. "Looks like I've entered the Twilight Zone. Hello, long lost twin." She takes a look around as she enters, her riding boots squishing into my creamy, plush carpet, hands at the waist of her leather pants.

I stand with my hand on the doorknob. "Simone, what are you doing here?"

"Why are you always surprised when I show up? Shouldn't you be happy to see me?"

She removes her jacket and tosses it on the sofa, making a beeline for the fridge.

"Nice!" she says, peering inside. "Somebody's struck the mother lode." She pulls out the orange juice and starts chugging.

"Look, Simmy," I say as I shut the door, "of course, I'm excited to see you. I just—"

She cuts me off with a nice long belch. "I was in town for this stunt double audition and thought I'd swing by to ensure my tragically boring sister hasn't crocheted herself into a cocoon of loneliness." She checks out my empty kitchen sink and vacant living room. "Yep. Just as thrilling as I imagined."

I cross my arms. "Actually, I was just heading out."

"Oh, yeah?" She glances over my camisole and skirt. "Where ya headed? Bible study?"

I roll my eyes. "No. In fact, I— Wait a minute, you said you're here for a *stunt double* audition?"

She nods, returning to the hunt through my fridge. "Yeah. I connected with Kyle in San Francisco, and we kicked it for a bit. But then he started going on and on about *catching feelings*, and *settling down*, and '*I've never felt this way about anyone before*.'" She scoffs, chuckling at her own imitation. "Anyway, it's some knockoff, Marvel-style, superhero, chick-flick. The heroine looks just like me—or us." She tosses me a glance and continues rummaging. "What's with the new look, anyway?"

"Indigo thought I should update my style." I play with my curls, beaming expectantly. "Don't you like it?"

She looks me over as she pulls out some grapes. "You look like you're trying too hard."

I purse my lips.

"Besides," she says. "You've never been big on change. Why switch it up now?"

I shrug, pulling my elbows into my sides. "Legend likes it."

"Didn't he like you before?" She smirks, popping a grape into her mouth.

"Well—"

"Forget I asked." Crossing the room, my grapes in hand, she drops into the gray accent chair and swings her legs over the arm. "I saw the little viral video of your lover boy, singing his heart out for the Ice Queen. Looks like he got what he wanted."

Warmth crawls across my cheeks as I drop my gaze. "Yeah. I guess so."

"So what are you gonna do about it?"

I glance up, blinking. "Huh?"

"Eleven hundred miles, Sam. You drove *eleven hundred miles* to be here for him. After everything you've dragged yourself through, the *least* he could do is give you some."

My mouth opens, but no words come out. I hate to admit it, but my crazy sister's got a point. I sink onto the sofa and bury my face in my hands. "Simmy, I'm trying but—"

"Yeah, right! Both of us know that's bull, Sam. The boy should only have eyes for you by now. Instead, he's falling all over himself for Little Miss Insta-whore."

"I don't know what to do, Simmy." I sigh, the words already too heavy. "I want him to be happy, and sometimes I feel like I should just head home. But every time I'm near him, I get weak."

Not that I have all that much to head back to anyway.

I shrug, dropping my hands in my lap. "They asked me to join them for dinner tonight, which is the *last* thing I wanna do."

Simone raises her hand. "Wait a minute, wait a minute. There's a dinner?" I nod. "And he's paying?" I nod again. She tosses the grapes on the coffee table and grabs her jacket.

———————— ·✦✦✦✦✦· ————————

Thirty minutes later, we're strutting up to some bougie Italian restaurant with mood lighting and a name I can't pronounce. Simone holds the door, grinning like we belong here.

I tried to talk my sister out of coming along, but she wasn't having it. "*And pass up the opportunity to meet* the Legend Blake? *No way!*" she said.

The hostess escorts us through a sea of burgundy dining chairs and white-clothed tables to a private room at the back. Alex and Lorenzo are guarding the door.

Simone whistles low as we approach. "Hey, fellas."

Lorenzo barely spares her a glance. I lift a hand in greeting, and he nods for us to head inside.

"Ooh, you know him?" asks Simone. I shush her, steering her toward the door. On the way, she pats the middle of Lorenzo's burly chest. "I'll see you later, big boy."

Legend's eyes lock onto mine the second we enter. He rises from his chair, a handsome smile spreading across his face. And for one reckless second, I think that smile is for me.

But my heart slams to a halt when I take in the rest of the table. To his right is Indigo, draped in a glittery minidress—her cleavage on full display—and across from him is Cam, of course. However, I didn't expect Kelly to be here. And Victoria Austin, of all people, is sitting at the head of the table. I swallow hard.

Indigo jumps up too. "Sam, thank God! I thought you'd never get here!" She strides over and gives me a Hollywood peck on each cheek but pauses when she notices my nearly identical twin standing nearby. "Who's this?"

"Um, Indigo, this is my sister, Simone. Simone, this is Indigo Taylor."

"'Sup?" says Simmy, tossing a half-hearted wave.

Indigo eyes my sister up and down, lips pressed tight. Then she cuts her gaze to me. "Can I speak with you for a second?"

She pulls me over near the restrooms.

"Sam, what the hell?"

"I know, and I'm sorry. She dropped in, out of the blue, and invited herself along. If you want us to leave, I completely understand."

She rolls her eyes. "You can't leave now! Victoria-fuckin'-Austin is here. Are you *trying* to make me look like a cold-blooded bitch?"

"I'm sorry—"

She waves her hand. "Save it. Just… don't embarrass me, okay?"

That'll be easier said than done. I promise anyway, and we start heading back. "So what's going on? I thought it was just a group thing?"

She nods, crossing her arms. "When I said group, I kinda meant meeting with the managers and Kelly. Maddox should be here any minute."

My knees go limp as I watch her return to the private room.

At the table, Kelly cuts me a look that says everything while Indigo makes the official introductions.

"Everyone, this is my new assistant, Samara." Indigo takes me by the hand, pulling me to her side of the table. "Sam, you've met Kelly. And this is Legend Blake." Legend and I exchange awkward nods.

Cam nods too. "What's up, Sam?" He smiles, waiting for my return tagline. I gnaw my lip, wishing he'd said *anything* else.

Indigo looks back and forth at the two of us, her golden ponytail swishing across her shoulders. "You two know each other?"

Cam blinks at her and me, then Legend. I hold my breath.

Legend turns to Indigo. "Well, all of us met at the Japanese restaurant after my surprise went belly up, remember?"

"Right!" says Indigo. The four of us softly chuckle.

Good save!

"It's nice seeing you again, Sam," says Legend. His eyes sparkle as he shakes my hand, and an electric wave shoots through my arm.

"You too," I squeak.

Simmy, who has already settled into a seat at the table, snorts.

"And this," Legend gestures toward Victoria, "is the woman that makes the world go 'round. Victoria Austin, my manager."

I've seen her on TV a thousand times. As the executive producer of *Lucky Star*, she was one of the main judges on the show. She's a full-figured woman with rich cocoa skin and voluminous curls that frame her face perfectly. Today, she's rocking a daring snake-print designer suit that makes a statement.

"It's a pleasure to meet you, Ms. Austin," I say.

She gives a tight smile as I shake her hand. "Likewise."

Simone leans forward, dramatically clearing her throat. "And everyone knows I'm Sam's sister, Simone. Can we eat now?"

We're about to place our orders when Maddox Barnes, Indigo's manager, rushes in, his phone still to his ear. "Yeah, yeah. I know. But if he ain't willing to put in the work, I might just have to sign somebody else."

Maddox is a solidly built man with deep brown skin and a clean-shaven head. His grin is as polished as the high-end suit he's in. He waves at everyone as he tells his associate he'll have to call him back.

"Sorry. Y'all know how it is." Everyone nods in understanding. He directs his attention to Indigo. "You look beautiful, as always."

Indigo waves him off with a smile and introduces Simone and me. "Her sister's in from out of town, so I figured the more, the merrier."

She glances at me, a brief, knowing look passing between us. Maddox greets us as the servers arrive with wine.

Legend orders for the table, telling the servers to put everything on his tab, then smirks at Indigo as the waiters head out. "You're cool with gluten this week, right?"

Indigo sucks her teeth, giving him a playful shove. The boy practically glows staring back at her.

"Wow," mutters Simmy. She takes up her glass, throwing me a pointed glance. "Why not twist the knife a couple times, see how much you'll bleed..." I glower at her.

"Can we get on with this already?" Victoria folds her hands at the table. "We're all here for a reason, and I've got a meeting at ten o'clock."

At the bite of her tone, Indigo sits up straight. Legend, on the other hand, leans back, a finger to his temple.

"Now," says Victoria. "This was supposed to be a private meeting, but since Legend and Indigo have decided to turn it into a party, we may as well get to the point."

Indigo and Legend glance at each other, and for just a moment, he grins at me.

"No offense, Indigo," says Victoria. "But you know how I feel about the two of you being... romantically involved." She practically gags when she says *romantically*. "It was doomed from the beginning. And I think we could all agree that the two of you are better off apart."

Simone slaps a hand over her mouth as she nearly spits out her drink with laughter. I smack her arm.

"Now, hold on, Victoria," says Maddox, shaking his head. "If these two have decided to enjoy each other's company, who are we to—?"

"We're their managers," says Victoria. "And it's our job to ensure neither of them makes a foolish mistake that could be the end of their careers."

Legend lets out a sharp exhale. "It's not your job to manage my life, Victoria."

"Like hell, it isn't," she says, raising a glass of wine to her lips.

Legend's jaw tightens as Indigo rests a hand on his arm, an unspoken understanding passing between them.

I hate how easily they turn his life into strategy. Like he's a brand, and not a person. And with Alex and Lorenzo out by the door, I'm the only one who can actually look out for him.

But I'm not the one at his side.

Maddox clears his throat. "Look, our opinions really don't matter. What matters here is that Indigo and Legend have decided to reunite. And the fans love it."

Victoria gives a gentle nod, taking another bitter sip.

"So, we wanna make the most out of the situation," says Maddox.

"You mean capitalize," says Simone.

I jab her with an elbow, but Maddox is chuckling. "Yes, sweetheart," he says, tossing her a smile. "I suppose you could say that."

"*Sweetheart?*" Simone bats her eyes. "If you're gonna call me that you better buy me dinner first."

Maddox is already checking her out.

"The point is," says Victoria, from the other end of the table. "Maddox and I think that Legend and Indigo should record a duet."

Indigo gasps, clapping her hands. But Legend's not matching her energy.

"Nah. We ain't doing all that."

Indigo pouts. "But Legend—"

"We just got back together," he says. "Give us a minute to work things out."

"*Work things out?*" Indigo narrows her eyes. "L, what is there to work out?"

"It's just—" Legend glances at me and gazes at the table. "We need time. That's all."

Victoria laughs. "Legend, how many times do I have to tell you: Time *is* money. We can't afford to lose either one."

"That's right," Maddox chimes in, his voice full of businesslike enthusiasm. "With that little video going viral, the Indies are *clamoring* for more. I bet Legend Blake fans are too."

Victoria agrees with a nod.

"And a new song and music video would be the *perfect* way to go public," says Kelly.

Indigo beams, wrapping her arm around Legend's. "She's right, honey. There's no better way to officially announce how we feel to the world."

Legend stares at her, then looks at me, his eyes pensive and soft. He shakes his head, studying the table. "I don't know. This is a lot."

Simmy elbows me again and again, whispering, "You saw that, right?" I slap her arm, trying to keep up with the conversation.

"Oh, please," says Victoria. "An album release and a tour through Europe are *a lot*. What we're talking about is one song, Legend. Two days in the studio. Record and done."

"That's what y'all always say," he snaps. "Then comes the video, the rehearsals, the promo. Next thing I know, y'all got me doing another tour. And I just wrapped up the last one. When am I supposed to get a break?"

Indigo scoffs. "Legend, you'll be with me. It'll be like a… honeymoon or something."

His head snaps back. *"A honeymoon?"*

"Well, you know what I mean!" Indigo laughs much harder than necessary as the servers return with our food. She slaps Legend on the shoulder, and he casts an awkward glance my way.

"Indigo's right, Legend," says Maddox, the servers setting a large plate of roast prime rib before him. "Think of it as a... vacation, where you get to serenade your dream girl a few times a week."

I smile like I'm not bleeding.

Legend looks back at Victoria. "So y'all already decided that we're doing this? I don't get a say?"

Victoria grins at him with a frosty gaze. "You got a say when you decided to join this business, remember?" She and Legend lock eyes, both of them frozen in a quiet standoff, as if they were chess players calculating their next move.

"This is better than WWE," says Simone, leaning forward as she chomps on croutons. I shush her.

"I think this is the perfect time," says Indigo. "Sam, do I have anything major in my schedule for the next few weeks?"

I hold her gaze, unblinking. She doesn't break eye contact. And the faintest tilt of her chin tells me all I need to know: if I screw this up, I'm fired. I risk a glance at Kelly, desperate for some guidance, but she gently shakes her head, offering nothing. I'm on my own.

"Uh..." I dig into my purse. "Let me just check."

"What the hell, Sam?" Simone slaps me on the shoulder. "This is supposed to be your job!"

Indigo drums her nails on the table.

"Legend, why do you have to be so bullheaded about this?" asks Victoria. "It's a couple songs. A six-week tour, at the most."

Legend arches a brow. "Oh, it's a couple of songs now?"

"Well, obviously, you have to sing the song you wrote for Indigo as well. It'll get tons of streams on Spotify."

They talk about streams and videos like love is a marketing plan.

"So let me get this straight," says Legend. "Somehow, one little duet has already transformed into two hit songs, a music video, and a six-week tour around the country. And you expect me to do all this during my back-to-school fundraising campaign?"

"Actually, that's been canceled, boss," says Cam, presenting the calendar on his phone. Legend glares at him, and Cam promptly sinks back in his seat.

"I still say it's too much, too fast," says Legend.

"Ah, here it is," I say, pulling up Indigo's schedule. "Besides a few interviews and a charity event, Indigo is free." I breathe a happy sigh, giving myself a mental pat on the back. But Legend isn't smiling.

"Oh, crap," Simmy whispers. "Take it back, Sam. Quick!"

"Look," says Kelly. "It might be inconvenient, but it's best for both of your careers. Legend, the world already *adores* you. Surely, you want it to love Indigo again too." Kelly shrugs. "Honestly, the ending to that viral video didn't paint her in the best light. She needs the promotion, L."

He stares at the table pensively.

"Then it's settled," says Victoria. "We'll record next week, schedule a shoot, and I'll start planning the tour."

+ + + + + +

All of us gather outside the restaurant after dinner. Maddox needs to rush off but expresses that he enjoyed meeting us. He asks Indigo for a chat on the way to his car. She follows in tow, leaving my sister and me with Legend and Victoria.

"Ladies," says Victoria. "I wish we could've met on better terms."

"Us too," says Simone.

I'm gonna slap her when we get home.

Kelly steps over with a nervous chuckle. "Victoria, how about I wait with you for your car. I wanted to get your advice on some optics anyway."

Victoria nods, giving Simone and me a chilly once over before saying goodbye.

Everyone's shoulders relax as they leave.

"Good riddance," mutters Simone, turning back to Legend. "Is she out of prune juice, or is she always that constipated?"

Legend snorts and smiles at me. "Man, your sister is hilarious."

"Yeah, to some." I toss a glare at her. But Legend's staring at me as he nods.

Well, it's nice to see him smile again.

Suddenly, everything's gone silent. And all I can see... is him.

Simone leans forward, her gaze ping-ponging between us. "So, do you two do this eye thing all the time?"

Heat rises in my cheeks as Legend scratches behind his ear, his gaze wandering to the parking lot. Indigo is deep in conversation with Maddox, her back turned toward us.

Legend clears his throat. "You told her about us, huh?"

"*Us?*" Simone repeats, cocking her head like she just stumbled into a soap opera. "There's an '*us*' now?"

"He means our friendship, Simmy." I sigh, trying to untie the knot in my stomach. "He means the two of us... being friends." I look at Legend again, but he's not making eye contact anymore.

"Oh, my bad," says Simone, turning to him with an innocent smile. "Don't worry, Legend. I have a big mouth, but not *that* big. I mean, if I did, I totally would've told you about the *major* crush Sam had on a boy who looked just like you in high school. Worked backstage just to watch him prepare for the talent show."

My jaw drops as Legend's brows knit together.

Simmy looks between us, an evil smirk on her lips. "Oops."

Nothing functions. I want the sidewalk to crack open and swallow me whole.

Legend stares at me, eyes widening like he suddenly under-stands. "You…"

"Sorry, guys!" Indigo returns and throws an arm around Legend. "Always a meeting to follow up the meeting, right?" She marks Legend's cheek with a kiss.

His smile falters as he looks at her, then shifts back to me, eyes flicking over mine like he's trying to read a secret.

If only I asked for a doggy bag. At least then I could cover my face.

Indigo is none the wiser. "Thanks for your help in there, Sam. But next time, let's not turn it into a hot mess, mmkay?" I nod. She lifts her gaze to Legend, her eyes glowing beneath the streetlights. "Shall we?" I've never seen the girl in such an incredibly good mood.

"Where are you two headed?" asks Simone. "Stargazing in the mountains? Quick jet to Aruba? Private luxury resort where you can have endless sex on the beach?" I jab Simone with an elbow, but Indigo cracks up laughing.

"I love her, Sam! You should bring her around more often!"

Legend drops his head. I can't tell if he's cringing or blushing. If only he could stay.

Some of the tension seems to melt from his shoulders as the guards pull his car around. "Goodnight, ladies."

"Goodnight," we call, as they head for the car.

I shove my sister hard as Legend opens the door for Indigo. But we're sure to give a polite wave as he glances back.

16

*T*wo weeks later, I've got my hands full at work, my phone delicately balanced between my shoulder and my ear.

"So... is she still treating you like lint, or have you finally earned a human nod?"

"Um... yeah. It's a lot better."

My mom's voice is low as she presses her mouth into the phone. I can practically hear the giddy smile on her face. "Is it true that she gets all of her underwear dry-cleaned?"

"Mom, you know I can't answer that."

"Sorry, sorry."

That reminds me, I need to swing by the dry cleaners this afternoon.

My phone nearly slips into the sink of sudsy water. I catch it with a wet hand and dry it off on my shirt. Pulling a lacy red thong from the bubbles, I curl my nose. I suppose I'll put it back and swish a little more.

"Have you heard from Simone?"

I'm not all that surprised that Mom is asking. The two of them rarely talk. "Yeah. She got that stunt double job she auditioned for.

The studio's putting her up at one of those hotels with buffet breakfast and unlimited room service. She's in love."

Mom sucks her teeth. "I just hope she doesn't get herself hurt. She's always tossing herself into these *risky* situations."

"She'll be fine, Mom." Though, honestly? A few bruises might do her good. I'm still annoyed with her attempt to blow up my spot with Legend a couple weeks ago, but Simone swears she was only trying to encourage some progress between us. Unfortunately, for me, there hasn't been much of that.

"Anyway," says Mom. "Everything's going good with Trey and the girls. The new app is just about ready for beta testing, and the girls— *Hey! Hey girls, knock it off!*" I wince at the sound of my mom's shrill voice piercing my ear. "Sorry," she says. "I'm counting down the days until they head back to school."

"I know, Mom." I toss the thong into a separate sink to soak, then move on to the black G-string.

"You know, I'm still searching for that Squatty Potty." Mom lets out a lengthy sigh. "You sure you don't remember seeing it?"

"No, Mom." I gnaw at my lip, scrubbing the panties between plastic gloves.

"That's really too bad… Trey's been awfully cranky lately, and—"

"Hey, Mom, I gotta go. But let me know if you find it." I hang up before she can respond.

⁘⧫⧫⧫⁘

A little while later, I'm making my way up the hall when I hear it. Soft music, low and moody, leaking from Indigo's bedroom.

> *"Let's jump off with both feet and dive in,*
> *My love, my sweetheart, my friend.*

And for once I won't put up a fight,
You're the one thing I know I got right..."

Indigo and Legend's duet, "Dive In," was released last week, and as expected, it went viral. According to Indigo, everyone's thrilled about her and Legend getting back together. Everyone besides her haters anyway... Guess I'm a hater.

Indigo's leaning back at her desk, her heels up on the giant fluffy ottoman. She plays in her curls, giggling. "I mean, of course, they're saying we got back together for publicity, but I really don't care. I'm doing what makes me happy."

My stomach twists.

"And I'm glad you're happy, darling." Maddox is on speakerphone. "I just want you to stay on your toes."

Indigo flits her eyes my way as I head across the room, gathering more laundry for Eva.

"This ain't the time to be getting saddled with a couple of Hollywood babies," says Maddox.

My hand slips on the laundry bag.

Babies? Plural? As in stroller-stuffing, career-ending, TMZ-headlining?

I stare at the wall like I've been slapped.

Every DM, every daydream, every what-if suddenly feels like a cosmic joke.

Indigo laughs. "Seriously, Maddox? How dumb do you think I am?"

"I know," he says. "I just don't want you getting caught up. You can't afford all that right now."

Indigo scoffs. "Please! The way I see it, this whole thing is a win-win. Legend gets the *baddest* chick in Hollywood back on his arm, and everyone sees that I'm still *that* girl."

I should've known it was never about him. I shove a crumpled T-shirt into the laundry bag, pressing my lips together to keep from saying something I'll regret.

Maddox lets out a low chuckle. "So maybe the headlines aren't that far off. Sounds like you're both getting what you want."

Indigo smirks, her eyes glinting. "Let's just say... we'll ride this wave until a better opportunity washes up."

Maddox chuckles too.

I choke down the fire clawing up my chest, willing it not to reach my face. Not here. Not in front of her. With my heart thudding against my ribs, I head for the door.

"Speaking of opportunities," says Maddox, voice dropping to a conspiratorial tone. "I've got a *great* one if you're free tonight. He's from London, and his name is—"

Indigo takes him off speaker and puts the phone to her ear. She gives me a tense smile as I head out.

What the hell was that about?

She's still giggling as I make my way down the hall. "Mmhmm. Yeah, I could show him a good time..."

It almost sounds like a date or something. But she wouldn't... or would she?

For the most part, things have been a lot better with Indigo lately. With her dating Legend, the girl's been in a much better mood. But she's still a brat, demanding that the world revolve around her simply because she's *the* Indigo Taylor. And frankly, I'm over it.

Simone says if this little summer adventure and breaking off a seven-year commitment are going to be worth it, I need to go after what I want. And there isn't a doubt in my mind, I still want Legend. After everything I gave up, he's the only thing that makes sense. Of course, I want him to be happy. I just think he'll be happiest with me. Now, if only I could convince Legend of that...

A couple hours later, Indigo's just settling into her bath when I receive the call of a lifetime.

I check over my shoulder to find Indigo already in La La Land. I slip out and answer my phone.

"Hey...you. Long time, no hear."

Legend chuckles on the other end. "I know, I know."

I can't help grinning as I tug the door behind me and step into the bedroom. I've barely heard from him since our bizarre meeting with my sister and Victoria. And honestly? I missed him so much that it hurt.

He'd texted me the next morning...

> **LEGEND:** *High school, huh?*
> **SAM:** *I swear, I'm gonna kill my sister for bringing that up!*
> **LEGEND:** *WOW.*

Fifteen full minutes passed.

> **LEGEND:** *I'll holla at you later.*

He didn't hit me up that day, or the next. When he finally did respond, it was mainly a cordial:

"'Ey!"

"'Sup?"

The occasional*"How ya been?"*

But we haven't had a full conversation since. This honestly might be worse than the last time he dated Indigo. I'm surprised that he's calling me now.

"What you up to these days?" he asks.

"The usual: Kickin' butt and cleaning up messes."

Legend laughs. "More like getting *your* butt kicked! Di-Di told me all about your 'incompetence.' Not a single blow during Jiu-Jitsu? *Tsk, tsk, tsk,* I thought you were tougher than that, Sam."

I roll my eyes, straightening her bed. "Please. I don't get paid enough to risk that kind of backlash from the Indies."

"You got a point," he says with a chuckle.

I smile, glancing around the room. I've got a window, and I'm not about to waste it.

She left her phone on the desk.

"Anyway," he says. "Sorry I haven't caught up in a minute. These rehearsals are no joke. And when I'm not doing that—"

"I know," I say, lowering my voice. "You're busy wining and dining Indigo." *That... among other things.* I cringe thinking about the red lace panties I had to launder earlier. Indigo doesn't want Eva touching her *delicates.*

Legend lets out a nervous chuckle, and then the two of us fall silent.

Yeah. This is *way* worse than when they dated the first time.

And he needs to remember there was a reason it fell apart back then.

"But I'm free tonight," he says.

"Oh, yeah?" I pick up Indigo's phone, my thumb hovering over the screen. Curiosity tugs hard... but I drop it back down. I've already crossed enough lines.

"Yeah. Indigo has some sort of meeting. You know what that's about?"

Somebody's still looking for intel.

I should probably be more bothered by it. But it's *his* voice. *His* attention.

How could I deny him a thing?

"I haven't seen anything on my calendar."

"Oh." He sounds slightly disappointed. "So, what kind of plans you got?"

"Me?" I release half a chuckle, daring to pick up her phone again. "I think there's a rom-com and a Snuggie with my name on it."

"*What?*" He sucks his teeth. "You should chill with me tonight," he says, his voice soft and sexy.

I go still as my heart does a flip. It's been forever since it was just us.

No drama. No Indigo.

I can hardly contain my smile as I search Indigo's browser history.

I know better. I do. But I'm still scrolling… There isn't anything in her calendar either.

"Mmhmm," I say, teasing Legend. "Let me guess, hiding away in your palace again?"

"It doesn't have to be here," he says with a seductive voice, tempting me.

"Oh, really? You think you could handle being seen with a lowlife like me in public?"

"I'm the lowlife for not making more time for my best friend."

My cheeks grow warm at the sober tone of his voice. He's never called me that before.

Before I can smile about it, I pull up Indigo's latest Google searches:

Willard Evans – London Film Producer

The Arrow – Hottest Nightclub in Hollywood

"So, what's up?" says Legend. "Anywhere you wanna go, I'm down."

I lean against the wall, a smile creeping to my lips.

———————— ✦✦✦✦✦ ————————

Legend and I make our way inside a little past eleven o'clock, the rhythm of the night pulling us deeper into the chaos of the Arrow. Like most exclusive spots in Hollywood, it has a secret VIP entrance that's even more hidden than the front. The faint scent of expensive perfume and cigar smoke clings to the air as we step inside, mingling with the cool blast of air from the AC. Just enough to cut through the heat of the packed night.

Legend guides me past bouncers, their eyes scanning for trouble, and a sea of thirsty patrons hoping to catch a glimpse of anyone famous. My pulse thrums in my ears, matching the beats echoing from the speakers.

The club isn't nearly as packed as the one Indigo took me to, but it still holds its own. Tufted leather booths line the walls, their dark hues reflecting the soft glow from tall, illuminated pillars. The dance floor stretches out, alive with bodies moving, lights flickering in hypnotic patterns. The air feels thick with anticipation.

But all I can focus on is the steady pressure of Legend's hand holding mine, pulling me toward the bar. The sticky surface beneath my fingertips as we move through the crowd, the neon glimmer of bottles reflecting off the glass. It's all too much and not enough. Like slipping into someone else's dream.

Legend leans in my ear, speaking over the trap music. "I'll get us a table." His lips brush the curve of my earlobe, just enough to make my breath hitch.

I nod, and he gives my hand a squeeze before heading on his way.

With a deep breath, I try to relax the knots in my stomach.

Okay, Sam. You summoned the storm. Don't hide from the lightning.

I scan the dance floor, searching for platinum blond curls. *She's gotta be here somewhere. I just hope this works.*

Purple and fuchsia strobe lights slice through the haze, flickering across a sea of grinning faces. Bodies move in sync to the deep, pulsing beat that shakes the air.

Jeez, I thought my black jumpsuit was bold, but these girls strutting by in barely-there miniskirts and push-up bras? They're giving me a run for my money. At least Legend told me I look gorgeous. But he says that all the time.

I take a few steps toward the VIP section, scanning left and right, but I don't see her anywhere. Maybe that's for the best. Maybe I should make up an excuse for Legend to take me somewhere else. Somewhere romantic where we can catch up... alone.

Among the sea of dancing bodies, my eyes find his. He flashes that smile—the one that's pure magic—and starts heading my way. My heart skips, but then a wave of panic hits.

I can't do this to him.

If I don't get him out of here fast, this'll crush him.

I sigh as he approaches. "Hey, maybe we should go."

He squints as if he can't hear me. He leans closer. "What?"

"Maybe we should—"

But his gaze shifts past me. Latches onto something.

And just like that, the light dies in his eyes.

Just a few feet behind me, in a plush VIP booth, is Indigo, flaunting her pink corset minidress like it's her personal spotlight. She's falling all over some guy with curly hair and bronze skin, drinking and laughing, all up in his face. His arm is around her as he leans in close, whispering in her ear. Indigo laughs and gives him a playful shove, eyes dancing.

This wasn't how I pictured it. But now that it's happening, I can't look away.

Legend's jaw locks, his eyes darken. Suddenly, he's moving like a man who's been sucker-punched by the past.

"Legend!" I catch his hand before he can take another step. "Don't!"

By some miracle, he halts, his eyes zeroing in on mine. They flicker with a pain that hits me like a punch in the gut.

I wanted him to see what I see. But not like this. It's been less than a month… and I've already broken his heart twice.

He exhales, his voice rough. "Let's get out of here."

✦✦✦✦✦

He drops me off at the front of my place and tells me he'll meet me upstairs.

The building glows under the soft halo of streetlights, its gold-trimmed glass doors gleaming like they've never known a crack.

A warm breeze and the hum of Sunset Boulevard fades behind me as I step inside. Marble floors, spotless glass, recessed gold lighting. Everything feels too perfect for a girl who just shattered something priceless.

My heels click against the tile as I cross to the elevator, each sound a countdown. He's coming up, and I don't know how to look him in the eye.

Ten minutes later, he's at my door.

I try to keep things light. "No Lorenzo tonight, hmm?"

He doesn't crack a smile as he enters. He tosses his blazer on the sofa and makes a beeline for my bathroom. He's rinsing his face in the sink when I peer inside.

I open my mouth to speak but no words come out. I was hoping to stir some drama, but I never expected to strike gold. Maybe this is all some big misunderstanding? Though I have no idea how Indigo's gonna explain this one.

Legend breathes a heavy sigh, gazing at himself in the mirror. His eyes fall on my reflection.

I stand up straight, grasping for something, anything to say. But I've got nothing.

I move aside as he makes his way into my bedroom. He sinks down on the bed with his hands over his face.

"Damn. I really let her play me twice. That's gotta be some kinda record."

I sit next to him. "I'm sorry, Legend."

He glances at me with a wry smile. "I feel like you've said that more since you've been here than you have since we started talking." I duck my head, a soft laugh escaping before I can stop it. His eyes don't move, just stay locked on me. "You always apologizing for everyone else's mess. This ain't on you."

I stare back at him, shame coiling tight in my stomach. I asked for this. Plotted it, even. So why does it feel like I've just kicked my own heart in the teeth?

He breathes a heavy breath, gazing down at his hands. "Victoria's gonna be in stitches when she hears this one."

"L, you don't know that. Who says she even has to know?"

"There's no way she *won't* know," he says. "I'm done with Indigo's bull."

My entire world stops as I stare at him, heart fluttering like a hummingbird's wings.

"Wait, you're... done? Just like that?"

He nods, pensively staring out my window overlooking the city skyline. "It's like a damn record playing Indigo's greatest hits." He drops his eyes, shaking his head. "The irony of her doing this shit again."

His mouth turns down and his brow crinkles, neck tensing... I move closer and rub his back, wishing I had something more to offer.

He settles into my arm, allowing the massage to soothe him. "Man," he sucks his teeth, "the first time around, I made every excuse for her: *She's stressed. She's bored. That's just how my girl is!* I went back to her place, ready to move on—as if her G-string wasn't all over *Page Six*. And you know what she did?" He looks at me with piercing eyes. "She dumped me, Sam. Told me she didn't need *another damn relationship*, whatever the hell that was supposed to mean."

My hand stays on his back, slow and soothing, while my stomach twists with something dangerously close to hope. Sure, it sucks what he's going through. But I can't help feeling just a little relieved that he's *finally* seeing the light. The question is, will he see me at the end of the tunnel?

"She *always* does this, Sam. It's like the only person she gives a damn about is herself!"

I nod as I rub in circles, knowing I helped set this whole thing in motion. And still… he's here. With me. Hurting, yes, but leaning on me like I'm the one who gets him. I should feel awful. And I do. But also? I've never been this close to having exactly what I want.

Legend's eyes pin on mine. "You're never like that, Sam." His gaze drifts into my hair and down to my lips. Then he looks away. And my heart cracks in two.

Right now, all I want is for him to see me. *Want* me.

The way Justin did.

To make me feel chosen. Secure.

I'll admit it. I might've walked away from a good thing. A *really* good thing.

But Legend's the dream. The fantasy. And he's right here. Right now.

I just need him to want me back.

Like an answer to prayer, he looks again. I give a crooked smile, and he answers with one full of heartbreak.

"Thanks for having my back," he says. "If you didn't stop me, I might've caught a case tonight." He cracks his knuckles, his shoulders rising and falling. I start rubbing his shoulders too.

His eyelids slide shut as he releases a satisfied breath, indulging in my fingers. "Damn," he says. "That feels good."

I let out a light chuckle, wishing I could press my nose into the crook of his neck, inhale every ounce of his wonderful, fresh spring scent. "You have every right to be upset," I say. "If she wants to see other people, the least she could do is tell you so."

"Exactly. I mean, she would want me to do the same, right?"

I nod. But he's staring at me again.

The silence stretches, thick with everything we're not saying. My heart hammers against my ribs, wild and wanting. I don't move. I don't even breathe, skin tingling under the weight of his gaze. Then his focus returns to my lips, softening with something that makes my breath catch.

Without another word, he leans in and kisses me, deliberate and slow, his hand cradling my chin. The world blurs. It's like standing in warm tidewater, my breath stolen by the rush, the pull. His lips are soft, searching. His tongue tastes like salt and citrus, dangerous and sweet.

His lips on mine feel like a *yes* I've been chasing for *years*.

He lowers me onto the pillows, mounting me as his mouth trails to my jaw, then down the curve of my neck. A happy sigh escapes me as he caresses my hips and waist, his firm hands exploring unconquered territory.

Yes! I am ready to be discovered!

He returns to my lips, groaning with every taste. The sound makes warmth bloom at my collarbone.

OMG, are we seriously doing this? Right here? Right now?

My heart's sprinting. My brain's a mess.

Oh, man, I should've shaved my legs!

But just as quickly as it started, he pulls back.

I blink up at him, breathless. *Please, don't stop.*

He stares at me like he's trying to find the right words in a language he barely speaks.

"Sorry, I—"

"No, it's okay. I—"

He backs away, settling on the pillows. "I didn't mean to—I mean I did, but—"

"Yeah. No, I get it." *I think.*

He gnaws his lip, avoiding my eyes.

I'm still trembling. The room hasn't even stopped spinning. I want to beg him to come back. But he just pulled away like it was all a mistake.

Like I was a mistake.

I steady my voice and act like it didn't shatter me. "You wanna head home now, don't you?"

He shakes his head. "Actually..." He reaches for my hand, threading his fingers through mine. His thumb brushes over my knuckles, gentle and steady. "Would it be cool if I stayed for a while?"

My breath catches. "You wanna stay?"

He nods, moving a little closer. Close enough to share a secret. "I miss talking to you."

I stare at my hand in his. "Talking to me?"

He smiles softly. "Yeah."

A thousand thoughts race through my mind, half of them screaming. *This is really happening.* The kiss. His hand in mine. The way he's looking at me like I'm more than the PA who launders his ex's panties.

I swallow hard, trying to play it cool even as my stomach flips. "Yeah. Okay."

He rests his head on the pillow, and I do the same with mine. "So... tell me more about your dad," he says.

"Hmmm..." I smile. "Did I tell you he was a baseball fan?"

His eyes light up with genuine enthusiasm. "For real?"

"Oh, yeah. *Huge* fan."

The two of us chat late into the night about everything and nothing. And for the first time in weeks, I talk without trying to impress him. I just... talk.

He tells me how fame sometimes feels like a cage, how he doesn't know who to trust anymore. I admit how lost I've felt since graduation, like I'm always waiting for someone to tell me where I belong. We even talk about my secret high school crush.

"Why didn't you tell me?" he asks, voice low and quiet.

I want to now. I want to tell him I used to imagine moments like this... before Justin. Before I knew what love really felt like. Back when it was just a crush, harmless and distant.

But now? It's something different.

"I guess I always hoped you'd remember that hot chick you helped off her ass backstage."

Both of us laugh.

"But you never forgot?" His eyelids are heavy, lashes brushing the tops of his cheeks, that drowsy grin softening every sharp edge of his face. He looks unfairly good like this. Like something out of a dream I forgot I once had.

I shake my head. And the corners of his mouth twitch, like he's not sure whether to smile or apologize.

And the two of us talk and talk... until we finally drift off to sleep.

17

I woke up first.

I've been studying his handsome face for at least an hour, and I swear, he looks even more beautiful while sleeping.

OMG... Legend Blake is in my bed!

I should feel guilty. Maybe I do, a little. I mean, I *did* manipulate the whole situation to get him here. But right now? All I can feel is the electric thrill of finally having what I've dreamed of for so long.

I take a chance and run my fingers across his soft, curly goatee, just below the sinful lips that kissed the common sense right out of me last night.

His breath is still on my skin. I want to bottle it. Keep it.

I release an incredulous sigh as his shoulders rise and fall, the golden rays of the sun shimmering behind him.

I guess my wish came true after all.

He stirs, and I quickly drop my hand, pretending I wasn't just tracing his face like a lovesick teenager. I prop myself up on one elbow, adjusting my jumpsuit. Like waking up next to a superstar is no big deal.

His eyes flutter open, still heavy with sleep, and he gives me a lazy smile. "'Sup?"

My stomach flips like a thousand butterflies just got the memo. "Morning, sleepyhead," I say, way too soft.

He chuckles, warm and low. But then the room settles into stillness. That kind of silence that feels like it's holding its breath, waiting for something neither of us wants to say out loud.

What if he regrets what happened? What if he tells me it was all a mistake? What if he says he needs some space to think and just never calls me again? Say something, Sam. Quick!

"Could you imagine how awful we'd feel if we got hammered last night?"

He blinks as I start chuckling, and I calm myself down.

Okay, maybe that wasn't the best way to go about it.

What if I misread everything last night? What if it wasn't hours of connection but just a rebound for him? I'm not built for flings. If this was just one night, how am I supposed to go back to pretending I don't care?

Silence stretches, hot and awkward.

I want to ask what he's thinking, but I'm terrified the answer will wreck me.

Finally, he excuses himself to the bathroom, and I fall back on the pillows.

Oh man, what is happening right now? Maybe it's my breath!

I run into the kitchen and slice a lemon. I gag, scrubbing it on my teeth and tongue. I gargle some sparkling water and dash back into the bedroom, just before he steps back out.

I'm pretending to straighten the bed. "Isn't it a gorgeous morning? I honestly never thought I'd miss rainclouds."

He looks out the window like he's somewhere else already.

He's having second thoughts. He thinks the whole thing was a mistake. Even though we talked all night, our hands intertwined, he's regretting the whole thing.

"You know," he says, his eyes resting on me. "I never truly appreciated home. At least, not until I got caught up out here."

I nod with a soft grin.

He takes out his phone and starts scrolling, eyes flicking fast. Probably tons of texts. Plenty from *her,* I'm sure. He sighs.

"I should head out. Lorenzo's already tripping over not knowing where I'm at."

"Okay."

He slips on his shoes and grabs his jacket as he heads for the door.

I follow, my heart aching with every step. "Look," I say, my hand on the knob. "About last night—"

"Last night was great," he says.

I blink in disbelief.

But before I can respond, he leans in. He kisses me soft… like it's a secret he wants to keep. And the rush of waves returns.

When we part, he offers a quiet smile. "I'll call you. All right?"

I nod, heart already betraying me.

He leaves, and I fall against the door, swooning. I press my fingers to my lips, trying to convince myself it wasn't all a dream. I want to scream with joy and cry into a throw pillow at the same time.

This is it! I think he's falling for me. This isn't just a crush anymore.

Finally, he sees what I see! And pretty soon, just maybe, we can make this thing public. I mean, sure it'll seem sudden to some people, and I might need round-the-clock security to protect me from the Indies, but it'll be worth it. I'll have to ask Legend if we could get away for a little while. Maybe go up to the mountains in Colorado or something, just until things calm down.

I fall across the sofa with a sigh. I can't believe I'm finally getting what I want!

Then my door buzzes, slicing the moment in half.

He's back! I glance in the mirror, fixing my hair, and open the door.

But my body goes stiff, like someone poured wet concrete through my spine.

"Indigo? What are you doing here?"

Her lips are pouting, and her eyes are wet. Clearly, she didn't use her waterproof mascara. It looks like a couple of miniature racecars have made skid marks down her cheeks.

She rushes into my apartment. "Close the door before somebody sees me." Her voice is thin and shaky. I do as she says. Thank God Legend didn't see her. But wait... she didn't see him?

She paces back and forth, twisting the tassels of her clutch. Just like me, she's still got on her clubbing ensemble from last night, but she doesn't seem to notice or care.

"I don't know what to do, Sam." She shakes her head, making tracks in my dining room. "I don't know what to do! Legend's not answering my calls, and I think... I think I'm in deep shit."

My heart stops at the sound of his name. "Legend?"

She pauses, staring at me with raccoon eyes. "I went to the Arrow last night... and I think he was there."

I swallow hard. "How'd you even know where I live?"

"I'm a fuckin' celebrity. I know where all my employees live." She sniffs as she glances around, observing my living room and kitchen. "This place is actually a lot nicer than I expected."

"So, wait, you think you're in trouble or something?"

"No, seriously," she says with a frown. "I don't pay you enough to live in a place like this."

"Indigo, what's going on?"

She storms across the living room and plops down on the sofa. Her face disappears into her hands, blond curls spilling through her fingers. "Legend. I think he's seeing somebody else."

A shiver shoots up my spine and I shift on my feet. "Somebody else? What—what would make you think something like that?"

She drops her hands, staring at me like she's waiting for a punch-line. "Somebody told me he was at the club last night. He saw me with Willard..."

Willard. The same name that popped up when I was snooping through her phone. I was wondering if that was him at the club, and now here she is, dropping him into conversation like I should already know. I try not to look too interested, even though I'm practically salivating for context.

I cross my arms, taking a seat in the armchair. I sit forward with scrunched eyebrows. "*Willard?*"

She nods. "This producer from London who smells like coffee and mothballs." She rolls her eyes, practically gagging. "Maddox asked me to schmooze him for some big movie deal coming up, and... I owed him a favor."

I watch in silence as she falls back on the sofa, running her hands across her makeup-streaked face.

"I didn't think it would be a big deal! But if Legend showed up..." She exhales shakily, looking on the brink of new tears. "They said they saw him leaving with some other chick."

The words hit me like ice water. *Some other chick.* I fight the urge to look away, to squirm under the weight of the lie that's clinging to me.

The lump in my throat refuses to budge. "Did they know who she was or anything?"

Indigo shakes her head. "But I swear, if I ever find out, I'm gonna drag her out to Santa Monica Pier by her tracks!"

Goosebumps bloom up and down my arms.

Indigo looks back at me, nostrils flaring. "I'm sick of this crap, Sam! I'm done!"

I rub cold, damp palms across my thighs. "Done? Done with what?"

"*This!*" She flings her arms in the air in disgust. "I'm sick of playing the tramp all the damn time. It's not who I am!"

I nod slowly, careful not to give anything away. Let her vent. Let her scream. Just don't let her see the mess I'm hiding under this calm.

She throws her face in her hands. "Haven't I done that shit enough already?"

Wait—what is she saying? Where is this going?

"You know... I know you wanna be me."

What... what does she mean? Has she heard something? *Felt* something? Seen the way I look at him?

She glances back at me, eyes heavy, voice thick with something between sleep and sorrow. She shrugs, like the truth's old news.

"Everybody wants to be me. But nobody wants to pay the price."

"The price?"

She nods, gazing at nothing in particular, her lip curled in disgust. "It starts with one secret meeting. One topless audition... Next thing you know, you're begging just to stay in the room." She rolls her glistening eyes my way. "Anything to keep that spotlight on you." Her voice is barely a whisper, like the truth might shatter if she says it too loud.

So, the casting couch rumors are true?

Her eyes flicker toward the floor, the bravado drained from her frame.

She's always been larger than life. Brilliant, bold, untouchable. But now? Now she looks like a girl unraveling at the seams, fragile beneath the weight of everything she's traded for applause. The silence between us stretches, heavy with things I'm not ready to know. I want to offer grace, a soft place for her truth to land. But the words catch tight in my chest, caught between judgment and the ache of knowing she's not the only one who's been used.

"I'm in love with him, Sam," she says. "But this time, I think I went too far."

The room blurs for a second.

Love?

I honestly didn't think she knew the meaning of the word. Not like me. Not like Legend. Not like *us*.

Last night felt like something new. Something *real*.

And now, Hollywood's heartbreak queen is sitting here, telling me she's felt the same way all along?

The weight of it all settles hard.

I clear my throat, trying to push down the guilt. My voice comes out tight.

"Are you saying you slept with Willard?"

She waves her hand. "No. Thank God! But Legend's not home, and nobody knows where he is." She gnaws her lip with the saddest eyes. "I think he's done, Sam."

I lean back, guilt gnawing at the edges of my conscience. This is awful for her. Really, it is. But my heart's too tangled up to pretend I'm not relieved. She's spiraling. And all I can think about is how close I am to having the one thing I've wanted for *years*. I hate myself for it… But I can't let Legend go now, not when I'm so close.

I aim to keep my voice steady, reassuring. "Whether you end up together or not, the two of you will be fine."

She looks up, her eyes boring daggers into my soul. "What the hell is that supposed to mean?"

I swallow. "I… Well—"

"You think he's gonna dump me? I'm gorgeous!"

I open and shut my mouth, searching for the right answer. But frankly, nothing that comes to mind feels safe.

She shoots to her feet, arms flailing. "You think Indigo Taylor can't keep a man? 'Cause I can keep a fuckin' man, okay?" She storms over to my fridge and grabs a bottle of sparkling water. Chugs it like some drunk in a bar.

I nod with just the right amount of sympathy. She needs reassurance, not reality. And I need her distracted, not suspicious.

"You know, I bet you're right. He'll probably realize the whole thing is a big misunderstanding." *Though I pray to God that he won't.*

Her phone rings, and she leaps like some sort of parkour athlete trying to get to her purse on the sofa. Her eyes flash like a paparazzi camera as she answers. "Legend!"

The way she lights up when she says his name? That's probably how I look when I see his texts. That's how I *felt* when I woke up beside him.

But he's calling her. Not me.

My chest aches as I hold my breath.

"Yeah, I wanted to tell you—" She drops her head, pacing with the phone to her ear. "I know, but—If you'd just let me explain—" Her eyes glisten as she swallows, gazing up at the ceiling.

I smooth a throw pillow that doesn't need straightening, calculating every second of their conversation. Trying to read her expressions like a script.

What if he's asking her to meet up? What if I was just the plot twist in their love story?

I shut my eyes, inhaling, exhaling, praying.

When I look up, she's bobbing her head, blinking as the tears fall. "I know!" she shouts. "But if you'd just let me talk! Damn!" She huffs, throwing back her head. "Thank you."

Indigo connects eyes with me, pointing toward the bedroom. I nod for her to go ahead.

She continues as she makes her way back. "Look, I owed Maddox a favor, and…"

I fall back in my chair, letting out a hot breath.

What if he forgives her? What if he takes her back?

What if they run off to Vegas, get married, and move to Liberia where they'll adopt fifteen babies, and he forgets all about me?

My pulse spikes, and I squeeze my eyes shut, trying to hold on to the image of his sweet, soft lips against mine. But it's slipping, fading faster than I can control.

Every second she's in there on the phone with him feels like confirmation. Like he's repenting, choosing her, deleting me. My stomach flips. I can't tell if I'm nauseous or just pathetic. Maybe both. I feel like I'm about to snap in two.

I'm pulling out my hair and tapping my foot by the time Indigo returns. She stops when she sees me, and I jolt to my feet.

"Is… everything all right?" I ask.

She averts her gaze as she heads for the sofa and snatches up her purse. She leaves without another word.

I stumble back to the bedroom, running my fingers through my curls.

What the hell just happened?

Did he tell her about us? Am I gonna have a job on Monday?

I sink into my mattress at a complete loss.

Did I misread all of it? Was I just a distraction while he figures things out with her?

Goodness, Sam, what were you thinking?

You're not her. You'll never be her.

Then my phone chimes. I dig it out of my purse with trembling hands.

LEGEND: *It's over.*

I throw a hand to my mouth.

What's over? And with who?

I stare at the text like it might grow wings and fly away if I blink. His second message only fuels my anxiety...

LEGEND: *Meet me for dinner and I'll tell you all about it.*

18

The night started like a dream: Legend sending a car, a velvet-wrapped rose with gold edges, the promise of something magical. But dreams don't typically include back-alley entrances, security checkpoints, and exhaustion so thick it makes your eyelids heavy. I gather the hem of my off-the-shoulder dress as Lorenzo leads me down a dim hallway, the glamour already fading.

Ugh! Why the hell did I wear slingback stilettos? My feet are killing me!

Just as my heels start to ache and my patience thins, light spills across the floor like a stage cue. I round the corner, and the scene opens like a movie set sprung to life.

It's a restaurant. Or a beautiful lie pretending to be one.

Little golden lamps flicker along the walls, casting a warm glow over velvet drapes and elegant Vienna chairs. Every table glimmers with golden flatware and tall taper candles, flickering softly. A full staff stands in place like actors awaiting action: servers in crisp black, a maître'd with perfect posture, and not a single hair out of place.

It's Hollywood's version of a Parisian dream. Scripted, surreal, and stunning.

I throw a hand over my mouth as I approach. *What is all this?*

Then I freeze. He rises from the table, sharp in a designer suit, smile slow and easy.

My cheeks grow hot as I approach with wobbly knees. "Where are we?"

Legend throws out his arms, taking in the scenery. "Just a random back studio lot. Don't you like it?" I chuckle as he kisses me on each cheek. He pulls out my chair like a perfect gentleman.

Immediately, servers glide toward me like I'm royalty, offering crystal flutes of champagne and linen napkins with a flourish. I release a soft laugh, shaking my head in awe.

"So," I say, glancing around at the candlelit fantasy, "what's on the menu—besides sweeping a girl off her feet?"

Legend smiles, his eyes sparkling with mischief.

"That," he says, raising a finger, "will be revealed one course at a time. There are seven, after all."

I giggle. "You've done this before!"

He gives me his signature Bond-esque brow. "A Hollywood star never reveals his secrets."

The two of us laugh and raise our glasses.

"To a lovely evening," he says. "And even lovelier company."

A warmth blooms across my cheeks as our glasses meet with a soft chime.

It isn't until we're starting on the second course, shrimp bisque, that I jokingly ask, "So where are all the extras?"

Legend lowers his gaze, stirring his soup in slow, deliberate circles.

That's when it hits me.

"Did the servers have to sign an NDA?"

He doesn't answer. Just lifts his glass and sips, eyes still down.

I tilt my head. "So... this whole thing is one giant secret."

He winces. "Well—"

I raise my hand. "Not a question."

A *secret*. The word coils in my chest, thick and heavy. A bitter laugh escapes me, but something uneasy squirms under my ribs.

I want this—*man*, I want this—but why does it already feel like I'm breaking the rules just by breathing the same air as him? I chomp down on my dry crunchy toast.

"Come on, Sam. Don't be like that." He reaches across the table, but I don't give him my hand.

"Do you know how exhausting it is to make your way through secret passageways and up multiple flights of stairs after switching cars twice?"

He nods. "Actually, I do." I glare at him. "But not in heels," he adds.

So much for a wish come true.

I take a swallow of champagne that tastes more like reality than romance.

"Look, I know it's a lot." His gaze softens, warm enough to melt steel. "But I think it's best, for now, to keep things private. As far as the public knows, Indigo and me are still together. How's it gonna look if somebody spots me taking out another woman?"

"Like you've moved on."

I could tell him. I could mention what Indigo said—that people are *already* talking. But I hold it in. The last thing I want is to spook him. Not now. Not when I finally have him sitting across from me like this.

He stares back at me, his eyes a little sad. "And like a jerk," he says. "Besides, I don't want you to lose your job."

I feign a pout as he returns to his champagne. But the truth is, it hits differently now. Just weeks ago, I couldn't have cared less about this job. It was just something I had to get through. For him. But now? I actually want to be good at it.

"I mean, she's your girl, right?" He shrugs. "Isn't this like, a violation of girl code or something?"

I stir my soup, thinking about the way her voice cracked this morning. "Actually, she might trust me more than I thought... She was at my place when you called her."

He chokes on his drink and starts coughing. "Excuse me?" He wheezes, pounding on his chest.

"She popped up just after you left, actually. I'm surprised you two didn't see each other in the hall."

Legend gapes at me. His panicked gaze shifts to the table. "What are the chances?"

"My thoughts exactly."

He sits up, clearing his throat. "So... you were there when we broke up?"

I nod.

He leans his elbows on the table. Then sits back again. He shrugs, feigning casual. "So, I mean, how'd she take it?"

The servers return, exchanging our empty bowls for two servings of *le poisson*. In this case, it's grilled halibut. "She didn't seem too happy," I say, picking up my fork to dig in. But he doesn't.

"She say anything about it?"

It's the concern in his eyes that stings the most. Like I'm not sitting right here across from him.

I lean back in my chair, tapping my fork against the side of the plate. "She stormed out as soon as she got off the phone. Didn't say a word to me."

He gnaws his lip, watching me sample the fish. Surprisingly, it isn't half-bad. But I can't help wondering how much better it would taste if this weren't turning into a third-degree interrogation.

Legend hasn't touched his plate. His brow pulls tight, worry etched deep.

"So like, what was the point of her popping up in the first place? She ever been there before?"

I push the fish around my plate, the bite I took suddenly feeling heavier than it should.

"Never. It was completely out of the blue. I didn't think she even knew where I lived." I grab some more fish with my fork. "She was freaking out about you."

He stares at me. *"Freaking out?"*

I nod slowly, the words catching in my throat before I speak. I don't want to talk about Indigo. This was supposed to be our moment, the one I'd replay in my head a thousand times. But the look on his face makes it impossible to stay silent. And I care too much to let him blindly walk into whatever mess is brewing.

"She was pretty shaken up," I say quietly. "Devastated when she thought you might've been at the club."

I pause, tracing the rim of my glass.

"She heard you left with some other chick… but nobody seems to know who."

As expected, the blood drains from his face. "You didn't—"

"Of course, I didn't tell her, Legend. You think I'd be breathing right now if I did?"

"You're right," he says, finally picking up his fork. "I'm sorry." He takes a bite of his food and pensively chews for a good long while.

Maybe this is all too fast. I should've given him a week or two.

He looks up and swallows. "You like the fish?"

"L… if you're not ready—"

He drops his fork, waving his hand.

"Nah, Sam. This ain't on you. I made my choice, and I think it's for the best."

But it *is* on me.

I stare at him, my jaw tight, the sting settling behind my eyes. I keep thinking about the way he looked last night. Shattered, like something vital had just slipped through his fingers. The sadness in his eyes when he collapsed onto my bed still hasn't left me.

He takes a long gulp of champagne, but it doesn't dull the weight in the air.

This isn't right. This isn't how it's supposed to be.

Not when I finally have his attention, and all I can feel is the ache of what he's trying not to feel.

He offers his hand again, and I reluctantly take it. "Sam, you've always been one of the coolest chicks to me," he says softly. "I knew from that first DM that I liked you. But with you in Seattle, and me here, I figured nothing would ever come of it. So I was cool with being friends. It was better than nothing."

I remember feeling the same. Telling myself friendship was enough, even when my heart wanted more. Even when I hoped he'd read between every line I sent.

"But then I saw you that night at TK's Seafood and... my feelings for you were much stronger than I thought they'd be. I wanted to see you again. And lucky for me, you agreed to come to LA and help me out." His eyes scan my face, lingering on my lips. "The more I saw you, the more you made me laugh. The more you made me smile... Suddenly, I'm entertaining all these thoughts I never really had. But with everything going on with Indigo, I just didn't know how to handle it. Ya know?"

Of course. Indigo will always be there, hovering in the quiet corners of his mind. Shaping his choices, even when she's not in the room. And maybe that's what stings the most.

Because I've dreamed of a moment like this: him, sitting across from me, saying all the things I've wanted to hear. Confessing that he thinks about me. That *I'm* the one who makes him smile.

But somehow, even now… she's still here. A ghost between us.

It's no wonder he backed away from me last night.

He gives my hand a squeeze. "Listen, about last night…"

I lift my eyes to meet his, wondering how he's reading my mind.

"It was nothing against you," he says. "You know that, right?"

I nod, averting my gaze. *It's hard not to take something like that personally.*

"I just—" He sits back, releasing my hand. "You remember how I said I never visit my dad?"

"Yeah, ever since he left your mom. And he respects your boundaries."

He goes quiet for a second, the weight of memory settling in his eyes.

"Well, this one time—the first Thanksgiving after they split—I went to his new place in Seattle." Legend drops his eyes, a curl of disgust on his lips. "Really, it wasn't new, it was his *alternate* house, with his *alternate* family. His side chick, who was about to become his wife, was there. And so were his three other kids: Clef, Solo, and Melody. And I thought my brother Denero and me had wild names."

The two of us share a light chuckle.

"Anyway, I did my best." He shrugs, grief sinking into his gaze. "My mom insisted that if I was gonna go, I needed to be respectful. But a *whole* other family? A *whole* other house? Watching this dude kiss up on some other chick the way he would with my moms? I couldn't handle that shit."

My throat tightens at how close his feelings hit to home. It's the same way I felt when Mom replaced Dad with Trey. I know that kind of loneliness. The kind that doesn't just haunt you but rewrites you.

Once again, since being out here, I see past the headlines and fan posters. Legend Blake isn't a fantasy. He's real. And he's hurting in a way I understand too well.

I look him over, returning to my food with zero appetite. "So what'd you do?"

"I told him off. I didn't plan it or nothing, but he followed me out to my car as I was leaving and I just… I had to let him know, Sam. He ripped our family apart with no concern for anybody's feelings. *'Whoops! I didn't mean to cheat. Whoops! Didn't mean to make a baby. Then another. And another…'*"

I cover my mouth, trying my best not to giggle. "You didn't say that to him, did you?"

"What you think?" His voice is low, eyes locked on mine.

"Damn." I shake my head. But he isn't smiling.

"I swore that day I'd never be half the asshole he was. That's why I wanted to wait last night—make sure I closed that door with Indigo. And I wanted to make sure my feelings were legit, not just act on impulse. Ya know?"

I nod. That makes total sense. He's such an incredibly sweet guy.

He sets down his fork and reclaims my hand. "After talking to you and ending things with Indigo, I knew for sure. This is what I want, Sam."

My heart flips. A grin tugs at the corners of my mouth, wide and hopelessly girlish. There's a spark in my chest that I can't quiet.

Is this real? Is this actually happening? I want to scream, cry, run a lap around the block. But I just sit here, nodding like a normal person.

"Well," I tease, my voice a little breathless, "and exactly what is it that you want, Legend Blake?"

He smiles, the sparkle returning to his handsome eyes. "I want you, Sam."

My brain throws a parade. Confetti, cymbals, the whole nine.

He traces my fingers like he's reading them, slow and reverent. Then he leans in, gaze locked, lips parted—just enough to make me forget how air works.

And when he kisses me… it's quiet devastation.

Tender but unshakable.

Like he's sealing something we'll never come back from.

<hr />

We're making out in the back of a limo—*his* limo—as the car eases to a stop in front of my building. The windows are tinted, the partition is up, and Legend Blake's lips are still on mine like we've got nowhere else to be.

It's dizzying. Unreal.

Legend Blake. Hollywood heartthrob. I used to scream at his music videos. Now I'm the one he's holding like a hook in a love song.

He kisses like he's trying to memorize me. Like I'm a secret he doesn't want to forget.

It's overwhelming in the best way…

But I need air. Need to think.

I tap his shoulder, breathless. "Wait. Just… give me a second. I need to remember how to *function*."

He gives a crooked smile, gazing out the window behind me. "Damn. We're here already?"

I giggle, trying to comprehend the warm sensation of his arm wrapped around my waist.

His gaze follows the curve of my body, like he's deciding how fast to ruin me. "There's a secret entrance around the back if you want me to come up," he says, voice hungry and low.

My breath escapes me. *Does he seriously want to....?* My heart races at the invitation, heat creeping up my neck as our eyes lock in a charged silence. The air between us pulses with anticipation, the kind I've only ever imagined in fanfiction and daydreams.

But just as I open my mouth, his phone chimes.

His smile falters as he checks it out, and I know without asking. It's Victoria.

Legend sighs, reading her message out loud: *"Austin Studios. Mandatory meeting at seven o'clock tomorrow morning. DO NOT BE LATE."*

I meet his pout with a weak smile. "Rain check?"

He exhales through his nose, then slowly releases me, fingertips trailing like he's reluctant to let go. His eyes follow me as I reach for the door.

"It was a pleasure, beautiful," he says, voice low, velvet smooth.

I chuckle like a dork. "See ya."

With a gentle wave from me, his bodyguard shuts the door, and Legend's handsome face disappears behind a black window. I say goodnight to Lorenzo, and he gives me a nod before returning to the driver's side.

A breath escapes me. Heavy, shaky... maybe even relieved.

Sure, I want him. My god, do I *want* him. The way he looks at me, the way his lips feel against mine. It's electric. I've dreamed of this for so long.

But going there? Right now? Inviting him into my bed? I'm not sure I'm ready for what happens after. Because as much as I want him—and I want him *bad*—I also know how easily this could fall apart.

Despite everything he says, I'm honestly not sure how much he means it...

What if he isn't over Indigo? And what if I'm not...

++++++

On Monday morning, I head back to Indigo's place. I tried to check on her by text, but all I received were blunt responses like: *Tramp. Leave me alone.*

She never said I was fired, so I assume it'll be business as usual.

Kelly's just stepping out of her Porsche when I pull up next to her in the driveway.

She rolls her eyes, joining me as I get out. "Fifty bucks says she's on her face again."

I scoff. "Come on, we're all she's got... Seventy-five says it takes smelling salts to wake her up."

We shake on it, and Kelly opens the door.

We can already hear the bass echoing from her room.

The two of us are heading up the stairs when we stop mid-step, gazing at the sexy chocolate man making his way down as he browses his phone. His leather jacket is open, exposing a perfectly chiseled chest.

Wait a minute, is that...?

He nods with a wink, passing on his way. "Ladies?"

Kelly manages a small wave, but I'm frozen. Our eyes are glued until the handsome celebrity has strolled out the door.

I swallow. "Kelly?"

"Mmhmm."

"Was that—?"

"Yes, Sam. It was. And *that* is exactly why Indigo Taylor is the *baddest* chick in Hollywood."

We find her in her room, sprawled across the bed in fishnet stockings and a bustier. But she's not on her face. Kelly and I exchange knowing glances. She passes me fifty bucks.

Indigo snaps her head in our direction, frizzy curls dancing over her eyes. "Ugh! What are you two doing here?"

"Same as always," says Kelly, switching off the music. "Trying to rescue you from your own disgraceful demise."

"*Disgraceful?*" Indigo sits up on the bed, shaking her head at no one in particular. "Ain't nobody, dis—dis..." She hiccups. "Indigo Taylor don't take nothing from nobody, mmkay? I do whatever the hell I please, and *whoever* the hell I please!"

Kelly folds her arms. "Yeah. We passed your latest delicacy on his way out."

Indigo raspberries, blowing curls out of her face as she stands. "He was boring as hell. If he didn't look so good, I doubt I would've had fun at all." She grabs a tall bottle of vodka off her desk and lifts it to her lips.

Kelly snatches it away before she can toss it back. "That's TMI, and it's nine a.m."

Indigo stares at her with sleepy eyes. "Idk if it's p.m. or a.m. or PMS. I ain't got crap to worry about anyway, so give me my drank!"

Kelly shakes her head. "Indigo, that isn't true. Just because Legend broke things off doesn't mean your career—let alone, your life—is over."

"You don't know the half of it." Indigo scoffs. "Legend ain't just ditching me. He's ditching the duet, the music video, the whole damn tour!"

I stare at the floor, lips pressed tight. Legend told me about the meeting with Victoria and the execs yesterday. He laid it all out, no filters. Said he didn't care how much they fined him.

The personal conduct clause was supposed to protect the label's image, to shield them from scandal. But after Indigo got caught partying with some guy who *wasn't* Legend while still publicly tied to him? Legend wasn't the liability. She was. And that gave him just enough leverage to walk.

He was done. Personally. Professionally. Publicly. No more fake smiles. No more Indigo.

And honestly? I don't know if I should be proud... or terrified.

"Just like every other time," mutters Indigo. "I'm about to be a damn laughingstock." She swipes for the bottle, but Kelly backs away, rolling her eyes.

"Come on, Indigo! You know as well as I do that you've been through worse. Don't do this to yourself."

"Yeah, I been through way worse," she says. "And nothing hurts as bad as this shit. Now, bitch, give me my drank!" She attempts to grab it, but Kelly keeps it out of reach before swiftly placing the bottle in my arms.

My eyes widen in disbelief. I shake my head at Kelly, who's already returned to her poker face. But Indigo? She's staring me down like *I'm* the one who owes her an apology.

Indigo sneers, stepping toward me. "You..."

I swallow, moving near the foot of the bed. "Yes, ma'am—I mean, Miss Indigo. Can I do anything for you?"

She strolls my way, her teeth flashing like a Siberian tiger's. "This crap is all your fault!"

I'm stammering, backing against the bed. "M-me, Miss Indigo?"

"Yes, you!" she growls. "If it hadn't been for your scrawny ass with all your little questions and your beady little Chihuahua eyes, I never would've let him back into my life. This is all your fault!" She takes a swing, and I duck! She tumbles into the bed, falling flat on her face.

Kelly steps over to me, and I pass back her fifty bucks.

However you look at it, this is bad. And Indigo's not wrong.

Muffled whimpers are escaping her now. "My life is over. I'm a washed-up child actress that fell off half a decade ago. Even Legend has given up on me…" Her body convulses with sobs.

I did this. I destroyed Hollywood's sweetheart.

I cringe, looking to Kelly for help. She sighs, throws me a look, then perches on the bed, one hand rubbing slow circles across Indigo's back.

"Honey, I know it seems like the worst, but this too shall pass, right?" Kelly nods at me for confirmation, and I nod back.

"Mmhmm."

"I mean, I know that's how I felt when I left my ex," says Kelly.

Indigo looks up at her, eyes swollen, face streaked with tears and snot. "Did you find love again?"

Kelly lowers her gaze. "Not yet."

Indigo throws her face back into the mattress, a dramatic wail escaping her. Kelly pats her back, eyes wide as they flick up to me, her expression a mix of concern and panic.

"But that doesn't mean I never will!" says Kelly. "I'm only thirty-two."

"That's old as hell!" cries Indigo. "Pretty soon, I'm gonna be old as you and ain't nobody gonna want me. They'll make me one of the options in *Hump, Marry, Kill*, and up against Angela Lansbury they'll kill me every *time!*" She lets out some sort of high-pitched screech, like a car with bad brakes.

Kelly shakes her head, seeming at a complete loss.

I have to do something.

I set down the precious bottle of vodka and join them on the bed. "Miss Indigo… Maybe you're right."

Kelly stares at me, wide-eyed, lips parted in panic. But I've got to get the girl's attention.

Thankfully, it works. Indigo sniffs and wipes her face on the blankets. She gazes up at me. "I am?"

I nod. "To some people, that's all you'll be—some washed-up child actress who randomly pops up for SNL cameos. They probably won't even invite you to the after-party."

Kelly frantically swipes her hand at her neck, gesturing for me to cut it off, but I'm not done. Indigo gives a somber nod.

"But to people like me—and all of your Indies—you'll forever be a star. When most kids were still trying to figure themselves out, you blazed on the scene at twelve years old, ready to take on the world. And you've been doing that ever since, Miss Indigo." I count off on my fingers, going over the list. "A *brilliant* dancer, a *phenomenal* actress... You killed everyone with that duet of yours!" Indigo smiles to herself with sad eyes. "And even though the guy might have the name, it takes a *true* legend to bounce back like you always do. Everyone knows that."

Indigo sits up, wiping at her tears. "You really think so?"

I nod. Kelly stops glaring at me long enough to nod at her too.

Indigo lets out a pensive sigh. "Maybe you're right. Maybe it's time I let him go."

"Exactly," I say.

Kelly exchanges a cautious glance with me. But why quit when I'm ahead?

"Look at how gorgeous you are... Look at this frickin' mansion!" I fling out my arms dramatically, and Indigo nods, totally sold. "You're on top of the world, Miss Indigo. And if you can learn to enjoy it again, you can do whatever the hell you want!"

Indigo stares at me long and hard. Kelly does too.

Sure, I want her off Legend's trail. But that doesn't mean it's all an act. Because somewhere along the way, I stopped hating her. Maybe even became a fan.

A grin breaks across Indigo's face "You're right!" She laughs. "You're so damn right!" She springs out of bed, struts to the window, and throws open the drapes. Sunshine floods the room, catching her bare behind like a spotlight. "Indigo fuckin' Taylor is here to stay, bitches!"

"Thank God," Kelly says, relief flooding her voice. "'Cause I've got news."

Indigo turns back, her eyes dancing again. "Shoot."

"The duet, plus your latest scandal, has created a buzz in town," Kelly announces, standing. "You'd be surprised how many people are taking your side."

Indigo surveys her, crossing her arms. "Really?"

Kelly nods, stepping her way. She pulls up something on her phone and holds it up for Indigo to read along. "A few comments from the Shade Room: *Indigo's too good for Legend. She NEVER should've settled.* *Homegirl's not his dog. Why's he trying to keep her on a leash?* *Indigo is a gorgeous butterfly. The chick was meant to fly.*"

Indigo snatches the phone from her hands and starts frantically scrolling. Her smile grows with every second.

"So," says Kelly. "Your agent plans to give you a call this afternoon, but I told her I'd give you the heads-up. There's a big audition for a crime drama coming up, and *you* are a shoo-in for co-star."

Indigo turns, her mouth hanging wide open. "You're kidding me, right?"

Kelly shakes her head. "They say you'd be perfect for the part. All you have to do is clean yourself up."

Indigo nods, glancing back at me. She's never looked so uncertain. "You think I could do it, Sam?"

Up until recently, I never imagined I'd be rooting for Indigo Taylor. In my mind, she was just a threat—an obstacle between me and the guy I wanted. Of course, I wanted to refocus her attention.

But now, seeing her like this, unsure and vulnerable... I'm actually kinda hoping she pulls it off.

"Of course you can," I say, and this time I'm serious. "I mean, you're Indigo Fuckin' Taylor."

19

The orchestra swells, strings and synths colliding in that unmistakable ABBA sparkle. The audience claps as the opening notes of *Honey, Honey* pour through the speakers, playful and sugary sweet.

Somewhere onstage, people are probably dancing. Singing. Kissing maybe.

But I wouldn't know.

Because Legend's mouth is on mine. And he kisses like he's starving. His hand cradles my neck, thumb stroking behind my ear like he already knows that's where I melt.

A laugh escapes me—breathless—between kisses.

"Can we focus, please?" I say with a giggle. "You paid a lot of money for these seats!"

"Yes, I did..." He trails kisses down my jaw like he's cashing in.

I snort as he tickles my neck with his tongue.

We're in a private theater box, checking out a matinee performance of *Mamma Mia!* Or at least that's what we're supposed to be doing. Right now, he's saturating my jaw with kisses, his fingers playing in my curls.

This week, despite walking away from the deal with Indigo, Legend's had his hands full with all of Victoria's assignments: meeting with perfumers, magazine interviews, brooding thirst traps on social media. The poor boy hates it. But after everything he's put her through, Victoria claims it's the least he could do.

And the least I could do is be a comforting stress reliever... even if it means missing one of the *greatest* musicals of all time.

Legend reclaims my lips, kissing me sweet and soft. "You wouldn't believe how long I've wanted to do this," he whispers against my mouth.

"Couldn't be longer than me..." I murmur with a moan, the truth slipping out before I can stop it.

And it *is* the truth.

Three years of midnight messages. But more than that. Because it started before I ever hit send. Back in high school, back when he was just a voice in my headphones, a tiny photo in my notebook. I've imagined this moment more times than I can count. The music swelling beneath us, the taste of him on my tongue, the weight of his hands on my hips.

He cups my cheek as he deepens the kiss... exactly how Justin used to hold me. Like I might break.

And just like that, something tugs at the edge of all this sweetness. A thread I don't want to pull.

Because while my mouth is on Legend's, my mind flashes to another pair of lips... ones I used to know by heart.

Justin's.

Kissing me outside that greasy diner on our first "official" date. Grinning as he wiped hot sauce off my cheek like it was some sacred ritual. Holding my hand like he thought we had time.

I pull back just an inch, and Legend stills beneath me. His brows knit, barely, like he feels the shift in me.

"You good?" he asks, voice low.

I nod. Too fast. Too practiced.

It's a different man, a different city, a different life. But muscle memory doesn't lie.

"Yeah," I whisper. "Just...so much to take in."

Legend brushes a curl from my face and kisses my cheek, gentle now, like he's letting me set the pace.

And I'm grateful. Because I want this... I think.

A loud pounding on the door jolts us apart like we've been caught doing something we shouldn't.

I blink, dazed, trying to catch my breath. Below us, *Mamma Mia!* barrels on. Glittering lights, peppy harmonies, the cast dancing like nothing in the world could go wrong. But up here, everything feels suspended between what almost happened... and what still haunts me.

Justin's face. His smile, the way he used to kiss me...

It feels like an anchor I can't shake.

"What the hell?" Legend jumps up and peeks out the door. "'Sup?"

"We got a situation," says Lorenzo. He lowers his voice, saying something about groupies and evacuating now.

Legend returns with a heavy sigh. "We gotta go."

"But we haven't even made intermission—"

"I know," he says, glancing out at the stage. "And I'm sorry. But right now, we gotta get outta here." Reluctantly, he extends a hand to me.

⸱⧫⧫⧫⧫⸱

Forty minutes later, we're on a hill that feels plucked from a movie set. Rolling green, the lake shimmering like it's been filtered, downtown LA ghosting the horizon. Legend felt guilty about our date at the theater going belly-up, so he brought me to this somewhat secluded spot for an impromptu picnic instead. I purse my lips, adjusting my shades. This isn't the dream date I imagined. And not just because our time at the theater got cut short.

As the city buzzes quietly below, I can't help but wonder if I'm still tethered to something I thought I let go.

A soft smile. Callused hands. The smell of cinnamon gum and aftershave from the corner store. A man who used to kiss me like he was grateful I existed.

A ways down the hill, Legend is standing in line at a hot dog stand, a baseball cap on his head, sunglasses on his face. He claims that he likes to do this sort of thing from time-to-time—hiding in plain sight. Every now and then, people glance as they pass, seeming to question if he's someone of significance. But he keeps his head low, browsing on his phone, pretending to be as ordinary as the rest of us... If only that were the case.

Things were going great at the musical until we were interrupted. It turns out that some fans caught wind that Legend Blake was in the building. People were lining up outside the venue, hoping to get a glimpse of the megastar. Alex and Lorenzo insisted it wasn't safe for us to stay any longer. They hustled us out through an underground passage.

The two guards are at their posts now. One sitting on a bench, pretending to check out his phone, the other standing in line at an ice cream cart.

Legend is just placing his order when a young woman steps up and taps him on the shoulder. Alex and Lorenzo inch forward, on high alert, but it's just a harmless fan. Legend nods, agreeing to a selfie. He gives the girl a light hug and returns to the cashier.

That was nothing to him. But I know too well what it's like to belong to everyone but yourself. To be under that constant pressure to perform, to please, to be *on* all the time. I couldn't imagine dealing with all this on such a major scale every day. I'd be exhausted.

I release a heavy breath as I check my email... Still no messages from Justin.

The sun is warm on my legs. Atmosphere couldn't be more chill. I've seen more palm trees and Teslas in a week than I have in my entire life.

But even with all that, sometimes I find myself longing for the scent of fresh rain, the pitta-pat of droplets against a window, rolling over in the sheets of my full-sized bed in the loft... a familiar charming smile awaiting me.

I tap out a text without thinking:

> **SAM:** *You'd hate it here. Everything's loud and filtered and fake. I miss*

But I don't finish the sentence. What would be the point? My thumb hovers, breath shallow. Then I hold it down and press delete.

Sometimes, I just wanna go home.

"Expecting something?"

I jump and my phone slips from my hand at the sound of Legend's voice. I struggle to grab it before it can hit the ground, but it keeps popping out of my grasp, like a slippery bar of soap. It tumbles into the grass.

Legend chuckles, taking a seat next to me. "My bad. Didn't mean to scare you." I give him a crooked smile as I dust off my phone. He passes a hot dog my way. "Mustard and relish, as you requested."

"Thanks." I take a bite and let out a happy sigh. I can almost hear my dad's chuckle on the breeze.

Legend leans over, nudging me with his shoulder. "For someone who's terrified of trying new things, how'd a girl like you end up liking relish?"

"My dad. He insisted I try it at one of our baseball game outings and… to my surprise, it wasn't half-bad." Below, people blur past on wheels—laughing, weaving, free. I shrug. "Been doing mustard and relish ever since."

Legend's still got on his shades, but I can feel his gaze on me as he chews. "You miss him, don't you?"

"Every day." I glance at my phone and set it face down in the grass.

Legend doesn't look away. "Missing anything else?"

I glance at him and shake my head. But the truth curls under my tongue like steam. There's a version of my life that felt simple. Socks on warm floors, the smell of cinnamon in old mugs, the quiet hum of someone knowing me without asking questions. The rhythm of a life that, for all its mess, felt like mine.

Out here, even the sun feels staged.

I take another bite of my hot dog, and Legend scoffs with a light chuckle.

"Wow, Sam. We lying to each other now?"

I stop and swallow. Even behind his shades, his gaze is piercing. My tummy twists like a pretzel.

"Okay," I relent. "I was checking to see if I heard from my ex. I told him about my friendship with you *weeks* ago, and he never responded."

Legend nods, looking out at the shore. He starts working on his hot dog too.

"You mad?" I ask with a wince.

"Nah. I get it. He reminds you of home." He glances my way as he chews. "Same way you do for me."

I give up on eating and plop my hands in my lap. "I just miss talking to him, that's all."

Legend shrugs. "It's cool." An uncomfortable silence hovers between us. Alex and Lorenzo are at both ends of the knoll behind us, ensuring our privacy.

I hate to admit it, but there are still times I want to return to what's familiar, what I know. As if nothing's changed, as if my old life is just waiting for me to come back. But that's the thing. Nothing's waiting. Not anymore.

I shouldn't be torn. But I am.

"Y'all go way back, huh?" says Legend, eyes on the horizon, until they shift to me.

"Elementary school, actually."

Legend's brows rise. "So you and him was playing *Hide and Go Get It?*"

"What?!" I bust out laughing, and so does he. "No way! I didn't even know he liked me until after I—" I drop my head. "Until after I... met you."

Legend leans back, a soft grin on his lips. "Sounds like I just got in the way."

"It wasn't like that! It just... happened."

"Maybe for you," he says. "I bet homeboy was checking you out at recess." The two of us laugh, and I give him a light shove.

"He just wanted to be a friend." I look out at the park, the memories rushing back like waves on the shore. "We were in second grade, and I was *never* a social butterfly... I'd had a little trouble adjusting to the new school year. New teacher and all that. I'd spent the entire first week eating lunch in the classroom. But one day, my second-grade teacher had an emergency, and I had no choice but to confront that dreaded cafeteria.

"I found a *mostly* empty table, kept my head down, shoveling my sandwich into my mouth. And out of nowhere, this plump boy with shoulders as broad as my dad's plops down next to me, introducing himself."

Legend arches a brow, trying to recall. "Justin?"

I nod. The kind of nod that comes with memories you can't shake, even if you wanted to.

"Justin." I sigh, a familiar weight pressing on my ribs. "So I'm sitting there, staring, taking a long hard sip of my juice box. He's happily munching on one of two sloppy joe sandwiches, practically swallowing the thing whole. Then he looks at me, and asks my name... I just tell him, *Sam.* And he gazes at his sandwich—the contents dripping across his plate like some sort of brown sludge—and says, '*I do not like green eggs and ham. I do not like them, Sam I Am.*'"

Legend busts out laughing. "What?!"

"That's exactly what I said!" I smile at the memory. "He's been calling me that ever since."

"So hold up, *hold up!*" Legend raises a hand. "You're telling me this dude picked you up with a line from *Dr. Seuss?*"

I can't help smiling, the memory flashing before my eyes like a photo album I haven't opened in years. "I guess you could say that." I lean back, feeling the weight of nostalgia pressing into me. "My dad used to read that to me at bedtime. *Every* silly rhyme, *every* comforting cadence... And when he never came home from that flight across the Pacific, Justin was there. Making me laugh when I wanted to cry. Nudging me forward when I wanted to hide."

Legend nods, his smile softening. "Sounds like a cool dude."

"Always has been." I stare at my hands, thinking about all of my meltdowns and anxiety, and how he was there, extending a hand to me every single time. "At least until now."

"Damn," says Legend. "Sounds like a brotha will never measure up."

I gaze at him. "I think that's how I felt about Justin when it came to you."

Legend's grin wavers, a hint of hesitation in his eyes. "I don't know if I should feel flattered or guilty."

I wave a hand. "It isn't your fault."

Legend returns to his hot dog. He meditates as he chews. "I guess I get it. For a long time, that's how I felt about—well, you know... Put her up on this golden pedestal, thinking she could *do no wrong.*" He lets out a half-chuckle, a sad grin passing over his lips. "I remember this one time when we first started going out, I took her to one of them Cook & Sip classes. It was a private one—just us and the chef. And I tell you, that chick is a terrible cook."

We share a quiet chuckle.

"Like, seriously," he says. "She could burn salad. Anyway, she was doing her best to act all chill and stay camera-ready. But really, I knew she was freaking out. Especially when the chef asked us to make bread rolls from scratch."

I gasp. "How'd she do?"

He tosses a lazy grin my way. "What you think?"

Knowing Indigo, I'm surprised she didn't walk out on the whole thing—after throwing the dough in the chef's face, of course.

Legend chuckles, reflecting. "It was the highlight of my day watching this girl attempt to knead dough with acrylic nails, her nose scrunched in a little ball." He puts on a high-pitched, girly voice. "*Legend, this better not mess up my new manicure!*'" I can't help smiling at his imitation. "So, I took a handful of flour," he says. "Slapped her on the back of her Prada sweater, telling her we'd get through it all together."

My mouth falls open.

"I swear," he says. "Her head did a full three-sixty. I couldn't help cracking up as I apologized, brushing a little more flour on her nose."

I choke on air. "You didn't!"

"I did." He chuckles. "Before we knew it, we were in a full-out food fight. And trust me, the instructor was *not* happy." He stops and studies the hot dog in his hand. "But for once, we were having fun, not worrying about what anybody thought, or who might snap a picture. I scooped her up in my arms before she could throw another crumb. And her eyes... they did this thing where they kinda dance, and shimmer in the lights..."

My heart aches, recalling the spark in her gaze on the small occasions she'd go on and on about Legend, and all of their magical evenings together... How she said she... loved him.

"And that's when I knew—" Legend stops himself, gazing out in the distance.

But he doesn't have to say... *That's when he knew he was falling.*

He clears his throat. "Anyway, having someone you can go to with all your shit is... invaluable." He tosses me a heart-stopping smile. "At least that's how it's been for me."

I nod, more to myself than him. "It's even better when you can squeeze out some benefits along the way, huh?"

He chuckles first. And I follow.

Then he looks at me and says, "I gotta admit, there's nothing like friends with benefits." He gnaws on those luscious lips of his, leaning my way. I can't help smiling as I lean in to kiss him.

But abruptly he stops short. His smile flickers, just barely, before he drops his head. That tiny shift punches the air right out of my lungs.

My stomach sinks, and without thinking, I pout.

He shrugs, glancing around at the empty park. "Sorry, it's just— no matter how hard I try, the paparazzi are *always* lurking."

I run my tongue across my teeth. *How could I forget?*

"Thanks for understanding, Sam. I owe you another matinee."

I glance down as he gives my hand a gentle squeeze, letting myself feel it. The warmth, the weight of his touch, the way it settles something shaky in me.

I lift my chin, sticking a finger in his face. "You know I'll hold you to it!"

20

*A*few days later, I'm in Indigo's kitchen, hard at work. I blow curls from my face, measuring the second teaspoon of vanilla.

Indigo throws back her head on the living room sofa, gazing at me upside down. "Can we do this already? I need to get to my afternoon bath."

I nod, checking the setup of her phone on a tripod. "We're all set."

Within minutes, she's jumping in front of the camera. "What's up, Indies!" She throws her arms out wide, her Gucci tracksuit dangling off her shoulders—revealing her sports bra and perfectly toned tummy. "Thanks for all your responses to my survey! Most of you wanna see me bake cookies, so here I am. And..." She grabs my hand, yanking me in front of the camera. "I brought along my assistant, Sam! Say hi, Sam."

I paste on a smile as I give a timid wave, but my skin prickles under the camera's stare. "Hi." *It would've been nice to have a heads-up. I must look like a wet terrier right about now.* I brush some hair behind my ear and swallow hard.

This whole thing was Kelly's idea. She says that an impromptu video on social media would make Indigo appear more *approachable*.

Indigo slaps her hands together, a flirty smile on her lips. "Today, we're making chocolate chip cookies. So let's go!" She moves around the counter as I reposition the tripod. "Y'all let me know what's your favorite cookie in the comments," says Indigo. She turns to me with a bright smile. "So where should we start?"

After fifteen minutes of guiding Indigo step-by-step, I'm stirring the dough with a hand mixer as Indigo takes questions.

"I mean, I'm not gonna lie," she says in response. "I don't get to do it *all* the time, but I *love* when I can make a few things from scratch. Pancakes, pasta, that sorta thing. Yeah, Indieforever21! Believe it or not, a girl like me gets in her carbs!"

I gnaw at my tongue, keeping my head down. She knows she's lying as well as I do.

We scrape up balls of dough with one of those stainless-steel cookie scoops and place them on a rose gold baking sheet. Indigo casts a seductive glance over her shoulder as she pops them in the oven.

"And in ten minutes, we'll come back and indulge." Stepping over to the camera, she blows a kiss. "See y'all then!" She grabs the phone from the tripod the second I turn it off. A huge smile spreads as her eyes dance over the comments. "Perfect."

I start cleaning up as she makes her way toward the stairs, still gazing at her phone.

"Should I record you taking out the cookies later?"

"Nah." She waves her hand. "I'm not gonna eat them anyway."

I press my lips together and drop the dishes in the sink.

Hours later, afternoon sunlight slants through the library's arched windows, gilding the rows of sponsored gifts spread across the table. Glossy bags, perfume bottles, and luxury skincare clutter the space, and I'm halfway through sorting them when my phone vibrates. Legend's name flashes across the screen.

I smile as I answer. "Hey."

"Hey, beautiful. Saw your live."

My stomach drops. I'd roll my eyes, but the heat rising in my cheeks betrays me. "Please tell me that isn't true."

"Unfortunately, it is. But you looked amazing."

"Thanks," I say flatly, though my pulse is still pounding.

The image of me, frizzy curls in my face, caught in Indigo's spotlight, makes me want to crawl under this table and disappear.

"So since our plans fell apart last weekend, I was hoping that maybe I could make it up to you."

"Oh, really?" Things cooled down between us after the heart-to-heart about our exes at the park. I still have no idea what possessed me to vomit up all those memories about Justin. Of course, before we started going out, I probably would've had no problem talking to Legend about that sorta thing. That's… if I weren't completely infatuated with him and terrified of missing out on a chance to make him mine.

After our time at the park, Legend dropped me off with a sweet kiss and promised to make it up to me. Frankly, I was a little surprised he didn't ask to come up to my place again. But I suppose it was for the best.

"Yep. I know about this *hot* pool party that's going down tonight, and the host is specifically requesting your presence," he says.

"A party?" I narrow my eyes, voice dropping to a conspiratorial tone. "Is this party at some celebrity's mansion?"

"Not just any celebrity. The *sexiest* R&B singer on the planet."

"Mmhmm." A slow grin spreads across my lips, warmth blooming in my chest. "And will there be other guests at this party?"

"Nah." He lowers his voice, whispering seductively. "It's exclusive VIP. Know what I'm saying?"

Heat floods my cheeks, and I bite my lip. This should feel like a dream invite, but my chest tightens instead. A hot tub with him sounds *amazing*. Terrifyingly amazing.

But am I ready for that sorta thing?

"Just make sure you wear a bikini," he says. "His jacuzzi can get pretty... steamy."

I bite back a laugh, my hand brushing over my lips as if that could keep him from hearing how much he's getting to me.

He chuckles too. "So what do ya say?"

I take a deep breath, trying to calm myself. "I'll have to see. Indigo's got a lot going on today."

"Aw, for real?" I can practically hear him pouting through the phone. He sighs. "All right. Hit me up later and let me know?"

"Of course."

"I'll be waiting, beautiful."

I smile as we hang up.

"Who was that?"

My heart lurches at the sound of Indigo's voice! The phone jumps out of my hand and tumbles into a box of diamond-encrusted spa headbands. I forego a proper search, spinning on my heels. "Indigo."

Her shadow cuts across me like a stage light snapping on at the wrong cue. She's mere inches away, her gaze sharp, one brow arched with suspicion. "Who were you talking to? And why were you talking about me?"

I open my mouth and close it again. I swallow hard. "Um, just..."

"It couldn't have been Kelly. She's at a resort in Jamaica this week." Her eyebrows rise. "That was Legend. Wasn't it?"

My eyes dart left, then right. "Uh, I... Hmm?"

She slaps me on the arm, a grin on her face. "It was! Sam, you sly chick!"

A jolt of panic twists in my stomach, but I force a laugh, matching her energy.

Is this trouble? Maybe. But with Indigo's eyes sparkling, I'm pretty sure she thinks this is all about her.

"You know me..." I say with a crooked smile.

She steps back, her hands on her hips. "No way!" A brilliant smile lights up her face. "What'd he say?"

"He, um..." I clear my throat. "He was just checking on you. Making sure everything's all right."

She tilts her head in this really ditzy kind of way. "Really?"

"Mmhmm."

Good thing it rarely rains around here. Lightning would've struck me by now.

Indigo throws a hand over her chest, tears coming to her eyes. She blinks her false lashes again and again. "That is so... incredibly sweet." She fans her face, stretching her eyelids wide. She sniffles. "He has always been such a gentleman, Sam. You have no idea!"

If only she knew...

She nods, that dreamy sparkle returning to her gaze. "So what'd you tell him?"

"I told him you're good. Working hard, focusing on your career and Jiu-Jitsu."

Her face drops. "You didn't tell him I was upset?"

"Was I supposed to?"

Her nostrils flare, and I force a casual shrug.

"I mean, wasn't I supposed to? 'Cause of course I did. I told him it hasn't been easy, but you're taking it day by day."

She nods, looking me over. "And what'd he say?"

"He said, he feels awful and hopes to make it up to you." I gnaw my lip, wishing I were a much better liar.

She sucks her teeth. "So that's why you were going on about my schedule and crap?"

I nod. "He wants me to pick up a gift for you later. Wanted to know when would be the best time."

Indigo's gaze locks onto me, unblinking and intense. Her leg starts bouncing, the frown deepening on her face. "A gift?" She blinks at me, more tears welling in her eyes. Out of nowhere, she snatches up one of her sponsored boxes of nail polish and flings it into the wall! My shoulders shoot up into my ears at the sound of the crash!

"That asshole breaks my heart *twice*, and he wants to send a fuckin' gift?! *I have enough fuckin' gifts!*" She seizes another box and launches it across the room. "*Fuck him! Fuck him and all of his damn gestures!*"

Boxes fly like grenades, perfume and nail polish exploding against the wall. Every crash feels like my deadline coming early.

My eyes bounce between her and the door. I'm weighing my chances of making an escape before she remembers I'm here.

Shoot! I can't leave my phone...

Her rabid red eyes flash at me. She's back in my face in two giant steps. "You're gonna fix this. And you're gonna fix it now."

I blink. "Excuse me?"

"You heard me, tramp. You've gotta get closer to him. Gain his friendship and talk some sense into him." She nods, mostly to herself. "Kinda like you did me. You're good at that sorta thing."

I rub my neck, wincing. "You want me to hang out with Legend Blake?"

"Hell yeah!" She's up in my face, her wet eyes beaming. "He already trusts you enough to confide in you. What's a couple meetings?"

I stare at her, my stomach churning.

Maybe I should tell her the truth. She's got all this hope in her eyes. A familiar-looking pain is behind her gaze.

"Indigo, I—"

She raises a hand. "I'm not letting you back out. You're my assistant. You have to do it."

I exhale, the weight pressing harder against my chest. I can't break the poor girl's heart again... not more than I already have. Her wide, desperate eyes lock onto mine, and the guilt claws deeper. I nod. "Yes, Miss Indigo."

She giddily claps her hands and brushes away her tears. "Great. And find out who that chick was at the club." She marches off, her kimono robe flapping behind her. "Start with the gift thing! Arrange someplace to pick it up."

***

The sun is already beginning to set when I finally stumble into my apartment, exhaustion clinging to me like the city's humidity. I kick off my heels, each step leaving a trail of scattered thoughts as I send Legend a text.

> **SAM:** *Sorry. Boss lady kept me late. Tomorrow?*
> **LEGEND:** ☺*'Til then, beautiful.*

I breathe a heavy sigh and face-plant into the sofa. Yeah, only twenty-four hours until everything I've built this summer comes crumbling down. I sink my cheeks into the cushions and shut my eyes. The only cure for this kind of stress is a long, merciful nap.

I'm just starting to doze when someone buzzes at my door. They're pounding before I can make it to my feet.

"All right. All right!" I shout, yanking the door open.

My sister smiles and wiggles her eyebrows. "This a bad time?"

I groan, swinging the door closed, but she catches it and strolls right in.

"No, seriously," she says, stretching her neck, glancing back at the bedroom. "I was hoping to catch him here with his pants down."

"Shut up." I yawn, tramping back over to the sofa. "He isn't here. And even if he were, we're not like that."

Simone gasps, this horrified look on her face. She rushes over to me and presses a hand to my forehead. "Honey, tell me you're joking!"

I stare at her with dead eyes.

"No!" She shakes her head, her curly ponytail swishing back and forth. "No, no, no. You can't *possibly* mean that! The boy's singing is trash, but even *I'd* screw him one good time." She tilts her head, squinting in my face. "Sam, are you okay?"

I smack her hand away. "I'm fine, Simmy. I just... I'm just not ready. Okay?"

"But he is?" she asks, brow arching high.

I shrug, and her jaw falls open.

"Oh! You have got to be the *dumbest* chick I've ever met."

"Thanks, sis. I love you too."

She stands and makes her way to the fridge as I gaze at my reflection in the coffee table.

I lift my temples, stretching my eyes thin. "Do I look like a Chihuahua to you?"

"A little." She buries her head inside the fridge, inspecting the shelves. "So you and the hot star finally stop dancing around and smash lips, he's taking you on the town to hidden rooms and phony restaurants, and you mean to tell me that *now* you're refusing to give it up?"

"It isn't like that." I scratch my head, pain thrumming behind my eyeballs. "We just haven't found the right moment, that's all."

"Kinda the way you and Justin couldn't find the right moment until Mom was out of town with Trey for the weekend?"

I fall back on the sofa, staring at the ceiling. "What do you want, Simmy? Shouldn't you be... tumbling off a building or something?"

"Actually, we just wrapped up recording this afternoon." She emerges from my fridge with a bottle of water in one hand, a slice of cheese in the other. An apple is under her chin. She shuts the door with her foot. "The director wants me to audition for another role next week."

"You gonna do it?"

She collapses in my chair and starts happily munching on her apple. "We'll see. I may or may not be available."

Leave it to Simone to find flaws in one of the most exciting jobs in the world.

"I mean, I like it." She shrugs, popping open the bottle of water and taking a swig. "But I'm thinking about heading back to San Fran for a while."

"San Fran?"

She nods, a little grin playing on her lips as she chews. "Kyle and I have been talking and... he really misses me."

I lean my elbows on my knees. "Really?"

She nods again, a pensive look in her eye. "He's settled down on this little ranch his grandpa left him, and the last time I went to visit it was really chill. We sat on the back porch eating sunflower seeds and watching chickens."

"Sounds like *I* should be checking *your* forehead!" I chuckle. "Who are you and what have you done with my sister?" She flicks some water at me, and I duck, laughing.

"Shut up!" She shouts, before wagging her tongue. "Anyway, what's going on with you and Romeo? I thought things were going great."

I'd much rather keep it to myself, but frankly, I could use the advice. With a sigh, I fill her in. I tell her about Indigo catching me on the phone with Legend, and her giant meltdown due to my lies. I tell her about the hesitations between Legend and me, and Indigo's little plan for me to spy on him.

Simone leans back, polishing off what's left of her apple. "My, my, how the tables have turned."

I toss a pillow at Simmy, and she knocks it away with a laugh.

"Don't you have any advice for me?" I grumble, half-expecting some wise little sister speech.

"I do." She leans back, crossing her arms with a smug smile. "Never date a guy on the rebound."

I snatch another pillow and launch it at her. This time, she catches it and fires it right back, clocking me in the head.

"Look," Simmy says, more serious now. "I get it. You've been friends with him for a long time, and you wanna be there for him. But you're not wrong to feel the way you do. He chose you, and he should act like it. That means not bringing up Little Miss Goldilocks."

"Right? I mean, this is *my* time with Legend. I should be enjoying it!" I huff, crossing my arms. "Maybe it's my fault. I was the one who brought up Justin. I mean, not directly, but…"

"Sam…" Simmy presses her palm to her eyes. "Tell me you did not bring up your ex while you were with Legend."

"I mean, we were at the park, and all these feelings kept popping up…We'd been making out in the private box seats for *Mama Mia!* when all of a sudden, Justin kept popping into my head! I couldn't stop thinking about him. And somehow, it just… slipped out."

Simmy gapes at me. Then her expression shifts to one of scandalized awe. "So, let me get this straight. You were making out with your celebrity crush in a dark theater, and you still found a way to ruin it by thinking about your ex?"

She says it like I've committed a felony against womankind.

I groan. "It wasn't on purpose!"

"Sam..." Simmy leans back, crossing her arms with a dramatic sigh. "You need a strong drink. Or better yet..." She grins, wide and wicked.

I shake my head immediately. "Nuh-uh. No!"

"I'm just saying," she sings, wiggling her eyebrows, "the easiest way to get over Justin is to get under somebody else."

My jaw drops. "Simmy!"

She busts out laughing, and I hurl another pillow at her. It's a direct hit, but she just laughs harder. "Oh, come on! You two were making out at a matinee! That's *hot*! Do you know how many people I've tried and failed to hook up with in a movie theater?"

I bury my face in my hands, but I'm smiling now. "Simmy, stop!"

"I'm just saying, it might not hurt for you to... *loosen up!*" My sister cracks up laughing, even as another pillow sails her way.

21

The next afternoon, I find myself standing in front of Legend's sprawling modern estate, nerves buzzing under my skin. As soon as I knock, the door swings open, and Cam greets me with his signature grin.

"What's up, Sam?"

"Not much, Cam!"

The two of us laugh, exchanging a hug.

Cam has always been a gentleman, but even more so since he almost slipped and let Indigo know that we knew each other at our dinner meeting with the managers. Like the rest of the staff, he's aware that Legend and I are a *little* more than friends these days. And just like everyone else, he's sworn to secrecy.

He gives me a once-over, eyes sparkling. "Hey, don't tell the boss I said this, but you lookin' *good!*"

A laugh escapes me, heat rising to my cheeks. I glance down at my peach sarong, the gauzy fabric fluttering around my legs. "Thanks. You headed out?"

He holds up a couple of sleek suits draped over his arm. "Yep. Dry cleaners run for Boss Man before my hot date tonight."

"*Another* one?"

He shrugs. "You know me."

From what Legend tells me, Cam stays in a tiny bachelor pad near Franklin Village. But that never stops him from entertaining a *fine* variety of women who are more than thrilled to spend time with Legend Blake's assistant. I guess the job has its perks.

Cam points over his shoulder. "L's down in the studio." I thank him, and we say goodbye.

As I head downstairs, the usual bass-heavy beats that rattle the walls are noticeably absent. The quiet is eerie, almost foreboding. A shiver creeps up my spine. I pause, listening, then catch the low murmur of Legend's voice.

"One post on IG and it's a wrap," he says. "All I gotta do is say the word."

A familiar, haughty chuckle drifts from the studio. *Victoria.* "You really think I'd give you that sort of power?"

I step lightly, listening in.

"Try me," she says. "And we'll see *exactly* who has the kill switch."

Kill switch? What the hell is she talking about? I move in closer and peek inside. Legend and Victoria are standing near the recording booth. He's gazing at the floor as Victoria looms over him, her back facing the hall. His brow is crinkling.

"Now, are you done having your little tantrum?" she asks. "Or should I call in reinforcements?"

There's a long pause before he responds, voice low and resigned. "I hear you."

"Very good." She pats him on the shoulder. "I'll send a car around on Tuesday morning. Don't be late."

She turns, and I duck, holding my breath.

"But what if I want out?" asks Legend. Victoria turns back.

Taking advantage of the opportunity, I slip into the billiard room, crouching low to listen.

"That's not a part of my vocabulary, sweetheart." Victoria's voice is dark and foreboding, a chillier bite to its tone than I've ever heard. "Going forward, if you want to do so much as hold your breath for ten seconds, you sure as hell better ask me first. Do you understand?"

Before long she heads out. I press myself against the wall, counting heartbeats until she's gone.

Legend's still studying the floor when he notices my arrival. His eyes lift and land on me, the darkness quickly melting away. "Dang, beautiful! Look at you!" His grin is wide, but there's something forced in it. He pulls me into a hug, his lips brushing against mine, but his gaze keeps flicking to the hallway.

"Sorry I'm late," I say, trying to steady my voice. "Indigo had some handbags she needed organized."

"Cool." His nod is automatic, distracted. "How's she doing anyway?"

"She's... doing okay. For the most part."

His brows knit. "Everything all right?"

Shoot. Not how I wanted to start our date. I force a smile, waving my hand. "Yeah. We can talk about it later."

He nods again, still glancing out to the hall. The boy seems so troubled.

"L, is everything okay?"

"Of course... You pass Victoria on her way out?"

"I saw her, but she didn't see me."

"Cool." His shoulders drop, but there's still a tightness in his voice. Finally, he really looks at me, a grin breaking through the shadows. "Ready to go swimming?"

It doesn't take long before I'm perched at the edge of the pool, soaking in my own private reenactment of Legend's cameo on *Heist in the Hills*.

He emerges from the water like a sexy crocodile, muscles slick, brown eyes locked on me. Droplets trace slow paths over his shoulders and abs, shimmering before they dive back into the sparkling blue.

"Cut!" I wave both hands, grinning. "That's all wrong! Run it back, and we'll try again."

Legend throws out his hands, his wet biceps glistening in the evening sun. "How could that intro be any more perfect?"

I shrug, my gaze trailing over him with a playful pout. "If you'd rather be replaced by Idris Elba, that could be arranged."

His mouth falls open. "You got jokes, huh?" He dives, resurfacing beside me in record time. "I'll show you who deserves the part!" His hands find my waist, and before I can wriggle free, he pulls me in with a splash.

"Ahhh!" I squirm, water rushing over me, but his arms are like steel, holding me close. He peppers my neck with cool, damp kisses, each one sending a shiver down my spine.

"Legend, stop!" I gasp, laughter bubbling up as I weakly protest.

"You want me to stop, huh? For real?" He leans back, eyes smoldering under wet lashes.

"Okay, don't stop!" I giggle, and he doesn't need any more convincing. His lips return to my neck, trailing lower. Heat blooms under my skin, the cool water doing nothing to stop it.

It's been a whirlwind, finally dating Legend Blake. Private VIP entrances, hushed conversations behind tinted car windows. A dream turned reality. But even paradise has its shadows. Dodging Indigo's suspicions, sneaking around, hiding this... us. I can't help but wish we could just be normal. Movies, carnivals, or even a cheap bowling night like I used to have with... with Justin.

I push the thought away.

Soon, Legend's pressed me against the pool's edge, his flawless body warm against mine, a contrast to the cool water. His mouth finds my lips, tasting me bit by bit, each kiss stealing my breath.

My fingers thread through his damp hair, pulling him closer. His chest is firm against mine, his hands sliding down to grip my thighs, pulling me tighter against his waist. I feel the hard press of his body, heat and strength wrapping around me. He groans against my mouth, a low, hungry sound, and my pulse races.

Oh man, this is a dream come true... I should forward chain letters more often!

"Mmmph..." His lips part mine, his teeth grazing, his tongue teasing, and I feel the ache between us—desperate, electric. His touch travels, slipping under the water, tracing my thighs, my waist, each caress a promise.

Damn... This is... This is... much more than I can handle.

I try to come up for air, but that only encourages him. His mouth trails to my collarbone, heat against my wet skin. A low moan slips free before I can stop it.

"Maybe we should take a breather."

"Oh, yeah?" Legend doesn't miss a beat, his lips brushing my shoulder, his hands roaming my waist. Goosebumps prickle my elbows as our wet bodies sway in the water. His breath is warm against my neck. "You sure you wanna stop?"

Oh, I don't wanna... But I need to. "Something happened yesterday with Indigo."

He pulls back like a record scratch, his face a canvas of confusion. "Indigo?"

And just like that, the mood is killed.

He releases me, water rippling between us. "What about her?"

"She kinda... sorta... heard us on the phone yesterday."

Panic flickers in his eyes, his jaw tightening. "Sh-she did? Like, how much did she hear?"

"Just the end, really. She heard me making plans to meet you. She wanted to know what it was about."

Legend's gaze drops to the water, his brow furrowing. He looks back at me. "What'd you tell her?"

"Not much. I said you had a gift for her. A sort of apology. That you wanted me to deliver it."

"A gift?" He blinks, then squints at me. "So you didn't tell her about us?"

I shake my head. "She thought you were just checking on her, and... I sorta went with it."

For a second, a hint of a grin tugs at his lips. "Really?"

I nod. Legend crosses his arms, staring at the water, tension rippling off him. I know I should keep quiet, but it's clawing at me.

"Legend..."

His gaze lifts to mine, guarded. "Yeah?"

"She wants me to spy on you."

His jaw goes slack. "Spy on *me*?"

I nod, feeling like I've dropped a grenade between us. "She wants me to become your friend. Get into your head... Find out who you're dating."

He lets out an incredulous chuckle. "Wow."

"I know, right?" I force a laugh, but he's already looking past me, eyes fixed on the rolling hills beyond the pool. Silence falls, thick and heavy.

So that's it. He's not over her. Not even close. And if he isn't... how is this ever supposed to work?

"You know," he starts, voice low, "with all the chicks in my DMs, I never stepped out on her. Not once. It's like she's desperate to convince herself that I never really—"

He stops himself. But I finish for him. "Loved her?"

His eyes meet mine, and he reluctantly nods.

Suddenly, the cool water is making me shiver. The two of us bob in silence, the soft pool waves dancing to the R&B crooning in the distance.

This is not what I had in mind. This isn't what I pictured at all.

Legend shakes his head, swimming back to me. His thumb sweeps across my jaw, a gentle touch. "But that doesn't mean I don't care about you, Sam."

His dark eyes search mine, lingering on my lips. "I've always cared about you."

My heart stumbles. I want to believe him. I need to.

He leans in, capturing my mouth with his, and for a moment, I forget the cold, the doubt. It's just his lips, warm and insistent, coaxing a fire to life inside me.

But I've gotta know.

I pull back, staring into his handsome brown eyes. "So what do we do?"

He nibbles his lip, his fingers tracing the curve of my waist beneath the water. "I guess we'll have to start hanging out in public. Make it look like you're doing your assignment."

I scrunch my nose. *He can't be serious.*

His forehead presses against mine, his tongue flicking over his lips. "Though I gotta admit, I *really* enjoy our privacy. Don't you?"

And before I can answer, his lips claim mine again.

✦✦✦✦✦✦

It isn't long before we're tangled on a lounge chair, the sky darkening, pool lights casting an electric blue glow over us. His hands roam, warm and confident, sliding along my hips, my thighs. His body presses against mine, heat and strength, his mouth hungry. He runs a hand up my waist and over one of my breasts. He commands my body's attention with a firm squeeze.

Man. This guy knows what he's doing... And I am sooo in over my head.

A sigh escapes me. My tummy twists in knots. *What the hell am I doing?*

My chest rises and falls beneath his touch, a rush of heat tangled with nerves.

Justin was my first... my only. But Legend? He's been with some of the finest, most beautiful, and most *experienced* women in Hollywood, including Indigo.

A rush of doubt chills me.

Legend pulls back, his brow furrowed. "You okay?"

"Mmhmm. I just... need some air."

He backs away and I sit up straight.

Inhale. Exhale. Oh, I might pass out...

Legend watches me with concerned eyes. "Look, Sam, if I'm moving too fast—"

"No! Of course not! I just... might need a paper bag." I throw my legs over the side of the chair and drop my head between my knees.

He rubs my back as I gasp and exhale. *Oh my gosh, this is so frickin' embarrassing!*

It takes a good minute, but finally, my nerves subside. I look back, and he's got a grin on his lips. I close my eyes and groan. "I'm sorry!"

He chuckles to himself. "I gotta say, I'm pretty flattered. I've never had a girl nearly pass out on me before."

"Ha. Ha." I lean back, covering my face. "I've ruined everything, haven't I?"

"Nah." He rubs my thigh and gives me a pat. "Maybe it's not the right time."

"That sounds awful when you say it out loud."

He shrugs. "If you feel rushed it wouldn't be right. I'm cool with taking our time if you are."

Relief floods me. I didn't realize how much I needed to hear that. "Really?"

"Yeah. In the meantime, how 'bout I take you out?"

———————— ·++++·· ————————

Over the weekend, Legend has a charity concert, and I've got a prime viewing spot backstage.

I can't help fangirling, watching him command the stage, his voice a warm, rich current sweeping over the crowd. A vintage leather jacket hugs his broad shoulders, his guitar hanging low as he strums, a grin flashing like stage lights. He lifts a hand, and the audience mirrors him, an ocean of swaying arms and raised voices.

The final chord fades, and applause swells, rolling over the crowd as he bows.

"Thank y'all for coming out!" He waves and jogs offstage. His charming smile only beams brighter as he approaches me. The second Cam takes his guitar, Legend throws an arm around my shoulders. "How'd I do?"

"It was aiight," I say, forcing a casual shrug.

He tickles my neck, and my laughter tumbles out, bright and breathless.

"Legend."

His name lands like a stone, and his smile vanishes. Victoria strides toward us, a vision of crisp elegance in her blazer dress with golden buttons, her gaze slicing right through me.

"Sup, Victoria?" His voice loses its warmth. "Didn't think you were gonna make it."

"Had a little extra time." Her eyes settle on me, assessing. "And who's this?"

Oh, wow. She doesn't even remember me.

Legend almost seems relieved as his arm drops. "This is my friend, Sam. Just came to check out the show."

Friend. The word punches cold in my chest.

Victoria looks me over. "Have we met before, dear?"

Legend answers before I can. "You're Victoria Austin. Who *haven't* you met?" He forces a chuckle, so I do too.

Victoria smiles, continuing to examine me. "Well, Legend, I have a few things I'd like to discuss before your interview on Tuesday. How about I treat you and your friend to lunch?"

Legend's jaw tightens. He told me about the radio interview she scheduled without his consent. The host is itching to drill him with questions about the breakup with Indigo. He never said either way, but I suspect it was the source of their little disagreement in the studio the other day.

"Actually," he says, his smile stretched thin. "We're heading out with the crew. Maybe we can talk later?"

Victoria's gaze flicks to me, then back to him. "Nice meeting you, Sam... if we haven't already."

"Of course." I shake her hand, my smile polite but slipping fast.

The second she's gone, I smack his arm. "What the hell was that?"

"What'd you want me to do? Remind her that you're Indigo Taylor's assistant?"

I stare at him with parted lips. I guess not. But just the same, he introduced me as his... "friend." I sigh, my shoulders drooping.

"Look..." He pulls me close, his voice low and serious. "Victoria finding out about us? That's a whole mess we don't need. Way worse than Indigo knowing." His gaze searches mine, steady and urgent. "You know what I'm saying?"

I nod, though my chest still feels tight, that word still lodged like a stone in my throat.

With a sigh, his arm slips back around my shoulders. "Now, let's go eat!"

•••••••

Before long we're at a restaurant just outside Crenshaw with his entourage. Legend's laughter blends with the chatter, his smile flashing bright as he cracks jokes with his friends. But he hasn't touched me. Hasn't even glanced my way the entire afternoon.

This isn't a date. I'm a tagalong. Another member of the team.

Hunter slings a muscular arm around Jackie, who glares at him. "Boy, you ever heard of personal space?"

"I'm just saying..." He looks her over, his eyes settling on her plate. "If you ain't gon' eat them fries, what's a brotha gotta do to get a bite?"

She smacks him in the chest and trades plates with him. Legend and Cam are cracking up as he digs into his second helping.

I chuckle too, trying my best not to roll my eyes.

Justin used to eat like that all the time... at least before he changed.

I'm just picking over what's left on my plate when Legend nudges me. "You good?"

I offer a stiff smile. *This is not what I had in mind at all.*

But he's already turned back to Cam, who's launching into some wild Vegas story. Their laughter swells, filling the space, pushing me to the edges.

I drop my fries. Appetite gone.

The server is just taking up our plates when I excuse myself and head to the bathroom.

I think I just might cry.

Inside a cramped stall, I sit, elbows on my knees, trying to re-member what I thought this would be. A dream come true? It's barely even a date. At least Justin made me feel seen… even when things went south.

I wash my hands, fix my curls, studying my reflection. A cropped V-neck and ripped jeans.

Is this really what I want?

With a sigh, I step out, and before I even spot the table, someone grabs my hand, tugging me around a corner! I find myself in a nook with an empty, rusted-out payphone cradle.

Legend's grin is boyish, his lips stealing a quick kiss.

"Legend, what are you doing?" I swat his chest.

"I missed you." When I scoff, his eyes narrow. "What?"

I spot Lorenzo at the end of the hall, guarding Legend's privacy as usual. I lean back, crossing my arms. "Has it occurred to you that you've treated me like I'm just another member of the crew the *entire* afternoon?"

He looks me over and shrugs. "That a problem?" I roll my eyes and turn to leave, but he snatches my hand, pulling me back. "Hey, what's going on? I thought we were having fun."

"Is that all this is for you? *Fun?*" The word scrapes out of me, raw.

Legend blinks. "I mean, nah. But… clearly, you're not down."

I purse my lips. *He'd never hide his relationship with Indigo like this. Maybe this whole thing was a bad idea.*

He pulls my hand from the crook of my arm, intertwining his fingers with mine. "Look," he whispers. "I know it isn't ideal, but I think we should keep things quiet for now. I mean, what if paparazzi catches on, and Indigo finds out—"

"Yeah, Legend. What *if* she finds out?"

He shushes me, glancing out to the hall. "Come on, Sam. You're always so chill."

I shrug. "Maybe I'm tired of being chill."

He gazes at me, completely dumbfounded. But I mean it. If he doesn't want to admit that he has feelings for me then what the hell are we doing here?

He drops his eyes and sighs. Nods more to himself than to me. "You're right. I'm sorry. Just— Give it a little more time. I don't want the media dragging me through the mud." He gives me those lost puppy dog eyes…the kind he saves for his most killer heartthrob scenes in all his music videos.

My tummy flutters and takes flight. "You're *so* lucky you're Legend Blake."

He smiles. "Only 'cause I got Samara Allen on my arm."

He takes my giggle as an invitation to kiss me again. And the soft graze of his lips makes me forget why I ever questioned him.

✦✦✦✦✦✦

A few hours later, we're tucked inside an empty ice cream shop just outside the city, his bodyguards posted outside like shadows. Legend paid a hefty sum for this—an hour of neon lights and sweet cold treats, minus the chaos.

"I know it isn't perfect," he says, licking a vanilla cone. "But you gotta admit, the ice cream's pretty damn good."

I nod, working on my scoop of chocolate. "I suppose you're right."

He reaches across the table and takes me by the hand. "You forgive me?"

I lift a shoulder, licking my cone. "I'll think about it."

He chuckles, but there's something softer in his eyes.

The place is a retro dream—pink and white booths, a fifties-style jukebox humming low, candy toppings gleaming behind glass. Fresh-baked donuts sit in perfect rows. The staff's on break, the manager hiding out in the kitchen. We're alone, but the quiet doesn't feel peaceful. It feels like a spotlight.

"Be careful what you wish for…"

Legend frowns, curious. "What do you mean?"

I look up, meeting his gaze. "I made a wish on a chain letter… that I'd get a second chance with you."

"A *second* chance?"

"The first was that day you helped me off my ass when you were rehearsing for the talent show."

He snorts as it comes back to him. "That was your chance, huh?"

"If your dad hadn't popped up, who knows where things could've gone!"

He drops his head, trying to calm his chuckles. "Yeah. Come to think of it, I'm sure sparks were flying."

"Shut up!" I nudge him with my foot. "Anyway, I got this stupid chain letter from my old boss and made a wish. Next thing I know, you're asking to meet."

"Just like that, huh?"

"I kid you not, it was within *seconds.*"

He gazes at me, the smirk still on his lips. "Looks like you got your wish."

I give a dry grin, returning to my ice cream cone. He tilts his head. "You disappointed with the results?"

I wince. "Wouldn't I sound ungrateful if I admitted that?"

"You're not wrong to feel how you feel." His voice is steady, understanding.

We eat in silence for a moment, the air thickening.

"Legend, I really like you. I've *always* liked you."

"I like you too." His smile is a little more guarded. "So why do I feel like I'm about to get dumped right now?"

"What?!" I slide out of my seat, crossing to his side of the booth. His arm wraps around me instinctively, and I lean into his warmth.

I like how it feels here. It almost feels like...

"You know," he says. "I remember feeling that way with Indigo. Like I made a wish, and it came true. But not the way I wanted."

I chuckle, though it's tinged with bitterness. "Really?"

"Yeah. Believe it or not, I was still kinda new to the game. And of *all* the guys in the world, Indigo Taylor wanted to date *me*. This one time, I rented a yacht. Wanted to treat her to a private weekend, just the two of us. But just as we were boarding, she decided to snap a picture and post about it. Ended up in some ridiculous digital war with a troll named AngelFire29."

"I remember that!" I say, eyes wide. "*Oh*, it was ugly..."

"Was it? 'Cause all I remember is sitting on the deck of this luxury yacht, clear blue sky, stuffed mushrooms and clams laid out... and her glued to her phone, raging at some rando online." He catches a runaway drop of melted vanilla on his tongue. "Definitely not what I imagined."

"That's awful."

"Right?"

I watch the light in his eyes, that easy spark of amusement as he recalls it... this memory of her. A warmth that lingers, even in frustration

"And you should *seriously* stop talking to me about your ex."

Both of us laugh.

"You're right." He plants a tender kiss on my forehead. "That's my bad."

His lips find mine. And for a moment, there's nothing but us—*just us*—tasting sugar and sweetness.

And for once, it almost feels real.

22

"And we're back, keeping it *real* with Legend Blake this morning!" shouts the radio host. "All right, L. You promised to give me some answers after the break. You ready?"

Legend chuckles, leaning into the mic. "As ready as I'm gonna be, man."

Indigo rolls her eyes, leaning back at her desk, attempting to touch up her nails. Meanwhile, I'm reviewing the most Indigo-focused news articles to share with her later as we listen to the interview online. I can tell by her pursed lips that she's terrified of what he might say.

The radio host continues. "Now, rumor has it that you were actually *at the club* the most recent time Indigo stepped out on you. That true?"

Legend pauses a moment before answering. "Yeah, man. It's true."

Indigo's golden cheeks flush pink as she shakes her head. "I knew it."

The radio host lets out an exaggerated gasp. "*Yo!* You serious? Dude, how did you keep yourself from pounding that guy's face in?"

"I don't know," says Legend with a thin laugh. "But I *will* say I came close."

The radio host is falling all over himself as if he's somehow struck gold. "Okay, okay. Now, tell me this...did you *really* leave with another chick that night?"

My fingers freeze over the laptop's keyboard, breath caught.

There's another lengthy silence. Indigo leans forward, her elbow perched on the back of her chair.

The host busts out laughing. *"Ah, man!* That response tells us all we need to know!"

"Look," says Legend, the slightest waver in his voice. "I was there with my friend. And it's a good thing she was there, 'cause she helped me keep my cool."

There he goes, calling me his friend again. My teeth press together as I clip another article for Indigo.

Highlight, save, minimize. Like it's routine. Like I'm not sitting here feeling invisible.

Indigo sucks her teeth. "Friend, my ass! Who is she, Legend? *Tell us her damn name!"*

I swallow hard.

The radio host seems to be digging too. "So you tryin' to tell us this *mystery girl* you left with was *just a friend?* You didn't go kick it with her that night?"

"Well..." Legend pauses, most likely for dramatic effect. "I'm a gentleman, so I'd never share the intimate details of our—"

"What?! *What?!"* The radio host claps with a haughty laugh. "Legend, you hit that?! You *so* hit that, man!"

"You know, I can't confirm or deny—"

"Ah, man! You don't have to! Any girl that's good friends with Legend Blake should get *all* the benefits," says the host.

My cheeks burn as heat floods my ears. I know it's just locker-room banter, but I'm not some groupie. I'm not his secret indulgence. I'm...

"Hey, shut up, man!" Legend is laughing too.

Indigo shakes her head, vigorously filing her nails.

There's a tightness in my chest, but I can't help wondering what else he might say.

"Okay, okay," says the host. "One more question—'cause I already know if she's hanging with you, she's gorgeous. Y'all still kickin' it?"

Legend lets out a sigh. "Yeah. We're still cool."

My heart drops. I'm thrilled that he's willing to admit that much. But if Indigo or the paparazzi even come close to putting two and two together, I am so dead.

There's no way he'll be taking me out in public now.

The radio host explodes with excitement, slapping fives with Legend in the studio. "That's my man! Movin' on and movin' up!"

Indigo breaks her nail file in half. The radio host is just wrapping up the interview when she tells me to turn it off. I rush to do as she says.

I don't know whether to smile or pout considering what was said. That's the closest Legend's ever come to sharing details about me with the public. At the same time, judging from Indigo's glowing red face, it's probably for the best that he didn't say more.

Indigo sits as still as a statue, gazing at the wall. If it weren't for the occasional rise and fall of her shoulders emerging from her slouchy t-shirt, I'd think she were dead.

I set the laptop aside and take a tentative step her way. "Miss Indigo. Is there anything I can do for you?"

She nods. "Tell me the truth."

My heart stops in my chest. "Excuse me?"

Her dark eyes meet mine. "I said... tell me the damn truth. You've met with him twice. What do you know?"

Shoot. I was hoping to hold her off a little bit longer. Legend and I agreed that a diamond pendant necklace would be the perfect apology gift. It's around her neck right now. And she knows all about us heading to lunch with his entourage after the charity concert last weekend.

She stands and approaches me, her gaze heavy and fierce. "What do you know, Sam?"

"Miss Indigo—"

"Did he tell you about her?"

"Um—"

"Was she there?"

"Well—"

"Tell me, Sam!" Her voice is a thunderclap, so loud it reverberates through my bones. Spit clings between her teeth like venom.

I wince, rocking back on my heels. "Okay, look… It's been tough. He's not exactly an open book, ya know—"

"Tell me *now*, or you're fired." She crosses her arms, nostrils flaring.

Great. Even though she needs my help with reading the frickin' news, I know she's just crazy enough to terminate me. But if I tell her the truth, Legend will *never* forgive me.

Besides, it's actually been kinda cool getting to know Indigo Taylor. I'm not ready to walk away quite yet. In spite of her crazy tirades, I've almost enjoyed helping her out. It's almost like we've become… friends.

She stares me down, waiting for an answer.

"Okay, so…" I avert my eyes, trying to steady my breathing. "While we were chatting this weekend, he did mention a little something…"

The girl's icy gaze instantly melts. "Go on."

"Well, he brought up the time you got in a digital war while the two of you were out on a yacht. Do you remember?"

She gazes up at the ceiling, nodding. "Yeah. What about it?"

"He just sorta mentioned how worked up you were that weekend, and that it frustrated him. He'd gone out of his way to get that yacht and present all this delicious food for you, and you were too busy... being a drama queen to notice."

Indigo scoffs. "He called me a drama queen?"

"More or less."

She drops her head, thinking. She starts pacing the floor. "So, what? He's trying to say I'm too dramatic for him now? He knew that shit when he signed up to be with me."

I casually cross my arms, shaking my head. "Men, right?"

She stops and looks at me, sadness sinking into her gaze. "So is that it? He's fed up with me and all my... drama?"

And the sorrow in her eyes has me all twisted up inside.

Legend is supposed to be mine. He's supposed to belong to me...

So why do I feel so guilty?

"Indigo, look—"

"That's it, isn't it?" She nods to herself, pacing again. "That boy was always bending over backward to treat me like a princess. He's never been anything but sweet to me. And just like always, I had to go and screw it up."

Her hand trembles as it combs through her curls. And then, without warning, she screams and sweeps everything off her desk! Papers scatter, perfume bottles crash, her favorite ceramic mug shatters against the wall.

I stumble back with a yelp.

"That's exactly the kinda shit he's talking about! Ain't it?!" she yells, spinning on me, cheeks stained with angry tears.

I press against the wall, nodding weakly.

Falling down on the bed she throws her hands over her face. "Ugh! I am so sick of myself!" Her shoulders sag as she sniffs again and again.

And for the first time, I see it. The exhaustion buried under her rage. Before long, she's whimpering.

I close my eyes and let out a heavy breath. I take a seat next to her, patting her on the knee.

I never thought I'd be the source of so much heartbreak. Three hearts shattered in three months, and every shard seems to be stuck in my hands.

"I didn't get it," she says, her voice muffled behind her hands.

"What do you mean, Miss Indigo?"

"I didn't get the part…" she says, shaking her head in quiet devastation. "They said, they *decided to go in another direction.* Which is code for: *You're not half the star we thought you were.*"

I pat her knee again. "I'm sorry, Miss Indigo."

She shrugs. "Don't bother. The only way I can command anyone's attention in this town is by actin' a fool or taking my fuckin' clothes off." She drops her hands, revealing eyes full of tears. "Mamí taught me that from the very beginning."

I stare at her in silence. Indigo *never* talks about her mom.

She sighs, looking back at me. "Did you know she escorted me to my first audition, as busy as she was?" I softly shake my head, knowing anything I add could risk escalating matters.

"I was twelve," she says. "And I was *so* excited. She and my daddy were hardly ever home. So when I woke up that morning and saw her sitting at the foot of my bed, it may as well have been my birthday."

She sits up straight, wrapping her arms around her tummy, this soft glimmer of melancholy in her eyes.

"We pull up to the place, and in this really sad sort of way, she says, 'Mija, *don't let anyone or anything get in the way of your dream… There's nothing you can't do.*' I didn't know what she meant at the time, but it wasn't long before I found out… She didn't come inside.

"As expected, the execs *loved* me, and I only had one more meeting. But..." She drops her eyes, her lips trembling. "It wasn't how I thought it would be... I thought I looked good enough. I thought I *was* good enough."

She rolls her eyes, a bitter grin on her face.

"But I got that damn part."

My jaw aches as she studies the floor. She struggles to maintain her smile.

She doesn't have to say it out loud. What she's implying sounds awful.

Indigo nods, staring at nothing. "I been fighting to stay on top ever since... even if that meant hurting the man I love."

Is that what all this has been about? Her attempt to stay in the spotlight?

She looks at me, a tear rolling down her cheek. "Sometimes, I think it would be a lot easier to be a nobody like you."

I drop my head, and she chuckles. But before I can react, she lunges forward, throwing her arms around my neck.

I freeze as her sobs soak into my shoulder, her entire body trembling.

What have I done?

Slowly, I hold her tight, rubbing her back. My own eyes sting. And before I know it, I'm crying too. "I'm so sorry, Indigo."

I really, really am.

"I just..." She whispers between heavy gasps. "I just miss him so much."

23

The hum of the engines is deafening. Or maybe it's my pulse.

I press my back to the seat, nails biting into the armrest like a lifeline.

"You all right?"

Legend's voice is soft as the private jet taxis the runway, but I can't look at him. I can't move. I'm too busy waiting for the sky to swallow us whole. Like it did my father.

"Mmhmm." My lips are glued shut, just like my eyes.

It's Legend's birthday, and at his request, I asked Indigo for the weekend off. Not that I told her what I actually had planned. What I *didn't* know was that his idea of celebrating involved four straight hours of psychological warfare... thirty thousand feet in the air.

Legend chuckles softly, then gently peels my fingers from their death grip on the leather. He laces his hand through mine, warm and steady. "Sam, look at me."

I wince, barely shaking my head. "I can't."

"Yes, you can, Sam. Look at me."

I force one eye open. Just one. My shoulders drop half an inch at the sight of his face, brown and beautiful, calm. His grin is the kind you give a puppy trembling in a thunderstorm, soft and just shy of a laugh.

"Why didn't you tell me you were scared of flying?"

I shrug. "It never really came up."

"That's why you drove to LA, huh?"

I nod. No point in denying the truth. When your dad disappears over the ocean mid-flight, you don't exactly jump at the chance to board another plane.

The wheels bump over something on the runway, and the whole cabin shudders. I flinch hard and squeeze Legend's hand like we just hit turbulence.

"Okay, okay... Ouch!" he says through a strained laugh. "That crap *hurts*. Like, for real, you 'bout to break my hand."

I loosen my grip, face burning. "Sorry."

Legend exhales slowly. "Look, I know you're nervous. But flying is one of the *safest* ways to travel. The chances of us crashing are slim to none."

"Yeah. Tell that to the people who were flying with my dad."

He stills. "You're right. I'm sorry." He reclaims my hand. "But I promise, I'd never put you in danger—"

"Even though you are."

He snorts—actually *snorts*—and I whip my head toward him.

"Are you laughing?" I stare at him in disbelief. "We could die right now, and you're *laughing* about it?"

"Okay, I'm sorry. It's just..." He bows his head and kisses my fingers. "It's my birthday, and I wanted to enjoy this time with you. Away from all the groupies and cameras."

He lifts his gaze, lips twitching.

"You mean to tell me you'd rather stay behind and slave away for Queen Indigo?"

I purse my lips, thinking about the endless list of assignments she'll have for me when I get back. "I guess not."

Legend leans in and presses a soft kiss to my lips, lingering just enough to make me forget we're preparing to be slung into the clouds.

"Try to relax," he murmurs. "We'll be there before you know it."

He calls over a flight attendant who's standing by with a bottle of champagne. She promptly pours us two glasses, and Legend raises a toast.

"To a bomb birthday with no regrets."

I smile. "Agreed."

Our glasses meet with a soft clink.

―――――― ⁘⁕⁘ ――――――

To my surprise, once I get over the sheer terror of being tilted on my back and hurled into the sky at two hundred miles per second, flying doesn't feel so bad. It's almost as relaxing as riding in a car.

I lounge back with a complimentary tablet in my lap, idly flipping through *Star Magazine*. Meanwhile, Legend paces near the widescreen at the front of the cabin, voice low and tight as he argues into his phone.

Victoria, of course.

Despite Legend being on his best behavior—and that painfully personal radio interview two weeks ago—she's still yet to back off. He could promise the woman his firstborn and she'd probably ask for twins.

"It's my birthday," he snaps. "And if I wanna take a quick trip, I can. You're not my mom!"

A beat.

"I know, but—"

Another pause.

"Look, I'll be back by Sunday morning, I promise." He hangs up and gives me a crooked grin. "Managers, right?"

He drops back into his seat, dragging a hand down his face.

"You didn't tell her about our plans?" I ask with a hint of sarcasm.

As far as I know, she still thinks I'm just the assistant, no idea I've graduated to the woman who's memorized the rhythm of his tongue by heart.

"I shouldn't have to," he says with a frown. "Between my concerts and movie deals, I'm making her *hundreds of thousands* every month. The least she could do is let me have two days to myself."

There goes that crinkled brow again.

I rub behind his neck. "One day, you'll be running your own label, and Victoria Austin will be nothing more than a footnote in your memoir."

That makes him smile. "You really think so?"

"I know so."

We lean in and meet halfway, trading a quiet kiss that says everything we don't.

Since the radio interview, things between Legend and me have been... better.

Even though I didn't love him implying we hooked up the night of Indigo's scandal, it was really sweet that he was willing to admit my existence. Plus, Victoria said it was great for his image—made him look like "*less of a simp.*" But when she pushed for more details about his *mystery girl*, Legend refused to get into it. He better pray she doesn't dig any deeper.

Legend settles back in his seat and throws an arm around me. "Man, I don't know what I'd do if I didn't have my girl in my corner."

My heart stops, but I casually glance up at him. "Your... girl?"

He blinks, unbothered. "Well, yeah. What else would I call you?"

I grin, trying to keep it light, even as my chest tightens in the best way. "I'm just so used to you calling me your *friend*. You keep saying things like that, and people might start to wonder."

He studies me, eyes trailing from my hair to my nose... then my lips, slow and unhurried. "Well," he murmurs, voice low, "maybe that's not such a bad thing."

And this time when he kisses me, it's deeper... bolder. Like he's claiming something he's done pretending not to want.

+ + ◆ ◆ + +

By some miracle, I survive the horrifying experience of landing in a plane—like seriously, I have no idea how we didn't crash into the pavement—and we check in at our New York hotel. Actually, Alex is the one who takes care of everything at the front desk, while Lorenzo ushers us through a private back entrance.

We share a light dinner, then spend a little too long in the penthouse—lips and hands learning each other all over again—before changing and heading to an underground club in Brooklyn.

Burgundy light washes the room, white spotlights slicing through the haze like search beams. The dance floor is packed wall-to-wall, bodies twisting in rhythm, sweat and music thick in the air.

Legend moves like he owns the place, slapping hands, nodding at familiar faces, a star among stars.

The DJ layers an Usher remix over a trap beat, the bass heavy like it's trying to shake the floor loose.

I glance over my shoulder, wishing Lorenzo and Alex hadn't agreed to stay in the car. They usually put up more of a fight. But Legend made it clear that he wants his privacy this weekend.

He suddenly stops, grinning wide as he spots someone across the room. Grabbing me by the hand, he leads me to the bar, where a young guy with short locs and a stack of iced-out chains around his neck is nodding to the beat, drink in hand. The two of them slap fives, then hug like it's been years.

Legend pulls me closer with a quiet kind of pride. "Sam, this is my brother, Denero."

My mouth falls open. *He could've told me he'd be here tonight.* I wave, trying to shout hello over the music.

A slow smile spreads across Denero's face as he wraps an arm around my neck, embracing me. "Heard a lot about you," he says. "Glad my brother finally stopped being a punk and made a move."

Made a move?

Before I can respond, Legend tugs his brother back by the collar of his Louis Vuitton track jacket. "Hey, that's enough. Give my girl some space."

They both crack up.

If Legend were a few years younger and grew out his hair, they'd be damn near identical.

Legend told me a while back that Denero's attending NYU—said he wanted space from all the West Coast drama and wanted to make a name for himself in New York. He's studying music production and already has a handful of local rap artists prepared to work with him.

Denero offers to buy us drinks and turns to the bar.

Legend slides an arm around my waist, fingers brushing the satin of my minidress. He leans in and kisses my forehead like we do this every day.

I blink up at him, wide-eyed.

He shrugs. "What?"

"Aren't you scared that someone might see?" I ask, glancing over my shoulder.

"Not here. People are cool." He pulls me closer. "Besides, who cares?"

I try not to smile. But I fail.

———————— ·•◆◆◆•· ————————

We're tucked into a VIP booth before I even realize it. Low lights, velvet seats, and an obscene amount of bottle service crowding the table. Legend sits with his arm slung around me like it's just another Friday night, while Denero lounges across from us, perusing every melanated woman who struts by.

I have to remember to close my mouth when Denero pulls a blunt from his pocket and lights up. I glance around, trying to act unfazed.

Is that even legal in here?

Denero takes a long drag, then holds it out to Legend.

Legend smirks but waves it off. "You know I don't do that junk anymore, man."

Anymore?

Denero laughs, exhaling a thick cloud toward the ceiling. "I know, I know. Gotta stay clean for them movie roles and shit. But hey, it's your birthday. If you can't chill now, when will you?"

Legend glances my way. But I know he won't. He's not that kind of guy.

Then, without a word, he takes the blunt. No smile. No joke. Just a smooth inhale like it's second nature.

I watch in dismay as he nods with satisfaction.

Wow. That cannot be good for his vocal cords.

It's a struggle not to gag at the thick, skunky smell.

Legend leans back, visibly relaxed, and takes another drag. He looks to me, teasing a lazy smile. "You want some?"

Justin would never...

I politely decline, my dad's voice ringing in my ear. *"It'll rot your brain,"* he'd say. I never questioned his judgment.

"Ah! She's a good girl!" Denero laughs as Legend passes the blunt back. "Be careful, Sam. You gotta know how to party when you're running with *the* Legend Blake."

Legend chuckles, dry and drawn out. "Shut up, man."

I never knew he smoked. In fact, he's never mentioned anything about his party life. What else hasn't he said?

I shift in my seat as he rubs my shoulder—slow, rhythmic. Like he's trying to pacify me.

"That reminds me," Denero says to Legend. "Them twins we took to my place last time you were here? They know you're in town."

The room doesn't tilt. I do. But Legend is chill as hotel ice.

"I wonder who told 'em that." He doesn't even blink.

Denero grins, all teeth. "Hey! They been asking about you. Neither one of 'em can get you off their mind. Know what I'm sayin'?"

Legend's arm tenses and he glances at me.

"You trying to make me look bad, man?"

"I'm just warning you, dude." Denero takes another lengthy drag. "Don't blame me if two chicks run up in here and start swinging on your girl."

What? My eyes race around the room, checking for the nearest exit.

Legend pulls me close as his brother busts out laughing. "Ignore him," Legend mutters. "He's just clowning around."

Denero raises his full eyebrows with a bold smile. *"Am I?"*

Legend snatches a flyer off the table, balls it up, and launches it at his brother. Denero ducks, still cracking up.

Maybe I should pivot.

"So… Legend, Denero, Solo…" I say, leaning in. "Your dad gave all of you such interesting names. How could you not be successful, right?"

The shift is instant. Both brothers go still.

Legend scratches his head. Denero just stares.

The smile slides right off my face.

Did I say something wrong?

Legend clears his throat. "We don't bring up the sperm donor around D."

"Yeah," says Denero. "Besides the name and some decent DNA, that dude ain't done shit for us."

My stomach twists. *Okay. Definitely touched a nerve.*

"Sorry." It tumbles out, awkward and unsure, like I already know it won't land right.

"We good." Denero takes a sip of his drink and nods at Legend. "You told her about the night we found out?"

Legend glances at me, lips pressed into a thin line. He shakes his head at his brother.

"Oh, fa' real?" Denero leans back, and some chick in a pink ruched mini skirt plops down in his lap like it's her assigned seat. She whispers in his ear, and he smiles up at her. "Aiight. Give me a minute." His eyes linger on her behind as she sashays off.

It's a full ten seconds before he remembers what he was saying.

"Night of the *Lucky Star* finale, the four of us are backstage." He stops and points Legend's way. "Bruh just crushed it. About to sign the contract of a lifetime."

Legend nods, brows tight. He tosses back his drink.

Wait a minute. Why haven't I heard this story before?

Denero stares at Legend, a smirk on his face. "Mr. Sensitivity over here can't shake the fact that our moms looks pissed. He keeps asking what's up, and she breaks down crying." He rolls his eyes, curling his lip. "Finally, that old fart confesses. Says he's got a *whole* other family and it's time he *move out.*"

I blink at Legend. He told me things fell apart after the show... but not *right* after the finale.

Legend gazes at his empty glass, then flags for another bottle.

"Since then," says Denero. "I ain't had two words for the dude. Told L to stay away too, but you know how he is. Had to get smacked around a couple more times before he finally stopped fooling with his old ass."

I remember the story he told me about their last Thanksgiving together. How carefully he'd chosen his words. Now I know why.

Legend's tired eyes meet mine. "And now you see why we don't talk about you-know-who around my brother."

We don't talk about him much at all.

Legend's frown deepens as he pulls out his phone. He rolls his eyes, leaning over to me. "Victoria's tripping. She just called for the fourth time."

I swear, that woman keeps him on a leash so tight I'm surprised he can breathe.

Not that I couldn't use a breather myself... especially after the emotional grenade Denero just tossed into the booth.

Legend starts to rise. "Let me step out and see what's up. You think you'll be good?"

I nod, trying to hide the tension in my expression. "Sure."

"Don't worry," says Legend, giving Denero a pointed look. "My brother's got you. Right, man?"

He nods... or is he just bobbing his head to the music?

I look back, and Legend is gone.

I grab my glass and toss back what's left of my champagne, the bubbles hitting harder than I expected.

Denero waves over a server, and she tops off my glass. "So what you doing in Hollywood?" He takes a drag of his blunt. "Singing? Dancing? Everybody over there got a thing."

I let out a light chuckle. "Not me. My job is to help the people who have a... thing."

He arches a brow, exhaling smoke. "Like an assistant or something?"

"Indigo Taylor," I say, my voice stretching across the bass-heavy music like cellophane.

Denero freezes, holding his blunt mid-air with wide eyes. He throws back his head and busts out laughing. "Ah, man! You know about her and my brother, right?"

I nod, lips tight.

Frankly, I'm surprised Legend hasn't told his brother all about his little plan to get me out to Hollywood.

"Now, *that* chick was a trip," he says. "I never got what he saw in her, really."

"Me neither," I say, lips curving like it's a joke we're both in on.

"You know, I flew in a while back to visit, and he said we couldn't meet up 'cause *she* had other plans?" Denero shakes his head. "That chick had him *whipped*, fa' real! I thought he'd never get over that one."

He isn't the only one.

I take another sip of my drink, the bubbles cutting just enough edge off my mood. "She farts during Brazilian massages."

Denero chokes mid-drag. "Yo..."

I lift my glass. "You're welcome."

The two of us are still wheezing with laughter when some tall, dark guy with big ears and a high-top fade slides in next to me, slinging a bulky arm around my shoulders.

"What's up, Denero?" he says. But his eyes are locked on me. He gives me a slow once-over, tongue dragging across his dark lips. "Who's this diamond?"

"Hey." Denero shakes his head, attempting to wave him off. "You don't wanna do that, bruh. She's taken."

"Not for long." The guy smirks, raking his gaze down my body like he's already claimed it.

"Nah, man—" Denero's interrupted when his previous female candidate returns, having lost all patience. She grabs him by the hand and pulls him off into the crowd.

Great. Now what do I do?

Dark and Scary looms over me, his whisky breath hot against my neck. "Come with me, and I'll make you forget all about your man."

I lean back, swallowing hard. *Where's Lorenzo when you need him?*

Peering over his shoulder, I raise my hand and wave. "Oh, there he is!"

I give the guy a pat on his boulder of a shoulder. "Nice meeting you." Before he can say another word, I duck out.

The crowd swallows me like a living thing—bodies pressing, twisting, grinding, impossible to navigate. I bow my head and push forward, weaving through the chaos like it may never end.

Ugh! Isn't there anything else these people like to do for fun? Why couldn't we just go to a movie or something?

Just when I'm about to give up, the sea of dancers parts, and I stumble back to the bar. I exhale hard and lean into the counter, dropping my head into my hand like I've barely survived a war.

"Can I get you something?" asks the girl behind the bar.

"Oh, uh—"

"I got her."

The voice is warm, confident—almost commanding. A distinguished-looking man steps up beside me, low-cut fade, a tight curly goatee. The kind of posture that says he handles things. His dark blazer fits snug over broad shoulders, paired with crisp jeans and just enough swagger to pull it off.

He extends one of the two neon blue drinks he's holding my way.

"Thanks," I say. "I hate bars."

The bartender gives me the meanest side-eye.

"I mean... except this one!" Swiftly, I take the glass and lift it in mock salute. She's not amused. I toss it back anyway.

Whoo. Fruity. With a tangy buzz.

The guy's smile is almost too perfect as he extends his hand. "Colton," he says, all smooth and sexy.

"Samara," I say. His grasp is firm, his gaze curious.

"Have we met before?"

"Nah." I gesture vaguely, my hand floating midair. "Just flew in from LA."

His brows lift, intrigued. "So I've seen you on TV?"

I giggle for absolutely no reason. "No. I'm not... I'm not—" I hiccup and slap a hand over my mouth. "Excuse me!"

Suddenly, I'm warm. Like, *Snuggie in the summer* warm. I set aside my drink and smooth my hands down the front of my red dress, just to be sure I'm not wrapped in fleece.

"It's humid in here. Don't ya think?"

Colton laughs softly as he sets down his drink and places a steadying hand on my back. "You wanna step outside? Get some air?"

"Actually"—a familiar voice cuts through the buzz—"she's with me."

Legend appears at my side, arm slipping around my waist like it never left.

Colton lifts both hands in retreat, that slick smile still in place. "My bad. Nice meeting you, sweetheart."

Why's he gnawing his lip like that?

Legend grabs my hand and pulls me toward the dance floor. "You good?"

"Mmhmm." I press my head into his shoulder. His leather bomber jacket feels so nice. So cool and shiny. "He was cute."

Legend stops and looks at me. "You trying to make me jealous?"

I bat my lashes at him, all sexy. "Is it working?"

He laughs low and pulls me close. "Let's dance."

I throw up my hands, swaying to the melody, the bass pulsing straight through my veins.

Oh. This is fun.

The music doesn't just play, it *moves* through me. Over my arms. Down my hips. Around my legs. Who knew music could feel so good?

Legend steps up behind me, wrapping his arms around my waist and pulling me into him. His breath skims the curve of my neck as he slow-grinds to the beat.

Man, I could get used to this. My eyelids draw shut.

Who needs Justin with all his sweet little gestures and walks down memory lane? I'm doing just fine without him. Yes, I am.

Suddenly, something sparks in me. A rush of boldness I've never felt. I've never been much for dancing, but tonight, I am *invincible!*

I spin on my heels, grab Legend by the collar, and pull him in with a grin.

Indigo Taylor ain't got nothing on me.

I pull Legend close, lips pursed, flushing hot. Then I spin out—channeling every video vixen I've ever secretly admired—and roll my hips to the beat, slow and bold. My hand trails down the front of his jacket as I head south, teasing...

Before I can reach my destination, Legend grabs my wrists and pulls me upright, glancing all around. "Sam... what are you doing?" he mutters.

"I'm dancing," I say with an extra shimmy. "Don't act like you don't like it." I laugh, but I'm wobbly now. My heel slips slightly.

Legend catches me before I fall, steadying me against his chest. "Okay. I think we oughta get out of here."

Next thing I know, I'm in our hotel bed.

Everything's a blur. I *think* I remember saying goodbye to Denero... maybe the car ride too. But mostly, it's flashes—Legend tugging me by the elbow, mumbling apologies to strangers as we headed out. I'm pretty sure someone carried me into the room.

And suddenly, like a sexy chocolate angel, he materializes at the foot of the bed. But his face is hard as stone.

"Drink," he says, pressing a glass into my hands.

I take a sip and gag. "Ugh. What is that?"

"Water."

I stick out my tongue and set the glass on the side table. At least, I try. The table shifts. Or maybe I do. Either way, the glass tips and water splashes across the carpet.

"Oops."

Legend groans, dragging both hands over his face before sinking onto the edge of the bed. "Sam. It's my birthday. You picked *tonight* to get wasted?"

"Wasted?" I let out a dramatic laugh that ends in a snort. "I am *so* not wasted! I am totally sincere... I mean, sober."

I give him what I hope is a seductive look, and somehow, he splits in two.

"Oh, *shit*..." I slap a hand over my mouth and collapse into giggles, rolling onto the pillows.

Legend presses a palm to my forehead. "Did somebody slip you something?"

"Don't!" I swat him away. "It's hot... It's *so* hot." I pull down the straps of my dress.

"Sam...wait." His hands fly up in panic. "Wait!"

But my dress is already down around my hips. "Mmm. That's better." I sink back into the pillows, eyes fluttering shut as the low hum of the air conditioner lulls me.

When I finally open them, Legend's still watching me—elbow on his knee, finger pressed to his temple.

I grin, glancing down at my strapless push-up bra. "You like what you see, lover boy?"

He cracks a smile as he nods. "Oh yeah. I love it."

I push up onto my knees and snake my arms around his chiseled bicep. "How about you grab some ice, and we can have some fun?"

That signature brow of his lifts, cocky and intrigued. "You are hella sexy when you're intoxicated."

"I'm not intox—intox...uh—whatever. I'm just loosening up... in *all* the right places."

He laughs, low and rough. Then leans in and kisses me like I'm the only thing on the planet that can calm the fire he's been holding back all night.

Man... Have his kisses always felt this good? Every single peck sparks a fire between my legs. Oh! It's so hot... He's so hot!

I help him rip off his T-shirt and the two of us dive into the pillows. He caresses my thighs, burning my cleavage with sizzling kisses.

This is it! We are doing this! "Oh my gosh! Legend Blake wants to bang me!"

Wait. I think I said that out loud.

Legend chuckles, making his way down my waist. "I'm about to make all your dreams come true, *Mamí*..."

Yes! Everything I've ever wanted is finally coming true!

And I laugh and laugh... until my vision tunnels. And everything goes black.

24

unlight stabs through the curtains, dragging me out of
sleep. I blink hard, once... twice... everything's too bright.

Man! My head is pounding... What the heck did I do?

I sit up slowly, taking in the room. Forest green furniture accents
the wine-colored walls. Massive windows line half the room from
floor to ceiling. Birds chirp outside. And the shower is running. I
swallow hard.

Carefully, I lower my gaze... Bare arms, bare shoulders, wrapped
in Egyptian cotton sheets and blankets.

*Oh no... No, no, no! There's no way I finally hooked up with Legend
Blake and totally missed it!* I squeeze my eyes tight. *Stupid, stupid, stupid!*

I take a deep breath and peer beneath the sheets. To my surprise,
my bra is still intact, and I'm dressed from the waist down. I throw
my head back, releasing a heavy sigh.

"You look kinda relieved," says Legend. He's leaning against the
frame of the bathroom door, a very lucky terrycloth towel around his
waist. His perfectly sculpted chest glistens in the glow of the sun.

I narrow my eyes. "Hmm?"

"Seems like you're thrilled that nothing went down last night." He steps toward the bed, raking a hand through his damp curls, muscles rippling. A few lucky droplets glide down his abs and disappear into his towel below.

But wait. I sit up in the sheets. "It didn't?"

He sits at the edge of the bed with a weak chuckle. "After you passed out, I covered you up. Called a private medic to come make sure you were okay. She said you were definitely slipped something besides alcohol last night, but with a couple winks you'd be all right."

I pout as the thoughts of the club return to my memory. "Stupid, Clinton... or was it Keaton?"

"Happy birthday to me," mutters Legend, eyes fixed on his hands.

"I'm sorry, Legend. I just wanted to loosen up."

"Where have I heard that before?" He stands and crosses over to the armoire.

His statement hits like a slap, sharp and insulting. "Are you comparing me getting roofied to Indigo's wild partying?"

He swings open the doors and pulls out a blazer and jeans, his tired eyes drifting back to mine. "You did enough of that yourself, after that... bizarre seizure you had on the dance floor."

"Seizure?"

"Look, I know you were overwhelmed when I introduced you to my brother, and I'm sorry I didn't give you a heads-up. But between your fangirling and fear of flying, I just didn't want you to freak out any more than you already were." He lays his clothes out on the bed, pulls a pair of Oxfords from his suitcase. "Instead, I end up leaving my own party, apologizing for bringing another chick that can't hold her liquor."

I blink, stunned by the venom in his voice. "Excuse me?"

"If you don't want people comparing you to Indigo then maybe you shouldn't imitate her." He shrugs, casual as hell.

"And if you don't want me thinking you're a jerk then maybe you shouldn't act like one!"

He glowers at me as he grabs his undershirt, then turns to the window as he pulls it on. "Fact is, if you were cool, you wouldn't have tossed back a drink from the first dude that looked your way."

Something pinches behind my ribs. He's not just mad. He's judging me. Like I'm some reckless fan who threw herself at him. After everything? The late-night texts, the voice notes, the way he looked at me when he thought no one else was watching...

This is what he really thinks of me?

The thought stings. And the sting hardens into rage before I can stop it.

"It was *your* idea to drag me out here," I say, heat rising in my chest. "*You* were the one who begged me to move to LA! And *you* kissed *me* first. I tried giving you space—offered to give you time—but you insisted that you were over Indigo... So why does it always come back to her?"

He scoffs under his breath, fingers moving stiffly over the buttons of his dress shirt. "Look, we got somewhere to be, so..." He gathers his things and heads to the other side of the suite, shutting the doors behind him.

An hour later, I'm gazing at a romantic table for two, a silk tablecloth with linen napkins. A crystal bud vase with a single red rose at its center.

Empire State Building with mimosas, watching the sunrise over Manhattan...

Not exactly what I pictured.

The sun gleams through mile-high windows on every side, shimmering across a glossy black floor. Soft rock music echoes somewhere above, the clouds drifting by outside. So maybe the top deck observatory isn't the secret floor, but at least we have the whole 102nd floor to ourselves.

Legend leans back in his chair, sipping his drink, his eyes focused on his plate of biscuits and jam. Thanks to my hangover, we totally missed the sunrise, and my food is cold.

"You like the eggs?" He doesn't quite meet my eyes, fiddling with the edge of his plate.

I give my best grin and take another bite.

This isn't half the fantasy I'd imagined. *I bet if he were with Indigo he'd be all smiles.*

"I guess that maybe you're right." His words escape on a sigh as his shoulders finally drop.

I glance up, fork hovering midair. "I am?"

He nods, tapping his glass once before setting it down. "I spent so much time obsessing about her—trying to figure out how to make things work. At the end of the day, it wasn't all it was cracked up to be. But that didn't mean the dream disappeared."

His eyes linger on mine. Soft, worn.

I glance away, bracing against the heaviness rising in my chest. Because I get it.

I know what it feels like to hold on to something so tightly, to shape your whole world around a maybe… only to realize the dream won't love you back.

And somehow, that doesn't stop you from wanting it.

"After she broke my heart for the *umpteenth* time, I was done. I refused to get burned by her again, and I knew I needed to move on." He stops and extends an arm across the table. And against my reservations, I place my hand in his. "And meanwhile, here's this really cool chick, who's *wild* about me—and gorgeous too... And I find myself thinking... *Why not?*"

Why not?

"Why not give it a shot with someone who thinks the sun rises and sets with me... instead of the other way around?" His thumb skims my knuckles as he shrugs, but there's a vulnerability beneath it. "And for the record, I owe you an apology. That shit I said this morning was totally out of pocket. You ain't deserve that."

My eyes fall on our intertwined hands, his thumb still grazing over my skin. The apology softens something in me, though a faint ache lingers. I nod, letting the words stand, but I can't stop wondering what made him go for the jugular like that in the first place. Though, I suppose I can let it go. For now.

His hand steadies me, but the bruise from this morning refuses to fade. For all the hours he spent stretched across my pillow, talking like we were brand new, there are still shadows I can't reach. Last night with his brother made that much clear. There's still so much of his world that's closed off to me. Places where outbursts like this morning are born.

The weight of everything unspoken presses harder than his touch.

"You never told me about the night of the finale," I whisper.

"The finale?" He frowns.

"Of *Lucky Star.* You've never said anything about what went down with your dad."

It hurts, realizing how much of him I still don't know. If he would just open up...

Instead, he trades my hand for his drink without so much as a glance.

"Wasn't all that much to tell," he says, before taking a sip.

The words land flat, hollow in my ears.

"But you've shared it with Indigo, haven't you?"

A long beat passes before he nods, once.

Something clenches in my chest. But before I can compose how to respond, Legend stands, extending a hand.

"Let me show you something."

With the help of a guide, he leads me up the stairs to the 103rd deck. When the door opens, a sharp breath escapes me. The balcony is tiny, suspended over the sprawl of New York. The East and Hudson Rivers extend to a peak in the distance, bordering Central Park. Birds pass on the horizon, dancing through the air. Car horns drift up from below as traffic shuffles between the Lego-like buildings.

Legend's eyes slide shut as he leans into the railing, the cool breeze brushing our faces. I press close, gripping his arm, trying to keep my bearings over the dizzying view.

Clearly, he's done this before.

"My earliest memory," he says, "is sitting on my dad's lap at the age of five, pounding on piano keys, random notes ringing out, my ma giggling at the sound. I swear, I knew back then that it was *exactly* what I wanted to do for the rest of my life... make people smile with my music." He grinds his jaw, then lets it go, eyes fixed on the horizon.

He has no idea how lucky he was to figure things out so early.

He studies the railing, stretching his fingers across the banister. "From that day on, he put me to work. Piano lessons every Tuesday and Thursday. Voice lessons every Monday and Friday. And practice was *non-negotiable*," he says, voice slipping into a fatherly baritone. *"An hour every morning before school. Two more before dinner...'* It wasn't long before he managed to suck every drop of fun out of it."

Thinking about the awards and endless crowds of fans, I ask, "Was it really that bad?"

His sober gaze connects with mine. "The only time I could find joy in any of it was during those performances. Girls screaming their heads off, everybody applauding like I was *the* greatest in the world. It

wasn't long before I was chasing that high. But deep down, I knew...
without my skills, nobody would care... especially him."

I rest my hand on top of his. "Legend, that's not true."

"Then why did he leave us?" He stares at me with a crinkled brow.
And I don't have that answer.

He lets out a heavy breath, looking out at the bustling city below. "You know, I could tell from the moment you set foot in LA,
you couldn't stand it. It's crowded. It's loud. It's *hot*. And everybody's
too busy trying to make a name for themselves to care about anyone
else's shit."

I nod, more to myself than to him.

"I could tell that deep down you *hated* Hollywood, Sam." He looks
at me, his eyes growing sad. "Sometimes, I don't like it either."

"You don't?" *I thought it was all he ever wanted*

He returns his gaze to the horizon, something delicate and unspoken shifting in his expression. "You remember Kristina Gray?"

How could I forget? A gorgeous girl with ice blue eyes and dark
wavy hair. She was one of the top three contestants in *Lucky Star*. She
posed a major threat to Legend and Travis Torres until the week before
the finale.

"Kristina and I had a thing for each other," he says.

It hits me like a slap I didn't see coming. Of all the things I expected him to say, that wasn't one of them.

"We started hooking up around week three. We were still together
when she—" He drops his head, refusing to say more. But I remember... They said she OD'd.

"Everybody thinks she was partying too much, but nobody men-
tions the shit they put us through."

He swallows hard, the motion tight and visible in his throat.

"They had a sex tape on us."

A cold rush shoots through my chest. The words drop like a floor caving in beneath my feet.

"I'm sorry, what?"

He shrugs. "Some people—some really important people—had planted a secret camera, and... they were threatening to leak the whole thing to the public if we didn't do what they said." His mouth turns down, his jaw trembling. "That was the night she—" He stops and drops his head. A tear escapes his eye.

I rub his back, laying my head on his shoulder. I had no idea.

Legend sniffs, brushing the tear away. "The whole thing was rigged, Sam. They wanted her to go home, and she refused to give up after fighting so long." He looks at me with glassy eyes. "She was supposed to be the winner, Sam. Not me."

"Legend..." I throw a hand over my mouth, at a loss for words.

"If I had known it'd come to that, Sam... I would've walked away from all this shit, I swear." More tears escape his lashes. "If it weren't for me, she'd still be alive—"

"Shhhh," I whisper, wrapping my arms around his trunk. "It isn't your fault, Legend. It's not."

"It is, Sam. If only you knew..." His voice breaks as he sinks into me.

And as he sniffles into my shoulder, falling into my embrace, it finally hits me: *Lucky Star* didn't just crown him. It cost him.

25

*T*he city blazes beneath a lavender dusk as our limo slides to a stop in front of the Selene, a soaring glass tower trimmed in gold, its marble steps flanked by paparazzi and velvet ropes.

Just hours ago, I was wrapped in hotel sheets, nursing a headache and secrets.

Now? Heels. Lashes. Lip gloss. Again.

I stifle a yawn as we ease to the curb.

Legend shoots me a sideways grin, adjusting the cuff of his designer blazer. "Please tell me you slept on the plane."

"Not all of us can rest easy forty-five thousand feet off the ground." I rub my neck, squinting my eyes. *The jet lag certainly doesn't help.*

He chuckles, taking me by the hand. "Thanks for sticking by my side. I know it's a lot."

"Hey, it's your birthday weekend." I squeeze his hand, pushing back the drowsiness in my brain. "Wouldn't miss this for the world!"

Speaking of…

I reach below my seat and reveal a small box. "I meant to give this to you sooner but never found the right time."

He accepts the gift with a crooked smile.

I hold my breath, barely able to contain myself as I wait to see his reaction to the stainless steel Movado watch.

But he freezes as he opens it.

"Oh no. You don't like it."

Legend clears his throat as he shuts the box. "No. I love it. Fa' real. It's just... I have this exact same watch at home."

"Of course, you do." My shoulders sag in disappointment.

"But I never wear it." He opens the box, gazing at the watch again. "My dad gave it to me just before I won *Lucky Star*... I had no idea it would turn out to be a parting gift."

Great. Leave it to me to pick out the absolute worst thing I could give the guy.

"After he left, I never bothered putting it on," he says, flashing a crooked smile. "Didn't want the reminder, ya know?"

"Legend, I'm sorry. I'll take it back." I reach for the box, but he holds it out of my grasp.

"Nah. I'll keep it. It'll remind me that time heals all wounds."

I purse my lips, sighing through my nose. "First, I get your brother all twisted up about him, and now you."

"It's not your fault," he says, gingerly slipping on the watch. "Everyone grieves differently, ya know?"

When it came to the loss of my dad, we all had our way of coping: Me with my daily rituals, Mom with her obsession with As Seen on TV products. Even Simone.

The poor thing used to be super shy. But after dad died, she started spouting off at the mouth every chance she got. She's been embarrassing me ever since.

Legend holds up the watch, cracking a genuine smile. "How's it look?"

"A perfect fit."

He kisses me like we've got all the time in the world... No cameras. No crowds. No past to outrun. Just this moment. And for the first time in days, I let myself believe it could be enough.

A quiet smile plays on his lips as he studies my face, stroking my curls in his hand. "You're great, you know that?"

"I try."

A light chuckle rumbles from his chest. "Let's make it official. Tonight," he says softly.

My breath catches, just slightly, as my gaze searches his. *Official?*

"You mean at your party or... something else?" A balmy wave washes over me as I think about how close we came to *sealing the deal* last night. Though... I may have barely remembered if we had.

His eyes dip low, dancing over my plunging violet mermaid gown. He licks his lips, voice husky with promise. "Why not both?"

My cheeks tingle as I bust out laughing. "Yeah... Maybe. Okay."

"*Maybe? Okay?*" He tilts his head, amusement dancing in his eyes. "*This* is how you respond to an offer from Legend Blake?"

The two of us chuckle as Lorenzo opens the door.

Legend jumps out and offers his hand to me. "Let's go knock 'em dead, beautiful."

••••••

The party is being held in an enormous ballroom with a tulle-draped ceiling, plush wall-to-wall carpet, and fancy cocktail tables. A massive seven-tier cake is on display in a corner, and a DJ's mixing on a large stage up front.

The crowd parts, and Victoria glides up with a champagne flute in hand, her embroidered ball gown sashaying behind her. "Legend! Sweetheart!" She kisses him on both cheeks. "I thought you'd *never* get back. Happy Birthday!" Golden light gleams off her proud smile, the kind of smile that says, *This was all me.*

Legend nods, scratching his nose.

"I see you brought your friend," says Victoria, her sugary-sweet gaze zeroing in on me.

Legend and I exchange glances.

"Yeah," he says. "Actually—"

"*Happy birthday, Legend!*" Two girls—one with blond locs and the other with red—rush up kissing all over him.

It's Nalorie and Nataki, a sultry Neo-Soul duo, known for their club mixes and electro-pop songs. Nalorie does most of the singing, while Nataki syncs the beats.

"It's been *forever!*" says Nalorie, shoving him in the shoulder. "How ya been?"

"Good," says Legend, tossing a crooked grin my way. "Really good."

"Hey! You still owe us that yacht trip you promised," says Nataki, batting her lengthy lashes.

He nods. "I know, I know—"

Nalorie jumps back in. "You heard about that new album DJ Khaled's working on, right?"

"Yeah," says Legend. "I'm on a couple tracks."

The girls gasp like twins. "*Fa' real?*"

He nods as the three of them drift toward the crowd.

"We're hoping to get on there too, but our manager's tripping..." says Nataki.

I'm starting to follow when I feel a light hand on my back. My heart stutters as Victoria's tight smile appears in my view.

"Why don't you help yourself to some refreshments, dear?" She nods, gesturing across the room. "The champagne fountain is right this way." She guides me in the opposite direction of Legend, not waiting for my reply.

"You *do* seem familiar," she says, squinting at me. "Have you been working in Hollywood for a while?"

"I, uh…" I glance over my shoulder, but I can't see Legend anymore. Sure, honesty would be the best option, and we did just agree to make things *official.* Legend also said Victoria finding out about us would be much worse than Indigo learning the truth. And I'm not sure that's a reveal I could survive without round-the-clock security. It wouldn't be wise to get ahead of him here. "I've worked with a couple celebrities before. Rihanna, Keke Palmer…"

"Ah!" Her pencil-thin eyebrows rise with interest. "So, you're a stylist?"

"Assistant."

She nods, looking me over. "That makes sense."

Wow. Polite on the surface, but sharp enough to leave a scratch.

We arrive at the massive gold-trim fountain, and I grab a glass of champagne off the table nearby. I start to toss it back, but Victoria's eyeballing me. Recalling my disastrous results from last night, I take a few small sips instead.

"You and Legend have been friends for a while, hmm?" She swirls her champagne with practiced ease, studying me over the rim of her glass.

"Mmhmm." I take another sip. Then one more. "We go a few years back."

"So you're in town to help him out?"

"Mmhmm." I repeat, praying I can keep this up for as long as her little interrogation might last. But suddenly, it occurs to me, *I never told her I was from out of town.*

Just then, a coordinator with a headset rushes over. She whispers something in the manager's ear, and Victoria rolls her eyes.

"You'll have to excuse me," says Victoria, tossing me an apologetic smile. "Enjoy the party!" She disappears just as quickly as she came.

What was that about? Maybe I have a weird accent or something.

I search the crowd, looking for Legend, but I don't see him anywhere around. Great. I cover my mouth as a yawn escapes me. Between the lack of sleep and this trap music, my head is spinning.

Laughter flutters from behind the fountain, pulling my attention. Just over my shoulder, two brunettes bump into the table.

"Shit!" one hisses. "Hurry up before somebody sees!" The other brunette pulls a tiny vial from her clutch and sprinkles white powder onto the back of their hands.

In perfect sync, they each take a sharp sniff.

I jerk my gaze forward and swallow hard. *I better get out of here.*

Weaving through the crowd, I make my way toward the front of the room, scanning for any sign of my date. Gorgeous models and celebrities flank both sides, chatting, laughing, effortlessly at ease.

I don't belong here. None of this is me.

I miss lounging at home, watching dumb movies like *Keanu.*

But Legend hates *Keanu.* He doesn't get its appeal at all.

Fingers wrap around mine, pulling me back to the present. Despite my reservations, relief floods through me at the sight of his handsome face.

"I thought I lost you," he says.

A breathy laugh escapes me. "Same here. This party's wild."

His eyes dance around as he gazes at all the people and golden oversized balloons. "I guess it's *aiight.*" The two of us laugh.

I keep smiling, nodding... but inside I'm screaming. I want to be here. I really do. But this world? I don't know if it was ever meant for me.

Some guy that's a dead ringer for Justin Bieber walks up and he and Legend slap fives. "Happy Birthday, man!" Legend thanks him, and the guy keeps it moving.

"I can't believe you know everyone here," I say, leaning in his ear.

"I don't," he says with a grin… but there's apprehension in his eyes. I've got a feeling he's thinking a lot like me, but for a very different reason.

"Legend, if you're not ready—"

He shakes his head, cutting me off. "I'm good. Fa' real," he says, taking me by the hand. "Let's go introduce you to a few people."

We're just starting to make our way through the crowd when the music dips low, and the DJ leans into the mic. "How y'all feelin' tonight?"

A loud cheer erupts around us.

"Let's take a moment to recognize the man of the evening— *Legend Blake!*"

A spotlight flares, casting a golden glow over him. Legend drops my hand without thinking and steps into the light, a bashful grin spreading across his face. A few guys slap him on the back, hollering birthday wishes as he nods, thanking them all.

I stay a few steps behind, half in shadow.

This is his world. I'm honestly not too sure how much I fit.

"Tonight," says the DJ, his voice booming through the speakers, "we've got a *very* special gift for you, Legend." He raises a tattooed arm and gestures across the stage. "We present to you… the very lovely *Indigo Taylor!*"

No. No, no, no. My heart slams against my ribcage. *What is she doing here?*

The crowd erupts in wild applause as she steps to the center of the stage, draped in a red sequin halter gown that catches every spotlight. Her updo is sleek and elegant, not a strand out of place. She's flawless. Of course, she is.

Legend doesn't move. He stands frozen, lips parted.

She shouldn't be here. This is my moment with Legend. Mine. Not hers.

And just like that, their eyes meet. Locked. Suddenly, it's like no one else exists.

Not even me.

She nods at the DJ. The lights shift.

Then the soft piano chords of her biggest hit, "Your Kiss," float into the air.

She wouldn't.

Not now. Not like this.

Legend blinks once. Then again. Each flutter slower than the last, like he's being pulled under... already slipping into some kind of trance.

> *"Been on my own here for quite a while...*
> *Happy and satisfied.*
> *Then, you come along, with your charming smile*
> *I know that I'm in for a ride..."*

Couples wrap their arms around each other, swaying in time with the beat. The room softens, tilting toward romance.

But Indigo's eyes are fixed on *him*. Every note is for Legend. Every word, a thread pulling him closer. There's this soft gleam in her gaze. Part apology, part promise.

And Legend just... stands there. Motionless. Spellbound. Hands shoved in his pockets, a slow, almost involuntary smile creeping across his lips.

My chest caves in.

Then I see her. Not on stage. Not in the spotlight. But just beyond it. Victoria.

Standing off to the side, her expression as slick as oil. Her eyes lock with mine, and a knowing smirk curls her lips as she raises her glass in some sort of silent toast.

She planned this.

> *"Insecure… falling in your lure,*
> *Though I've never felt quite like this…*
> *But I knew for sure,*
> *The moment I felt your kiss…"*

The floor blurs beneath my feet as the truth settles in—slow, heavy, cruel.

As much as Legend and I have laughed, talked, kissed like there was no one else in the world… it doesn't matter. Not now. Not with *her* here.

Whatever we had, it's over.

The final note fades, and applause breaks out across the room like confetti. Cheers, whistles, claps.

Legend joins in too. Clapping. Smiling. Eyes locked on the woman who just hijacked his party… and perhaps his heart.

With a light, satisfied sigh, Indigo gracefully hops off the platform. She doesn't even scan the room. Just makes a beeline for him, that same confident grin playing at her lips.

I should move. Maybe say something. Do anything but stand here like some starstruck assistant in a clearance-rack gown. But my feet won't budge.

Because deep down, I already know how this ends.

Not with a speech. Not with some grand gesture. But with a quiet unraveling.

A slow fade.

I want to believe he'll turn to me. That he'll remember the late-night texts, the inside jokes, the way we fell asleep in my bed after gazing into one another's eyes like it meant something.

Like *I* meant something.

But right now, in this room full of champagne and celebrities... I've never felt smaller.

Suddenly, phones are buzzing and chiming all over the room.

One by one, people stop recording and glance down at their screens. Conversations hush. A low murmur spreads through the crowd like fog rolling in.

There's a shift in the air... Gasps. Quick glances. Fingers pointing.

People look from their phones to me... then to Legend.

What is going on?

I slip my hand into my purse, my pulse tapping at my temples. My phone lights up with a flood of notifications:

LEGEND'S MYSTERY GIRL REVEALED! PHOTOS INSIDE!

My face is all over *Page Six*... and *Media Take Out*... and *TMZ*. *No... No... No!*

Pictures of me holding Legend's hand. Pictures of him stepping out of my building. Pictures of the two of us kissing in New York!

Oh my god. Oh my god! How did this happen?

The articles detail the scandalous affair Legend Blake's been having with Indigo's personal assistant, Samara Allen. Quite possibly since before they broke up.

My face... *My* name... How the hell do they know my name?

At some point, Legend woke up from his hypnosis and took out his phone too. He stares at the screen long and hard, the blood draining from his face.

Seeming to catch his fallen expression, Indigo halts her approach. She blinks, noticing me for the first time. "Sam? What the hell are you doing here?"

I take a small step back.

Clearly irritated that her big moment's been hijacked, Indigo strides over and grabs Legend's hand, yanking his phone to see for herself.

The second her eyes hit the screen, she stiffens. Her lips part, but no words come out. Just this tight, stunned breath like she's trying not to choke. And then her gaze lifts to me, sharp and furious, blazing with betrayal.

Like *I'm* the villain at the center of all this.

I hold up my hands in surrender. "Indigo, look—"

"Di-di..." Legend steps in front of me. "Don't blame it on her, okay? This was *all* me."

Indigo isn't moved. She steps around him, her eyes laser-focused on me. "I trusted you," she mutters. "I thought you were my fuckin' friend."

"I was." I nod frantically. "I mean, I am!"

Indigo's face twists, nostrils flaring. Jaw clenched so tight her cheekbones could cut glass. Her fists ball at her sides as she glares at me like I've ripped the floor out from under her.

My heart pounds loud enough to drown out the gasps around us. I hold my trembling hands higher, guilt thick in my throat.

I didn't mean for it to go this far. At least, I don't think.

Everyone's frozen, eyes bouncing between us, just waiting for her to pounce.

But instead, Indigo inhales sharply and blinks, taking in the room... the whispers, the flashing lights. Her lips twitch. Not with rage, but heartbreak. Then, without a word, she spins on her heels... and walks out.

I exhale so fast my whole body caves inward. A weight I didn't even realize I was carrying drops hard in my gut.

I honestly can't believe she didn't kill me just now.

Legend stares after her, a quiet ache clouding his eyes.

Great. I've done it. Broken two hearts in one night. And lost someone who, for all her flaws, *was* my friend... maybe even two.

It takes a long beat before Legend seems to remember I'm standing here. Finally, he turns to me, voice low. "You all right?"

I nod. But his gaze has already drifted back to the door.

The DJ fumbles to fill the silence, cueing up the next track and urging the crowd to get back on the dance floor. But no one's really in the mood.

I watch Legend, my mouth parting, a dozen apologies and explanations crowding my throat. But his eyes are fixed on the ground, like it holds answers I'll never understand.

And then my phone chimes.

I don't know why I'm surprised when I see the message.

INDIGO: *You're fired.*

26

I stumble out of the hotel's grand entrance, lungs tight, mind spinning. Neon-lit palm trees sway above the boulevard, casting crooked shadows on the sidewalk. Beneath a canopy of LED strips that pulse like a heartbeat, valets in tailored uniforms slip behind the wheels of Bentleys and Benzes, retrieving them with mechanical grace.

I need air. Real air.

I drift to a concrete bench near the revolving doors and drop onto the cold slab. The chill seeps through my dress, grounding me.

Well, I'm definitely not sleepy anymore.

There's gotta be at least ten different angles of that disaster floating around already. I'm probably a meme by now. And yet, miraculously, the paparazzi haven't swarmed me.

Maybe they're too busy chasing Indigo. Or maybe they're just waiting to catch me ugly-cry in public. I bury my face in my hands.

How the hell did I get here?

Arms folded tight, I stare out across the valet lane. A chauffeur jogs around a glossy black BMW, pulling the door open with polished ease. Out steps a vision. Flawless red hair, legs for days, and a sheer feathered dress that looks like it costs more than my rent. She doesn't glance back as the driver nods and returns to his post. She's already gliding inside, heels clicking with intention, ready to conquer whatever ballroom magic lies beyond those doors.

I wonder what her thing is.

I smile to myself, recalling Denero's words. *"Everybody over there got a thing."*

Rubbing my temples, I sigh through my nose. *Everybody but me.*

Legend barely registered my voice when I told him I was going to step out. He just kept staring at the floor, lost.

"How did they even know?" I asked.

"I have no idea," he said. But then, his gaze slid past me, straight to Victoria. A slow, knowing look.

Whatever was going on between them, I didn't want front-row seats. I backed out before I lost my lunch.

Maybe she'll help him figure things out. Though that smug little smirk she shot my way is still crawling down my spine like a centipede in heels.

A cool breeze slips under the canopy, and I shudder.

I came here to help Legend. To be a friend... Maybe more. But somewhere along the way, I started chasing his attention like it was oxygen. And in the long run, I only made him more miserable.

And Indigo... damn it, I actually like her. She's messy, but she's real. And now? I'm sure she hates my guts.

I close my eyes and pinch the bridge of my nose, willing back the tears.

What the hell am I doing? None of this is me!

"Sam?"

I lift my eyes and see... a ghost. "Justin?"

He's just a few feet away, looking like a man plucked from a *GQ* spread—tailored suit hugging his frame, Italian leather shoes gleaming under the lights. On his arm is a golden-skinned super-model with cheekbones for days and short wavy hair that glints like polished bronze.

"Wow. What are the—" He tucks away a stunned expression, lips twitching in an incredulous grin. Then, turning to the woman, he murmurs, "Why don't you wait in the lobby? I'll be right there."

She smirks—not in his direction, but mine—scanning me from curls to heels before clicking off, her perfume trailing like smoke.

Justin stands back, hands in his pockets, staring like I'm a paint-ing he's not allowed to touch.

"For a second, I thought you were your sister…" His gaze is slow as it travels over me. "But she'd never be caught dead in a dress that gorgeous."

"Thanks." My cheeks burn as I glance down at my low-cut gown. "I'm here for a party, actually…"

Justin steps closer but stops short, as if he's not sure how close he's allowed to get anymore.

"You here with somebody?" His voice is gentle now. Curious, almost hesitant.

I nod faintly, eyes drifting down to the pavement.

I was. At least, I thought I was.

The silence stretches a beat too long.

"How about you?" I ask, glancing up.

"Hmm?"

I nod toward the Halle Berry clone who just stepped inside.

"You here for a date?"

"Nah." He shakes his head, that same bashful grin tugging at his lips… the same one from middle school when he'd ask to borrow a pencil when we both knew he had five. "I mean, yeah, but… I came for a conference and bumped into her. We kinda hit it off, and I figured, I'm single, so why…why not? Ya know?" He lets out a light chuckle, but it fades too quickly. His throat bobs as he swallows the silence.

Single.

The word lands like a punch to the chest.

I try to nod. Smile. But suddenly, it hurts to look at him.

With a brief glance toward the lobby, he swiftly takes a seat at my side.

He still smells like everything I used to love… clean laundry, vanilla cologne, and something new I can't quite place. And he looks incredible. Like he's been doing overtime at the gym, sleeping eight hours a night, hydrating like it's a full-time job.

Meanwhile, I'm out here covered in other women's vomit and broken promises.

"You doing all right?" he asks gently.

"Honestly…" I blink fast, trying to hold back the tears. "I've been better."

Between Indigo's breakdown, Legend's silence, and the way Victoria keeps circling like a vulture, tonight's been a mess. And the one person I want to fall apart with is sitting inches away, smelling like comfort and memories. And I can't even lean on him.

Justin nudges me gently with his elbow, like he has dozens of times before. "Wanna talk about it?"

Goodness. I forgot how easy it can be with him.

"Well, for one…" I say on an exhale. "I just got fired."

"*Fired?*" He pulls back, laughing in disbelief. "You're joking, right? 'Cause ain't no way anybody with a brain is firing Samara Allen."

"Hmm, typically I'd agree with you." I let out a dry, humored breath. "But this time… I think it might be justified."

So I tell him everything—from the night Legend Blake asked me to come to LA, to the scheme we cooked up to get Indigo to hire me, to the half-lies and full-blown manipulation I justified in hopes of winning Legend's heart.

Justin cringes as I complete my tale, reviewing how I've just become a hot tabloid topic.

"Wow," he says, stretching his hands across his knees. "That *is* a jacked-up situation."

"You're telling me."

"Too bad too. 'Cause I seen the way you work with Indigo," he says. "She's gonna miss having you around."

I blink, confused. "What do you mean you've seen the way I work with her?"

"I checked out that video of y'all baking cookies together." He lets out a low chuckle. "The poor thing couldn't add chocolate chips without your help."

"*You* follow Indigo Taylor?"

"No. But I follow Legend Blake. He was promoting the video." *Like that's any better.*

"You follow Legend Blake?"

"Mmhmm." He says it as casually as admitting he likes bananas with his cornflakes in the morning. Like it isn't the least bit strange to follow the man who—while not officially—might as well be sleeping with the woman he once promised forever to.

I gaze in the opposite direction, pressing my lips into a thin line. But Justin nudges me again.

"So," he asks. "What are you gonna do?"

"Honestly?" I shake my head, blinking away tears. "I don't know. I mean, I moved out here, thinking it would be the easiest choice. I wanted to give this whole thing a shot. Instead, I found myself in way over my head. And... It's just not what I thought it would be, ya know?"

Justin rests his elbows on his knees. A small, pensive chuckle slips out. "He's why you turned me down, huh?"

I study his profile, searching for bitterness. But he doesn't look at me. Just stares out at the road, scratching the bridge of his nose.

"Makes sense that you would turn down a boring guy like me when you had this exciting life waiting for you out here."

"Justin, that's not true. You were never the boring one... I was."

He lets out a soft laugh, but it's more breath than sound. Like he doesn't quite believe me.

"Just the same." He shrugs. "I should've known better than to ask you to come out to Silicon Valley, or even to..."

He trails off, a faraway look settling in his eyes.

"Anyway, it was this... feeling. Always sitting deep down in my gut, ya know?"

"*A feeling?*" I tilt my head, genuinely thrown by the softness in his voice.

He nods.

"A feeling that you had to settle for me. Like I was never your first choice."

I wince, placing a hand on his arm. "Justin, I—"

"C'mon, Sam. We both know it's true."

He looks back at me, no anger, just grief. The kind that comes from watching someone you love slip through your fingers without even fighting.

Okay, so maybe I was scared. Not of Justin. But of what it would mean to stay in something good when I didn't feel good enough to hold it. For the longest, I never would've seen it any other way. We shared too much history. I couldn't imagine us apart. As far as I knew, Justin had always loved me, and I couldn't help but... I study the ground with a swallow.

"But I never settled for you, Sam," he says, recapturing my gaze. "To me... you were the prize."

And my chest cracks... because part of me believes him.

I open my mouth to respond, but the words won't come. Because how do you explain leaving something real... for something that might never have been?

A wave of nausea rolls through me as the reality curdles in the pit of my stomach.

What if I walked away from the one thing that actually saw me—flaws and all—for the chance to be someone... I'm not even sure I like?

Before I can work it all out, Justin pats my knee and stands.

"I better get inside."

I watch him go, my eyes tracing the familiar curve of his shoulders, the easy way he moves... like he's already slipping back into a world I'm no longer a part of.

The word tumbles out before I can stop it. "Teddy?"

He pauses, turns, and flashes that crooked, charming smile that used to undo me.

Goodness. It still does.

Seeing him here, like this—in this rock bottom moment—my tongue betrays me again. And I can't speak.

"It was good seeing you, Sam I Am," he says, soft and almost teasing. "Feel free to hit me up sometime. Promise, I won't ghost."

And then, he's gone.

The second the door shuts behind him, I crumble, returning my face to my hands.

Ugh. When did I become this girl?

I used to be steady. Loyal. Thoughtful. Now I'm just... a mess with a heartbreak trail.

I deserve every single thing that's happened to me. And I don't deserve Legend, or Indigo's friendship... I never even deserved Justin.

I deserve to be alone... Old, alone, and boring.

And suddenly, it hits me.

The way Justin was speaking just now, he sounded *exactly* like Legend does when he talks about Indigo. If Justin saw me as his prize... then how could Indigo be anything *less* to Legend?

And after everything Legend's done—every headline, every sacrifice, every bit of pain he's shoved down for the sake of success—How could I stand in the way of that?

How could I be so incredibly selfish?

Without another thought, I dart back into the party, heart pounding as I scan the crowd for Legend.

I need to fix this. Now. It's the only way he'll ever truly be happy.

But he's nowhere in sight.

Instead, I find Lorenzo posted up by the door leading to the lobby, arms crossed like a bouncer with better posture.

I stand on my tiptoes, straining to speak in his ear. "Have you seen Legend?"

He leans back with that usual blank expression, nods once, and says nothing.

"Seriously?" Why is everyone in LA allergic to direct answers? I tiptoe again, louder this time. "Where is he?"

There's a beat. I half expect him to crack a joke, give me the runaround. But instead, Lorenzo scans the crowd, then leans down just enough to be heard over the music.

"Mr. Blake had to step out," he says, his Boston accent low and firm. "Told me to escort you home."

⸱⸱✦✦✦✦⸱⸱

The ride back is quiet. Too quiet.

I sit alone in the back of the limo, the leather seats cold against my skin, the city lights blurring past the tinted windows like ghosts.

I pull out my phone and try calling Legend. It rings. And rings. But he doesn't pick up.

My chest tightens. I shoot him a text instead.

SAM: *Hey, can we talk?*

Minutes pass.

Nothing.

I throw my head back against the seat and squeeze my eyes shut, willing the tears to stay put.

Ugh! Why was I so incredibly stupid? I wasn't trying to hurt anyone. I was just... trying to keep up.

Mom had Trey. Professor Natalie got back with Paul. Even Simone seemed to be pulling her life together. And Justin was moving forward, becoming this... version of himself I couldn't recognize.

And I felt stuck. Still the same girl. Still waiting for the future to start.

I thought if I didn't do something—if I didn't *leap*—I'd get left behind. By him. By everyone.

So I reached for the one thing that didn't remind me of who I used to be: Legend.

Because staying meant standing still. And I was so afraid that if I didn't find myself *soon*, I'd disappear altogether. But in trying to become someone else, I might've destroyed everything that ever made me... real.

Now, I might lose Legend too. The one person I gave it all up for.

This entire situation is a dumpster fire. Where's Olivia Pope when you need her?

And that's when it hits me. I fumble with my phone and dial Kelly's number.

She answers with a smile in her voice. "Let me guess, you need a crisis manager who will clean this mess up?"

"Very funny," I say dryly. "But I *do* need your help."

"Okay. Shoot."

"Do you have any clue where Indigo might be headed? I need to talk to her."

"Hmmm." Kelly clicks her teeth. "Are you sure that's a good idea? 'Cause honey, I saw the videos. It's a miracle you were within six feet of that girl and lived to talk about it."

"I know, I know. But I've gotta make this right."

Kelly lets out a slow, measured sigh. I'm just praying she'll take pity on me.

"Look," she finally says, lowering her voice. "Don't tell anyone, but after she started passing out in clubs, I had to keep a closer eye on her. I've been tracking the girl's phone for years."

Relief floods my chest as she taps the screen.

"She should be... at home," Kelly confirms.

My eyes slide shut, a wave of tension finally loosening in my spine.

"Thank you, Kelly."

"Mmhmm. And next time you wanna hook up with a hot celebrity, maybe double-check he's not dating your boss, mmkay?"

I thank her again and hang up.

"Hey, Lorenzo?"

"Yes, ma'am?" He glances at me in the rearview mirror. All casual, like he hasn't been eavesdropping this entire time.

"Could you swing by Indigo Taylor's? I need to speak with her."

Technically, I'm the one calling the shots here. But the way he pauses and eyes me again in the mirror, makes it clear he's not sold.

"I was assigned to take you home, ma'am."

My stomach twists, but I square my shoulders anyway.

"And you will," I say, steadying my voice. "Right after a quick detour."

He doesn't respond.

But I have to do this… even if I'm scared.

I lean forward with a hopeful smile. "Please?"

27

I hop back into the limo with a frustrated huff.

Lorenzo shuts the door, slides into the driver's seat, and checks me in the rearview.

He says nothing.

"Obviously, Kelly's GPS is out of date," I mutter, buckling in.

There isn't a single light on at Indigo's place. Not one. Guess Eva has the night off.

I sigh through my nose, my fingers twitching in my lap. The silence feels like a dare.

Where the hell could she be?

Lorenzo starts the car, and I rub my chin, staring out the tinted window as we pull away.

At night the estate looks different. Less glamorous, more haunted. The towering sycamores cast long shadows across the stark white concrete walls, turning the house into a cold, modern shell. Art deco, sure. But right now, it feels like a mausoleum.

I didn't come this far to give up now. I square my shoulders and pull out my phone, then dial Cam on speaker.

"What's up, Sam?" he says, picking up on the first ring.

"Not much— Actually, a whole lot. Were you at the party? I didn't see you there."

"Uh… I was around. Just a little preoccupied, if you know what I'm sayin'."

With a lady friend, I'm sure.

"Look, I'm trying to hunt down Legend or Indigo. Have you heard from either of them?"

"Nah. I heard there was some sort of blow-up at the party, and both of them took off."

If he hasn't heard the details of the "blow-up" by now, Cam is the last person who could help me.

"Thanks anyway."

"Hey," he says, before I can hang up. "If you could get a hold of Lorenzo, he could probably help track down Legend. He always knows where the brotha's at."

"Really?"

Lorenzo's dark eyes meet mine as I hang up and cross my arms.

"Okay, Lorenzo. Tell me where he is."

He scratches his coarse beard, focusing on the road.

"Oh, come on, Lorenzo!" I'm whining now. "I really need to find him! I've gotta fix this!"

He pulls up to a red light, jaw tight, his grip on the wheel just shy of annoyed. He doesn't look at me this time. Just stares straight ahead like he's trying to decide whether I'm worth the headache.

I rack my brain, searching for the right mix of desperate and charming. What's it gonna take?

Tears? Bribery? A heartfelt playlist?

"I was supposed to have the rest of the night off," he mutters, softly shaking his head as he stares at the traffic light.

"Right… I totally understand."

Now don't mess this up, Sam. One wrong word and he's back to his strong, silent era.

"It's just this one thing. Please!" The light turns green as I clasp my hands, staring at him with pleading eyes.

Not much later, we're winding up the hill to Legend's place.

Even at night, the mansion looms over LA like a monument to ego and excess. Sleek lines, mirrored panels, and glowing accent lights that make it look more like a luxury spa than someone's actual home.

Perched this high above the city, it doesn't need gates or guards. Privacy comes built in.

I half expect paparazzi to pop out of the hedges as we pull up, but the place is dead quiet.

"Look," Lorenzo says, glancing back at me. "I'm not gonna hang around when the boss told me to get lost."

"I completely understand. I'll get home on my own." I gather my things, already halfway out the door. "Thanks, Lorenzo. You're amazing!"

He takes off the second I'm out, tires barely whispering against the concrete.

I charge up the walkway, eyes fixed on the massive front entrance. The exterior lights are on, but behind the glass? The house is mostly dark.

Maybe he came back to clear his head. Or stare at the ceiling in one of those moody man-thought spirals.

I take a breath and press the buzzer. A lengthy beat passes, but there's no answer.

Come on... Come on! He's gotta be home. I promised to help Legend, and I will, if it's the last thing I do.

I'm just weighing my options of giving up or trying again when the door buzzes open. I rush inside. But I'm met with a blanket of darkness. The first floor living room and breakfast area are silent and dormant, the table and bar seemingly untouched from our weekend away.

Where is he?

"Legend?" My echo bounces back to me. But then I hear his voice, faintly crooning downstairs.

> *"How about you and me?*
> *Can you think of us together..."*

He must be in the studio. I hurry down the stairs, lifting my dress just enough to keep from face-planting. Glancing around the studio, I call out over the music.

Of course he's in here. This is where he always comes to clear his head. To work through... whatever he can't say out loud.

The booth door is cracked. I move toward it and step inside.

"Legend?"

A muffled grunt comes from the corner.

I whip around to find him tied up... bound and helpless on the floor.

Wrists behind his back. Ankles strapped. And tape stretched tight across his mouth.

Like someone hunted him. Like he's prey.

"What the—?"

A hand clamps across my mouth from behind. Darkness swallows my scream!

And I...

Everything's fuzzy when I wake. There's throbbing in my wrists. My ankles burn. I try to move, but my limbs are stiff…tight. I'm lying on something soft but unforgiving.

The studio floor?

My vision starts to clear… and there he is. Legend. Hands tied behind his back, head bowed like it's too heavy to lift. His ankles bound. Just like mine.

So it wasn't a dream?

"Legend?" My voice scrapes out, dry and raw. "Legend, what's happening?"

His head lifts fast, eyes locking onto mine. There's panic there. But also something softer. Relief. Like me waking up is the only good thing that's happened in hours.

He grunts behind the tape and starts inching toward me with everything he's got. I sit up straighter, heart hammering.

"Legend, what happened?" I whisper. "Who did this to us?"

His eyes hold so much regret it nearly knocks the breath out of me. He leans his forehead gently against mine, and lets out a low, pained sound. Like an apology he can't say out loud.

Slowly, he shakes his head, as if to say *I'm sorry. I didn't see this coming.*

I stare back, my pulse thundering in my ears, trying to piece it together.

What is this? Is someone robbing the place? Does Legend owe someone money?

The music has stopped, and voices are debating in the hall, low and tense.

"I was prepared to get rid of one, ma'am," says a deep, measured voice. "But I might need reinforcements for two."

Get rid of one? My stomach flips as I glance back at Legend.

He's still shaking his head, slow and heavy, eyes glassy, jaw tight. No words. Just guilt. And warning.

Oh dear God. What did I walk into?

"I don't care what you have to do," says another voice—low, commanding... and unmistakable. "This stays between us. And you know the consequences if it doesn't."

Victoria.

A second later, the sharp *click-clack* of stilettos echoes down the hall. She steps into the studio like she owns it, because of course she does. A tall man in black follows behind her, silent as a shadow.

"Ah, look who decided to rejoin us." Her voice is all sugar and venom, a delighted smirk tugging at her glossed lips. She folds her arms across her gown... a 9mm in her hand.

"Victoria, what the hell?!" I scramble back, pressing instinctively against Legend's side.

"Aw, Legend." Victoria lets out a low, sinister chuckle. "Didn't you tell your little girl what this life was all about? The poor thing looks terrified."

Legend casts a glance my way, brief but loaded. He returns his gaze to the floor, refusing to respond.

"That's my boy," Victoria says with a grin. "Always selling the dream."

I look between them, my pulse hammering in my ears. Then my eyes dart to the tall man behind her—the way he stands too still, like he's waiting for an order.

What is she going to do? Is this about the party? About Indigo?

"I don't understand," I whisper. "What's going on?"

"Well," Victoria says, positively gleeful, "what we have here is a breach of contract... and an unfortunate lapse in judgment."

She strolls forward like she's presenting a runway show, gun still loose in her grip.

"Legend seems to have forgotten what happens when he tries to get clever."

He grunts behind the tape, jerking his chin toward her—angry, but helpless.

That's when I notice it.

There's blood. A slow trickle trailing from the back of his head, matting into his curls.

I choke on a breath, panic tightening in my chest.

"What he's trying to say is..." Victoria rolls her eyes like she's already bored with the conversation. "He made the foolish mistake of trying to walk away from his owners. And now, he'll have to pay the price."

"*Owners?*" I glance at Legend, but he won't look at me. "Victoria, surely there's another way—"

"Uh-uh." She lifts a single finger, slicing the air like a blade. "You've already served your purpose, fangirl."

I blink between her and Legend, my throat suddenly bone-dry.

Served my purpose?

Her heels sink into the carpet with each slow, deliberate step, quiet, but somehow more threatening for it... too graceful for how dangerous she looks.

"You really thought he could sneak his little cyber girlfriend out here and I wouldn't find out?"

My stomach twists. How long has she been watching us?

"It wasn't like that, ma'am," I manage. "We were just friends."

"Sure you were." Victoria paces in front of us, her ball gown swishing at her heels as she taps the side of the gun against her elbow. "I tried to let it go. Thought maybe it would do him some good. Help him get over that *pathetic* little obsession with Miss Indigo Taylor."

I glance at Legend again, but he won't look at me. His head stays down like he's taking every word, every insult, and just... absorbing it. As if he deserves it.

And for the first time... I see it. It's not just his fame she's feeding off of... It's his *heart*. The very thing that made me fall for him is what made him a target.

Victoria continues pacing, her scarlet lips pursed.

"But the more time he spent with *you,* the less he picked up *my* calls," Victoria says, pacing with venomous grace. "He started talking back, making demands. Insisting on *doing his own thing.*"

She stops, twirling the gun lazily at her side.

"And tonight? He chose the birthday party *I* threw him—the one *I* planned, paid for, and packed with press—to announce he was *quitting.*" She lets out a cold laugh. "You know what they say about biting the hand that feeds."

My brain stalls, like it missed a step.

Legend finally decided to walk away? It's no wonder she's so upset.

Victoria's not just mad. She's *humiliated.*

Legend's told me that she can be controlling. But this? This is punishment.

She stares down at Legend like she's trying to decide which limb to shoot off first.

Legend groans through the tape, shaking his head like he's trying to wake up from this nightmare. His body jerks as he struggles against the bindings, but he can't do much more than thrash in place.

Victoria sighs restlessly and flicks her hand toward the looming man behind her.

"Let him talk."

The guard steps forward and grabs the edge of the tape, yanking it off in one quick, brutal motion. Legend winces with a pained grunt, his lips parting in a sharp gasp as he catches his breath. Then his eyes, wild and desperate, lock onto mine.

"Sam," he breathes. "I'm sorry. I never meant to drag you into this—"

"Save it," Victoria snaps. She tilts her head, smirking. "The least you could do is be honest with her in your final moments."

My heart stops.

"Final moments?" I look from her to Legend in a panic. "What does she—what does she mean, *final moments?*"

Legend lowers his gaze, and his throat moves, slow and tight.

One shallow breath. Then another. Like he's counting them.

"Oh, yeah." Victoria chuckles to herself. "You wanna tell her what happened to the last chick you tried to hide from me? Hmm?"

"Look," Legend mutters, voice low. "She knows about Kristina, all right?"

"Oh, I *highly* doubt that, sweetheart." Victoria flashes him a smile, sharp and gleaming.

But... he *did* tell me about her. Didn't he?

Legend's eyes flick nervously from her to me and back again, like he's waiting for someone to yank the floor out from under him.

"You see..." Victoria slides the piano bench across the floor, the legs dragging with a soft *thud* against the carpet. She sits down wide-legged, gun still aimed casually in our direction. "What most people don't know is that Legend had a chance to save poor little Kristina's life."

She leans forward slightly, a devious smirk on her lips.

"And he didn't take it."

I look at Legend, searching. But he keeps his eyes fixed on the floor, like even meeting my gaze would cost too much.

"Victoria, it's bad enough as it is," he mutters. "Can you please just—?"

"Legend!" She stares at him in feigned disbelief. "If you care about your friend as much as you say you do in *all* your little DMs, the least you could do is let her hear the truth."

My mind spins. *What truth?* What has he kept from me? And what exactly is she planning to do with it?

I stare at the two of them, pulse pounding, watching the way she lounges on the piano bench, like a predator perfectly content to wait while her prey bleeds out.

"You see, Sam—can I call you Sam?" Victoria nods before I can answer, a smile curling at the corner of her mouth. "On the night of Kristina Gray's death, Legend was right there in the hotel room—"

"And so were you," Legend snaps, his voice low and sharp. His eyes finally lift, pinning her with a glare. Hard. Unflinching.

"Sure," she says, lifting a careless shoulder. "All she had to do was pack her bags and go home like she was told. But Kristina got bold. Started talking about 'justice and integrity.' Like this was some *noble cause* instead of a business deal. She threatened to blow the whole thing wide open. And, obviously, we couldn't let that happen."

What is she *talking* about? Kristina OD'd... didn't she?

"Legend..." she chides, her full lips curled in a disapproving pout. "I thought you told her."

But his gaze returns to the floor, like the truth might crush him if he lifts his eyes.

"Oh, this is *rich!*" Victoria throws her head back in a howl.

I flinch as she claps the gun between her hands. As if I'm in on the joke, she tosses me a grin.

"Honey, let me tell you, that poor little thing couldn't have been more than a buck-fifteen. She stands up, asking Legend to come with her, and together they'll make their grand declaration—expose the *dark side* of my life's work. Do the right thing." She leans forward slightly, as if sharing a juicy piece of gossip. "And for a split second? He *hesitated.*"

No. I blink at Legend, waiting for him to say it's not true.

But his eyes stay glued to his feet. Still. Silent.

"That's right," Victoria purrs. "Left homegirl hanging. 'Cause at the end of the day, Legend Blake only puts one person first... and that's *Legend Blake*." She bursts into laughter as his jaw tightens.

"You didn't have to kill her," he growls through clenched teeth.

"What else was I supposed to do?" she says, like she's recapping an inconvenient business deal. "Let her destroy my empire?"

My stomach flips.

It's as if Kristina's life was just... collateral damage. A minor glitch in her flawless career. And Kristina was *somebody*. Just days away from breakout fame.

If Victoria could erase *her* that easily... How much less would she care about a nobody assistant from Seattle?

Victoria sucks her teeth and waves a dismissive hand.

"Legend, don't be so dramatic. She needed to be silenced, so... that's what we did. It wasn't supposed to be *permanent*." She pouts with seemingly innocent eyes.

"That's bull," Legend snaps, nostrils flaring. "The way that guard grabbed her? Y'all *never* intended for her to walk out of that room alive!"

"*Puh-tay-to, puh-tah-to*," Victoria sings. "She should've known better than to cross Victoria Austin... And so should you."

She raises the gun, steady and deliberate.

"Wait a minute! Wait—no, no, no!" I lurch forward, panic slicing through my chest.

"Oh please," she sneers, flipping her curls. "Another pocket-sized rebel with a savior complex? Legend, if you wanted a lapdog, you could've bought one."

"I'm sorry, Sam," Legend says, eyes locking on mine like he needs me to believe it. "You were never supposed to get dragged into this."

Victoria snorts. "So much for that."

"You blackmailed me," he spits, glaring at her with fire in his eyes. "You *knew* I wanted out. You threatened to pin everything on me if I didn't sign your *damn* contract. You been running me into the ground ever since!"

I dig my fingers into the carpet, knuckles tight and trembling. I thought I knew everything there was to know about him... But I was so very wrong.

"Well, like I said before," Victoria says, too calm for someone with a gun in her hand, "you want out? That can be arranged. But maybe I'll start with your little friend. We can't have any witnesses, after all."

She swings the gun my way, and the whole world narrows to a black circle I can't escape.

"*No!*" Legend screams.

I squeeze my eyes shut, bracing for the pain, for the end, for... whatever comes next.

Buzz.

The intercom crackles to life.

"Damn it!" Victoria hisses, stomping her heel into the carpet as she glares toward the door. "Who is it this time?"

The guard exits the booth and checks the security monitor. "It's Indigo," he says.

Her voice slices through the static: "Legend... Legend, I know you're in there!"

Relief and dread collide in my chest. Of all the times for Indigo to humble herself enough for a heart-to-heart...

Legend's eyes slide shut. He drops his head against the wall behind him like he's silently praying she'll leave.

Victoria stands, clicking her tongue. "What kind of spell do you have these girls under, Legend? Even after my entire exposé on your little love affair, Little Miss Thirsty is still at your door?"

"So it was you?" I whisper, resentment tightening in my throat.

Victoria rolls her eyes. "Keep up, honey."

"What do you want me to do, boss?" asks the guard.

No. Not Indigo too. Fear spikes through my chest.

Victoria grins slowly, wicked and amused.

"Let her in," she says, eyes never leaving mine. "Three's company, too."

28

*B*y the time Indigo starts down the stairs, Victoria has already slapped duct tape over our mouths. Legend and I exchange anxious glances as Indigo's heels echo faintly up the hall.

Victoria's guard looks to her for direction.

"Take her down," she says.

Legend groans, yanking hard at the restraints. My pulse quickens. Indigo has no idea what she's walking into.

The guard draws a Glock from inside his blazer and moves toward the door like a shadow. Both Legend and I struggle to get free, muffled protests humming from both of us.

With a sinister smile, Victoria presses a finger to her lips.

My ears strain for Indigo's voice. Maybe she'll turn back. Maybe she'll sense something's wrong. *Please, God…*

"Legend?" Indigo calls. "Are you in the studio?"

There's a gasp, a shuffling of feet. The guard grunts. Then a scream—Indigo's—cut short by a sickening *thump*.

POW!!!

Legend and I jolt in place.

We scream through the tape, thrashing like wild animals, but our cries are useless. There's still movement outside. A crash. Wood splinters. A dull thud against the wall. Another body hitting the floor.

Victoria lifts her gun and creeps toward the hallway... Then, like a roach at the first flick of light, she whips around and darts back inside the booth, pressing herself behind the door.

I look to Legend for answers, but he shrugs, seeming just as lost as me.

We freeze as the footsteps draw closer... slower... deliberate.

Then Indigo steps into view: sweats, sneakers, a broken cue stick gripped in one hand like it's an accessory. Legend and I both exhale, shoulders sagging. She's alive.

But Victoria's behind the door.

At the exact same moment, Legend and I start hollering through the tape, frantically shaking our heads.

Indigo narrows her eyes, taking in the situation as Victoria slinks out from behind the booth door, gun raised.

Before she can aim, Indigo spins, grabs her wrist, and twists, disarming her in one practiced snap. The gun clatters across the floor, landing just inches from my feet.

Legend and I exchange glances. I shuffle forward, trying to grab it with my toes, but Victoria lunges toward me. I curl into a ball, bracing for pain. But it never comes. Only the sound of a guttural gag. Victoria flails as Indigo wrenches her back, cue stick tight across her windpipe.

Legend juts his chin toward the gun at my feet, encouraging me to try again.

Stretching my legs, I scoot forward. One kick. Then another. The pistol slides out of reach... but also away from Victoria.

Victoria cries out as Indigo whacks her in the shoulder, causing her to stumble back. Indigo grabs the other end of the stick, trapping

Victoria in a headlock. In one swift move, she flips the woman flat on her back, smashing the piano bench into pieces.

Oh my.

Victoria groans, sprawled in a mess of limbs and splintered wood.

Indigo stands tall, her curls wild, her breath steady. She drops the cue stick and blows a strand of hair from her face.

"You two good?" she asks, voice cool as ever.

Legend and I stare at her in stunned dismay, but she shrugs.

"All the creeps in this town? A girl's gotta stay ready."

———— ✦✦✦✦✦ ————

In no time, Indigo frees us. We get Victoria and her unconscious guard tied up, wrists bound with speaker cables and a shoelace Legend found behind the amp stack. Legend locks them in the studio while I slip into the billiard room to call the police.

When I return, Indigo and Legend are in the hall, wrapped in a long, uneasy silence. She stands with her arms crossed, staring back at the studio. He rubs his palms against his dress pants like he's trying to scrub off what just happened. They both look rattled. And honestly, I don't blame them.

Still, I feel like I've just walked in on a conversation that wasn't meant for me. I swallow as I approach.

"The cops are on their way," I say, voice soft.

They nod. Nothing more.

For a second, the three of us just stand in place, quietly studying one another—none of us quite sure where to begin. Indigo is the first to break.

"Sorry about the drywall," she says, pointing to the gaping hole in the hallway. "He came at me with that gun. I'm lucky it wasn't my face."

"It's cool," Legend mutters, like she just told him she spilled a drink on the carpet. He gnaws his lip, then adds more quietly, "Thanks. For real."

Indigo's expression shifts, lips twitching at the edges. With the roll of her eyes, she waves a hand. "Please. Tuesday in LA."

It's painfully obvious what's going on between them. Based on the goo-goo eyes they're exchanging, you'd never guess the tabloids just tried to cremate what's left of their relationship.

It's like he's seeing her the way he did the night they met... draped in silk, eyes full of stars, daring anyone not to fall in love with her.

I swear, a full minute passes before they remember I'm still standing here.

"Um, it is a *pretty* big deal, actually," I say, voice lighter than I feel. "You saved our lives."

They both turn to me with sober eyes.

Got it. "Look, I owe both of you an—"

"Sam, don't," says Indigo, clearly over it. "It is what it is."

"And what is it, exactly?" asks Legend, his unapologetic gaze locked squarely on her.

Indigo meets his stare and swallows, her arms crossing tighter.

Meanwhile, I stand between them like the world's most awkward party crasher.

But the thing is... I *want* him to be happy. I really do. He deserves that.

And so does she.

So finally, I take a step back. "I should probably wait upstairs—"

But Legend grabs my hand as I turn.

"Sam, wait. Don't go."

I look back, and his eyes meet mine, wide and hesitant, like a kid afraid to let go of his mom's hand on the first day of kindergarten.

Indigo watches us, her gaze fixed on where his fingers wrap around mine. She silently rubs her arm as if trying to console herself. I've never seen her look so... helpless.

"Legend," I say, voice tight with tears I refuse to let fall, "you asked me to do you a favor, and that's what I came to do. I never meant to get in the—okay, maybe I *did*. But it was wrong. You were happy, and I—"

"Messed it up?" he finishes for me.

I glance between them, heart climbing.

"That night at the club... you knew she'd be there. You *wanted* me to catch her with that producer." Legend lifts a shoulder, eyes lowered. "Took me a second, but yeah... I figured it out."

So Legend knew. And still wanted to be with me?

My throat dries as I shift to Indigo. She's not glaring. Not pacing. Just... wounded.

I hear her voice from the party again, sharp and bitter: *"I thought you were my fuckin' friend."*

Friends don't do what I've done. Enemies do.

"Indigo, I'm sor—"

She holds up a hand, gentler this time. "It's cool. If I hadn't been wilin', there wouldn't have been anything to catch."

But there's so much more I need to say.

"Sam..." Legend's voice is quiet. Frayed. His eyes don't leave mine—remorseful, unsure, like he's clinging to something slipping fast. "You make me happy too."

I hold his gaze, searching, then look back to Indigo. "I'll never make you happy the way she can."

He and Indigo lock eyes. Something passes between them—old, unresolved. He looks down.

"L..." I reach for his cheek, brushing it gently. "This time with you? It's been a dream. Well, except for the part in New York. That was kind of a nightmare."

He huffs a laugh, eyes glassy. It warms me more than it should, knowing I can still make him laugh like that.

"But she's your dream," I say, glancing at the platinum-haired goddess I'll never be. "And if you two can make it work, you *should.*"

He hasn't let go of my hand, so I squeeze his lightly. Just once.

"I'm the safe choice… but she's the right one."

Their eyes meet—hesitant, but full of hope.

I slip from his grasp and step back. "The two of you should talk."

I turn and head for the stairs, my heart aching with every step. But deep down, I know, this is what I have to do.

"Look, I get it," says Indigo, as I make my way up the stairs. "I screwed up. Royally. But I never meant to hurt you, Legend. I was just so—"

Thankfully, he shushes her.

"We've got a lot of catching up to do," he says softly.

A beat passes, and she sniffles.

"Will you forgive me?" she asks, her voice cracking with emotion.

"As long as you forgive me," he murmurs.

Despite the knot in my chest, I glance back one last time, only to find them gazing at one another's lips.

I turn away and give them their moment. Because sometimes the bravest thing you can do is let go. And I think, maybe—just maybe—we're all right where we're meant to be.

<hr>

A few days later, I call my mom.

To my surprise, Trey picks up the phone. "Sam! How's it going?"

"Hey, Trey." I exhale through my nose, steadying myself. "Is my mom around?"

"Yeah, I'll grab—"

"Actually," I cut in gently, "I wanted to talk to you." I swallow, surprised by my own words as they leave my mouth. But I know why I'm calling.

A few seconds pass. "Okay. Sure. What's up?"

I take a deep breath, pressing my eyes shut for a beat.

"I just wanted to say... thank you. For everything you've done for my mom. For all of us, really. It hasn't always been easy having someone step in and take my dad's place. But if it had to be anyone... I'm glad it was you."

The line goes quiet.

For a moment, I wonder if the call dropped, but then I hear him breathe. Soft. Measured. Almost stunned.

"Thanks, Sam," he says, his voice thick. "It means a lot to hear you say that."

A smile slips across my face as I twist a curl around my finger, Indigo style.

"And if the offer still stands, I'd love to go to a baseball game with you sometime."

He chuckles. "I'd love that, Sam."

With a quiet "hold on," he hands the phone to my mom.

"Sam, you will not believe what I found!"

I gaze at the ceiling, a grin tugging at my lips. "Let me guess. The Squatty Potty?"

"How'd you know?" She gasps, genuinely surprised. "It was in Tatiana's room, under the bed. Can you believe that? I don't even know how I—"

"Me either, Mom." I laugh softly, a wistful ache blooming in my chest. "But I'm glad you found it."

Goodness, I've missed them. Trey with his techie tangents. The girls screaming over spilled cereal and TikTok dances. And Mom never quite being able to get her head on straight in the mess of it all... at least not until it really matters.

She lets out a happy sigh on the other end. I can picture her now, flopping into the kitchen chair like she just ran a marathon.

"So, how are things in LA?"

"Good... Actually, I'm heading back soon."

"Really?" Her tone shifts, a flicker of concern rising. "Is everything okay? I thought things were going well with Indigo Taylor."

Since Daddy passed, she's never been one to keep up with the news. Definitely not entertainment news.

"Yeah, but... it wasn't the right fit for me. I think I'll apply to a few different places closer to home. Maybe try PR or marketing." A small smile touches my lips. "Who knows? Maybe I'll finally give broadcast journalism a shot."

"*Now* you're sounding like your sister." Mom chuckles. "Have you talked to her lately?"

"Last I heard, she's moving in with Kyle. Got a steady role as a stunt double on some crime drama."

"Hmmph." Mom exhales. "I guess we all need a little change sometimes."

I breathe in deep, letting it settle. This strange, soft feeling of finally letting go.

"Yeah, Mom. I think you're right."

An announcer calls over the PA system.

"Hey, I gotta go," I say. "But before I do, I just want you to know... I get it."

She's distracted, probably picking up after one of the girls. It takes her a moment to respond. "You get what, honey?"

"I get why you married Trey," I say slowly. "Why you started over."

I don't know why I feel the need to say it. Maybe because I finally understand what it's like to love someone... and still choose yourself.

FALLIN' FOR THE FAME

"You think I started over?" she says softly.

"In a way, yeah. And I used to resent you for that. But now I see it... you were just trying to find joy again. And I don't blame you."

Another beat passes before an astounded breath escapes her.

"Thanks, honey." Her voice cracks a little. "That means the world to me."

Another call from the PA system echoes overhead. I glance toward my gate.

"I'll see you in a couple days, okay?"

"Wait. Sam, where are you? It sounds like you're in an airport."

"Yep."

"But honey," she lowers her voice, as if she's in on some conspiracy, "you hate flying."

"I know, Mom. I know. I'll be home after a short detour."

I end the call and head for the terminal.

The gate agent lifts the mic as I approach: "Now boarding all passengers for flight seven-forty-nine, destination: Silicon Valley."

29

"**O**h, come on!" I shout at the guards. "I'm in love! Haven't you ever been in love?"

Each of the guards maintains his stance outside the headquarters' entrance, not budging an inch. People stroll by with their MacBooks and Apple thermoses, shaking their heads at the latest sideshow on display. It's me. I'm the sideshow.

"*Please?*" I sag my shoulders and pout. "I have to see him now! Otherwise, my whole grand gesture will be a bust. You don't wanna ruin that, do you? *Do you?!*"

The tallest guard, a Hispanic guy with a buzz cut, breathes a heavy sigh, connecting eyes with me.

"Ma'am, as we said before, no visitors are allowed at headquarters without a pass. Now, if you'd like to wait at the Visitor Center—"

"I don't want to wait at the stupid Visitor Center! I came to *surprise* him!"

"That's not gonna happen, ma'am."

I blow the curls out of my face with a hot breath and turn away like I'm done.

But the second they relax I pivot and take off running! They catch me by the elbows before I take three steps. "Ugh! Let me go! This is ridiculous!"

———————— ✦✦✦✦✦ ————————

They're still holding me hostage in the lobby when Justin comes out. He blinks a few times as he strolls down the stairs. "Sam?"

"Justin!" I breathe a sigh of relief. "You wouldn't believe what I've been through. I trekked across campus, stole a bike. Justin, I nearly got taken out by *three* joggers."

He presses his hands into his pockets, looking over the two giant men holding my arms. "They said some crazy chick was out here try-ing to get in, but..." He chuckles, flashing that charming smile of his.

My heart pounds in my chest. *If only I could get to him.*

"Justin, will you please tell these two men they're being ridiculous and that I wouldn't steal a thing. I don't even like Apple products—" the men stare at me—"all that much, I mean."

Justin bows his head, scratching his nose. He points to some benches outside. "Let me talk to her out there, fellas."

By some miracle, they let me go.

"Stupid guards..." I rub my arms as we walk. "Messing up all my plans..."

"Sam," Justin stops to face me, eyes steady, voice soft, "what are you doing at my job?"

The question lands harder than I expect. My throat tightens, and I blink fast, trying to hold it together... but the tears push through anyway.

"Justin... I made a mistake. A really stupid mistake. After I saw you at the hotel, it was all clear, and I wanted to make things right.

But then everything went crazy, and I nearly got shot, and if it hadn't been for Indigo—"

"Wait, wait…" Justin lifts a finger. "You almost got shot?"

"Listen, I know it sounds wild, but I went to LA because I was scared. I was scared of marriage, and a career, and… babies, I guess. So I ran off to Hollywood and tried something outrageous. Something both of us know I would *never* have tried in my right mind."

He bobs his head, eyes fixed on the sidewalk like it's safer than looking at me.

"But I don't want that life, Justin. I don't want that life at all. I wanna be boring, and ordinary, and… I wanna watch *Keanu* with someone who actually laughs at the same dumb parts I do."

He finally looks up. And the way he gazes at me, quiet and bruised, nearly unravels me.

"Justin, I know it must've hurt like crazy when I revealed my secret friendship with Legend—"

"Yeah," he says. "Learning that the woman you love has actually been talking to some other dude she's been fantasizing about for *years?* Not exactly a walk in the park." His jaw tightens as he looks at me—disappointed, guarded, like he's trying not to bleed all over the pavement.

And I get it now.

That gutted, left out feeling? That aching question of *why wasn't I enough?* I lived it… chasing something that was never meant for me.

But Justin was. And I still hurt him.

After everything we shared… after everything he gave me… I know exactly how deep this must've cut.

I drop my gaze, too ashamed to meet his.

"I see your point. But—Teddy, you've gotta believe me. He may have been the man of my dreams… but you're the love of my life."

I shake my head, tears slipping down my cheeks. "And I couldn't go another day without flying out here, and letting you know—"

"Wait a minute." He raises his hand again. "You *flew*? On your own?"

I nod. "But it'd be a whole lot better flying with you."

For a second, I'm terrified he won't forgive me. That maybe I broke us beyond repair.

He just stares, like he's seeing me for the first time... and remembering everything we were.

Then, without a word, he takes my hand, pulls me in, and kisses me. Slow. Sweet. Certain.

Like forgiveness. Like home.

Every ounce of fear dissolves into the warmth of him. Goodness, I've missed this. I've missed *him*. The way his lips fit against mine. The way his presence quiets the noise in my chest.

I blink up at him, tears clinging to my lashes. "Do you still want me?"

He smiles. "You're all I've ever wanted, Sam I Am."

He kisses me again, and just like that, the chaos fades. The fear. The shame. The ache. It all dissolves into the warmth of his lips and the steady beat of hope returning.

I pull back, breathless, and glance around. Half the guards and crew are frozen mid-task, watching us like they're waiting for the credits to roll.

"What is it?" asks Justin.

"I just pictured this happening with a round of applause or something."

"Honestly, I think they're just waiting for us to leave," he says.

"Right."

The two of us head up the sidewalk.

"So," he shrugs. "How about lunch at the visitor center?"

EPILOGUE

By spring, we make it official.

Teddy and I say *I do* beneath a canopy of soft florals and wide blue skies. He pulls me into a kiss—slow, reverent, and full of every promise we made.

We face the crowd as the minister announces, "I present to you, Mr. and Mrs. Justin Clark!"

We gaze out at all of our family and friends as they stand from the white folding chairs in my mom's backyard: my sisters, Mom and Trey, Kelly, Cam, Legend, and Indigo—not to mention several cousins, aunts, and uncles. I've never felt more complete.

———— ✦✦✦✦✦ ————

Before long, the floral arch and custom aisle runner are swept away, the white chairs transformed into elegant table settings under strings of twinkling lights. Justin and I take our place in the center of the yard for our first dance, swaying in rhythm as Legend and Indigo serenade us with their hit duet, *"Dive In."*

The garden glows in soft hues of coral and mint, poppies and garden roses blooming all around us. Justin gives me a spin, then pulls me close, his hand pressed to the small of my back as our friends and family watch with teary eyes.

Later, we steal away to the ledge overlooking the pond. He wraps me in an embrace from behind, and I lean into him, breathing in the warm, spicy scent of his cologne.

The old willow tree dances in the breeze as the sun dips low, spilling amber light across the water. From the far side of the yard, a pianist begins to play a soft instrumental of *"Just the Way You Are,"* each note floating through the evening like a blessing.

It's been a perfect wedding... and an even more perfect beginning.

"Just a couple more hours before we set sail," says Justin. "A few days at sea, and then it's back to Silicon Valley."

I nod, studying the koi dancing in the pond below. "It'll be nice to head home."

We moved into our new house a few months ago. Things were getting a little crowded with his roommate anyway.

"Did I ever tell you how grateful I am that you came back?" Justin rests his chin on my shoulder, his arms wrapped snug around my waist.

I give him a pointed look. "Did I ever tell you how grateful I am that you *took* me back?"

The two of us chuckle.

"Sam!" We turn and see Professor Natalie and her new husband, Paul, approaching. She hugs me tight and smiles, looking over my trumpet wedding gown. "You look *gorgeous!*"

"I completely agree," adds Justin.

All of us laugh, and I give a humble nod.

"Thanks," I say. "So do you!"

We all say hello as she officially introduces her husband.

"I wish you'd had a wedding," I say. "You know we would've jumped at the chance to take a trip across the pond."

Her eyes widen with delighted surprise. "You? Flying across the pond?"

I laugh. "Shocking, right?"

Back in school, she used to dare me to drive across state lines. But now? I don't mind flying at all.

There's something about being thirty thousand feet in the air with snacks, legroom, and a window seat that feels... freeing. And hey, it's still better than sitting in traffic.

"You know how it is sometimes," she says with the wave of her hand. "When you know, you *know*. Who wants to wait for the formalities?"

Justin and I exchange a knowing glance. After all the chaos leading up to this day, there were plenty of moments I was ready to scrap the whole thing and head straight to the courthouse. But Mom wasn't having it. She said she *deserved* to see at least one of her daughters walk down the aisle in a real dress—especially since Simone went and eloped without so much as a save-the-date.

That reminds me... I haven't seen Simone or Kyle since the ceremony.

They *better* not be upstairs.

"We're happy for both of you," says Justin. "And thanks for flying out."

"It's the least we could do," says Natalie. "If it weren't for Sam's support and encouragement, I may never have made my way back to my true love."

It feels good to know I made a difference in her life even half as much as she's made in mine.

"Thanks for your reference, by the way," I say. "I got the job at 112 FM in Silicon Valley, no problem."

"Happy to help," says Professor Natalie. "Though... I'm sure the references from Indigo Taylor and her publicist didn't hurt either."

She's got a point there.

Natalie places a hand on my cheek, a warm grin on her face. "I told you you'd find your way, and here you are. Congratulations, sweetheart."

I nod, and Professor Natalie and Paul head back to the party as Justin rubs my back.

"You gonna be all right?" he asks.

"Yeah." I turn, snatching the handkerchief from the pocket of his vest, and blow my nose. "It's just an... emotional day."

Justin smiles, rubbing my shoulders.

"Honey?" My mom trudges over in her bare feet, concern etched in her face. "Are you okay?"

"Yeah, Mom." I dab at my eyes, thankful once again for the invention of waterproof mascara. "Have you seen, Trey? I wanna thank him for walking me down the aisle."

"He's around here somewhere," she says, glancing over her shoulder. "Probably chasing after your sisters."

According to Mom, Trey's had a lot more time to bond with the girls now that his new app has successfully launched. She still gets overwhelmed trying to keep up with the little ones, but he ensures she gets a chance to take a load off every Thursday night, and sometimes on the weekends too.

I made good on my promise last week and joined Trey and the girls for baseball.

Justin came too, and even Mom tagged along. And I've gotta admit, between the crowd's energy, the salty breeze, and the perfect hot dog in my hand—mustard *and* relish, obviously—it wasn't half bad.

Mom smiles beside me, a soft gleam in her eyes. "I know your dad would've loved to see you walking down that aisle today."

I glance up at the sky, throat tightening as I swallow hard. "Come on, Mom," I say, blinking fast. "I'm already struggling as it is!"

She chuckles, squeezing my hand.

"I'm just... thrilled to see you so happy. And to finally have this boy for a son-in-law!" She reaches over and pinches Justin's cheek as he beams proud.

"Speaking of which, have you seen Kyle and Simone anywhere?" she asks.

"Um…"

All of us were shocked when Simone showed up at Mom's door for Christmas. She had Kyle on her arm and a ring on her hand. *"Merry Christmas!"* she said. All of us spent the holidays together. But that didn't stop the two free birds from slinking off to enjoy their little honeymoon every second they could. Mom was appalled when she stumbled across the two of them fooling around in her laundry room.

I frown, thinking about the icky possibilities, as a burst of laughter cuts through my thoughts. Talia and Tatiana come tearing across the lawn, screaming and giggling in their coral flower girl dresses.

"Girls!" Mom throws a hand to her head. "What are you—?"

Kyle and Trey race after them with Super Soakers in hand. They've removed their jackets and ties, and their sleeves are rolled up to their elbows.

"You better run!" shouts Trey. "We're gonna get you good!"

Mom's jaw drops as she looks back at me.

"Did you know about this?"

I shake my head, equal parts innocent and amused.

All of us jump when Simone sprints by with two mega water pistols of her own, her mint green Matron of Honor gown hiked up around her knees.

"Simone the Cyclone is here to stay! *Feel my wrath!*" She dives to the ground and does some sort of *007* somersault before taking off after them. I raise my arms in surrender as Mom turns to me in dismay.

"As long as they stay away from my dress and the cake, I'm good," I say.

Mom breathes a heavy sigh before stomping off after them.

"That's not gonna end well," says Justin, throwing his arm around me.

"Twenty bucks says Mom ends up drenched."

The two of us shake on it.

"I'll go divert them from the cake." With a quick peck to my temple, Justin heads across the lawn.

I drop my head with a laugh. I honestly don't know what I'd do without this wild, utterly ridiculous family of mine.

"Sam, now I see where you get it!" Indigo shakes her curls as she and Legend approach. "That kooky family of yours is something else."

"I know."

"Wish we all could be so lucky," Legend adds, his voice warm as our eyes meet. We trade a grin, quiet and knowing.

"Sooo, let me see it!" says Indigo, snatching up my hand. She nods, approving my two-carat ring. "All right! Mr. Justin didn't do half bad." She glances back at Legend. "You know mine has to be at least double this, right?"

Legend exhales through a crooked smile, lifting his champagne glass with a slow, exaggerated sip. He nods with mock solemnity.

To this day, people on social media are still shocked that the three of us get along so well. But after clearing the air and establishing some boundaries, we've all become great friends.

Legend was the first to call the day after the incident with Victoria. He asked if I was sure about leaving. I told him it was for the best, and eventually, he agreed.

"So, why do I feel like I'm losing my best friend, right now?" he said, sighing into the phone.

"Well, maybe you are," I said. *"But you're gaining a really great one in Indigo. And you know I'll always have your back."*

Indigo, on the other hand, didn't call until a few days after I reconciled with Justin.

"Sam, what the hell? Are you gonna tell me why you were all over Page Six *with my man? I know he's fine, but damn!"*

Guilt clamped down on my chest as I closed my eyes with a sigh.

I told her the truth. How I'd crushed on Legend since I was fifteen, how the chance to be near him felt surreal, irresistible. How I never meant to hurt her, and how much I'd come to respect her, both as an artist and as a woman. I told her I was sorry, truly. For crossing a line. For betraying her trust.

And honestly, I wouldn't have blamed her if she never forgave me. She'd already been burned so many times before.

After a lengthy beat of silence, she said, *"Did you sleep with him?"*

I couldn't have been happier to honestly tell her the truth. *"No."*

"It's no wonder you were able to walk away," she muttered.

"What?"

"Anyway, I'll hit you up later." And she still does to this day. In fact, she calls even more than Legend. Sometimes for my opinion on interviews or appearances, or just to rant about the way she's being portrayed on TV.

People were so enamored with the story of her rescuing Legend and me with her "superhero" skills that a reality TV show was inevitable. It's called *Life with Indigo*, and the filming crew is across the lawn, waiting to resume shooting right now.

Kelly appears, tablet in hand, wearing her signature power heels and no-nonsense expression.

She gives Indigo a pointed smile. "They're almost done with touch-ups. You're on in five."

Indigo turns to us with a smirk, her whole vibe more relaxed than it used to be. She smiles a lot more these days. Real smiles, not just the camera kind.

"I want you two front and center," says Indigo, pointing between us. "Sing along for the cameras, okay?"

"Yes, ma'am," I say, grinning.

"You looked amazing out there," says Kelly, squeezing my hand softly.

"Thanks," I say, dipping my head. "My knees are still auditioning."

She barely chuckles, but I don't mind.

Kelly glances between Legend and me, then checks her watch. "You've got about five minutes before they mic her and push her to the stage," she says, already shifting back into work mode. "Enjoy them."

Then she's gone—striding across the lawn, tablet raised.

I lift the back of Legend's blazer, peeking at his mic pack.

"Does it bug you, having to wear that thing all the time?"

"You get used to it after while." He shrugs. "But don't worry. I'm not turning the thing back on until they notice it's off."

Both of us laugh, and he raises his glass to me.

"It was a beautiful wedding… and an even more beautiful bride."

I snort, shoving his shoulder. "Stop! You're gonna get us in trouble."

"It's true." He chases the compliment with some of his drink.

Indigo's right. Legend could flirt with a wall and make it blush.

I study him quietly, letting the moment settle between us. "You're happy, right?"

He nods. "I mean… she's Indigo Taylor. She's gonna drive me crazy sometimes. But I couldn't see it any other way."

And just like that, it clicks.

All the chaos, the headlines, the tension between them. It makes sense now. They're fire and friction and somehow still exactly right.

"Plus," I add with a teasing glance, "you kind of owe her your life."

He chuckles. "Not a day goes by that she lets me forget."

Funny how something so chaotic ended up giving all of us the clarity we needed.

"Hey, it's gotta be better than answering to Victoria Austin every day."

"That is *definitely* true."

Now that he's launching his own record label, Legend's finally free to do what he really wants with his music, and at his own pace. There's still going to be a bit of battle in court, but Legend has faith that he'll win in the end. In the meantime, Victoria's gonna be locked up for several years for the conspiracy in Kristina Gray's death.

"I'm taking her to meet my dad for the first time tomorrow," says Legend, glancing over at Indigo. "Pray for me, all right?"

"I'm sure it won't be *that* bad!" I laugh as he arches a very serious brow my way. I nod. "You're right, I'll pray for you."

Especially if that camera crew's around.

Speaking of which, they have a camera pointed our way. Legend nods, directing me to face the pond with him. It isn't a ton of privacy, but at least they can't read our lips.

"I can't believe I signed up for this nonsense," he mutters.

"You know you love it... How are things with your dad, by the way?"

"Cool," he says. "We've been chatting every now and then for a while now."

That's great to hear. Legend picked up his dad's call, not too long after I left, and the two started things fresh. His dad even apologized for putting him in harm's way with Victoria. He said he just wanted a good life for Legend... and maybe himself too. Legend decided to let it go and forgive him, but he says Denero's gonna need more time.

"Everybody grieves in their own way." I couldn't agree more.

Legend glances back at Indigo across the lawn sucking in her cheeks, raising her head high as a stylist reapplies her blush. Another stylist touches up her hair. "You know, we're planning a trip to Hawaii this summer. You think you and Justin might wanna join us?"

"You sure Indigo would be cool with that?"

"It was her idea. We could rent a couple private suites at a luxury resort, hang out on the beach, have dinner. It would be fun."

"I'll check with my *husband*." I drag out the word, teasing him, and he throws back his head, laughing.

"Yeah. You do that."

The two of us gaze out at the pond rippling below. Among the rocks, copper and silver coins shimmer in the amber light. Tiny, hopeful treasures tossed in over the years by my sisters and me.

"I think your wish came true after all," Legend says, his voice low.

I turn to him. "The one from the chain letter?"

Legend nods, a small smile tugging at his lips. "And I'm glad it did." He glances back toward the yard, eyes landing on Indigo. "Otherwise, we'd always wonder, ya know?"

He's right. Even the messiest paths can lead you right where you're meant to be.

Legend's just pulling me in for a hug when Justin returns.

"All right, all right," says Justin, waving his arms. "Prince Charming is back, so you can step aside, pretty boy."

It's the highlight of my day watching the two men slap fives.

Justin was a little wary of Legend and I continuing our friendship, but when he learned that we never "officially" hooked up he was much more relaxed about it.

I place a hand on my husband's chest as he wraps his arm around my shoulders.

"Teddy, Legend and Indigo are inviting us out to Hawaii this summer."

Justin's eyebrows rise. "Fa' real, man? I'm still trying to digest the fact that you're lending us a luxury yacht for our honeymoon."

I glance at Legend, still not quite believing it myself. The same man who once blew up my timeline with shirtless selfies now casually hands out yacht keys like party favors. But then again, that's kind of who he is. Flashy, generous, and surprisingly thoughtful when it counts.

Legend shrugs like it's no big deal. "Consider it a wedding gift."

"Thanks, man," says Justin, extending a hand to Legend. "We'll think about the offer." The two shake hands with genuine grins.

"Been on my own here for quite a while...
Happy and satisfied..."

"There's your girl," says Justin, gesturing toward Indigo on stage. She leans into the microphone, mesmerizing the crowd with her angelic voice.

Legend glances back at her, then meets my gaze with a gentle nod.

The three of us are just making our way toward the front of the crowd when Justin takes me by the hand and gives me a spin.

"Teddy, what are you—?" I laugh as everyone clears and makes space for us to dance.

"I just wanna give you a heads-up," he says, pulling me in close as we begin to sway. "Now that you're my wife, you should expect a lot more surprises."

Here we go again. But this time, I'm not running.

I throw a hand to my head in mock despair as he rocks me gently side to side. "What have I gotten myself into?"

"*So* much trouble." He flashes that familiar charming smile.

Everyone looks on as the two of us dance to Indigo's melodious voice.

"You think you can handle it?" asks Teddy, gazing into my eyes.

I nod, certain. With him, I can handle anything.

And for the first time in my life, I'm looking forward to what the future holds.

ACKNOWLEDGEMENTS

To God, my Heavenly Father. You go first in everything. You covered me, sustained me, convicted me when needed, and guided me every step of the way. Without You there is no book, no breath, no story. Thank you for liberty and grace.

To Jaime. You were reading these chapters back when this story was the randomest idea in my head. You wrangled the kids when I was eyeballs deep in edits. You made it possible for me to finish. Thank you for always being home, no matter where I found myself.

To my kids, Jonathan and Isabella. Two of the biggest supporters of my dreams who continuously inspire me with your own. You celebrate me without question and remind me what all of this is for.

To my family and friends who showed up for me during my debut and still continue to show up now. You prayed, you checked in, you bought the books, you kept me steady. I see you.

To my Substack readers and everyone online who read, listened, commented, and shared this series. You lent your time, your voice, and your enthusiasm. You carried this story farther than I ever could have on my own. Thank you.

To my Black bookworm homegirls who have had my back from day one. You remind me every single time why I write us into stories of love, growth, and second chances.

And to the team who always has my back: my editors, cover designer, and formatter listed in the credits. I could not do this without you.

Here's to another one. Thank you all.

With all my heart,
Kimberly R. Vargas

WHAT'S NEXT
Feels Like Destiny

Some roles are earned. Some are fate. Some might cost everything.

Larger-than-life actress Jayana "Yana" Gardner arrives in New York certain her big break has finally come. She's got a casting director boyfriend, an ensemble role on Broadway, and just enough hope to believe things are falling into place. Then everything falls apart.

One breakup, one lost job, and one eviction later, Yana is suddenly single, unemployed, and unhoused in a city that does not slow down for anyone.

Just when she's convinced her dream has turned into a nightmare, a few serendipitous encounters with Broadway's grouchiest music director, Langston Washington, open a door she never saw coming. The star of his new neo-soul musical has vanished without warning, and Yana looks almost identical to her. Close enough to step into the spotlight. Close enough to keep the show alive.

Soon Yana's training in secret, learning the lead role, while studying a real-life celebrity's interviews and mannerisms to keep the illusion alive. With Langston by her side, offering private coaching, a couch to sleep on, and a belief in her she struggles to give herself, Yana's lifelong dream of fame just might be in reach… and perhaps a little romance too.

But the deeper Yana steps into Alexia Hyrd's shadow, the louder the whispers grow. The cast is nervous, the investors are watching, and the truth about Alexia's disappearance seems to follow Yana everywhere she goes.

To claim her destiny, Yana must trust her gift and decide who she is beyond the spotlight. Because Alexia Hyrd may be gone, but the past she left behind has yet to take its final bow.

ABOUT THE AUTHOR

Kimberly R. Vargas is a contemporary romance and women's fiction author who writes soulful stories about love, heartbreak, and second chances. She's the creator and voice of *The Next Chapter*, an audio newsletter devoted to healing and hope through storytelling. Her work centers captivating women of color who find joy against all odds and the tender romances that help them along the way.

When she's not homeschooling, editing, or chatting with the characters in her head, she can be found struggling to hit a Mariah Carey octave or dancing in her basement. She lives in Michigan with her husband and two children.

A NOTE FROM THE AUTHOR

If this story moved you, the best way to support my work is to leave a review on Amazon or Goodreads. Your words help other readers discover the book and make a real difference for independent authors.

Stay connected for updates, behind-the-scenes notes, and early chapters at: **www.kimberlyrvargas.com**

Follow me on IG, TikTok, and Substack:
@kvargasauthor